BY ALEXANDER FREED

Star Wars: Battlefront: Twilight Company
Star Wars: The Old Republic: The Lost Suns
Rogue One: A Star Wars Story
Star Wars: Alphabet Squadron
Star Wars: Shadow Fall

SHADOW FALL

NEW YORK

SHADOW FALL

An Alphabet Squadron Novel

ALEXANDER FREED

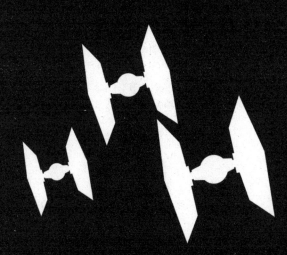

Published in the United States by Del Rey, an imprint of Random House, a division of Penguin Random House LLC, New York.

Del Rey is a registered trademark and the Circle colophon is a trademark of Penguin Random House LLC.

Hardback ISBN 978-1-9848-2004-4
International edition ISBN 978-0-593-15987-3
Ebook ISBN 978-1-9848-2005-1

Printed in the United States of America on acid-free paper

randomhousebooks.com

2 4 6 8 9 7 5 3 1

First Edition

Book design by Elizabeth A. D. Eno

For Stephen R. and Iain M.,
who'll never know and who aren't to blame

THE DEL REY STAR WARS TIMELINE

THE DEL REY STAR WARS TIMELINE

A long time ago in a galaxy far, far away. . . .

PART ONE

UNDER RAVENOUS HEAVENS

CHAPTER 1

SIX TRILLION SUNS AND NONE

I

On Polyneus, where Wyl Lark was born and lifted into adulthood by the Sun-Lamas of the Hik'e-Matriarch, the word *city* was synonymous with *garden*. Settlements on Polyneus grew on canyon walls like moss and sprouted from forest floors, cultivated and tended by their residents. In Cliff, where Wyl learned to fly the sur-avkas, the streets flooded and changed with every monsoon, and the residents rearranged their homes to suit what fate and drainage made of the landscape.

Wyl had traveled to many worlds since leaving Polyneus. On Troithe he realized he had never truly seen a city before.

The engines of his RZ-1 interceptor thundered as he banked away from a massive façade of midnight metal and gold-plated arches, hurtling between towers and under tram lines. Above the lines of digital billboards solar projectors cast their midday light. Bright against the black sky, they guided Wyl through the urban labyrinth.

"Tell me you're not running, brother?" The voice coming through Wyl's comm was barely audible over the noise of the A-wing. Nath Tensent sounded amused.

"Not running," Wyl said. "Circling around."

"That's a big circle. You're off my sensors."

"Maybe because your equipment is older than I am," Wyl returned, but he forgot to smile and he wasn't listening to himself. He angled his fighter into a cloud of smoke, specks of ash smearing his canopy as he reduced speed. He wrestled with throttle and repulsor controls, looking only at his scanner—visuals told him nothing—and his stomach lurched as the A-wing dropped a hundred meters and exited the cloud.

To his right, a multi-level speeder port rose out of view. Sections of three stories spewed jets of flame—the source of the smoke cloud—while crimson particle bolts sprayed another two levels, pockmarking metal and chipping duracrete slabs. Wyl veered away from the flames and into the storm of bolts, watching his shields shimmer as he banked hard and felt his harness bite into his side.

He glimpsed pavement far below and two groups clashing along the boulevard. The particle bolts battering the speeder port (and—at the moment—Wyl's deflector screens) were aimed at a UT-60D "U-wing" transport hovering twenty meters above one group of combatants and unleashing its weaponry onto the second. Wyl processed the image in less than a second, steering his ship with his body as his vision glimmered with spots. "Kairos?" he asked. "You need an assist?"

He avoided colliding with a metal spire—decorative architecture or obsolete technology, he wasn't sure—as a low tone sounded over the comm.

That's a negative, Wyl thought, and flinched at the roar of the U-wing's laser cannons.

"What she needs"—Nath's voice again—"is for us to handle our target. I'm making my attack run in about ten seconds. You want high or low?"

"High," Wyl replied, and swung his fighter down an avenue perpendicular to the main boulevard. His eyes sorted through structures filling the horizon—domed opera houses and shopping spirals, stacked spheres of cracked crystal that had once hosted sporting events—and focused on the titanic metal fiend striding toward him on four spindly legs. Its arched back led to an insectoid head bearing twitching gun barrels in place of mandibles, and its plating was scored by blaster impacts and coated in dust and ash. Though it was dwarfed by the surrounding buildings, it moved among them like a predator through grass.

Wyl had seen its kind in holograms. He'd heard Sata Neek and Sonogari tell stories of Imperial walkers marching in platoons capable of leveling spaceports. This particular monster might have been a cargo-carrying model—one of the ground troops had said as much—but one shot would still suffice to incinerate a dozen of the soldiers below.

So Wyl went *high*, streaking toward the walker's head to seize its attention before bobbing and rolling as energized particles ripped through the air. He went high despite the fact that the walker's fire would, if it failed to obliterate Wyl, tear into the neighboring structures. It would pierce the domes of opera houses and shatter crystal arenas; it would turn Troithe's history to dust.

But it would leave the New Republic infantry intact.

Wyl cut his throttle, allowing the walker's targeting sensors to track him. Cannon blasts screamed loud enough to shake his bones and illuminated the world like lightning. He rocked in his seat, flight helmet smashing against the headrest, and tried to stay one step ahead of his foe.

"You see it?" he whispered, and nearly bit his lip as the A-wing jolted. "Nath's coming. Just a few seconds."

A sensor blip grew brighter. "You talking to your ship again?" Nath asked.

Wyl laughed, loud and unembarrassed, as he spotted Nath's Y-wing bomber racing ten meters above street level. Wyl flew on past the walker, out of its targeting zone, and the bomber launched its ordnance with the sound of a thunderclap. He looped around, ready to provide covering fire to allow Nath a second firing pass, but crackling arcs of electricity already poured off the now-motionless walker's hull. "Ion torpedoes, direct hit," Nath reported. "Think I got it."

The walker raised a single leg, its metal struts and pistons trembling arthritically. Its head tilted and the machine's weight shifted. Gravity did its inexorable work. Wyl watched as—slow as a leaf drifting from an autumn tree, then swift as an avalanche—the walker toppled to one side.

A round tower walled in broken advertising screens, restaurant balconies, and boutique windows was poised to receive the brunt of the impact. The falling walker's body connected somewhere around the seventh floor, compacting the building's frame and tearing through metal support beams. Energy continued to ripple across the armored vehicle, briefly causing exposed power conduits and battery stations in the building's wall to flare. As the walker's head struck durasteel, the structure seemed to undulate and Wyl heard a noise like mortars firing as—story by story—the building began to disappear into a mass of rubble and fire.

A moment later the fallen walker burst as if stuffed full of flames; then it was completely buried. Dust made it impossible to see anything more, though the sounds of collapse and incineration continued.

Someone was cackling over the comm. "Pretty sure you got it. Appreciate the help, though." It was a woman's voice. Not one Wyl recognized.

Wyl brought his A-wing up and around, out of the dust cloud and back toward the ground troops. He forced himself not to look back. His canopy was plastered in soot.

"That mean your mission's done?" Nath asked.

"*Your* mission, you mean? We should be getting word from the insertion team soon," the woman said. "Kind of glad you downed that tower, though—would've made a perfect sniper nest."

Wyl checked his scanner, saw no one airborne but Nath and Kairos, then shot a glance toward the boulevard and the infantry. The band of soldiers was cautiously retreating from the blossoming dust cloud and passing out of the shadow of the U-wing. "No civilian sightings?" he said. He kept his voice level.

"Not in the six hours since we entered the district." The woman's voice dropped in volume as she shouted orders at her cohorts. Then she resumed: "This all used to be an entertainment center, according to the brief. Big investment when the Empire first came in, pretty well abandoned now."

Pretty well abandoned wasn't a guarantee. "Understood," Wyl said. "We'll hold position until you give the word."

"Copy that. And tell your U-wing she's blocking my light."

At this, Wyl managed to smile. *If only there were light to block,* he thought, but instead relayed the message to Kairos, who crept barely ten meters away from the squad. The illumination from the dimming solar projectors seemed no brighter.

"Feeling a little overprotective?" Nath asked.

Kairos didn't answer.

Wyl caressed his console absently in search of a rattling plate. The dust continued to churn and dissipate. His mind veered between thoughts of the destruction and thoughts of the insertion team descending through the undercity.

"You know we were careful as we could be," Nath said. He'd switched to a private channel. "She was a fine-looking building but not worth tearing up over."

"I know," Wyl said. "I'll be okay—"

"Target acquired! Three Imp guerrillas bagged, cuffed, and ready for interrogation." The woman's voice broke through. "Insertion team's done the job you flyboys are six tons too heavy for."

"Got it." Wyl focused on the console, adjusting his communications settings and linking to Troithe's long-range network. "Let's see if we can get a signal out—we've got people waiting."

II

Astrogation charts called Cerberon a system, and it was—but it wasn't a star system, because there weren't any stars within half a light-year. Instead, its planets and moons and asteroid fields orbited the Cerberon singularity: a black hole like a burning eye, its ebony pupil surrounded by an iris of fiery debris. In a few thousand years, Troithe, Catadra, Verzan, and the other worlds of Cerberon would be swallowed by the black hole's gravity—forces more powerful than any Imperial death machine. A few millennia more and the nearest stars would suffer the same fate.

Against the glowing heavens of the dense galactic Deep Core, the black hole had the distinction of being both the brightest and the darkest object in the sky. Chass na Chadic wondered how anyone could live in the system and not go mad. It hardly seemed like a place worth fighting for—but the New Republic higher-ups were terrified Cerberon could be used as a shortcut between Core Worlds, and it turned out being on the winning side of a war meant fighting for stupid things.

She tore her gaze from the eye and looked back to the asteroid field surrounding her, carefully rotating the primary airfoil of her B-wing assault fighter from above her cockpit to below. A slab of rock drifted lazily overhead; she'd been flying in atmosphere so often she half expected to feel the ship tremble in reply. She gave a burst of power to her thrusters, wriggled in her harness, and asked, "So what was I saying? Before the rocks?"

Through her comm, a woman's voice—rough as a charred bone out of a cook fire—replied, "The Slipglass Conglomerate."

"Right," Chass said. "So the Empire gives the 'Glom total control of transport on Eufornis Minor. Can't get on a tram without chaincodes, let alone a shuttle, and I'm stuck way out in the middle of muck-all. What do you think I do?"

"You need a vehicle of your own," the voice replied.

Chass laughed. "I do, don't I? So I've never flown one before but my host has this old Voltec skyhopper. Barely works. One night he starts asking about my *species* again and I decide I'm done, so I climb aboard and start examining the controls, one button at a time . . ."

The story was a lie—not every word but enough to qualify—and she stumbled through it joyfully, concocting increasingly absurd incidents while her ship drifted among the asteroids. She told of an arm-length parasite she found in the Voltec's engine compartment that speared itself on her horn-stubs; about maneuvering through a storm while on the run from planetary security; about firing on 'Glom droids as she landed on the outskirts of a spaceport. She was pretty sure the last part would draw questions—so far as she knew, Voltec had never made a skyhopper with weapons—but no objection came.

She squeezed her control yoke as an unexpected flash of crimson flared off her starboard side. She saw fragments of rock tumbling her way and heard the voice say, "Asteroid might have been trouble for you. Keep going."

Chass shrugged and did as requested. She took the story as far as it could go, ending with: "—finally made it offworld and managed to signal Hound Squadron. Felt good to be back, by the end."

You know *that's a lie,* she thought. *You have to know by now . . . Hound Squadron wasn't until way later.*

What will you let me get away with?

"I can only imagine," Yrica Quell replied.

Chass cackled, threw back her head, and nearly winged another asteroid.

"Something funny?" Quell asked without a trace of irony.

Maybe Quell was mocking her, Chass thought. Or maybe she was, for some reason, trying to make friends. Either way it was entertaining, but not what Chass expected from a woman as fond of chaos as a badly timed belch. She imagined Quell's face—blond locks tucked into her helmet, jutting nose and tawny skin, eyes straining humorlessly at the darkness.

"Nothing at all," Chass said. "Target's coming into range. We good to go?"

"Ground team gave the signal. Guerrillas captured, didn't get off an alert. Now—" She cut herself off. Chass heard a digitized beeping and an irritated curse.

"Still not getting on with the new droid?" Chass asked.

"It's fine," Quell said. "CB-9 just wanted to offer *input,* but as I was saying: Now we go after their supplier."

Chass adjusted course and yanked a control lever. Servos issued a grinding noise as her strike foils extended and reshaped the line of the vessel into a cross. She scanned status displays as the computer automatically redistributed power and heat. Ion cannons came online. The primary torpedo launcher registered fully functional; the secondary registered dead as it had since Pandem Nai, but Chass knew better. If she needed the secondary launcher, it would work.

Finally, she adjusted her comm system. A low drumbeat and swift, Huttese-accented lyrics splashed against static and filled the cockpit: Narvath retro-shudder, from a music chip she'd stolen off a drunk fool in the Western Reaches. Satisfied, she leaned into her seat and let her first torpedo fly.

The target was an asteroid the size of an orbital battle station. The torpedo, with a flare bright enough to blind anyone within a kilometer, shattered a small mountain's worth of stone and left the rest of the rock uncracked. Chass loosed a second torpedo before adjusting her systems and spraying particle bolts. She sang as she fired, let the music dictate the rhythm of the violence, and adjusted her vector so that she could batter the asteroid as she passed. Her scanner indicated Quell's X-wing maintaining its distance on her wing, ready to move in but not engaging.

She watched the torpedo novas, moved to the beat of the music, and periodically checked her depleting munitions supply. She barely noticed her scanner flash until Quell's voice broke through the music. "Fighters on the move. Break away from the rock and check your deflectors."

Chass looked between her scanner and the asteroid. A moment later she spotted the glinting vessels erupting like a geyser from a chasm, the spout compact closest to the asteroid before dispersing farther out. She counted at least a dozen ships—all basic TIE/ln fighters, with two broad, flat panels protecting the central cockpit eye.

In the hands of a skilled pilot, a TIE fighter was a knife—swift and slender and deadly against a lumbering beast like the B-wing. In lesser hands a TIE was a garbage pail strapped with guns. Clumsy and defenseless.

Alphabet Squadron had been in Cerberon long enough for Chass to understand what to expect.

"Look at them," Chass muttered. "They can't even stay in formation."

Quell grunted but didn't disagree. The TIEs broke into separate flights, sweeping away from the chasm as one last ship emerged: a cargo shuttle, boxy and asymmetrical with a four-winged design out of fashion for decades. Chass called out its coordinates and said, "Looks like it's running—you want to go after it?"

"No."

"This why we're out here?"

"Yes," Quell said. "With the hideout on Troithe gone, we know exactly where it's going. But we can't let it *look* like we're letting it escape."

Eight TIEs moved between the New Republic fighters and the shuttle, dividing into pairs and sticking close to the rocks. "Two ways of doing that," Chass said. "We're outnumbered, so we could run like idiots—or we could fight as hard as we can while trying not to win. You know my vote."

Chass expected she knew Quell's vote, too. But anything sounded better than returning home, lying in her bunk, and waiting for the next mission. The Narvath retro-shudder came to a close and a new song, squealed at high speed in a language she didn't recognize, began.

"Sixty seconds of fight time," Quell offered. "If we're hard-pressed, we blow one of the big rocks for cover and bail in the debris shower."

Chass laughed, boosted power to her deflectors, and tumbled toward the enemy. Maybe Quell had changed, but she liked her new commander. "Deal. Try to keep them off me, huh?"

The TIEs were using the asteroids for shelter. It wasn't a bad plan, but the counter was straightforward: Chass squeezed her trigger and filled the sky with particle bolts, raking the asteroids and sending granite shrapnel flying in every possible direction. Her own shields flickered as she was pelted by stone fragments. If she was very lucky, a shard would puncture an unlucky and unshielded TIE's engine, but all she was really looking to do was make a mess and reduce scanner visibility—and in that, she had succeeded.

She called out her target as Quell swept around, attempting to intercept the first pair of TIEs heading their way. Instinct told Chass what could happen next—told her a dozen ways she could win and fifty more she could die, but she'd learned in the past weeks that death was a broken promise. Verzan, the system's airless garrison world, had been a fortress that cracked open under the *Lodestar*'s fire and Alphabet's proton bombs. Catadra's temples and palaces had burned as its defenders spat impotent turbolaser volleys. The battle group had seized Troithe's main spaceport in less than a day of fighting. In Cerberon there was no sense that any lost battle could be the last in the war, as there had been with the Rebellion; there was no failure the New Republic couldn't recover from against a scattered and diminished Empire.

People died. Infantry died. But TIEs were in short supply and death was for the stupid and careless, not for heroes.

It wasn't what Chass wanted, but she figured she might as well enjoy it.

She adjusted her aim and fired at the first of the TIEs as Quell's X-wing tore through the second fighter. She hauled her control yoke to port, barely avoided a volley of particle bolts as her opponent sped past her, and rather than pursue, focused instead on the six fresh enemies closing fast. "Got to hit *one* of them," she muttered, and loosed quick pulses at the cluster.

"I'm taking a shot at the cargo shuttle," Quell said. "Hold on."

Chass half snarled, half laughed as the X-wing slipped between the asteroids and fired wildly at a target she could no longer see. The seven surviving TIEs changed course to surround her—she shot down one, grazed another, and watched emerald streak past her canopy. One of the nearest asteroids was burning, releasing some combustible gas from a punctured pocket. She put her aft to the flames and wondered how she would survive.

She transferred power to her forward deflectors. She wasn't surprised when the TIE closest to her exploded instead of shooting. The dagger of an A-wing interceptor cut through the blooming flames and then spun about, eliminating another opponent in a single maneuver.

"You knew they were on their way?" Chass asked, less irritated than she sounded.

"I knew," Quell said. "You got your sixty seconds."

Chass looked to her console. With the debris still cluttering the scanner readings, she couldn't make out the U-wing or Y-wing, but she was confident they were there, too.

"Good to see you, too," Nath's voice snapped through the comm. "Play us some music and let's save your butt."

III

The dying-animal squeal of Chass's music flooded the comm as Nath Tensent plodded toward the battle. T5 was reconfiguring his thruster output but he doubted the droid would squeeze much more out of the aging Y-wing. "Just keep us steady," he called, and the ship only seemed to buck harder.

If he was late to the fight, he thought, it would be for the best. After hitting the walker, he was short on ordnance.

Quell called out orders. Nath snapped off a few shots, coming close to actually hitting a TIE before Kairos, of all people, eliminated his target. She wasn't a showy flier or a tactical mastermind, and Nath had a habit of forgetting she was more than troop support, but she still packed a punch when on the offensive.

Chass, meanwhile, scrapped more TIEs than should've been possible by a B-wing. By the time Nath came into optimal firing range, all that was left was salvage and an asteroid that burned like a reactor core mid-meltdown. "You never know what's flammable around here," he said. "We all set? We need to hunt for survivors?"

"One crashed into that burning asteroid," Wyl replied. "I'll do a flyby, check and see."

Poor boy, Nath thought, and shook his head with a smile.

"Finish up quick," Quell said. "Kairos, stay with Lark in case he finds something. Chadic, sweep for reinforcements on my wing. Xion, scan all comm frequencies and make sure that cargo shuttle isn't sending a distress call."

Wyl and Chass called acknowledgments. Kairos moved into position. *Guess that makes me Xion,* Nath mused, but he didn't comment on Quell's slip and he let T5 scan as instructed. No one else seemed to have noticed.

"So, you pull off whatever convoluted spy job you and Adan had planned?" he asked.

"I'll let you know when it's done," Quell said.

Soon after they were finished and en route to Troithe, the five vessels moving in formation out of the debris field and their computer-adjusted velocities locking them in relative position as they swept toward the planet. They crossed over the broken landmass and a neighboring sea, then descended toward one of the unshielded sectors of the sprawling city-continent.

The solar projectors had dimmed from pale yellow to a twilight blue, suffusing the blur of decaying skyscrapers and disused industrial parks—a testament to millennia of development and transformation and vibrancy that had peaked long before the rise and fall of the Empire. Centuries earlier, Troithe had rivaled Coruscant as the Republic's cosmopolitan jewel, its city encompassing half a globe and teeming with billions of residents—more than a few belonging to the Republic's most respected aristo-mercantile families.

Troithe had been the sort of planet the rust worlds of the Mid Rim pretended to be: a place of invention and manufacturing, where a skilled artisan could develop a cognitive module in the morning, attend a trendy concert midday, and oversee the assembly of an innovator droid army at night. Troithe fell anyway: Coruscant, already the political center of the Republic, had drawn migrants from thousands of Republic member worlds and foreign allies and built sector after sector, level after level of new housing blocks in response. It began to outpace Troithe as an industrial powerhouse by virtue of its greater population, putting hands and minds from countless species to work.

And as Coruscant's production had waxed, Troithe's waned due to factors both unavoidable (the exhaustion of precious mineral resources on the broken continent; the Cerberon system's decreasing accessibility in a Republic expanding into the Colonies and the Inner Rim; the gradual decay of Troithe's planetary orbit as it spiraled toward the black hole) and tragically preventable (a short-lived civil war between the mixed-species underclass and the majority human population—a conflict manipulated in part by an ambitious aristo-mercantile family seeking to profit). By the Clone Wars, Troithe had settled into slow decline. Every year, its billions-strong populace grew a little smaller. Every year, another factory shut down or another residential district was abandoned.

Many of Troithe's inhabitants had welcomed Emperor Palpatine's promises of renewal and restored prominence for their world. Some of those promises had even been kept, and a substantial portion of the population still retained Imperial sympathies. That was one reason why the operation to seize Troithe had been slow going.

The skyscraper hills sloped into a basin filled with low metal platforms and webs of scaffolding, along with tents and prefab shelters packing the roads and runways. Past the refugee enclaves came hangars and tarmacs occupied by dozens of freighters, corvettes, and snubfighters. At the very center was the *Lodestar,* the aging *Acclamator*-class battleship that had carried Nath and his colleagues across half the galaxy and back.

"You can smell the carbon scoring from here," Nath observed. "Old girl hasn't moved for weeks and she's still waiting for a good scrubbing."

"Your kind of woman," Chass answered with a snort, and laughed to herself at length.

Instead of angling for the battleship, the starfighters curved toward a landing pad half a kilometer out while Kairos split off with her U-wing to join the other transports. Twenty minutes later Nath had lowered his vessel onto the landing pad, briefed his ground crew on his spent weaponry (he didn't trust them with more than basic maintenance), and extracted T5 for recharging. Finally, he reunited with Wyl under the black sky to begin their trek back to the carrier.

Sweat saturated both men's flight suits, though the day was cool and mild. Each carried his helmet under his right arm. Aside from uniforms and postures they bore little resemblance to each other: Where Nath was broad and muscular, Wyl was slender; where Nath's hair was dark, receding, and pulled back, Wyl's was brown and neat; where Nath's skin was tinged with brass, Wyl's was olive-toned. Yet despite nearly two decades separating them, both walked with the swagger of youth.

They spoke to those around them more than to each other—as they strode down tarmacs Wyl waved encouragement at two Hail Squadron pilots tinkering with their ships. Nath yelled good-natured insults and sly innuendos at passing speeder riders and received grins and ripostes in return.

"You see Chass anywhere?" Wyl asked after a while.

"She's gone wherever she goes after missions. Expect she'll be back by morning."

They didn't see Quell, either—Nath assumed she'd already gone to huddle with Caern Adan at his makeshift intelligence headquarters— but they crossed paths with Kairos as the *Lodestar*'s hull grew large on the horizon. If the silent woman ever sweated, it didn't show through the layers of fabric that swaddled her body or the riveted metal mask that concealed her face. She fell into step beside them as they maneuvered through a field of tugs, loadlifters, and equipment crates before marching up the boarding ramp. Inside, the vast hangar mirrored the civilian encampment outside; rows of multicolored tents, the smell of oil sizzling on heater plates, and the noise of a hundred conversations dominated. Soldiers ate and cleaned their rifles and played keep-away with someone's crumpled jacket.

"The heroes of Alphabet Squadron!" a burly sergeant with a stormtrooper's haircut cried. "You drag yourselves back here looking for applause?"

"We'll take it if you're offering," Nath said.

The sergeant—Nath vaguely recalled the other troops calling him Carver—scoffed loudly, swept his gaze past Wyl, and then gave a fierce nod to Kairos. "Only one who deserves it won't be the one to ask. Strike team sends its regards—good shooting out there."

Kairos didn't seem to hear, and strode toward one of the corridors leading off the hangar. For a woman who risked herself for the infantry as often as she did, she never seemed much interested in face-to-face encounters.

Wyl tried to excuse himself next, but Nath gripped him by the arm and pulled him into conversation with Carver and a dozen other ground troops. While Alphabet had been running jobs for New Republic Intelligence, the Sixty-First Mobile Infantry had continued its slow march through the districts of Troithe. The ground war was a war of attrition and the outcome seemed inevitable—same as throughout the galaxy, really, where there hadn't been a decisive triumph since Pandem Nai—but the stories were decent enough and it was best not to get on the infantry's bad side.

"Be charming," Nath muttered to Wyl as a jittery woman named Twitch described knifing Imperial guerrillas in an alleyway. "You get shot down, you're going to need these people."

"Troithe needs these people," Wyl returned. "General Syndulla needs these people. I need a shower before we're called out again."

"Suit yourself." Nath shrugged. "I can celebrate for the full squadron."

He could, too. He started to, making an effort to learn the names of Zab and Vitale and Junior, watching for exhaustion and boredom and fervor in the eyes of the grunts as he wove lies about how Alphabet had come together, why General Hera Syndulla had brought them to Cerberon aboard the *Lodestar* and joined the ground war. He could've gone on for hours, but eventually his comm buzzed and he was surprised to hear Quell's voice crackle through.

"Couldn't get through to the others," she said. "Pass the word—briefing tomorrow with the general."

"Good news or bad?" Nath asked.

"Adan and I have a plan," Quell said. "The *convoluted spy job* worked, and we got the intelligence we were looking for off the captured cargo shuttle."

"Sighting?"

She would know what he meant.

There'd been no confirmed sightings of the Empire's Shadow Wing since Pandem Nai. They didn't talk about the enemy they'd been assigned to neutralize anymore—had avoided the topic insistently since reaching Cerberon, with their efforts to assist the assault broken up only by the occasional inexplicable intelligence op.

"Not exactly."

"What, then?"

She didn't speak for long enough that Nath wondered if he'd lost the signal.

"We've been looking at the layout of the Cerberon system. We have the makings of a trap," she said.

Nath grinned.

Quell was a liar, a hypocrite, and a war criminal. But on her best days, the woman had style.

CHAPTER 2

AN HONEST DAY'S WORK

I

Soran Keize stood aboard the bridge of the *Aerie,* surrounded by tactical displays and viewscreens aglow with charts and status readings. He saw none of them consciously—he allowed his hindbrain to absorb the data and translate it into something visceral, staring instead through the viewport of a TIE in his mind's eye, listening to the imagined scream of the vessel's twin engines.

He saw junk rings glimmering in the sky above Jarbanov's barren soil, and the domes of a colony rising on the horizon like triple suns. From one of the rings, a glittering stream trickled into the atmosphere like a distant waterfall. Leather-winged birds prowled the air, dipping close enough to study the TIE before veering off in search of easier prey.

"Squadron Four is in position now, Major." The voice came from the comm. "What do you suppose we should do next?"

Soran let his eyelids flicker and banished the fantasy. When he returned to himself he spoke softly and deliberately, observing the reactions of his bridge officers to Captain Gablerone's evident sarcasm.

"Proceed as planned," Soran said. "We have you on monitors and will provide assistance if required."

"Acknowledged, *Aerie,*" Gablerone replied, before issuing commands to his squadron—calling approach vectors and assigning targets, ordering final systems checks before the violence began.

The *Aerie's* bridge crew, meanwhile, concentrated on their consoles and headsets, never glancing toward Soran. He'd met most of them only recently, but he recognized a stiffness to their professionalism. Officers comfortable with their duties showed it in their posture and the ease of their words. Chatter meant communication and cooperation. Quiet soldiers, conversely, were soldiers with unspoken fears.

He would return to that later. For the moment, his bridge crew was out of danger. It was his pilots who required attention.

Squadron Four struck its first two targets almost simultaneously. Lieutenant Seedia—the squadron's newest member, transferred and promoted after the death of Draige at Pandem Nai—and her wing strafed the colony's primary disassembly plant. Soran had suggested filling Draige's role with Arron, but Arron had died on a mission to someplace called the Oridol Cluster; a loss Soran blamed on his own recent absence. Lieutenant Kandende's flight, meanwhile, fired on the battery recycling facility nearly too late to inflict significant damage. Soran would have to interrogate that error during debriefing.

Give them time, he told himself, then chastened himself. Time was not on their side.

"Distress calls going out," Rassus announced from his station on the bridge, glancing backward at Soran. "Shall we attempt to jam them?"

"No," Soran said.

Rassus opened his mouth to argue, then returned his attention to his console.

Question me or be silent, Soran wanted to say. *Show confidence for the sake of the others.*

Perhaps the others wouldn't notice.

The fighters continued their brutal work, Gablerone's own flight spraying fire onto the roads and bridges. Soran had timed the attack precisely, allowing the colony's industrial hubs to release their workers from their afternoon shift. Civilian casualties (if one could call colonists supplying the New Republic military *civilians*) would be higher than if he'd chosen a nighttime strike, but that was incidental to Soran's goal. Fewer workers at their stations guaranteed greater *chaos*.

It was a lesson he'd learned in the aftermath of the Roona attacks, years before. The tactics of the Rebel Alliance had struck him as cruel, then. Perhaps attacking from a position of weakness required cruelty.

"Patrol craft sighted," Gablerone announced. "Enemies incoming."

"As we discussed," Soran answered. "Do not engage."

He turned his attention to the tactical maps and watched the TIE flights increase speed as they wove through the colony. The local militia was confined to atmospheric vehicles—according to the intelligence Soran had been able to obtain, there were no enemy starfighters in-system—but so close to ground level the TIEs had no natural advantage over armored cloud cars. The TIEs took evasive action through the streets, firing on targets of opportunity while avoiding closing range with the patrols.

Soran knew his people well enough to understand the restraint they exerted—none of them was comfortable *running* from a threat. Yet they maneuvered well. Outnumbered and in unfamiliar territory, utilizing tactics they'd lacked even a simulator to practice, they outflew their enemies with ease. An enemy patrol craft disappeared from the tactical map, and Lieutenant Seedia called out the cause: a collision with a garbage silo by an enemy attempting to outflank the TIEs. "Convenient," she added, "for whatever cleanup crew comes after." Soran heard pride in her aristocratic enunciation.

Afraid or not, doubting or not, the men and women who flew over Jarbanov were still pilots of the 204th. They were still Shadow Wing. If their execution was imperfect, it was because they'd flown through the gates of hell and returned to fight a war they hadn't trained for—not because a backwater colony militia could match them blow for blow.

"How much more time?" he asked, striding lazily behind Rassus.

"Three minutes. Maybe four," the gray-haired major said.

"Good." Soran clapped a hand on Rassus's shoulder and began to pace the bridge, attempting to project confidence.

He listened to reports of recycling yards burning and junker caravans scattered, updating his profile of Squadron Four and its pilots. Every call and response reminded him of how much the unit had changed—he had found Shadow Wing decimated, reeling from the loss of Colonel Shakara Nuress and with a roster of dead longer than any he'd predicted.

He'd called Nuress *Grandmother.* They all had once, in sly admiration of the woman who had made the 204th into one of the Empire's finest fighter wings. She had been his friend, and in honor of her memory—among other reasons—he had come to take command, to reshape the unit, after once refusing to shed his blood with his pilots in their darkest hour.

His homecoming had been . . . difficult. *Command* was not what he had been given.

He checked the tactical map again. "Captain Gablerone? May I make a suggestion?"

Gablerone paused for longer than Soran would have liked. "Go ahead."

"You're outnumbered. Crossfire situations are to your advantage. You may wish to adjust formation accordingly."

"I'll keep it in mind, Major," Gablerone said.

Gablerone did not adjust his squadron's positioning, and Soran didn't press the matter.

He had been a different man during his absence from Shadow Wing. He remembered being Devon and mourned the loss.

Devon had never truly treasured his own existence—his freedom from all responsibility, save for those he chose. He had not appreciated the luxuries of mercy and time.

"One minute!" Rassus called.

"Withdraw your forces when ready," Soran said.

Devon could never have survived in the 204th.

Soran watched Squadron Four shake its pursuers and skim the surface of the planet Jarbanov before rapidly ascending. Seedia hung at the rear of her flight, straying off course long enough to puncture a row of hazard vaults on the colony outskirts—an act Soran had advised against during planning, out of an abundance of caution. He tried to picture how the young lieutenant had bypassed the defenses and made a note to warn the ground crew.

"Congratulations, Lieutenant Seedia," he said. "You may have just rendered the entire Jarbanov colony radioactive."

"Do you object, adviser?"

Adviser. Her voice suggested no hint of disrespect, but even Gablerone had called him by his rank.

"I don't," he said, "but I suggest you remain in your cockpit until all trace radiation has been scrubbed from your ship."

"I'm comfortable in my flight suit," Seedia replied. "Proceeding with the extraction."

Someone snickered over the comm channel.

The single Republic corvette in orbit would attempt to intercept Squadron Four, but the TIEs had speed and planning on their side. They headed directly for the far side of Jarbanov's moon, where they would soon rendezvous with the cruiser-carrier *Allegiance* and jump directly to hyperspace. Escape would not be difficult, even if the squadron's discipline appeared lax.

Which meant Soran could turn his attention to other matters.

He looked from the tactical screens to the viewport, studying the massive junk field where the *Aerie* drifted. With its systems at low power and the colonists otherwise occupied, the vessel had maneuvered deep into the inner system, dangerously close to Jarbanov.

Jarbanov was on the outskirts of the junker systems—not officially affiliated with the guild, but nonetheless a major processing center for everything from starship wrecks to obsolete planetary mining rigs. It had taken Soran considerable time, effort, and expenditure of personal influence, but he had managed to make contact with a reliable ally inside the Jarbanov Orbital Sorting Association.

"Do we have a visual?" Soran asked.

Rassus nodded, flipping a switch on his console. "Activating the tractor beam now," he said.

The secondary viewscreen flashed, replacing an image of Jarbanov's moon with a low-resolution feed from the *Aerie's* main hangar. Beyond the magnetic field, outside the ship, local space was cluttered with unidentifiable plastoid lumps and pitted bulkheads. Moving toward the *Aerie,* caught in the grip of the tractor beam, was a salvage sled: an autonomous vehicle fifty meters long, little more than a spindly platform with magnetic clamps protruding from its body like a centipede's legs.

As the tractor beam urged the sled closer, the sled's cargo came into view: Attached to nine clamps was the wreckage of nine TIE/ln starfighters. One vessel was missing the solar collectors on its port wing, leaving its naked side albino white. Another lacked its cockpit viewport, as if someone had gouged out its eye. A third TIE had had both wings amputated altogether. All were smeared with ash and carbon scoring, and many dangled cables and piping from exposed wounds.

Soran looked from the viewscreen to his crew. He noted pursed lips; eyes that refused to observe. He voiced the sentiment that he knew was in their hearts: "We risked our lives for these? We risked our colleagues in Squadron Four and exposed ourselves to attack for—what? Junk?"

He shook his head briskly, waiting for Rassus and the others to turn his way. When they did, he continued.

"These are *our* ships. These are the vessels of the Empire, flown by pilots who gave their lives for their brothers and sisters. They will have the chance to fight again.

"We will make them *fly* again."

He timed his words carefully. He finished as the tractor beam deactivated and the sled gently tapped the deck of the hangar, then transitioned from speechmaking to command in an eyeblink. "Lock down the hangar and retrace our path through the field. Prepare for lightspeed jump."

Thankfully, the crew obeyed. Rassus hadn't yet questioned him openly. Someone whispered, "Let's just burn down a planet already," and Soran felt the *Aerie* vibrate beneath him as the cruiser-carrier's thrusters ignited.

Everything he'd said was true. It galled him to stage an operation solely as a diversion—solely so he could claim ships that the Empire would have incinerated rather than repaired. That even the *New Republic* had deemed unworthy of use. It pained him to put his pilots into action when they were barely a cohesive unit.

But the 204th was fragile. He had counted the TIEs and pilots surviving, and neither was sufficient to the task ahead. He could not lead a wing ready to break after a single blow; he could not save his unit without rebuilding it.

It would take time. But he would restore Shadow Wing to glory.

CHAPTER 3

PAST AND FUTURE GLORIES

I

"I called him Xion. In the middle of an operation, I called Tensent by Xion's name. I don't think he noticed."

"Would it be terrible if he had?" the droid asked. It dilated the red dot of its photoreceptor, in the accusatory way Yrica Quell had grown accustomed to. "Your squadron is aware of your past inside the Empire."

"Not really," Quell said.

"No. Not really."

The IT-O unit's spherical black chassis floated roughly two meters from Quell, above the emergency driver's pit of the tram car. Quell sat in the doorway opposite, where a heavy barricade should have sealed off unruly passengers from the cab's almost entirely automated controls. But the tram car hadn't run for weeks—not since the New Republic had secured Troithe's primary spaceport, and likely not during the turmoil preceding—and the reprogrammed interrogation droid had taken the car for its office, correctly presuming no one else would need the vehicle.

"I remember things all the time now," she said, and it was as difficult a confession as any she'd made.

In the Cerberon debris field Quell's mind had drifted to another mission—a patrol on the outskirts of Cathar, undertaken shortly after her graduation from the Imperial Academy. Back then she'd discovered during takeoff that her helmet had reeked of creamed longcorn and bile. She'd been new to her squadron and had said nothing about the stench. When she'd returned to the Star Destroyer *Pursuer* it had been another three shifts before Sergeant Greef found her scrubbing her flight suit; as it turned out, half a dozen officers and crew had known about "the incident" with Xion, who'd grabbed Quell's helmet at a moment of acute nausea.

Quell wasn't sure why the mission had dredged up that particular memory, but it had. The memories that came were often of unimportant things—of Shadow Wing pilots who had died a year into her tour of duty, or of the astringent aftertaste of Imperial rations stamped by Aldraig manufactories. Occasionally she remembered more distressing events—maneuvering through the clutterbomb-riddled passages honeycombing Tassahondee Station, or the day she'd nearly collided with an ejected rebel pilot in the vast emptiness of space.

Sometimes she thought about how, months before coming to Troithe, when she'd still belonged to the 204th Imperial Fighter Wing, she had taken part in an unforgivable crime. She had abetted—she had *performed*—an act of genocide on the planet Nacronis. Given the opportunity, she'd have continued in her role of murderer, of war criminal, of squadron commander. Only her mentor had saved her from that fate.

"Memory is a construct," the droid said. "For your species, an individual recollection is not a single clear recording but a reassembly of all relevant data. Before Pandem Nai, you suppressed the keystone to all of your memories with the 204th. Now that you have acknowledged your trauma, it is not surprising other memories would surface."

Major Soran Keize had told her as they'd surveyed the Nacronis wasteland: "If you would do *this,* then there's nothing that will drive you out." He'd spoken of a moral sickness destroying her, and warned that she would stay with the 204th until either the sickness killed her or the rebels did.

Keize had ordered her to leave, and she had. She'd lacked the spine to argue. She'd lied to the New Republic about the circumstances of her defection, lied to her comrades about attempting to thwart the genocide at Nacronis, lied to her new superiors, and lied to herself. She'd found that so long as she clung to the fiction of Yrica Quell, the righteous woman who'd been pushed too far and tried and failed to stop Operation Cinder, she could hunt down her old friends with barely a twinge of remorse.

But now someone knew. The droid knew. She could no longer lie to herself.

So she was beginning to remember.

"You witnessed a terrible act," the droid went on. "You feel tremendous guilt, and daily you deceive the colleagues with whom you entrust your life. The notion that this should *not* affect your health is absurd on its surface. The only question is whether you will permit us to heal the injuries you have suffered, rather than simply ameliorate them."

"I'm here, aren't I?" Quell said.

"You are. And I recognize that important step. Nonetheless, I'm not certain I understand what you expect from these sessions. I wonder if you know yourself."

"I want you to show me how to get my focus back. If you need to medicate me, medicate me."

The droid's primary manipulator twitched. The attached syringe was empty. "Medication is in extremely short supply. I will assist you in functioning day-to-day, but the symptoms are not the disease."

She stretched out one leg that had been folded beneath her and rubbed at the tattoo on her biceps showing the Alphabet crest.

She knew better than to argue with the droid. It meant well, but healing was a luxury. The only permanent solution was to finish her mission and get as far away from Alphabet Squadron and New Republic Intelligence and Caern Adan as possible. Escape the people who knew the truth, and the people who would judge her if they knew.

"What do you want to talk about?" she asked.

"I'd like to return to the topic of Nacronis," the droid replied. "Specifically, I'd like to talk about the story you concocted, and some of the details you decided upon. I don't know if you're aware, but you—"

The sound of a fist rapping on metal interrupted the conversation. Quell jerked up, ready to spring to a stand. The droid descended toward the control pit, depressing a toggle and activating the tram's intercom system. A woman's voice came through, low and lightly accented: "Gravas here. I'm looking for Yrica Quell."

"We're in the middle of a session," the droid said. "Can we alert you when we're done?"

"Mister Adan's very busy," the intercom replied. "So's the general. They're ready for her now." The language was civil, if not entirely courteous. The tone left no room for interpretation.

The droid acquiesced without further argument. "Car doors unlocked." Quell rose, swaying on the balls of her feet, and turned away from the cab. The synthesized, masculine voice of the droid called out to her, "You will return tomorrow?"

"If I can," she said. Which was true, and vague enough to bind her to nothing.

"We can seize the capital," General Syndulla said. The green-skinned woman raised her chin, her head-tails bouncing as her eyes swept the room. "The only questions are: *How long will it take?* and *How much will it cost?*"

They'd requisitioned the *Lodestar*'s tactical center for the briefing. It was less formal than the ready rooms, and with the battleship parked planetside there were no crew members making use of the transparent screens protruding like crystalline stalagmites from every surface. Instead, Quell, Caern Adan, and Syndulla stood at one end of a holographic display table, surrounded by flat images of urban topography and Imperial bunkers and planetary shield maps. Wyl Lark, Chass na Chadic, and Nath Tensent sat at the table's other end, eyes on the general or roaming the room. Kairos paced, moving from one screen to the next, studying the data.

Quell could've scolded her, but she'd accepted months earlier that Kairos was a woman of unusual habits. Besides, she was still shaking off the session with her therapist.

"Alphabet Squadron," Syndulla continued, "has been instrumental in the progress we've made in Cerberon so far. With Vanguard Squadron on special assignment in the Bormea sector, Alphabet, Meteor, and Hail are all we've got for the remainder of the campaign. However—" She looked among the pilots, even locking her eyes with Kairos's visor. "—I haven't forgotten Shadow Wing. I know you haven't, either. Officer Adan has shared the suspected sightings list with me, and I agree there is a danger."

Quell caught Adan's glance in her direction. He stood to one side holding a datapad, his antenna-stalks nestled in his coiled black hair, and looked simultaneously bemused and smug.

"Do we know what they're doing?" Tensent asked. He started to raise his boots to the tabletop, then appeared to think better of it. "Grandmother's dead. Did they find an Imp battle group still active?"

Adan tapped a key, summoning an array of images in orbit around the central holoprojector: the faces of men and women Quell knew as Shadow Wing's squadron commanders; an Imperial Star Destroyer; a pair of cruiser-carriers. Quell forced herself not to look away, instead staring past the azure light. "We have several theories," Adan said. "We don't think the unit's been absorbed into a larger armada, which means we can assume that they're rebuilding. Leadership would be easier to determine if we knew who survived Pandem Nai, but you've already seen Quell's roster of likely candidates."

"Until we have a better sense of their activities, my best guess is Major Rassus." Quell reached out to touch one of the holographic images and a middle-aged man with a sour expression bloomed. "Competent, obedient, and never extraordinary enough to draw attention or threaten anyone's sense of ambition. Most likely he's following Grandmother's last orders and keeping the squadron leaders pointed in one direction."

General Syndulla leaned against the table one-handed, studying the images and expelling a sigh. "Regardless of who's in charge, the threat remains. The last time the 204th followed the orders of a dead leader, millions died on Nacronis."

Again, Quell saw Adan glance her way. She expected him to twist the knife, to mock her with a comment about Operation Cinder only she would understand. Instead he looked back to the pilots and said, "Quell and I have proposed a plan to General Syndulla that addresses both problems—the situation on Troithe and the threat of the 204th. General, we don't mean to waste your time but if you could sum up the strategic situation?"

Syndulla swept away the holograms and turned to the screens. "Governor Hastemoor remains secure in his residence, with surviving infantry, cavalry, and air force close at hand throughout the capital and neighboring sectors. The system's space force has been virtually eliminated, but otherwise significant military assets remain to our foe. Meanwhile, the shield generators protecting the region are fully operational. Even if there weren't millions of civilians still living in the area, a bombing campaign wouldn't do much good.

"Ordinarily, then, we would take the enemy sectors surrounding the capital one by one, closing the noose over a period of months. By the end, only the capital sector itself would remain unsecured and the governor would find himself under siege. We might not be able to starve him out, but we could come blasted close." She scrolled through maps as she spoke, and Quell watched countless skyscrapers, skyways, gardens, and industrial districts blur together—thousands of kilometers reduced to the stroke of a finger. "This strategy would minimize allied casualties. It would give the enemy nowhere to run. It would mean that once we took the capital, Troithe would be *won*."

It wasn't truly that simple, even in the best-case scenario. Troithe wasn't Ryloth or Abednedo—it wasn't a world that had been straining under the Imperial yoke long before Endor. Quell had seen Adan's New Republic Intelligence analysts discussing the likelihood of loyalist guerrillas holding out for years, no matter what the outcome of the war.

General Syndulla knew it, too. *One battle at a time,* Quell thought.

The general continued. "Instead, we're going to move on the capital directly." She swept a finger over one screen, drawing a line from the New Republic territories near the spaceport into Imperial sectors of the city. "We'll need to move rapidly or else be surrounded and cut off. Both ground and air units will be at considerable risk. But the tactical droids agree that our goals are achievable. When the job is done—when we take down the governor and occupy the capital ourselves—the enemy will still control considerable portions of the continent. The planet will be in our hands, but anyone hoping to retake it would see an opportunity."

Tensent was the first to comprehend the implications. "Hell of a plan," he said. "You think the 204th would come all the way to the Core to retake Cerberon?"

Adan looked to Syndulla. Syndulla nodded to Adan. "I'm handling that side of things," he said. "I'll make sure they learn what's going on. They'll know Cerberon is valuable enough to fight for and they'll know precisely how to take it."

Syndulla picked up the thread. "We've got an idea of how to tempt them into action. We'll leave a back door open in the planet's defenses—something they won't realize we know about, that looks like the perfect way for a fighter wing to recapture Troithe single-handedly."

"Back door have something to do with that last mission, running down the cargo shuttle in the debris field?" Chass na Chadic asked. She was slouched forward, elbows on the tabletop and chin on her folded hands.

"Right now the details are need-to-know," Adan told Chadic. "But you'll be briefed when the time approaches. Suffice it to say that we'll be able to predict exactly when and where Shadow Wing will appear. I wouldn't worry about the final battle."

Tensent grinned broadly and nudged Chadic with his elbow. "Because whoever heard of a trap going wrong?"

Adan shot him a furious glance that Quell almost admired for its laser focus. Chadic cackled and Tensent waved it all off as he said, "I like it, though, I do. If we're taking down the 204th for good, I'd rather do it on our terms."

"What about reinforcements?" Chadic asked. "For us, I mean."

"Also need-to-know," Adan said. "But Lieutenant Quell has put her expertise to good use, and General Syndulla has vetted the plan."

"No one's going on any suicide mission," Quell said. She was surprised by Adan's graciousness, though she assumed it was for Syndulla's benefit. "We *can* defeat Shadow Wing. We've proven it before. We're just here to finish the job."

Chass na Chadic looked more bored than reassured. Quell couldn't guess why. Wyl Lark's fingers were locked together, and he stroked the tabletop as he asked, "*Couldn't* it go wrong, though?"

Adan began to answer but Syndulla held up a hand and waited for Lark to continue. After a pause, he did so.

"You said this was the riskier path. We almost lost Pandem Nai because we misjudged the situation. What if we endanger civilians again?"

Syndulla nodded in acknowledgment. "It's a fair point. But this *isn't* Pandem Nai, and we can learn from our mistakes while still judging every situation on its merits. I'm confident the civilian risk, while significant, isn't meaningfully higher than it would be using another approach. Frankly, it's our casualties I'm more worried about." Wyl began to interrupt but Syndulla silenced him. "Taking the capital this way . . . people will die. The ground troops will take hits they wouldn't absorb otherwise, no matter how hard we try to prevent it.

"But it's a good plan, and in war *any* action—inaction included—could lead to losses. We have to decide what stopping Shadow Wing is worth."

She didn't have to repeat herself. Quell heard Syndulla's words echo in her mind: *The last time the 204th followed the orders of a dead leader, millions of people died on Nacronis.*

Yet Syndulla wasn't finished. She shook her head gently and amended, "*I* have to decide what it's worth. That's my responsibility as a general, and I promise you I will do the very best I can."

The tactical center fell silent. Lark still looked troubled but he nodded to the general. Chadic shrugged, shoulders rising and falling with an exaggerated breath even as her eyes were on Lark. Tensent's gaze held on Quell, and she had to suppress a flinch—he was studying her, watching her as if he heard the same unspoken words she did.

Kairos stood staring at one of the tactical screens. She turned her body slowly—so slowly, like a tree imperceptibly rotating to bring its branches into sunlight—toward General Syndulla.

It was Adan who broke the stillness. "Besides," he said, "this whole system's a war zone. We can't make these people's lives much worse."

"I thought she'd call our bluff about the sightings," Adan said afterward at a narrow desk surrounded by printouts in his small office. He grasped the sleeve of the coat slung over the back of his seat and rubbed the cloth over a smudge on the datapad occupying his attention. "But you were right. It looks like the general is on our side."

"It wasn't a bluff," Quell said. She stared past him, through the semitransparent walls that looked out onto what had once been the tram tower's control center. Half a dozen beings reviewed data at workstations or murmured to one another in hushed discussion. Most were un-uniformed and unarmed, but though New Republic Intelligence wasn't part of the military hierarchy, it was surely part of the war. "We have data—"

"We have speculation." Adan shrugged. "Which apparently is enough."

He met her gaze as he darkened the walls to opacity.

Adan had been insufferable enough alone aboard the *Lodestar*, operating his working group with minimal support from the battle group and the general. Since Pandem Nai, however, Adan had become *respected* by both the military and New Republic Intelligence. It had masked his most vile traits—she hadn't seen him shout or curse for a while—but she couldn't help but read his easy confidence as smug arrogance.

Yet he also appeared more competent than she'd given him credit for. The assignments he doled out to Alphabet Squadron were sensible and consistent with the overall strategy they'd agreed to. His team of analysts regularly revealed paths to military victory that would've otherwise remained invisible. If he hadn't held Quell's life in his hands, she might have respected what he was accomplishing.

"I received word from my superiors about the reconnaissance question," he was saying, and Quell forced herself to watch his lips and listen to the words. "It's about what we expected—polite praise for our work and an emphasis that we're *in no way* to blame for the fact that virtually no New Republic battle group has captured an enemy system in weeks. But there's no extra resources to go around."

"Well," she said, "I'm glad the war didn't grind to a halt because of us."

"Reassuring, isn't it? But it means the working group is stuck here even if there's a lead to follow."

Adan was the only person Quell knew who still referred to Alphabet Squadron as part of the "New Republic Intelligence working group on the 204th Imperial Fighter Wing." She supposed he had the right; he had founded the thing.

"What about Vanguard Squadron?" she asked. "Any chance we can borrow them for a scouting op?"

"Possibly." Adan shifted aside a datapad blocking a holoprojector built into the desk. He tapped several keys and a series of images coalesced out of glittering blue dust—a star system, a shipyard, a technical schematic—along with lines of text that Quell couldn't read from her angle. "But Vanguard's on a mission to try to ameliorate the shortage of starships going around. *Special* mission, from Syndulla's *special* consultant Lindon Javes."

"Professional rivalry, or personal?" Quell asked.

It was a stupid thing to say, but Adan smirked. "The man likes to second-guess the rest of us, even when he's not invited."

"Frustrating trait in someone who's not always right." She decided she'd tested her leash more than was wise and quickly pressed on. "So we can't be sure the message will reach Shadow Wing. We're building a trap we can't bait with any confidence."

"We've got time, and I've got options. All I need from you is a list of possible sectors."

They turned to the real work of the day. Adan pulled up incidents that had been flagged—by his own analysts, by New Republic Intelligence HQ, by military droids—as fitting parameters indicative of Shadow Wing activity. One by one, Quell and Adan reviewed them together. They dismissed an ambush over Skako as too sloppy to qualify ("Even without Grandmother," Quell announced, "they wouldn't be stupid enough to get caught in the gravity well") and the disappearance of the *Bantha's Charge* on the Rimma Trade Route as too unremarkable ("If we start tracking down every lost shipment some merchant blames on TIE attacks, we deserve to fail," Adan grumbled).

Other sightings showed more promise. A mole inside the Pyke Syndicate reported that a badly damaged *Quasar Fire*-class cruiser-carrier had arrived at the Gyndine shipyards seeking assistance. The source was reliable but the information scant; Quell added Gyndine to the sightings map and tagged it with a medium-confidence indicator. New Republic agents at Jarbanov, by contrast, could offer numerous descriptions of the TIE fighters that had attacked that planet, but the strike lacked the typical signatures of a Shadow Wing attack.

"Whoever did it was *good*," Quell said as Adan pulled up images of burning disassembly plants and rescue workers in radiation suits crawling over downed patrol craft like maggots on a corpse. She was surprised to find her mind at ease, conjuring no images of carnage from her tenure with the 204th. "But there's no precision to the targeting. Poor pilot discipline, if you watch their formation. Nothing we'd normally associate with the unit, even if Grandmother is no longer enforcing standards."

"Possible they're changing tack?" Adan asked.

"Possible," Quell said. "But without a reason to think so, I wouldn't build a plan around it."

"I'll spare you the gruesome images of the radiation burns, then. I'm not concerned about their flying habits, in any event."

They marked the map, agreed to a low-confidence indicator, and proceeded to review a massacre at Anx Minor (thorough and bloody and entirely in line with what Shadow Wing had done at Beauchen, albeit distant from all other sightings on the map), and rumors of a repainted "Ghost TIE" along the Koda Spur. After looking at the details of the latter, Quell asked to see a list of known surviving Imperial aces to cross-check. "Not today," Adan replied, and that was the abrupt end of the topic.

When they'd finished marking the map, Adan wrinkled his nose and nodded. "We'll pass it to the droids, see if anything comes of it." He tapped a key, causing the holo to vanish with a flash that filled Quell's vision with spots. "We've got weeks before our deadline passes—that's a long time for a message to wind its way through the galaxy."

Quell nodded. "Anything else?"

"How's your squadron faring?"

She straightened her back and squinted at him. "Pardon?"

Adan stood from his seat and stepped to a cabinet at one end of the office. He opened the metal door, stared at the liquor bottles inside, frowned, and closed the door again. "Ito mentioned wanting to check in on the others. I don't want to waste their time unless it's necessary, so—as squadron leader, how are your people?"

"They're fine. Performing better than ever. Lark and Chadic are getting along. Tensent's no trouble. Frankly, I expect they're under less stress than they've been in years."

Adan snorted and leaned against the cabinet as if putting on a show of nonchalance. "Is that right?"

Quell tapped a finger against her shirt, feeling the bulge where a memory chip hung from a chain around her neck—the last scrap of D6-L, the droid that had been destroyed at Pandem Nai after dedicating its existence to Quell and her mission. "We're winning," she said. "They're used to being outnumbered and on the run. Now they're making bombing runs and returning home to a hot meal."

There was a knock against one of the walls. Quell could see a silhouette through the opaque surface.

Adan ignored it. "And Kairos?"

Quell tried to discern what, exactly, Adan was asking. Kairos had been the man's first recruit; she didn't know how long they'd worked together, though he clearly knew some of her secrets.

"Kairos is Kairos."

"Fair enough," Adan said, and opened a door in the opaque wall.

Nasha Gravas was waiting, staring into the office with gunmetal eyes. Her slight frame and smooth, fair skin gave an almost childlike impression, though Quell couldn't guess at the woman's real age. Certainly she had the jaded edge of a veteran. "Formal complaint just came in," she said. "The Children of the Empty Sun are feeling neglected."

"The cultists on Catadra? If we bombed one of their compounds, tell them to take it to General Syndulla," Adan said.

"Apparently, the same smugglers who were moving supplies to the Empire—the ones we just captured—were also assisting the cult." Gravas spoke without sympathy or judgment. "There's not many of the Children on Troithe, but they're enough to carry some weight with the civilians."

"Fine," Adan said. "See if you can smooth things over with the discretionary funds. You're in charge of the project."

Gravas nodded, flashed Quell a look like a sniper preparing for murder, and stepped out.

Adan shook his head in apparent disdain. "Religious types are springing up all over the galaxy. This lot says they're a *religious fellowship*, but 'cult' will do. Word from command is try to avoid interference."

"Lucky Gravas, getting the job to deal with them," Quell said.

"Considering where she transferred from, I'd say so."

Quell understood Adan well enough to know exactly what this meant: Not "let's talk about Nasha Gravas," but "I have secrets you don't."

"Does she know?" Quell asked.

"Does she know what?"

"Does she know about Nacronis? Does anyone on your team?"

There were many possible reasons for Gravas to disdain her, but the truth was the best reason of all.

"That's really not what you should be worrying about," Adan said, and when he smiled it wasn't half as oily as it should have been. "I'll make sure no one knows who doesn't need to."

It was a threat, in its way, because no one *needed* to know until Quell caused trouble. But this was how the conversation always went, no matter who she asked about: Gravas, or Adan's superiors, or General Syndulla.

They spent a few more minutes discussing the operations to come, and with her options curtailed Quell found it easier to concentrate on business. It wasn't until she left Adan's office that she found her mind wandering again.

Nasha Gravas escorted her to the turbolift, as if afraid Quell would peer over someone's shoulder at a classified data display. As she stepped through the doors Quell said, "Adan trusts me more than you do."

She waited for a reaction. She hoped to see some glimmer in Gravas's eyes—some sign that Adan had shared Quell's crimes with her, or not. Something to tell Quell how boldly she wore her shame.

Gravas only smiled darkly. "It's not about trust. Adan *likes* you more than I do."

Quell began laughing as the turbolift doors shut.

CHAPTER 4

SUBSURFACE ROT

I

As a child Soran Keize had visited the ruins of Navosh-Hul in the Warplands of Fedalle. The decay of ages had occluded that window into the planet's ancient past, as had the anachronisms—the custodial droids and velvet ropes and explanatory plaques—but he'd perceived grandeur nonetheless. Wandering those alien palaces, knowing that every vast chamber and kilometer-long passageway had once possessed a name, served a purpose for a forgotten people, he had felt *awe* for the first time in his young life.

Years later, when he had stepped aboard his first Star Destroyer, the broad, endless corridors had returned the metallic scents and glasslike chimes of Navosh-Hul to the forefront of his mind. He had felt awe again, knowing that a battleship required more workers to construct than even Navosh-Hul—that although generations of Fedallese lifeforms had carved and mortared and etched those palaces, tens of thousands of Imperials had worked factory lines and engineering pits to bring the Star Destroyer to life. Soran didn't think of himself as an artist or historian, but on a visceral level he was drawn to the Empire's grandeur as he had been drawn to the achievements of that lost Fedallese civilization.

The cruiser-carrier *Aerie* was not a Star Destroyer. It inspired no awe, and Soran was reminded as much every time he walked its cramped halls. It was an efficient, functional vessel, with equipment visibly packed into every alcove and cabling run close enough to overhead lighting fixtures to cast odd shadows onto every surface. No Imperial cadet, Soran thought, had ever aspired to serve aboard a *Quasar Fire*-class cruiser-carrier, no matter how useful such vessels were in the larger scheme of the navy fleet.

He descended a ladder on his way from the bridge and hesitated to drop his booted foot to the plating below. For an instant he considered taking an alternative path to the wardroom; then he dismissed the notion as cowardice and proceeded along his path, soon reaching a four-way intersection near the center of the deck.

Standing in the center of the intersection, oriented ninety degrees from Soran, was a humanoid figure cloaked in red leather and fabric. A plate of black glass served as its face, and it possessed a stillness that made obvious it was either statue or machine. Periodically, Soran knew, the figure would turn to face one of the other halls—like an antique timekeeping device cycling through the hours, or a primitive compass pointing to some place of galactic importance.

The intersection around the figure was decorated—*anointed*, Soran thought, distantly recalling lectures on the rituals of the Fedallese—with a hodgepodge of objects. Tucked into the space between piping and the corridor walls were rank plaques and officers' caps and bottles of contraband liquor. From a cable hung a line of medals and ribbons that swayed in reply to the thrumming of the *Aerie*'s hyperdrive. On the walls themselves, writing etched by utility knives and laser torches filled whole panels—names of the dead from the 204th and elsewhere.

It was as much a memorial to the Empire and its fallen as it was a shrine to the entity at its center—the red-cloaked Messenger who had come to Shadow Wing after the Emperor's death. The Messenger had spoken only once, so far as Soran knew, ordering the commencement of Operation Cinder before falling silent. Since then, it had remained with the unit, following Grandmother to Pandem Nai and escaping where she had not.

It had been in the same intersection aboard the *Aerie* when Soran had arrived. Its presence troubled him—it was a machine with out-sized influence, using the name and voice of a dead Emperor who had strangled the galaxy as much as nurtured it—but the reactions of the *Aerie*'s company disturbed him more. The shrine grew daily. Pilots bowed their heads and fell silent as they passed. Soran had considered proposing it be moved to a cargo bay, but he feared that would only create dismay and distrust.

He met the faceless gaze of the machine as he passed. It said nothing. Two minutes later he arrived at the wardroom.

The chamber was dominated by a single table and left barely enough room between table and walls for seats—let alone for the occupants of said seats. Outside, the *Aerie*'s corridors had been almost silent aside from the ever-present hum of the engine; inside the wardroom, a dozen voices competed for attention.

"These attacks on Yaga Minor are suicidal—"

"Cherroi's complaining about falling behind on that competition with Squadron Five! Is that really—"

"—rebel propaganda, all of it. Maybe they *are* winning, but the idea that we'd believe—"

Soran crept along the edge of the wall and took his seat at the head of the table. Gradually, the others fell silent. He swept his gaze over the faces before him: the 204th's six squadron commanders and the acting commanders of the cruiser-carriers *Aerie* and *Allegiance*. They all looked back at him, stoic or impatient or concerned.

He made an effort to even his breathing. He steepled his hands against the table's edge. He owed them all his best effort.

"The operation at Jarbanov was a success," he said, the acoustics of the room flattening his voice. "The objective was completed with zero casualties and minimal damage to our fighters. Our engineering crews report that no fewer than seven of the TIEs we retrieved can be restored to working order, while the remaining two can be disassembled for parts. That brings us significantly closer to a full fighter complement—a necessity for any further action."

Even to Soran's ears, it didn't sound like much of a victory. No one applauded.

He thought back to when Devon had rallied the citizens of Tinker-Town, teaching them to defend themselves against the local gangs. Life had been considerably simpler then.

"Successful or not, however," he went on, "we do have much to learn from the operation. No one here was trained to worry about the energy cost of missed shots; nor are we used to fighting an enemy capable of deploying vast forces at a moment's notice. Nonetheless, a failure to adapt will cost the wing dearly. We refine our methods with every mission. All of us."

There was silence in the room. A few of the squadron commanders nodded.

Gablerone stiffened in apparent discomfort. "I thought," he proclaimed from the far end of the table, "that this meeting was a state-of-the-war update."

Soran studied Gablerone. The commander of Squadron Four was round-faced and curly-haired, with a mustache that hadn't been in style in the Core Worlds during Soran's lifetime. Soran had known Gablerone for many years and still thought of him as the man Moff Coovern had sent to replace Colonel Nuress as leader of Shadow Wing; despite Nuress's stubborn unwillingness to retire, however, Gablerone had served adeptly and shown neither ambition nor disloyalty. No matter their differences, Soran respected him.

"I'd intended to leave that topic for the end," Soran said. "We can't do much good for the Empire if we can't stay alive ourselves. But—" He leaned back and dropped his hands to his sides, projecting indifference. "—I don't wish to overstep. I'm here to advise. If the consensus is to alter the agenda, so be it."

Gablerone had been the first to agree to appoint Soran *adviser* to the 204th. He'd also been the first to aim a rifle at Soran upon his arrival aboard the *Aerie* several weeks prior, accusing him of desertion. For this, too, Soran respected the man.

The assembled officers looked to one another. Gablerone finally answered, "Give us the Jarbanov postmortem first, then we talk about the war. My people want updates."

There were no further direct challenges. They reviewed footage from the Jarbanov attack, and Soran called Gablerone's second-in-command, Palal Seedia, into the conference to account for her flight's actions. Though it was certainly possible to find fault with the strike, Soran had no desire to make an enemy of Squadron Four; he encouraged both Gablerone and Seedia to lead the discussion, raising concerns only when required.

Where Gablerone was a thundercloud of emotion forever portending a storm, Seedia was stoic save for a hint of arch wit. Slender-bodied and crested by a fuzz of dark hair, voice projected through a medical vocabulator, she defended her flight's actions. When Soran brought up the fuel costs of tight maneuvering, Seedia argued that burdening her pilots with logistical worries could lead to fatal errors. Rather than answer with irritation, Soran agreed that the key was not in arbitrary limitations but to alter flight patterns in low-risk circumstances. He'd have raised the same objection in her place; he didn't fault her for defending her people.

He waited until a good fifteen minutes into the discussion before asking why she'd gone out of her way to damage the colony's hazard vaults. "We had all the distractions we needed," Soran said. "By the time you irradiated the colony, the act itself was unnecessary."

"Setting Pandem Nai on fire seemed unnecessary, too," Seedia answered. "Yet the rebels did so without hesitation. Wouldn't you agree?"

"Lieutenant," Gablerone growled.

"The concern is Jarbanov," Soran said, "not Pandem Nai."

But he let the jab go. He almost smiled.

By the time they'd dissected every shot fired over the junker world and every errant TIE-to-TIE transmission ("Assume that all comm traffic will be recorded, decrypted, and passed on to New Republic Intelligence," he warned them), Soran's people were growing restless. He dismissed Seedia and set to fulfilling his earlier promise. News of the war wouldn't lift the commanders' spirits, but it wasn't a subject he could avoid forever.

"The New Republic propaganda broadcasts are not to be trusted," he told them, "but as supporting evidence they have been useful. It appears Moff Pandion has indeed been killed, and that his forces have allied with Admiral Rae Sloane. Sloane's fleet is clearly growing, and she appears to be operating primarily within the Outer Rim.

"Our technicians aboard the *Allegiance* have also managed to access a newsfeed operated by former Black Sun agents—no more reliable a source than Republic propaganda, but with its own slant. Combined with the data banks delivered to us by my junker friend, we can safely assert that the New Republic is every bit as chaotic as one would expect—their military supply lines are stretched thin and pirate and raider attacks are at levels roughly sixty times normal. The Empire's been reduced to pockets of stability, but that stability seems real."

Teso Broosh, Squadron Five's commanding officer, had been staring at the wall during Soran's summary. Now he asked simply, "What about Coruscant?"

Major Rassus looked to Soran; Soran waved him to speak. "The system is still blockaded," Rassus said, "but the capital remains untouched by New Republic troops. No word yet from Grand Vizier Amedda."

Captain Darita, Squadron Two's latest commander, offered, "We could break the blockade. Not permanently, but we could make it to Coruscant. Aid in the fight, maybe extract Amedda himself."

Gablerone scowled. "If Amedda wanted to get offworld, he'd find a way. One TIE wing can't free Coruscant."

"If not Coruscant, what about one of the other territories under siege?" Phesh spoke next, leaning forward across the table. "There's still no news out of Anoat—the sector must be under control. We could pledge our services—"

"—and end up working for a power-hungry would-be Emperor who doesn't give a rip about the galaxy at large." Darita shook her head brusquely. "I'm not throwing in with some warlord outside the chain of command."

"Then pick a target!" Phesh cried. "If we're not rejoining the fleet— any fleet—then let's at least do some damage out here!"

Soran allowed the officers to debate—to sketch plans ranging from the cautious to the absurd in their search for a purpose for the 204th Fighter Wing. He listened without judgment until Rassus asked, "What about the Emperor's Messenger? If the droid's with us, it must have orders . . ." Then Soran stood, striking the tabletop with the palm of his hand.

"We won't solve this problem today," Soran said. "Nor should we try. Until we've recovered our strength and reestablished the unit, planning for the future is a futile gesture." Gablerone's lips were twitching and even loyal Rassus shifted uncomfortably, but Soran didn't stop. "I suggest we adjourn for the day and resume tomorrow."

The officers muttered and cursed but filed out of the room, edging around the table and knocking shoulders as they made for the door. When the door slid shut Soran was surprised to find Broosh still present.

"Why encourage debate if you won't accept their ideas?" Broosh asked.

He was a tall man, with a neatly trimmed beard and a face that seemed to have aged a year for every month since Endor. His voice was mild and puzzled.

"They don't trust *my* ideas yet," Soran said. "If they're going to question me, I'd rather them do it in the open so I can guide them toward— well, toward something that won't get us all killed."

Broosh laughed—politely, Soran thought, but with no genuine amusement. Soran had known Broosh long enough to distinguish one from the other. "Give me your judgment," Soran said. "You see the others from a clearer vantage."

Broosh sighed, glanced toward the door, then said, "It's not your ideas that are the problem. I don't think anyone here believes they can lead this unit better than you—hell, it's the only reason you weren't tossed out an air lock.

"It's *you*, Major. *You're* a problem for them."

"Proceed." There was nothing in Soran's voice to comfort or encourage Broosh. Nor was it necessary.

"You *left* us," Broosh said. "After Nacronis, you told the squadron commanders that the war was lost—that continuing to fight was pointless—and you deserted your unit." There was no rage in Broosh's voice that Soran could perceive—just a scolding, like a parent might deliver to a child caught in a lie. "You offered us a way out. Honorable, in its way, and I know you were attempting to set an example, but you left us at our lowest moment.

"And you didn't see what happened at Pandem Nai. You can't understand the pilots who want revenge instead of safety, and they won't understand you."

Shakara Nuress was a friend, Soran thought. *I want revenge as much as anyone.*

But he knew it wasn't true.

Leaving Shadow Wing had been a calculated risk. Soran had moved on to show the others that moving on was not only *possible* but necessary for survival. Yet they had learned nothing from his example and instead, Soran had discovered his assumptions had been in error. Leaving the battlefield had not given Soran a chance at peace; it had isolated him from allies while the New Republic had hounded him. His unit, meanwhile, had been exposed to the vehement spite of the Empire's old foes.

The soldiers of the 204th were wrong to think victory was a possibility. Wrong to think revenge could be wrought in any satisfactory way. They were not wrong to think the New Republic would never leave them be.

"I appreciate your candor," Soran said.

Broosh grunted. "I'm sure. Is—"

"One other question. What do you think of Lieutenant Seedia?"

Broosh arched his brow. "Speaking of revenge? Blowing the hazard vaults was a bad idea only she could've pulled off."

"High praise." Soran considered awhile, stood, and gestured to the door. "Thank you, Commander. Again, I appreciate your candor."

Broosh exited with a brusque nod.

He was right about everything.

Almost everything.

Yet another reason Soran had to do justice by Shadow Wing.

II

The X-wing cut a slash across the dark sky, its strike foils closed. Wyl Lark followed the faint light of its thrusters—fainter than stars under the strange heavens of Troithe—and tried to mimic its dips and spins while maintaining a steady distance. He chased it low among the planet's solar projectors, lower still over the near-invisible atmospheric ripple of the bombardment shield, and then into the upper atmosphere at speeds that left his head aswim and his vision glittering.

There, as he leveled out his ship and sucked in cold gasps of oxygen, he was struck by a revelation: He was a better flier than Yrica Quell. But she was the better starfighter pilot.

"Tell me we got the images," he said, "and that we're not making another pass."

"Confirming." If Quell was breathless, Wyl couldn't tell by her voice. "CB-9 confirms the cam rig picked up twenty-two hundred images of the target area. Assuming your equipment's functional we should have seventy percent coverage."

Wyl tried to recall the briefing. The target had been 63 percent. "Recon's over, then?" he asked.

He rubbed at the console as navigational data flashed onto its screens: a course looping them over the planet's northern hemisphere. "We're taking the long way around," Quell said. "Comm network is glitching today, so better not to pass over even friendly territory. No reason to scare anyone."

"Copy that," Wyl said.

He didn't need an explanation. He was glad for the excuse to soar—he hadn't left Troithe since the mission in the debris field, spending the past few days skirting rooftops and eluding surface-to-air missiles and shooting walkers. He'd escorted Kairos's transport through Cybersynth District foundries and drained his batteries obliterating fifteen stories of Glimmere Tower crawling with stormtroopers. Flying was a pure joy.

As if she understood his thoughts, Quell asked, "You enjoying the break?"

"More than anything," he said, though he was surprised to hear her ask. She'd never been given to unnecessary conversation, in or out of the cockpit. "Thanks for bringing me out here."

They sped eighty-four kilometers above the surface through a cloudless sky. With a gentle dip of one wing, Wyl could bring the vast cityscape into view. It wasn't as undifferentiated as it appeared from orbit, instead splotched with darkness where power grids had failed; banded in differing geometric patterns where architectural styles had shifted during the millennia of the city's expansion; compressed where underlying mountain ranges or waterways or deserts had forced the colonizers to adapt; tinted with beryl or rose or jade, depending on peculiarities of the solar projectors and pollution emitted by local industries, baking color into the composite metals of the metropolis.

"I meant the whole campaign," Quell said.

Wyl's thoughts crumbled apart like a clod of dirt from a drought-parched plain.

"Come again?"

She spoke with obvious consideration. "I don't mean to say things are easy. I know you're working hard as ever, and this operation has its challenges with Vanguard Squadron out-of-system and the need to appear vulnerable without losing outright; add coordinating intelligence with Adan and . . . it's a lot of moving parts.

"But compared with everything in the run-up to Pandem Nai? Compared with the Oridol Cluster, or before Endor?"

"It's different," Wyl admitted. He kept his tone gentle. He didn't want her to feel challenged or disbelieved, but he was genuinely puzzled by this turn in the conversation.

He glimpsed distant shimmering as they passed beyond the edge of the planetary deflector shields. The cityscape was severed by a dark ocean and replaced on the far side of the channel by a bleak expanse of rock. Lightning lit patchy clouds like gaseous obsidian. Here and there was the flash of something metallic, though whether he saw structures or merely stone polished to a sheen he was unsure.

This was the Scar of Troithe: a continent torn apart by mining machines, carved and honeycombed and chiseled until what was left lacked even the harsh beauty of a lifeless planetoid. Wyl tamped down instinctive revulsion—such devastation was anathema to the ways of Home—and reminded himself: *You find beauty in the city. This is the price these people paid—a graft of their world's skin, lifted from one site to sculpt another.*

"We haven't lost a ship in fifteen days," Quell said. "Not us, not Meteor Squadron, not Hail. General Syndulla suggested we might set a record."

He leaned into his seat and pitched his ship so that he could no longer see the landscape. "You're right," he said. "You're absolutely right. I'll still be ready for all this to end."

He found himself wanting to talk to her—to confess that every night he found it harder to dream of Home, and that he'd intended to leave the New Republic before Shadow Wing had murdered his friends. That he wanted to leave now and couldn't.

She was talking, however, and he made himself listen. "I've been where you are now. I used to fly escort on bombing runs all the time. You watch what happens and there's only so much you can do, but you fight to protect your comrades in the air.

"I was at Mek'tradi, Wyl."

There was a long pause. The galaxy seemed upside down, with darkness below and the blazing starlight of the Deep Core above. Wyl felt irritable and guilty at his own confusion—he remembered the destruction of the rebel outpost on Mek'tradi from the Shadow Wing files, realized there was *meaning* in Quell's words yet couldn't discern what meaning that was.

Ask her. If she's coming to you for support, ask her.

"What happened at Mek'tradi?" he asked.

But he'd waited too long.

"Nothing," Quell said, and they flew on through the endless night.

If there was a history of the Thannerhouse District worth knowing, it wasn't in the droid-generated tactical summaries sent to Wyl and the rest of the squadron. The district was old, at least—its borders were defined by the shores of the Thanner Lake, a massive reservoir so buried by towers, bridges, and platforms that it was invisible from orbit. From afar, the only evidence the lake existed were the massive pipes climbing housing blocks and the saucerlike balconies shaped like antique Mon Cala sea skimmers. These last, Wyl supposed, were affectations of the wealthy.

The residents had been warned for three days that New Republic forces would be moving through the district. Broadcasting the plan entailed little risk—by now Governor Hastemoor and his army had surely realized that General Syndulla and her forces were coming for him, and the direct path led through Thannerhouse—and the notice was delivered hourly via radio broadcast and orbital flare. Civilians were advised to evacuate or, as the time of the attack approached, to locate blast shelters and stockpile supplies.

In most of the previously targeted districts, evacuation warnings had resulted in kilometer-long trails of refugees making for New Republic territory. In Thannerhouse, for whatever reason, the residents remained put. Maybe it was out of loyalty to Governor Hastemoor's rule. Maybe it was out of fear of the same.

Either way, Alphabet Squadron was expected to escort the infantry caravan and provide air support in the event of a ground skirmish. Meteor Squadron was twenty minutes away in case of emergency, but recon suggested the district would fall without serious opposition and Alphabet's mixture of fighters and bombers—along with the U-wing transport—made it a surprisingly effective complement to midsized ground detachments. "We've found your calling," General Syndulla had joked before takeoff.

So they flew among the spires of the Thannerhouse District, observing the lambent sunset of tower lights while speeder bikes scouted paths far below. They listened to Chass's collection of Verpine pipe-glass ("My droid has better range and melody," Nath declared) as hover-tanks and stolen Juggernauts rumbled after the speeders, packed with infantry squads spilling out onto their roofs and leaving trails of fluttering ration pack wrappers like spoor.

When the first blast came, the thunder of Wyl's engine and the barrier of his canopy rendered it nearly inaudible. But he knew it for what it was by the screams over his comm.

It was a panicked minute before anyone located the attackers. The energy blast that had melted a Juggernaut and incinerated fifty-nine passengers had come from below—not from a bomber or a gargantuan AT-AT walker but from something below the surface of the water. A second beam erupted seconds later, then a third and fourth. The particle streams caused boiling geysers to erupt, scattered defenseless New Republic soldiers, and cut through buildings a kilometer aboveground. Whatever was below didn't aim for the starfighters, but that made their beams no less deadly.

"Astromech calculating beam trajectories. Attempting to locate their points of origin," Quell called. "Can't get a sensor reading but it looks like we've got six aquatic combat vehicles down there."

"*Kraken*-class deep lurkers," Chass muttered. "Seen them before."

Wyl's screens flashed as data from Quell's X-wing streamed to his console. He checked his weapons loadout and tried to do the math. "They're too far underwater. Concussion missiles won't penetrate that far—"

"Take Kairos and go," Quell snapped. "Get out of range, above the solar projectors. Neither of you is useful here."

Wyl growled and jerked his control yoke, pulling the A-wing away from a beam that left a molten streak across the façade of a corporate tower.

For an instant he thought it was raining. As Quell called orders and Wyl danced among the beams, his mind processed the droplets beating against his canopy and he realized that the enemy had punctured the massive water tanks drawing off the lake water. He was flying through a windless storm, navigating by instruments alone, attempting to escape the spray and find a purpose for his ship, a purpose for the death machine that could do nothing for the troops on the ground or his squadron in the sky.

"The battle didn't last ten minutes," Wyl said. He stood in the *Lodestar*'s observation deck, staring out at the peeling red paint of the maintenance bay and clutching the recorder in one hand. His voice was low, though that was a needless precaution—no one was up and about in that part of the battleship so late. "The lurkers were heavily armed but their plating wasn't any thicker than a walker's. We owe the win to Chass and Nath, mostly."

He described it as he remembered (and maybe, mostly, as it had occurred). Chass had broadcast a Snivvian rhythm-rhyme as she'd descended. Nath had struggled to pitch his Y-wing toward the ground without crashing. But they'd both launched guided bombs through gaps in the broken grating above the lake and annihilated the enemy below. Kairos had ignored Quell's command to get clear, instead evacuating ground troops clinging to shattered streets or caught by waves of boiling water. "Kairos packed thirty soldiers aboard her ship," he said, clasping the holorecorder between both hands. "People are scared of her—you don't know much about her—but I've never met anyone who fought harder to keep her allies alive.

"When it was over, and I got clear of the spray, and looked around"— his voice was soft and calm—"there was water everywhere. Spilling from the tanks and the pipes, running down the buildings. Kicked up from the bomb blasts. Someone had broken the dams, and I could hear the water rushing out. It takes a lot of water to hear over an A-wing's engines.

"We did a quick pass to check for other enemies, but we didn't find any. We listened to the ground troops checking in, and Quell told us we'd done well—we'd kept casualties low, under the circumstances. Chass laughed and said: 'If you sign up to be a ground-pounder you know what you're in for. If you're in the first wave *something's* going to kill you.' She didn't mean it to be callous. We've all seen people get hurt.

"After we finished with the aerial pass, I set down, just to see if we could lend a hand. Water had washed out whole floors of the big towers. One of them's bound to collapse from the damage, and that'll probably take down others. In a year the whole district will be ruins rising out of a lake.

"Nath set down, too, and we looked for anyone to rescue. I asked him, 'Why are we doing this?' and he knew what I meant. We were wading through thigh-high water, searching for missing troops.

" 'We get the capital, we get Shadow Wing,' he said."

They would do it, too. Wyl didn't know what would happen when Shadow Wing came, but he was confident they would take the capital. He'd seen enough of Troithe to realize that there was no defense Governor Hastemoor and the Imperial forces could erect that would stop the New Republic; all the enemy could do was delay the inevitable, to force the expenditure of lives for every meter gained.

Long ago, Wyl had been part of Riot Squadron. He and his colleagues fighting for the Rebel Alliance had seen more losses than wins. They had wept together and danced after missions no one would ever remember. (Missions only Wyl was *alive* to remember.)

"We're fighting a different war now," he told the holorecorder, "and I'm feeling a little sick."

In the early days after Wyl had left Home, he had often written to the elders of his birthplace, Cliff. He'd asked about the righteousness of killing and how to mourn his enemies without betraying his duty. He'd reaffirmed his commitment to fighting until the Emperor was defeated and Home was free. He'd been unable to receive answers, but it had been enough to quiet his mind.

Now he envisioned the recipient of his message—not an elder of Home, but a more nebulous figure—replying. He heard a voice smooth and low, backed by static and neither evidently male nor female. The voice was exactly as he had heard it months earlier, and it showed no sympathy for Wyl's plight.

What do you think a soldier is for, *Wyl Lark?*

He found nothing else to say. Nothing more he wanted to confess, even knowing that the message would never leave his recorder. He squeezed a button with his thumb and erased the data, as he had every time he'd prepared to contact Blink, his friend and enemy. Blink, the anonymous pilot of the 204th Fighter Wing; Blink, who had killed Riot Squadron in the Oridol Cluster and helped save a planet at Pandem Nai.

Even in his imagination, the Shadow Wing pilot would offer no escape from the ocean of blood Wyl swam through. Blink wouldn't listen; and the elders of Home would never understand.

III

Soran Keize dropped from the sphere of his TIE onto the hangar deck, listening to utter silence as his boots impacted the metal plating. He checked the seal on his helmet through the numbing thickness of his gloves and eyed the gauges on his chest plate in the dim emergency lighting. He wouldn't have nearly enough oxygen to explore the entire vessel—but then he didn't have much time anyway.

"Keize in position," he announced. "Minimal life support. Atmosphere twelve percent expected density. No alarms. Status outside?"

"Squadron Five is chasing the last of the rebel escorts." Major Rassus's answer was crisp and curt. "They're no threat but escape is a possibility. Broosh is ready to trap the bantha if we need to pursue through hyperspace—"

"No," Soran said. He thought of the *Aerie*'s journey through the Oridol Cluster, pursuing a rebel frigate into the depths of oblivion. He'd spoken to the pilots involved—heard stories of the enemy picking off hardened warriors as they'd raced through hellish, alien landscapes. "I

want to be done as swiftly as possible. Gone by the time rebel reinforcements arrive."

He strode through the hangar, testing the tug of artificial gravity
and passing a dozen other TIEs as Rassus spoke to someone aboard
the cruiser-carrier. Soran studied the vessels in the gloom, noting the
red-painted cockpit hatches and the bulky machinery half visible
through their viewports. *Drone fighters, every one.*

"What about Squadrons Two and Four?" Soran asked when the
murmuring on the comm ceased.

"Still performing flybys, per your recommendation." *Not "your instructions,"* Soran noticed. "No activity spotted, though Lieutenant
Seedia says she saw a light go dark in section fourteen. Could be a
glitch, even if it were real."

"Seedia doesn't strike me as a woman prone to imagining things,"
Soran said. "Don't you agree?"

There was a short pause. "I wouldn't know. We've never spoken."

Then leave the judgment to me, Soran thought.

"Patch me in to Squadron Five," he said. "I'd like to listen while I
look around."

The ensuing chatter was crisp and professional: targeting assignments and missile lock warnings and gruff words of approval from a
commander to his pilots. Soran found it soothing as he moved out of
the hangar and into the arteries of the Star Destroyer *Edict.*

They'd come searching for the ship guided by little more than hope.
The *Edict* had been a wreck even before the Battle of Endor—a vessel
past its prime, assigned to training missions and war games and
stripped to its core components. It was, Soran had known, one of rela-
tively few Destroyers that could've escaped engagement during the
weeks after the Emperor's death. If anyone had remembered its existence (*he* hadn't, at the time), they certainly wouldn't have considered
its retrieval a priority.

Through guesswork and the careful exchange of intelligence with
less-than-trustworthy sources, he'd managed to locate the *Edict* under
New Republic guard in the desolate expanse of the Pormthulis system.
Whether these efforts would prove profitable he wasn't yet certain.

The corridors were dark, but no dust swam in the rays of his glow rod. Soran unsealed blast doors and rerouted emergency power to turbolifts, navigating the labyrinth as he wended toward section fourteen. He permitted himself a smile when Squadron Five's Commander Broosh declared the last of the rebel forces destroyed, but he said nothing.

Section fourteen was primarily devoted to crew habitation—bunk rooms and messes and supply stations, with a scattered few turbolasers and point-defense cannons set into exterior bulkheads. Soran saw no indication that the area was in use—no unexpected power distribution, no sealed-off atmosphere, not even a tray out of place in the galley. He adjusted his comm as he walked.

"Keize to Seedia? Can you pinpoint the exact location of the activity you saw in section fourteen?"

"Negative." Static cut through the reply, but with Soran's helmet set to amplify and broadcast, it echoed even in the thin corridor air. "Would you like me to make another pass?"

"No need. If we have allies aboard, I have no wish to frighten them. If we have enemies, I will die with few regrets. Should I abruptly cut contact, open fire."

"Understood," Seedia said. But Soran was no longer listening to her.

The crew emerged slowly, like feral animals approaching a potential source of food and warmth. They crawled out of maintenance shafts and supply closets, wearing scuffed and grease-stained uniforms along with rebreathers and oxygen packs. Most wore cadet insignia and had an air of youthful uncertainty; three were noticeably older, white-haired or entirely bald. Twenty in total surrounded Soran, blocking the corridor in both directions.

"You hid from the New Republic?" Soran asked. He directed his question to a bejowled captain who fingered a blaster pistol. He did not raise his voice.

"If you're asking why we didn't fight—" the captain began irritably.

"No. Given your circumstances, you might have breached protocol—but adaptability is no flaw in a soldier. Did you hide?"

"We did." The captain nodded to someone behind Soran, perhaps indicating to one of the cadets to back away. Or come closer. Soran didn't turn his head. "But I don't appreciate being questioned by a TIE pilot."

"I don't fly much nowadays." Soran waited for a laugh, or at least a raised brow, but none came. He continued: "I'm Major Soran Keize, special adviser to the 204th Imperial Fighter Wing. We are diminished, as you have been, but we came here to bolster our unit."

He paused, watching the survivors of the *Edict* and grateful that his helmet hid his expression. He'd hoped that the ship would be abandoned—or better yet, crewed by naval officers hardened after months of fighting and already evolving to fight a war in dire straits. Instead, he'd found children and their nursemaids. They would tax his resources instead of contributing. All he really needed was their ship.

"If you wish to join us," he said, "you would be welcome."

It turned out the *Edict* was drifting through the Pormthulis system rather than being disassembled in a New Republic salvage yard because its hyperdrive had been offline for weeks. The *Edict*'s crew had been unable to mend it without a replacement generator, reactant agitator injector, coaxium suspension element, and twenty-eight Imperial-standard sealing bolts. The New Republic, upon capturing the Star Destroyer, had also been unwilling or unable to effect repairs.

Thus, it fell to Soran Keize to sacrifice the cruiser-carrier *Allegiance* so that the *Edict* might live. The *Allegiance* had served the 204th well but no one questioned the wisdom of the decision. The carrier's engine was disabled and disassembled, its parts gingerly guided down zero-gravity corridors into the hangar, out the magnetic field, and directly into the maw of the *Edict*. Under Soran's supervision, the cadets and their superiors proved that they possessed a measure of competence after all, restoring main power and lightspeed capability to the Star Destroyer within six hours.

The entire process reminded Soran of Devon's life aboard the *Whitedrift Exchange*, where Devon had partnered with young Rikton under the Harch to repair drive systems and malfunctioning thrusters and a hundred other problems with a thousand classes of starship. He was surprised by the ferocity of his desire to shove his hands into the Star Destroyer's guts. He was surprised he hadn't wondered where Rikton was before now, and wondered if he'd made a mistake sending the boy away.

But perhaps Rikton had a future ahead of him yet. He had been Imperial, but hadn't done the deeds Shadow Wing had.

After the disabled *Allegiance* had been stripped and obliterated by Squadron Three (the carrier's captain, Rogart Styll, objected, but sentiment was a burden the 204th could not carry forever), and *Aerie* and *Edict* had escaped from danger into the cerulean storm of hyperspace, Soran suggested a celebration to welcome the 204th's newest members and the addition of the Star Destroyer to the growing battle group.

It did not go as he planned.

"Andara has fallen!" Kandende declared, tipping the bottle of wine and letting the liquid spill from his lips onto the collar of his uniform and down to the tabletop on which he stood. "The New Republic declares victory once again, and we—"

Gablerone grabbed the young pilot by the ankles and tossed him from table to floor with impressive speed, but the damage had been done before the drunken toast. Soran could finish the sentiment himself: *—and we celebrate, having recovered a training vessel crewed by children.*

The news had spread before the celebration in the *Aerie*'s hangar bay. Rather than a crowd of festive soldiers sharing a precious supply of wine and "enhanced meal rations," Soran was faced with a grim-faced gang of squadron commanders and those pilots and crew who'd failed to find busywork elsewhere.

"Is that true? About Andara?" the bejowled instructor from the *Edict*—Soran had learned the man's name was Oratio Nenvez—asked.

Soran deliberately turned away from Gablerone's harsh discipline of Kandende. "That's the claim being aired on the propaganda networks. We'll need to confirm, but it does seem likely."

"Bastards," Nenvez spat. "You intend to strike back?"

"If Andara is lost, direct retaliation wins us nothing. We'll continue rebuilding the wing, hitting targets as opportunity allows."

"Rebuilding for what purpose?" Nenvez scoffed. "While we grow stronger the rest of the Empire is crumbling."

We can't save the rest of the Empire, Soran thought. *We can save ourselves.*

"Rebuilding so that when an opportunity arises, we may take full advantage of it."

Nenvez stared at Soran a while and then, with a curt nod, stalked away.

In the old days, aboard the *Pursuer,* Soran would have left the celebration. He would have sought out the pilots and crew who hadn't joined in, squatted next to them as they stripped engine coils or tested cannon chargers, and silently assisted until they admitted what troubled them. That had always been his method, and he was tempted to leave the celebration now.

But being second-in-command to Colonel Nuress had given him cover he no longer had. *He* had called this celebration, and if he walked out he would be abandoning those who'd come as well as lose what credibility he'd earned with the wing's leadership.

"See to your people," he murmured in passing to the squadron commanders present. They understood the message, each quietly gathering their own soldiers before departing. Darita hissed *"Fix this!"* to him as she went. Soran was left with the crew of the *Edict* and those from the *Aerie* and *Allegiance* who had lacked the sense to stay out of sight.

"Come," he called, sitting on an empty battery crate. "Let's tell our stories about Andara and about the *Allegiance.* If this is going to be a funeral, we'll do it right."

They did tell stories. Not pilot stories, but stories about repairing a power conduit on the *Allegiance* as Pandem Nai burned or about taking leave on Andara after the death of a sister. Soran stayed silent—his place was to listen, not to dominate—but he remembered his own brief encounter with Andara's security forces when he had been young and foolish. A month before his entrance into the Academy and he'd almost earned an arrest record that would've kept him out of the Imperial Navy forever.

"We can't let them keep winning," Creet said. She was a veteran of the 204th but no older than twenty-one. She spoke with a thick Twi'lek accent that Soran imagined had earned considerable mockery during her training among the ground crews. "You've seen what is out there, Major. They think they've already won. Do they not?"

"They do," Soran admitted. *Are they wrong?*

"We need to show them they haven't. Even if we are to bide our time—" He could see Creet fumbling with the language. The others were watching her. "—we owe the people of Andara. We need to be showing them all that people are still fighting. Fighting for them. Fighting for the Empire."

"We will," Soran said. "We *are*."

The answer satisfied none of them, but they nodded. "Tell us," Creet said, "what it's like under their rule."

He wasn't keen to discuss his time as Devon. But it was better than promising vengeance and bloodshed, and he gave his audience the truth: that the New Republic was a government that did not know how to govern; and that while scattered worlds might revel in their newfound freedom, more were suffering from food shortages and societal breakdown and criminal activity. He told them about Mrinzebon and Tinker-Town, where he had met an Imperial who'd fallen prey to the same corruption afflicting the rebels—a small, petty man who preyed on impoverished locals to enrich himself and his companions.

Soran found himself weeping gently as he told the story, though he hadn't wept at the news of Andara. He did not hide his emotion, and the others watched him with the gravity of youth as he described Gannory, the cantina owner who had befriended him; his students in Tinker-Town, who had learned to fight for their own survival when *someone*—the Empire, the New Republic—should have been protecting them.

And when he was asked again, "When will we show them we still fight?" he said, "Tomorrow."

The next day he scanned star charts and tactical maps and chose a target. He persuaded the commanders one by one and they flew to Mon Gazza, where Soran knew from his travels that the New Republic was establishing a planetary outpost. They reduced it to dust with particle cannons and proton torpedoes; they walked among wreckage and corpses to make sure that nothing was left undone, nor any evidence left behind, and Soran allowed an anonymous pilot to scrawl in the ashes: FOR ANDARA.

He doubted anyone would find it.

After he had showered (two minutes only, as water was still in short supply), he swept dirt and ash into the drain and sat in his office to review the latest intelligence skimmed from open comm feeds. This was not his specialty—he lacked the expertise of a dedicated analyst—but who else was available?

He browsed headers, satisfied that nothing regarding the capture of the *Edict* had made it into the public conversation, and paused when he reached a file of corrupted half messages sent on coded Imperial channels. There were the usual desperate cries for help from outposts under siege by entire New Republic fleets, but one—earmarked with an obsolete encryption code once used by the 204th—caught his attention.

A message from the Cerberon system.

He read the sections that had not decayed to gibberish with interest. He read it again and pulled up files on Cerberon, its worlds, and its military significance.

If his people insisted on risking their lives for a war already lost, the least he could do was give them a battle worth winning.

IV

Chass na Chadic didn't have her ship but she still had a mission. She tried to comfort herself with that fact as the U-wing's deck bucked beneath her and wind blasted her through the open loading door. *You could be back at base,* she told herself. *You could be dragging your butt through the refugee camp looking for a deck of cards. Or death sticks. You* volunteered *for this because this job didn't need another bomber.*

But as the ship rocked and she wedged the toe of her left boot into a seam to keep from falling a kilometer onto pavement, she couldn't bring herself to feel grateful. She shouted a curse at Kairos (one the pilot certainly wouldn't hear over the buffeting air) and pressed her face to the turret scope.

"Problems above?" The question came through her headset; sound vibrated through the ill-fitting earpieces raking her horns, worsening her temper. She couldn't remember the name of the speaker—one of the infantry troops, name of Vitale.

"Ignore our girl Chass," Nath's voice answered. "She's not in a happy mood."

Don't condescend to me, you surly bastard, Chass would've said, but she was wrestling the turret barrel into position, squinting to get a magnified glimpse of the street below. Parked speeders, uncollected garbage . . . occasional barricades that had to have been assembled by civilians. She hoped the computer-assisted aim would pick up anything she was missing; a walker could flash by and she might not notice.

The job was recon: Fly into enemy territory a few klicks ahead of the ground troops and scout the sectors nearest the capital. Scan for the governor's forces and identify a path to the shield generators. Chass risked a glance up at the faint shimmer in the sky, where the planetary deflector refracted the burning iris of the black hole. They'd entered below the energy field but so close to the ground that a single stormtrooper with a Plex rocket could take them down.

For the real assault to begin, New Republic forces would need to bring bombers into play. That meant eliminating the shields before anything else.

She spied the flash of a hovermine floating midway up the side of a tower, blocking a side street. She called it in.

"Ground team," Quell called, "you have enough to work with? They've likely spotted the U-wing by now, even with the baffles and jammers on."

"One more pass along the tram line and I'll feel more comfortable," the woman on the ground replied. "Sending a route to the pilot now."

Chass felt the U-wing's thrusters transfer power a millisecond before her field of view shifted. The transport banked and turned. She captured images of the tram line and the barricades—real barricades this time, duracrete and energy fields—erected along its length; spotted stormtrooper patrols in the distance marching through the streets. She felt her cheeks and nose go numb from the wind and spun the turret around, making an obscene gesture into the recorder lens before returning to the work.

"Charming," Quell said.

"You love it."

"Just make sure you get the images."

"Come on, Lieutenant, you know I'm good for it—"

"If you two are done flirting?" Vitale interrupted.

"Be grateful," Chass snarled, suddenly self-conscious. She didn't mind Alphabet listening, but strangers were another matter. "We're doing this work so *you* don't get killed."

"And we're going to get killed *why*, exactly? Why are we rushing into the capital instead of starving the governor out?"

Chass knew better than to mention Shadow Wing on an insecure channel. But not mentioning the trap didn't keep the thought from flashing through her head, and she shifted restlessly.

"Leave the speculation for another day," Quell said curtly. "Finish up and head home."

The U-wing adjusted course again and Chass moved on wobbling, wide-spread legs toward the loading door's control panel. She slapped it hard and leaned against the bulkhead as the door began to slide shut. "Bastards," she muttered, and her mind lingered on Shadow Wing—on Blink and Char and Puke flying through the clouds of the Oridol Cluster.

The clouds of Oridol became the flames of Pandem Nai as something erupted and thunder shook the transport. Chass was launched across the cabin. She turned her head in time to avoid breaking her nose against the far bulkhead, but her cheek hit hard and the studs of her horns were driven back into her skull through her left temple. Heat surged at her back, and when she twisted around she saw shards of rocket casing burning on the deck and the crew seats afire. The loading door had finished closing but rattled worryingly.

"We're hit!" Chass called. She smelled melting plastoid and fabric as smoke rose from the seats. She felt a flash of pain as her nostrils flared. "In case you didn't notice!"

The U-wing accelerated, abandoning all pretense of stealth. Chass could only guess that they were running from their attackers. She swallowed a mouthful of smoke and stumbled away from the wall, kneeling and fumbling at floor panels in search of the emergency compartment. She jerked at a handle, yanked with frustration until a plate came loose and she was able to retrieve the fire extinguisher.

Two minutes later the flames were out and Chass had kicked most of the rocket shrapnel into a corner. She stuck her head into the cockpit long enough to confirm that Kairos was alive and on course, but the masked woman acknowledged her with nothing more than a glance and a nod. "Nice that you were worried," Chass said, and returned to the main cabin.

When she went to return the extinguisher to the emergency compartment, she saw the trophies.

In the chaos of the fire, she hadn't noticed them. But they were lined neatly against the sides of the emergency compartment, tacked in place with adhesive. On one side were Imperial rank pins and comlinks and something it took Chass a moment to recognize as a cracked optical lens from a stormtrooper's helmet. On the other side were scraps of cloth that, beneath a layer of grime, displayed rebel starbirds and stylized beasts and smiling skulls. New Republic infantry patches, Chass guessed.

Most of the trophies were damaged, chipped at the edges or scorched by particle blasts. Some of them still had the rank odor of human sweat.

Kairos . . . what have you been doing?

She'd met a specforce grunt once who'd claimed he extracted the dead stormtroopers' fingernails to ensure some post-Imperial government could genetically catalog families involved in atrocities. She'd seen it as a mix of sadism and politics but figured she might've done the same if she'd been a ground-pounder.

Pilots didn't collect trophies. They never got close enough. They just kept score.

She peeled off one of the patches and rose from the floor. She caught a glimpse of Kairos's battered bowcaster as she ducked into the cockpit.

She dropped into the copilot's seat, shrugging off the pain of her fresh bruises. Outside, the U-wing was ascending away from a hexagonal pattern of city blocks and entering a thin mist of clouds. They'd left the capital region and the bombardment shield behind. The unnaturally bright glow of stars was diffused by the fog but not hidden altogether.

"You're a freak, you know?" Chass said.

Kairos increased thruster power and kept her visor oriented toward the viewport. Chass studied the woman's wrappings and the dull metal of her helmet. She appeared more battered than Chass had noticed in the past—her garment as scorched and ashy as her trophies, her mask specked with rust. Chass had *felt* the change in Quell over the past weeks, grown almost comfortable with the straight-edged defector, but any change in Kairos came too subtly to notice. *Like watching grass grow,* Chass thought.

She pressed the patch against the console, smoothing it with her fingers. It showed an emblem of the dead world of Alderaan orbited by a starfighter. "One of ours, right?" she asked. "From Thannerhouse, maybe?"

Kairos's gloved hand flexed on the control yoke. Her head turned a fraction of a degree. It was as much acknowledgment as Chass had expected.

"What about the Imp stuff? Those your kills? Ours? Someone else's? You save them for motivation, for memorials . . . ?"

Her hand had found its way to her sidearm. She thought back to Abednedo, where she and Kairos had slaughtered a pack of stray troopers. For all the damage Chass's acid rounds could do, Kairos had somehow done worse.

The U-wing pilot didn't react at all this time.

In a human, Chass would've seen the response as arrogant. If Quell had brushed her off that way, she would've raged. But Kairos had never acted like a human, and while Nath and Wyl might never have considered whether species made a difference, Chass was inclined to give Kairos the benefit of the doubt. She'd been on the receiving end of too many poor assumptions.

So maybe Kairos was a killer at heart. But Chass breathed in the metallic, floral scent of Kairos's gear—or her body, Chass didn't know—and made a decision. Kairos had saved her more than once, and Chass owed her a good turn.

"I won't tell anyone, obviously," Chass said. She peeled the patch back off the console, scratching off tacky residue with her fingernails. "You want my advice, though? You're thinking too much, carrying this stuff around. Reminders don't change the job. They just make focusing harder."

Kairos turned fully to observe Chass. Then she looked back to the viewport.

Chass rose from the seat and clambered back into the main cabin. "Look at me," she called as she stomped to the emergency compartment, sticking the patch against the metal somewhere close to where she'd taken it from. "*I* don't dwell, and I get by fine."

That was a lie. She dwelled on many things. Just never on the dead.

CHAPTER 5

A WINDING PATH TO VICTORY

I

Yrica Quell was laughing. It came naturally, though the sound was unfamiliar enough to surprise her and her own surprise amused her further, fueling the reaction like a hyperdrive melting down.

"It wasn't that funny," Caern Adan said. He was smirking as he spoke, though Quell suspected it was at her expense.

"It really wasn't," she agreed, and stifled her snicker. She flattened her affect in an instant. "You're not a funny man."

Adan arched his brow but didn't reply. General Syndulla looked between Quell and Adan, apparently as charmed as she was puzzled. "Let's continue," she said, and walked two meters around the display table and forty kilometers west through the holoimage of Troithe's surface.

The two weeks since beginning the march to the capital had gone well. Alphabet hadn't been grounded due to damage or mishap for more than a day. Meteor and Hail were assisting with all assignments requiring heavier firepower. There was the usual complaining from the Sixty-First Mobile Infantry—it was increasingly apparent the unit had never fought a traditional urban ground war, and Quell had spotted the captain arguing with Syndulla more than once—but Troithe was falling to the New Republic sector by sector.

Meanwhile, Quell found herself spending most of her non-flying hours with Adan and his analysts. With Adan, she didn't need to worry about slipping up and revealing her darkest truth. With Adan, she could be as cynical and honest as she had the heart for. She spent more time with the intelligence officer than she did with Syndulla, though the Twi'lek general seemed grateful for the sounding board that Quell had become.

Now they were on the verge of victory. The greatest challenge was leaving room for future defeat.

Syndulla took a sip of caf. Six cups and two thermoses stood guard around the room. "What if we hit the command centers on the way to the capitol building? That'll reduce the risk of the infantry being outflanked. Maybe even let us capture the governor, if we're lucky."

"We're already blowing the shield generators," Quell said. "The more military infrastructure we disrupt, the less likely Shadow Wing is going to want to take the planet back."

Adan grunted. "Not that I'm arguing for it, but do we *need* the infrastructure if enough of the Imperial Army is left standing? When the 204th studies the situation, they'll see an opportunity to rally—"

"No." Quell spoke only to Adan, leaning lightly against the table. "They're not grand strategists. Without Colonel Nuress, they'll be looking for a dramatic win achievable with a single strike. That only works if the infrastructure is there for the Troithe forces to reoccupy."

"So the infrastructure stays. My big worry is putting the infantry in a killbox," Syndulla said. "Air support can only do so much. We're already paying a cost in lives to bait this trap; but total failure is a real possibility."

Quell parted her lips to reply. Syndulla raised a hand, palm-out, asking for silence as she wrinkled her nose and studied the map.

Finally, the general nodded and drew up. "We'll have to hit the shield generators as fast as possible. Allied troops move in under the field first, enemy emerges from hiding to intercept. We wipe out the shields, bombers decimate the enemy before they can retreat back to the bunkers. The timing will be challenging but I don't see a way to make it easier. Not unless someone's got a Jedi hidden away."

No one spoke up.

"I can dream," Syndulla said, and her smile was sadder than Quell would've expected.

They spent another hour reviewing details. Adan's team had worked up a psych profile of Governor Hastemoor that did little to illuminate his strategies. Analysis of the U-wing's reconnaissance imaging had allowed the droids to plot out multiple "minimum-risk" routes for the ground troops. Quell read off inventories provided by Sergeant Ragnell of starfighter munitions (though Syndulla dismissed these—"If we win here, I'm not worried about running low on torpedoes tomorrow"; Quell disliked the principle but couldn't argue).

At last, General Syndulla announced that any useful discussion had ceased. "We'll close up shop and discuss outstanding issues tomorrow," she said, and began to collect the thermoses. "I'd say we've got about seventy hours before the troops are in position, so no need to burn out tonight."

Adan smiled wryly. "Why don't you head back? We'll save out the data. No need to keep you."

Quell gave Adan a surprised glance but didn't comment. She stayed where she was, bent over a console entering encryption keys for the tactical maps.

"I'm in no hurry," Syndulla said. "Besides, I wanted to talk with Quell for a moment."

"If you've got concerns about the working group—" Adan began, and Quell tuned out the words as Syndulla reassured the man he wasn't being shut out. She snapped off the holos and realized, looking between the two, that she was hoping Adan would win the argument.

Yrica Quell . . . when did you start wanting *to spend time with that man?*

Syndulla came out ahead, of course. Quell gathered an armful of mugs as they left the tactical center and began to walk to the galley. "I've been meaning to tell you," Syndulla said, "your squadron's come a long way."

"Thank you," Quell said. She didn't know what else she was expected to say.

"I mean it." The corridors of the ship were quiet. Without the background thrum of the engines, the *Lodestar* seemed emptier than it truly was. "You and I both remember when you couldn't get your people through a training mission without an accident. Now they're as strong a team as Meteor. Stronger than Hail Squadron, since we lost the twins."

Quell waited for the *but*. She thought of debriefings with Major Keize, who'd rarely spared her feelings. Syndulla was fluid where he'd been solid, and the unpredictability made Quell tense.

Or maybe it was the thought that Syndulla might yet realize what had happened at Nacronis. Or the thought that Adan had already told her.

They entered the galley and they began returning the cups and thermoses to their places. "The only advice I'm going to give you"—the general smiled wryly as she spoke—"is to keep an eye on them. Bringing them together was the start, but you have to keep doing the work."

"You notice something wrong?"

"Got a complaint from the ground crews about Chass joyriding in her B-wing and coming home intoxicated. Aside from the obvious, there's something going on with her. Might just be she's testing her limits."

Quell wanted to ask: *Why wasn't I told first?* But that was a complaint for the ground crew, not for the general.

Syndulla kept speaking. "It's the rot you don't see that does the most damage. Wyl, Kairos, Nath? Don't wait till the house collapses to check on them."

"I'll take care of it. Anything else?"

"Seventy hours," Syndulla said. "After that, it's going to be a chain of crises until we know this trap failed or until Shadow Wing is done for good."

They stood watching each other. Syndulla seemed to be waiting for Quell to figure out the rest.

"In the meantime . . . ?" Quell tried.

"Go bond with your squadron. Maybe take the night off."

"Try the green one," Tensent insisted, nudging the bottle across the table toward Chadic. "Go on."

"I'm not trying it."

"You're scared. You don't have to be scared—"

"Seriously? I'm not a puppet. You can't call me scared and make me jump into action."

Quell watched them snipe under the light of stars and the burning iris of the black hole. They sat at a long metal table in the civilian section of the spaceport, their faces warmed by heat lamps and their backs chilled by the evening breeze. Somewhere nearby, Empty Sun cultists were listening to holographic lectures and children were playing cards. Lark had brought them to a makeshift restaurant serving high-class "neo-Coruscanti cuisine" on sheets of recycled plastoid—he'd somehow met and befriended the chef, who'd taken his trade from the wealthiest region of Troithe to the refugees' tent city.

Quell wasn't sure where the chef had obtained his ingredients; she had her suspicions and chose not to investigate (a choice that made her feel more like Nath Tensent than the New Republic Intelligence officer she was supposed to be). They dined on curled slivers of gutterfish encrusted with spices; bread with the texture of sea foam and the taste of salted fruit; spoonfuls of organic metal dust drizzled in purple and green sauces kept in oversized squeeze bottles. The portions were small, but it was unquestionably the finest meal Quell had ever eaten.

She said as much to Lark, who sat beside her while they ignored the escalating argument between Tensent and Chadic. Only Kairos hadn't joined them for the meal.

"We had plenty of food growing up," Quell said, "but it wasn't something we talked about. Flavor wasn't something we analyzed, except for my father with his brandy."

"That's the most you've ever said about your family," Lark answered. "It's good to know."

Quell shook her head, certain that wasn't true but wondering if the cheap wine they'd been served in tin cups wasn't having an effect. "What about you?"

"We didn't import much from offworld, but we enjoyed our food. We—"

Tensent's hand came down on Lark's shoulder, cutting short the younger man's thought. "Sorry to interrupt. Think someone's looking for you."

He gestured past huddled crowds and tents, and Quell's eyes spotted a woman trekking through the dark in an infantry uniform. Her hair was braided in tight rows, and streaks of cyan paint dappled her dark skin. Quell didn't recognize her, but Lark politely excused himself.

"Who is she?" Quell asked.

"That's Vitale," Nath said. "Been teamed up with her a few times. Don't think she saw us, but the boy deserves a good night and they seemed to get along," Tensent said, and Quell laughed softly.

By the time their meal was finished, Lark had returned not only with Vitale but with half a dozen other infantry soldiers. There was no more food in the restaurant's stocks but the troops didn't seem to mind. Tensent produced an armful of Imperial rations out of nowhere—the good sort, the kind TIE pilots had traded favors for aboard the *Pursuer*—and handed them out, calling the troops by name and pouring the last of the wine. The gathering felt less intimate than before but that suited Quell: It allowed her to escape attention.

"Is it true we're going after the governor soon?" one of the soldiers asked, and when Quell inclined her head enough for him to infer agreement, he swore. "Means we actually might win this system, huh?"

"You rather not?" Chadic asked.

The man laughed and shook his head. He was human and gray-haired and olive-skinned, with a high-pitched lilt to his voice that seemed out of place. "Just means the next assignment comes sooner than I'd like. You know where we're going, right?"

Tensent laughed uproariously at something occurring at the far end of the table. Lark asked, "Where are you going?"

"The captain won't admit it," the man answered, "but everyone knows Troithe is just a test run. Command is trying out tactics, seeing what works. Giving us experience before they send us to the galactic capital."

"Coruscant?" Lark said.

"Coruscant," the man agreed. "Sooner or later, they're going to drop us in the thick of it. All this? Just practice."

Quell could have corrected the man. She nearly did, thanks to the wine and a sudden warm burst of poor judgment. But the working group's project was better left confidential, and she doubted he would prefer the news that Troithe was being used as bait.

Besides, he might've been right. Quell didn't know what was going on in the minds of General Syndulla and her superiors. She didn't know anything about the captain of the Sixty-First Mobile Infantry. Any reassurance she could offer would be false.

Instead she said: "Maybe it is practice. But you'd better get it right the first time."

The table erupted in laughter and cheers and mockery. Quell downed her cup of wine and wondered if she was as flushed as she felt.

They told war stories, pretending they were engaged in the natural give-and-take of conversation instead of one-upmanship. A man named Zab who had just returned from Catadra claimed that an incident there reminded him of the fall of Yordain Core, and recited an unlikely tale of survival and a priest-king's blessing. Chass na Chadic, in reply, told a story of the Cavern Angels in the days before she'd joined Hound Squadron. An infantrywoman told the story of Blacktar Cyst; Quell remembered the battle differently, but she said nothing about having fought there as part of the 204th. Wyl Lark spoke of Pandem Nai. Nath Tensent and two others swapped legends of the Battle of Hoth.

Talk of Hoth became talk of Darth Vader, the dead Galactic Emperor's chief enforcer. The strangers at the table gave their own tales before Tensent said, "A lifetime ago, I was Imp Navy. I could tell you what I heard—" Here he paused and jutted a thumb at Quell. "—but our commander's got better."

Quell wanted to strike him. No one blinked at Tensent's admission that he had been Imperial, however, and no one asked when she'd changed sides. They only looked at her and awaited a story.

"I never met Vader," she said.

Tensent grinned and shook his head so only she could see. The others groaned with disapproval or urged her on.

"Give!" Chadic shouted, and squeezed Quell's arm, nails digging into skin and Quell's squadron tattoo.

She bowed her head and gave what she could: lurid tales of Vader murdering subordinates who had failed, of Vader shooting down wingmates who got in his way during flight, of officers summoned to Vader's mysterious fortress and never permitted to return. "One of my first captains served with Vader right after the Clone Wars and said he'd changed over the years. That he'd always been violent, but he'd matured."

"*Matured*?" one of the soldiers asked.

"At the start, he'd kill you because he was frustrated. Later, he waited for you to make a mistake. Maybe a trivial mistake, but always a mistake."

"You know where he got his lightsaber?"

"I don't," Quell said. "Probably killed a Jedi for it."

Wyl Lark shifted uncomfortably, but no one save Quell appeared to notice.

Talk of Vader became talk of his master, the fallen Emperor, and talk of the Emperor turned to ghost stories. Quell silently prayed that no one would speak of Operation Cinder—that Cinder was Emperor Palpatine's own order was a fact that remained unknown to most. And as soldiers took turns describing what they would *do* to the Emperor's corpse if it were recovered from the ruins of the second Death Star,

Quell thought of the night she'd walked alone through the forests of the cold moon of Harkrova and been haunted by his presence.

"I wish he had survived," said a one-eyed Mon Cala who'd been lurking beside Zab most of the evening. The socket on the scarred side of his face was as large as a fist, and Quell forced herself not to stare. "I wish we could see him tried for every crime he ever committed, from his days as Naboo senator on. It would take a year, perhaps, but everyone in the galaxy would watch. Everyone would say *Never again shall such an empire rise,* and when they executed him at last, every Imperial who followed him would fear the justice of the New Republic."

Vitale raised her wine cup with a grin before spitting on the ground. "If they tried him first, every Imperial who followed would have a defense: *I wasn't as bad as that guy.*"

"Executions never brought anyone justice," someone else said, and Quell stared past Lark's shoulder into the crowds of refugees milling about in the starlight or heading to their tents. The conversation fractured, one half of the gathering arguing over the ethics of capital punishment while the other half offered ill-informed tactical speculation about the defenses of the Anoat sector and the Iron Blockade there.

"Come on," Nath Tensent said, and practically lifted Quell from her seat one-handed. "Let the dirt-stompers have the table—we've all got enough wine in us to enjoy the night."

She would've had an excuse if she'd been drunk. But only Chadic had imbibed enough wine to be more than *loose,* and Quell knew she was responsible for her choices as they made their way into the spaceport tram station and boarded one of the maintenance cars. Unlike the rest of the network they were self-powered and fully functional.

"We'll get shot down, and then what?" Quell asked as Tensent withdrew a code cylinder and activated the autonavigation.

"It goes half a klick outside the port," Lark said patiently. "If there are enemy troops targeting us this close in—"

"—we'd be doing the general a favor, luring 'em out!" Chadic said much too loudly, laughing as she did. She flung her arms around

Quell's shoulders for balance as the tram car lifted out of its moorings and hummed along an ascending mini line.

The four of them rode together, and Quell tried to put aside questions like *Why are we doing this tonight? Why am I here? What if an alert goes out?* and focus instead on the view and Chadic's warm, muscular arms against her.

Lark and Tensent were pointing out something below them. Quell didn't try to see what. She watched the lights of the camp grow smaller until they reflected the brightness of the starry sky. She watched the titanic cityscape become as unreal as a silhouette in the night, saved from total obliteration by scattered lanterns and distant towers blazing like distant beacons, detached from the dormant power grid. Quell felt what she could not see—the antiquity of the world, the billions of lives lived across hundreds of years, the masses still teeming in the darkness, and the utter weight of a world converted into a labyrinth of civilizations extending through time and space. Parts of her brain sparked like a loose electrical conduit, attempting to calculate the tonnage of Troithe's structures as a means to understand its scale. She didn't know how to begin.

She leaned against Chass na Chadic and heard conversation beside her, but she no longer understood the words.

It was a glorious evening.

It wasn't yet midnight when they parted ways. Lark said he needed to check on his ship before bed. Tensent winked and headed back into the refugee camp. Quell escorted Chadic back to the *Lodestar,* shivering in the night's chill. The Theelin woman stumbled all the way through the spaceport and into the battleship's halls, shrugging off Quell's offers of help and proceeding into a turbolift with a slurred "I do this every night."

Quell would have followed up—the notion raised alarms and reminded her of Syndulla's concerns—if she hadn't heard the footsteps behind her. She turned. Standing in the dim light of the corridor was Kairos.

Quell stiffened as if she'd been *caught*. Kairos hadn't been with them through the evening, hadn't lowered her guard, and now she watched Quell with her softly glowing visor as if she were ready to rebuke Quell for forgetting herself.

Quell opened her mouth and said nothing. She breathed in the floral scent of the strange woman.

Kairos took three steps until she was half a meter from Quell. Each footfall rang like a gong on the metal deck. Quell noted the tears in the woman's cloak; the rip in the leather of her left glove, which revealed only more fabric beneath.

The last time she'd been so close to Kairos, the woman had thrown her onto the floor of an airless cargo bay and pulled away Quell's oxygen mask. Kairos had been steady then, implacable, and Quell still didn't fully understand why the woman had spared her.

Kairos was not steady now, nor implacable. She was trembling.

A voice, low and wet and guttural, made sounds that Quell took full seconds to register as words: "They fall for us, so we may purge the shadow. The mission must succeed."

As if released from a spell, Kairos's shoulders slumped and she spun away, marching back the way she'd come.

Chass na Chadic was snoring in Quell's bunk when Quell finally made it to her billet, one of the Theelin's legs dangling off the edge and a blanket pulled halfway over her face. The unreality of Quell's encounter with Kairos dissipated like a dream. She had to hold back a laugh.

She couldn't imagine why Chadic was there. Once it might have shaken Quell—back when she'd first met the younger woman, when (she could admit it now) she'd felt a juvenile attraction crawling under her skin. She'd felt jealousy watching Chadic and Lark on the cold moon of Harkrova.

That crush was gone now, the intensity burned away in the aftermath of Pandem Nai.

Quell lowered herself to the floor, tugging over a corner of Chadic's blanket to use as a pillow. As she drifted into sleep, she thought about what Kairos had said: She thought of the masked woman flying above the Thannerhouse lake, hugging the water as she rescued soldiers in the face of certain death; she thought of Kairos killing with cannons and gloved hands.

There was meaning to be found in those half-cogent images, but by morning Quell had forgotten it all.

CHAPTER 6

A STRAIGHT PATH TO TRAGEDY

I

"**B**ombers in position?"

"Waiting for the fun to start," Nath Tensent said into his comm, though it struck him as he said it that this was the least *fun* he'd had in weeks. He called out his coordinates to the *Lodestar,* leaning back as the Y-wing rumbled around him. "How about you, Chass?"

"You know I'm in position. You can see me floating to starboard," she answered. "I'm the speck that doesn't handle well in wind."

Nath's display blinked and he read T5's commentary. His astromech droid had a foul imagination. He grinned and refrained from sharing the message for the sake of the flight control officer. "Just let us know when you've got work for us. We'll keep our eyes on the shield," he said, and ceased transmitting to the ground.

By now Wyl and Quell were streaking toward the capital, low enough to slip below the energy shield and make for the generators. Until the shield was down, though, there wasn't much for Nath or

Chass or Hail Squadron to do—their assault craft didn't have the speed or agility to follow the A-wing and X-wing, and the enemy wasn't stupid enough to send forces out from cover.

So they waited.

"You picking your songs?" Nath asked.

He heard the petulance in Chass's voice: "How long do you think it takes me?"

"So you're not busy, then? I've got a pack of cards—"

"Seriously?"

"Sure."

"You got a week's pay to bet?"

"Sure," Nath repeated.

His week's pay wasn't the same as Chass's, but she didn't need to know that. Caern Adan was still lining Nath's pockets, as he had been since the founding of the working group.

Originally, Adan had treated Nath as his personal agent, offering regular deposits of credits in return for the occasional side job. Now that Adan had a whole division working for him, both men understood the new deal without speaking openly of it: Adan's payments were meant to keep Nath silent as much as keep him on the squadron.

Nath had learned things about Yrica Quell that Adan was choosing to keep quiet. Nath was fine with that. He could use the extra cash.

Nath pulled a deck from under his seat. He and Chass played a slow, awkward hand of full open sabacc, occasionally pausing when someone announced progress on the ground. "What do you say about a side wager?" he asked. "Suppose the governor's got a surprise waiting for us down there?"

Chass laughed loud enough for the cockpit speaker to crackle. "'Course he does. No bet."

Nath shrugged and scratched beneath his helmet's chin strap. Chass wasn't the brightest member of the squadron, but she wasn't an idiot. "What's your prediction? For the whole battle?"

"My *prediction* is that Wyl and Quell fly into a firestorm. They scrape by, take out the shield generators anyway, and by the time we get down there it's all easy flying. Still a meat grinder for the ground troops, obviously."

"Obviously." Nath liked the troops of the Sixty-First, but he'd learned before ever joining the military that infantry didn't survive long. It was why he'd picked the navy instead of the army. "Guess in a few hours, the planet will be ours. Maybe Quell or Adan will share their plans for us, then."

He noticed the uncertainty in her silence even before her awkward reply. "Right."

Now, that's interesting.

"You figure they'll keep holding back?" he asked. It wasn't a question he especially cared about, but it was a probe fired off into the night.

"Probably," Chass said.

Nath turned the conversation over in his head and grinned. "You don't want to see Shadow Wing again, do you?"

Chass swore. Nath silenced her transmission and replied to a status update from the ground before he caught the end of her signal: "—you don't know what you're talking about."

"Sure I do," he said. "Don't worry about it. Truth is, I don't think Wyl much wants to run into them again, either."

"He tell you that?"

"Wyl's a good kid. He'll grow into a half-decent commander if he gets the chance. But he isn't exactly hard to read."

That got a snort from Chass, though she didn't say a word. Nath considered sharing what Wyl *had* told him but decided to keep the boy's confidence. They'd spent an evening together dancing around the subject, Wyl expressing his gentle frustration with the Troithe operation until it became obvious he was worried about another disaster like Pandem Nai. Worried about the price of another victory.

But Nath assumed that sheer terror played a role in Wyl's lack of enthusiasm, too. Wyl wasn't a coward, but he was only human. If he didn't want to face Shadow Wing again, of course he'd justify it as worry over the plan.

He wondered if he could get Chass to come clean. She was the last squad member he'd expected to have reservations—even if she'd gotten past her death wish, she sure as sin hadn't lost her grudge against Shadow Wing.

Before he could say anything, she spoke again. "What about you?"

He considered the question before saying, "I got my revenge, and those bastards nearly killed me twice. I'm not looking forward to it, either."

He left out the parts she didn't need to hear: That the *fun* was getting a pile of credits for very little work as the New Republic claimed its territory; that he was finding a lot of pleasure in playing air support to troops who would shout his name and drink with him and make a fuss when he landed. Taking the capital was a risk. Trapping Shadow Wing was going to be *work*.

"Well," Chass said. "Maybe we'll screw this mission up and we won't have to worry about it."

Nath would've answered, but another transmission came through first.

People were dying far below. The battle had started.

II

Over two decades earlier, following the ascension of Galactic Emperor Palpatine, Troithe's capital had been relocated from its thousand-year home in the Gloried Chalice District to the Troithe Planetary Defense Center. Before the Empire, the TPDC's role had been symbolic— private military companies had battled Separatist incursions during the Clone Wars while the TPDC's interplanetary missile batteries, stadium-sized ion cannons, and massive infantry barracks had sat abandoned—yet in an effort to restore planetary pride Troithe's first Imperial governor had razed or converted the obsolete weaponry to build bureaucratic processing centers and state-of-the-art broadcast facilities. Tram lines now ran between missile-silos-turned-luxury-apartment-complexes; modern turbolasers stood surrounded by bronze statues of forgotten Troithe war heroes; and the colossal shield generators that rendered an eighth of a continent invincible rose from army parade grounds between starkly glittering towers.

Even under the dark of the Cerberon skies, Yrica Quell was grateful for the polarized visor of her flight helmet as she navigated the TPDC. Beams of light lanced the air, originating from point-defense mounts and raking the skies in five-second bursts. The beams that failed to find a starfighter—and two had disintegrated Meteor Squadron X-wings already—either ripped through the tallest structures or splashed against the underside of the planetary shields, causing sparks and fire to rain down. TIE strikers (all spherical cockpit pods and bladelike wings, built for atmospheric combat) flew in the beams' wake, the last of the governor's air force. Quell swung her X-wing to and fro, fingers stiff around her control yoke and boots alternating pressure on her rudder pedals. She ignored the stream of complaints scrolling down her display from CB-9. The astromech was struggling to keep the ship stable, adjusting thruster output and repulsor power multiple times per second.

Keep it stable or we both die, Quell thought. She felt D6-L's memory chip on its necklace chain, cold against the sweat on her throat.

"Close strike foils," she said. Her scanner blazed in warning as a missile (surface-launched or from an enemy fighter, she couldn't determine) swept toward her. Blood rushed to her head as she rolled the X-wing and skimmed the outer frame of a tower. "See if we can buy more maneuverability."

The sound of an explosion behind her, powerful enough to rock her ship, reassured her that she'd evaded the missile.

"With S-foils closed you've got no weapons," a voice protested. Quell recognized the speaker as Meteor Leader and resisted snapping back before he continued: "We'll do our best to cover you."

"Understood," Quell said, and tried to find Wyl Lark on her scanner.

Lark was playing scout—his A-wing was faster than anything else in the air. As death pierced the sky from below and fell from above, he'd looped around towers and streaked down streets and tunnels, searching for a path to the shield generator that the X-wings could follow.

Quell found his blip half a kilometer ahead, no more than ten meters aboveground. She felt her ship's servos whir and the strike foils lock closed as she called, "Where to?"

"They mounted missile platforms on the tram lines," Lark returned. His voice was strained. "Trace my path *exactly.*"

CB-9 sent flight paths to her console. She didn't question them. She dived.

Gleaming metal blurred around her before she leveled out above an electrified transport track built for loads too bulky for trams. Current arced to violently interact with her shields, causing the energy globe to burn so bright she could see nothing beyond her canopy. In that moment—as she wrestled with her controls, using instruments to navigate—she was no longer on Troithe but skimming the surface of Yethra, the horrifying brightness of the sun reflecting off ice sheets and leaving her blind to the world. She wasn't sure if it was Lark's voice or Xion's guiding her, warning her of enemies swooping in pursuit; she watched on her scanner as Major Keize or Meteor Squadron sent the scorched metal chunks of her opponents crashing around her.

It didn't matter. She knew her mission. She barely knew who she was, but she knew her mission.

"Approaching the generator now," Lark said.

Reality re-formed around her as she sped down the track.

"Ground forces have engaged the foe," General Syndulla's voice announced. "Take those shields down, and take them down fast."

III

Wyl Lark felt his fighter lurch as he launched every missile he had.

The parade grounds were at street level but they seemed like the depths of a plunging abyss, dwarfed by towers on all sides and awash in gloom. Particle bolts streamed from turret emplacements around the perimeter, charging the darkness with crimson lightning; but the turrets were slow to rotate and their deadly output was simple to elude. The twenty-meter disks of the shield generators were caked in dirt and rust, crude in comparison with the sleek surrounding structures; the vast energy they emitted was invisible to a human eye.

Wyl saw only the first impact: The concussion missile struck between the disks and flashed, but he was already pulling up before the second missile hit home. Far above, he could see the faint, shimmering opacity of the deflector field. His spine dug into his seat. His scanners showed TIEs converging on all sides.

His missiles hadn't sufficed. If he was going to escape—if he was going to survive—it would be because Quell followed him and finished the job. If he died, he would die dashing his ship and his body against the deflector field they failed to destroy.

"It's okay," he breathed with what little oxygen his lungs could find. "It's okay."

"In position," Quell said, and Wyl closed his eyes and waited.

IV

"Bombers! Go! Go!"

General Syndulla's voice came through the comm, sudden enough to startle Chass. She straightened in her seat, checked her angle, and ignited her thrusters even before Nath called, "You ready?"

"Sure," Chass said. "So long as no one tries to shoot me, I'll be just fine."

"How's the rest of our squadron doing?" Nath asked.

The B-wing bounced as Chass adjusted its gyroscopics—she'd kept the cross upright while holding position against the wind, but in flight she was better off horizontal—and began a long, spiraling descent through the cloud cover toward the capital. Nath and the Y-wings of Hail Squadron were behind her now, but according to the flight plan they'd overtake her once they descended below shield altitude.

She was wondering if something had gone wrong when Quell's voice said, "Lark and I are intact and on our way to escort you. Kairos is giving cover to the ground teams."

"Great," Chass said. "We'll try not to blow her to bits."

When the cloud cover ripped away and the city came into view, Chass tapped a button. The rapid patter of a Loletian politi-folk singer filled the cockpit. The Y-wings followed her and she swayed with the breeze and the song, and the first proton torpedoes and laser-guided bombs dropped toward preassigned coordinates like the too-bright stars of Cerberon rattling loose from the sky.

Soon Chass would be close enough to see the devastation. Soon she'd be picking targets and evading fire while trying not to murder her own side's ground troops. She could forget the conversation with Nath—he'd sneered, *You don't want to see Shadow Wing again, do you?* but he was wrong about that; Shadow Wing didn't frighten her so much as what came *after* Shadow Wing.

The B-wing leapt as a proton bomb ejected from its launcher.

For now, she could do the thing she was best at. The only thing she was made for.

V

General Hera Syndulla of the New Republic stood in the tactical center of the *Lodestar* and observed as glowing dots on a screen shaped the fate of a planet. She listened to the chatter of pilots and ground troops, heard triumphant cries and anxious voices, and watched her subordinates clutch their headsets and snap replies. She tried to appear strong and confident and compassionate.

All to bait a trap.

Even if they won, she wouldn't know if it was worth it until Shadow Wing arrived. Until another battle had been fought.

"*Lodestar* is in position," her aide said as he drew up to her side. By the expression on his face, she could've believed Stornvein hadn't said the words in a dozen battles before; his unwillingness to become jaded was why she kept him on staff. "Even without the shield, there's not much room to descend, but we'll pick off any TIEs if they get close."

"Thank you," she said. "What about the video feed?"

"Some jamming activity," Stornvein said, "but it should be ready now."

Pixelated holo-footage from a soldier's helmet cam showed a telescope's view of chaos—too-close glimpses of a grand tapestry of destruction. Fires burned. Stormtroopers squatted behind barricades made of piled speeders. The frame of a scout walker slumped against a building. Streaks in the sky could have been starfighter cannons or torpedoes.

Hera should have been on the ground. Instead she'd chosen to remain at a remove, to coordinate forces too professional, too well organized to truly need a general overseeing them from orbit.

"Rotate the comm channels," she said. "I want to know what they're thinking."

She pieced together the state of the battle from audio fragments. Meteor Squadron was maneuvering to drive away TIE strikers and thwart enemy attempts to provide air support; she flinched as Meteor Two called for assistance and sighed in relief when his brother eliminated their pursuers. Infantry squads were calling in coordinates to Hail Squadron; glowing dots faded from her screens as walkers and tanks were annihilated by proton bombs.

She lingered on the feed from Alphabet. She recognized Wyl Lark's distress as he hissed, "If this goes on, there won't be anything left of the district."

"This is the plan," Quell said. "This is the only way we win."

Hera shook her head briskly. She'd grown to like the Alphabet pilots over the past months, though she didn't know them well. She'd been proud to see Quell take command and apply her skills as a tactician. But part of her—a very small part, one she wasn't thrilled with— wished they'd never brought their war with the 204th to her unit.

She'd approved Adan and Quell's plan because it was a good one. That didn't mean she liked it.

"What's going on there?" she asked as multiple dots on the tactical screen crept in sync away from the edges of the district, back toward the midpoint.

Stornvein huddled beside a comm officer. The two whispered urgently as Hera examined the maps. "The governor's ordered a retreat," Stornvein said after a moment. "Enemy ground teams are withdrawing toward the logistics center. Control for communications, data flow, civilian power grid. The 'Tri-Central Complex,' officially."

She recognized the name. She was puzzled nonetheless. "Why not the governor's mansion? Or one of the military stations? Tri-Central doesn't have much in the way of defenses, does it?"

"It's accessible via two major throughways under enemy control. It could just be a convenience—the easiest spot to regroup."

Hera started to swear, caught herself, and squared her shoulders. She stepped to one of the comm stations and keyed in a frequency override. "General Syndulla to all forces—we have to cut off their retreat. Do *not* let the enemy near the Tri-Central Complex."

A flurry of affirmative responses followed. A familiar, husky voice asked over the link, "What's happening, General?"

"Lieutenant Quell. So far as we can determine, whoever's commanding their forces just made a very stupid decision or a very smart one." She summarized what they'd seen and continued: "Either way, we can't afford to let them consolidate forces there."

"Understood," Quell said.

Hera expected she *did* understand. The battle plan was Quell's as much as Hera's own.

She watched the dots on the map. Very soon she would have a decision to make, but she feared it would be no decision at all.

VI

Quell heard General Syndulla order the bombers to break off as enemy ground forces approached the complex. She immediately recognized the reasoning. Predicting the consequences took her a moment longer.

Tri-Center wasn't a military installation, but the facility was essential to the planet's infrastructure network—holding it wouldn't win the war, and losing it wouldn't bring about defeat, yet if Tri-Center was reduced to ruins by the bombs and torpedoes of New Republic starfighters, Troithe would be left in disarray for months to come. No outside force would care to reclaim the planet for the Empire.

Therefore, Tri-Center had to be preserved, or else the working group's efforts to bait the trap—to lure Shadow Wing into attacking Troithe—would fail.

Quell wasn't prepared to fail.

She thought of all this as she escorted Chadic's assault craft out of the combat zone, pursued halfheartedly by a TIE striker barely able to stay aloft. She split her attention between her flight and the feeds blinking on her display—indicators of ground troop positions and enemy progress.

With the bombers pulling back, the New Republic infantry would be left without support. Tri-Center wasn't well fortified but it didn't need to be; allied and enemy ground forces were evenly matched, and a clash inside the complex would guarantee a bloodbath. Alternatively, if the New Republic infantry retreated, it would position the governor (or whoever survived to take command) to resecure the region and collapse the narrow corridor Syndulla's forces had been establishing from the spaceport to the capital.

Those were the options: hundreds of dead New Republic troops, or weeks—months—of progress lost in the campaign to take Troithe and trap Shadow Wing.

Quell knew what she would choose. She knew what General Syndulla would choose, too.

"CB-9?" she said. "I want to hear what the squads are saying."

The droid patched her into the infantry frequencies. Only a handful of squads were in position to intercept the enemy approaching Tri-Center, and they were sorely pressed—barely a dozen people were attempting to blockade the entrance against hundreds of stormtroopers and army regulars. The Imperial walkers and tanks, at least, had largely been destroyed or abandoned, but even at a chokepoint the New Republic wouldn't hold out long.

"What's the word, General?" the infantry captain called. "I can't stop them. I can buy you another minute. Maybe five, with a miracle."

Quell had met the captain, though she couldn't recall his name. He'd been younger than she'd expected, aware of the peculiarities of the campaign and insistent that Syndulla understand the cost in lives—but never refusing an objective. Never asking *why* they were taking the capital in such a manner.

She expected he would let his people die if ordered to do so.

Quell spoke, though she knew doing so was improper. "Would five minutes be enough to bring your people in from the rear? Flank the enemy, push them away from Tri-Center?"

"No," the captain said.

"Get them out of there, Captain, however you think best," Syndulla said. "I'm sorry, Quell."

Quell was protesting, but she couldn't hear herself. She saw the work she'd done, the sacrifices on the ground, the last hope of finding Shadow Wing burning away in the fire of the battle. There would be no second chance—everything she had built with Adan required that the trap be set *now*, not in a week or a month.

Her heart rate spiked. The air in the cockpit seemed thin.

Then a new voice broke into the comm frequency. She didn't recognize the speaker—one of the infantry troops.

"Captain? Got a U-wing coming in fast and taking a lot of damage. If that's our evac, not sure we can make it back *out*."

This, too, Quell immediately understood.

Kairos.

She pressed a rudder pedal hard, leaned into the turn and the pressures on her body, and made for the Tri-Center Complex.

VII

There were words Kairos did not understand. Even after years of exposure, she struggled to comprehend the intricacies of the language so demeaningly called Galactic Basic. But words were not always a barrier to *understanding,* and she knew what was occurring on the battle-field.

She knew why the ships and soldiers pulled back. She would not join them.

A single broad boulevard led to the Tri-Center Complex, joined by narrower tributaries. A horde of white-clad troopers pushed toward the front entrance—toward the once-transparent metal façade tower-ing like a cliff wall, pockmarked and ash-smeared into opacity where particle bolts had left their mark. Where the eternal gloom of Cer-beron enveloped the streets, the interior atrium blazed with light, il-luminating the trapped rebel soldiers who attempted to repel the invasion.

Perhaps they had a means to escape. A way out of the complex.

She swept in low above the boulevard, flickering particle lances from the horde shattering against her shields. Her vessel trembled as the electromagnetic field churned and coruscated—her ship the hatch-ling within her deflectors' invisible shell. She fired her cannons into the crowd, sending burning bodies flying into packs of survivors. There were too many for her to miss, even as they scattered.

Perhaps her allies did not need Kairos to save them. Perhaps she acted for her own sake.

She fumbled with her vessel's controls through ungainly gloves, smelling the rotting odor of her twisted body trapped inside her mask. She could not scent the smoke or charred corpses, though she could imagine both with perfect clarity. She angled her ship ten de-grees upward, exposing aft and underside to the continuing fire of the enemy and making for the transparent metal façade of the complex. She diverted all power from her forward deflectors and into her kill-ing cannons—an act of technical wizardry that possessed no deeper meaning, no resonance in the true world, yet proved effective for her needs.

Cannons flashed. The howl of torn metal resonated through her or-gans (somehow she could taste the tang of iron) and she entered the atrium through the newly created gap in the wall, shifting from thrusters to repulsors, turning ninety degrees, and floating ten meters above the startled New Republic soldiers.

Kairos had been at war with herself, her spirit sundered. She'd often thought of leaving her people—leaving the defector, leaving Adan. But she would not leave Adan.

Half sheltered by the fragmented wall of the atrium, Kairos accepted the blow of an incoming rocket against her flank. The vessel heaved and listed to one side; she saw on her console the damage to thrusters and repulsors, but she was still aloft. She gently adjusted a lever and climbed out of her seat, retreating to the main cabin. With the touch of a button, she opened the loading door and—stepping behind the turret gun—fired into the horde once again.

She understood that Adan and the defector sought to ensnare their foe in a trap—she'd comprehended those words well, after Adan had taken her aside and explained each step. The butchers of Nacronis and Pandem Nai and so many other worlds did not deserve to escape justice. Nor did the beast of Troithe who called himself governor—who unleashed monsters against his enemies—deserve to escape punishment. So she had accepted the strategy of a man wiser than she, and agreed to the price in blood.

She raked the stream of the turret through the gap in the wall and across the boulevard, tearing apart stormtroopers and black-clad troops, their faces sweaty and screaming. She could hear the battle clearly now, the shouts and the sizzle of bolts and the crackle of flames. As her foes returned fire and the deck began to shake, she thought that the horde seemed smaller.

Since their time on Troithe had begun, she had slaughtered and allowed noble warriors to be slaughtered. In her commitment to vengeance, to the scouring of her foes, she had accepted the sacrifice of the soldiers she was expected to preserve. She had agreed to the price. She would not, could not turn away now.

The deck jumped once to warn her that the ship was failing. She leapt from the turret to seize the crew seats as repulsors died and the U-wing dropped to the atrium floor. She heard only a cacophonous roar and saw nothing—her vision was obliterated by the stresses of gravity and bulkheads—and when sight returned her body was suffused with pain. Motion was rewarded with surges of agony. But she had suffered worse, and she scaled the wreckage of the askew cabin to retrieve her weapon.

She could not turn away. Never turn away. Not after all that had happened.

She didn't know what had become of the New Republic soldiers. She lodged her bowcaster against her shoulder and gurgled instead of screamed as it kicked back against her with every shot fired. The crash of the U-wing had left the atrium thick with smoke and flame, and the clouds glowed like the clouds of Pandem Nai, exquisitely scarlet, as they soaked up the colors of particle bolts streaming toward her.

She felt air against her skin. Her forearm wrappings were scorched. She had broken her last vow.

She fired into the smoke. She fired at the stormtroopers who hurled themselves toward her, piled body upon body—few in the grand tale of it all, few compared to those she'd killed in the past and those soldiers she'd failed to save—and kept on firing until she could no longer feel, could no longer stand. She heard cannon fire outside the complex but she could not raise her head to see.

She heard the calls of rebel soldiers still alive.

The last thing Kairos saw was the beautiful face of Yrica Quell—the defector, the traitor—looking down at her.

VIII

Caern Adan could hear the reports through the wall but he steadfastly ignored them. His staff was tracking every soldier's death, every meter gained by the New Republic infantry, as if there were something they could do to affect the outcome of the battle from their stations in the tram tower—as if the fight for the capital were part of their duties instead of a distraction.

Adan remembered a summer in the offices of the *IGBC Financial*

Review when his colleagues had made a daily habit of ceasing conversation one by one and tuning their consoles to the season's ongoing smashball tournament. Adan had possessed neither interest in smashball nor any local pride in Muunilinst's team (having only transferred there for the work); he'd found the practice relentlessly irritating. And though his time on Muunilinst seemed like a half-forgotten dream and he had much at stake in the battle at the capital, he was determined to make better use of his time than his colleagues past and present.

After all, it wouldn't be long before Shadow Wing arrived in-system. He intended to be fully prepared.

He told himself this even as his antennapalps stood rigid. The noise of comm chatter outside his office resonated in his skull. He ignored the reports yet he still listened. *What would Ito say, seeing you distracted?* he wondered, and snatched a datapad from his stack to review.

He buried himself in news of Vanguard Squadron's operations in the Bormea sector, taking diligent notes on the impact to Cerberon's defense capabilities until his console pinged and notified him he was receiving a direct transmission. The codes were military but the sender was unidentified. He activated his comm and waited.

"Adan," Yrica Quell said.

He hadn't expected to hear from her until hours after the battle. They'd been getting on better lately, though—she seemed *calmer*—and she *had* become more communicative.

He wondered on occasion if she was simply manipulating him.

"I'm here. What's going on?"

"Kairos is hurt," she said, her tone flat. "We're evacing now. I'm not sure of her condition. I thought you'd want to know."

"Send coordinates to my team," he said, and closed the channel as he stood. He paused long enough to grab his comlink, made it out of his office and halfway to the turbolift before it occurred to him to return for his coat, then forged ahead anyway. He ignored the stares from Nasha Gravas and the rest of his staff—they could supervise themselves for an hour.

He tried to snuff the anxiety in his chest as he formulated a plan. If her injuries were bad enough they'd take her to the spaceport, but only if she could survive the trip. Otherwise they'd move her to a field station, and he'd need a shuttle to get there. He tried to remember who was still available to fly him—who *hadn't* gone to the capital to fight?—and ran through a mental list of names as he stepped out into the spaceport proper.

Had he sent Kairos to die?

It had never occurred to him that Kairos could die.

If she *did* die—

Time became a blur. He spoke to Nasha through his comlink. He made arrangements for an airspeeder. He kept walking alongside the refugee settlement and out to the tarmac where a pilot met him. Thirty minutes later he was at a field site, and only then did he find the courage to alert IT-O. The droid would want to know, even if Adan didn't want to talk to him.

It had been the three of them in the camp, long ago. Adan owed and trusted Kairos, as she owed and trusted him.

The medical evac point was nothing more than a few oversized tents erected around a makeshift landing pad outside the flooded remains of the Thannerhouse District. Adan doubted anyone present, organic or droid, had the proficiency to treat Kairos. But he would put in the call anyway. He'd tell IT-O to unlock her files, to decrypt and declassify everything he had about Kairos's anatomy. He expected they'd argue about it, but IT-O would obey an order if it was given.

He'd worry about Kairos's reaction later. Yes, she trusted him. She would expect him to keep her secrets. But he *owed* her.

He was activating his comlink, breathing in the stink of polluted water, when someone behind him spoke his name.

"What?" Adan asked, not turning around.

There was no answer but the muzzle of a blaster against his scalp, an electrical crackle, and the sound of his own breath expelled from his lungs.

CHAPTER 7

SCHEMES AND DREAMS

I

He had chosen the timing carefully, waiting for a moment when the value of his guidance had become clear. Soran Keize didn't think of himself as a man proficient at politics nor one who enjoyed them, but he knew when he was liked and when he was loathed. Only a fool proposed a new enterprise when he was loathed.

Thus, the morning after the attack on Parozha VII, Soran called the leadership of the 204th into conference. It had been barely six hours since Squadrons Two, Three, and Four had swarmed the supply port, first annihilating every docked ship and then cracking open the station itself; suffocating the inhabitants and blasting open the cargo bays so that the *Edict*'s tractor beam might retrieve whatever bounty the crew could lock onto. It was an act of piracy more than an act of war, but the Parozha VII outpost had once supplied the Empire and now aided the enemy; before Endor, the Rebel Alliance had struck ports with less justification.

Word was that the outpost had been operated by the same family of

Parwans for generations—a forest of over seventy of the fungal creatures, left to drift in vacuum. The galaxy was a touch less wondrous without them.

The squadron commanders and senior staff of the *Edict* and *Aerie* sat at the *Edict* conference table where Soran sipped a cup of tea— a blend he didn't recognize, one of the few worthwhile spoils from the attack—and waited for their attention. "We have an opportunity," he finally said. "A chance to do more than simply restock, rebuild, and survive another month. I'd like to put forth a proposal."

The words carried risk—the phrasing was a concession to his status as adviser, yet there was no humility in his tone. He might well incite the commanders against him.

"The Deep Core system of Cerberon has been hard-pressed in recent months," he went on. "Once an Imperial stronghold, its planets are rapidly falling into rebel hands and we have received a plea for aid.

"The message was corrupted but it appeared to be from allies of Governor Hastemoor. It contained details of the enemy presence in-system as well as the remaining Imperial holdouts. Such distress signals have not been infrequent—" He raised a hand to forestall questions that didn't come. "—but all of them so far have been from parties too distant or desperate to be worth attending."

Now he did wait. It was Major Rassus who said, "I've seen the distress calls. I've never pressed to pursue them; there's little we can do for the Empire's gangrenous limbs. So tell us—what makes this call different?"

"Specifics," Soran said, "and a plan of action."

He tapped the control panel on the conference table. Lights dimmed and a hologram shimmered into being, displaying the layout and orbital paths of the Cerberon system—a tangled knot of satellites and planets and asteroids whipped around the mass of a black hole. A blinking halo accented a dot labeled TROITHE. "The sender suggested an unusual approach to the capital—a planet heavily shielded and under guard by enemy naval forces.

"The system's orbital dynamics are—as you can see—extraordinarily complex. The local government expended significant resources studying and modeling the effects of the black hole. Wartime activity caused additional disruption in the debris field, which in turn resulted in minor collisions between uninhabited planetoids." He paused and smiled long enough to make a show of humility. "I'm quoting the reports now—astrophysics isn't my field, but the *Edict's* main computer double-checked the math."

Lieutenant Seedia raised a single finger. Soran had expected her to challenge him again at some point—had invited her to the conference anticipating it, despite her rank—though now seemed an unusual time to do so. He acknowledged her with a glance and a nod.

"I spent a year in the astronomy department at the Institute for Quantitative Studies at Bothawui."

Not a fact that had been in her profile; he wondered if it was true. "If we decide to proceed, I'll make sure you have access to the data," he said. She appeared satisfied, and he continued:

"As of the Empire's last readings—and by last, I do mean *final*—it appeared that a small asteroid would soon traverse the debris field and approach Troithe at high velocity." The holo highlighted a second dot, drawing an arcing path toward the first. "As a weapon, it would prove ineffective even if we wanted to bombard the world. Troithe's planetary defense shields would be raised well in advance and hold against the impact. However, were a TIE unit hidden on the asteroid itself . . ." He paused, allowing them to come to their conclusions before he echoed them. ". . . it could approach Troithe undetected, then launch an attack near Troithe's orbit before alarms could be sounded or shields could be raised."

It was a plan worthy of the Rebel Alliance, and that was distasteful in its own right. But no frontal assault would take Cerberon, and Soran saw that his commanders understood. Darita appeared grudgingly impressed, eyeing the holo with pursed lips and crinkled nose. Teso Broosh sat impassive, as a man deep in thought. Gablerone watched Soran rather than the orbital map.

Soran might have swayed them then. He saw vulnerability. But there was another matter—one they deserved to comprehend before passing judgment.

"General Hera Syndulla's battle group has taken the lead in the New Republic invasion of Cerberon," he said. "Her flagship is currently at rest on Troithe."

Broosh flinched—not at the words, Soran suspected, but at the swiftness of the lash. Major Rassus's shoulders tightened. Only Nenvez, the *Edict* crew's representative, looked altogether puzzled.

"Syndulla led the attack on Pandem Nai," Rassus said, by way of explanation to their newest recruit. "I'm sure you know her by reputation."

She nearly killed you, Soran thought. *She killed Grandmother. She almost burned Pandem Nai to ashes.* But he didn't have the right to say it aloud. He hadn't been there.

"Last time," Captain Phesh—Squadron Six's commander—said, "we were at nearly full strength. No Star Destroyer, true, but the advantage of the turf and our defenses made up for the lack. Run a tactical analysis and I doubt you'll find we're in condition to compete."

"We wouldn't be going there to *compete*—" Gablerone began, but Soran didn't hear the rest of it. Arguments filled the air as suddenly as dead Parwans had poured from the Parozha VII supply port. He saw no wild bloodlust in their eyes, knew that all of them were too seasoned to think the choice was an easy one, but Wisp had lost almost all of her squadron at Pandem Nai and tapped her forefinger against the tabletop; Darita pulled files from the *Edict*'s data bank and pointed out that General Syndulla had *always* been a priority target, still was one; Broosh asked the others, one by one, how their squadrons would react, whether they would be inspired or intimidated. Phesh and Rassus discussed the strategic advantage of controlling Cerberon and whether the Imperial fleet would even make use of it.

Seedia remained silent, observing the others and observing Soran. When she spoke at last, it was with clarity sharp enough to cut through the bedlam despite her electronic vocabulator. "General Syndulla and her people murdered our comrades. Bringing home her head is the honorable thing to do."

This was why he'd brought her—because while he was fond of many of the pilots under his command, it was Seedia who would be bold enough to vocalize the sentiment too many of the squadrons felt.

By necessity, the commanders gravitated toward practical answers. Soran needed the support of the full wing for what was coming.

He judged the time was at hand. "We all have our reasons for wanting this. I desire only what is right for the 204th and I am willing to lead the mission personally," Soran said. "To take full command, as would be necessary."

They looked at him. He waited to be accused—accurately, he supposed—of using the moment to seize power.

"And can you give us victory where Colonel Nuress couldn't?" Rassus said.

"I can promise nothing," Soran said.

You desire victory. You desire revenge. This is the only way I can protect you and give you what you want.

"Do you advise us," Rassus asked, "to take on this task?"

"I do," Soran said, and rose from his seat at the table. "Will you accept my decision?"

They said yes, of course. After, Soran considered whether that was the outcome he'd truly wanted.

He returned to the *Aerie* from the *Edict*, where much of the 204th remained—with the *Edict*'s systems still barely functional, the cruiser-carrier was the more robust and adaptable ship. He listened at the doors to the billets, hearing his pilots debate and laugh and mourn, but he spoke to no one.

That Shadow Wing needed purpose was undebatable. He could save his people if they would let him—he could teach them to survive on the fringes of the galaxy, away from the war they'd already lost—but they'd committed to the delusions of vengeance and patriotic fervor. They wished to fight a war, and so he would find a war for them to fight.

He simply wasn't certain if this was the right one.

He paused as he rounded a corner and heard a voice whisper, "Help us."

The corridor intersection where the shrine of the red-cloaked Messenger lurked was ten meters away. The offerings to the droid multiplied daily, and now ashes and scorched wood from the ruins of Parozha VII joined other gifts at the machine's feet. Kneeling before the Messenger was a young man Soran recognized as Kandende—the pilot who'd disrupted the welcoming party for the *Edict*'s crew.

"Help us, Emperor Palpatine," Kandende said. "Guide us to something more."

Soran observed as Kandende withdrew a straight razor from his pocket, opened it, and pressed the blade into his palm. Blood the color of the Messenger's robes welled up, and Kandende took one of the droid's hands in both of his own, clasping the leather glove until red ran down Kandende's wrist; until red dripped onto the *Aerie*'s deck; until Kandende's pained expression broke and he pulled away, stanching the wound with the sleeve of his uniform.

The droid had not reacted and did not react now. Kandende turned away, stumbling down the corridor.

Soran recalled the Messenger's arrival. The machine had arrived aboard the *Pursuer* via shuttle—Soran still didn't know the shuttle's origins—and sought out Colonel Nuress. It had tested her blood with a needle that had erupted from its palm.

He thought of anthropological studies of primitive peoples exposed to galactic technology—cults that formed around moisture vaporators, believing that worship was necessary to activate the devices. He wondered if Kandende was the first pilot to entreat the Messenger so; the man's actions had possessed a ritualistic formality.

Soran decided it no longer mattered whether the war for Cerberon was the right war for the 204th. It was far better than the alternative.

II

"It's hard to hear it, I know—but it's good news."

General Syndulla spoke with the quiet authority that Yrica Quell had become accustomed to, sitting cross-legged on the hull of the

Lodestar half a dozen meters from the nearest maintenance hatch. The general had made a camp of sorts, with a blanket spread on armor plating, a heat rod glowing to one side, and a spread of datapads around her like a fortune-teller's cards. The battleship sat ensconced in the spaceport once again, and the burning light of the Cerberon singularity sank behind the city like the dying sparks of a distant battle.

It was three days since the invasion of the capital, and the news—as Syndulla said—was good. Yet Quell took no pleasure in it.

"Any word on an enemy counterattack?" Quell asked. She lifted her left foot, instinctively wanting to pace. Syndulla had already scolded her for that—*If you won't sit,* she'd said, *do me a favor and stand still.*

"We're watching for anything via satellite. They have no communications. No organized leadership, so far as we know. There are a *lot* of them—we left whole sectors of Imperial troops untouched for a reason—and this planet's going to have guerrilla trouble for a while. But I wouldn't worry about anything coordinated, at least not until—" Syndulla shook her head. "If the New Republic can keep the threat from organizing, I'm willing to call the planet stable."

"Until Shadow Wing," Quell said.

"No. We've got that under control. Forces are deploying. This was your plan, remember?" What should've been condescending in the words was somehow mitigated by the warmth in her voice. "*And* his. He knew what he was doing."

"Caern Adan is a bastard," Quell replied.

"I know. And you were just starting to get used to him." She raised a hand, forestalling any reply. "The New Republic *will* find him. His staff, his superiors, everyone's invested in the search. He's on the missing-in-action list, classified and declassified versions, so the troops know to look. I can't promise he'll turn up tomorrow, but everything that can be done will be done."

Quell nodded briskly. It was nothing she hadn't heard before, and she knew that the intelligence officer was most likely dead. He'd disappeared outside the safe zone—racing to meet Kairos's medical transport after Quell had chosen to contact him, which surely put a share of responsibility on her shoulders—and if he wasn't floating in the waters of the flooded Thannerhouse District, he was probably being interrogated by Imperial guerrillas.

To say that Quell *missed* him would be a misrepresentation. But she felt his absence.

"Any word on Kairos?" General Syndulla asked.

This time it was Quell's chance to offer platitudes. "She's in good hands. She's nonresponsive. They won't let anyone in to see her."

Syndulla waited for more, but it was all Quell had to give and the general smiled sympathetically. "Sit down, Lieutenant. Please."

Quell lowered herself onto her knees beside the blanket. Her bones felt as brittle as they had after Nacronis. She knew what was coming—she'd heard the rumors, seen reports that had been meant for Adan but had made it to her anyway—and she managed to say, hoarse but not disrespectful: "I understand you're leaving?"

The surprise in Syndulla's face didn't reach her tone. "I am. Not for long, I hope, but Vanguard Squadron needs support in the Bormea sector and I intend to give it to them. I'll need a few units with me, but the *Lodestar* will stay here. With any luck, I'll be back before the 204th comes out of hiding."

"Give Vanguard my regards," Quell said.

She'd never been *close* to Syndulla. They'd never been friends. The general certainly didn't owe her anything.

"The timetable's not an easy one to meet. But you have the plan. Your squadron knows what needs doing. The troops from the mobile infantry—they're ready and committed. You don't need me for this, Yrica. I'd love to cheer you on, but I can't do more than get in your way."

Quell nodded. She thought she nodded, anyway.

Syndulla slid across the blanket, almost serpentine, and Quell found the woman's strong arms wrapped around her. The general held the embrace until Quell's own hands limply touched the woman's back; then the two parted. "You've done more with your squadron than anyone could have hoped," Syndulla said.

"Good luck," Quell said, feeling utterly alone.

———

The torture droid didn't judge her. The torture droid was programmed not to judge, she assumed, or at least to keep its judgments to itself. Yet as she sat in the tram car she perceived a change in its demeanor—some invisible alteration to the way it hovered and stared with its red photoreceptor. "I should've stepped in earlier," she told it. "I should've known something was wrong."

"What sort of something?" the droid asked.

"She was—" Quell looked away from the red dot, out of the cab window and onto the tracks that went nowhere. "Something that showed she wasn't right."

"Some might say she acted heroically. Her actions gave the infantry time to scatter the Imperial forces and secure victory."

"We should've known it was something she'd try. I could've taken her off duty. I could've posted a gunner aboard her ship . . ."

The droid waited for her to trail off. "I've known Kairos for some years. I hold responsibility as well."

"So I should've consulted with you sooner?" She stood suddenly, took three strides to the window, and leaned back against the glass. Someone had spray-painted a cross inside a circle in the lower left corner; the symbol of the local cultists, the Children of the Empty Sun. "That makes me feel *so* much better."

"It was an observation, not an accusation. Nor are these sessions necessarily intended to make you 'feel better' immediately, as we have discussed in the past."

Because you're a torture droid? she wanted to say, but IT-O kept speaking.

"However, I would ask you this: If there was no sign that Kairos was in distress, and her sacrifice was in the service of a cause that you and your squadron had taken on, is it not possible that her injury—grievous though it may be—is most directly attributed to her *participation in a war*? Not the personal failings of anyone involved?"

The droid's simulated voice remained steady and stern. But it rarely spoke at such length. It was angry, Quell thought. The torture droid was angry, and she grew angry in return.

"She *spoke* to me," she said. "That's how I knew something was wrong."

She hadn't intended to admit it.

The droid's photoreceptor dilated. Its manipulator arm rotated in its socket, the servos whirring and the empty syringe turning in place. Clockwise, then counterclockwise, then clockwise again.

"It's possible," the droid said, "that I am incapable of providing care in my role as your therapist at the present time. This is not an indictment of your actions."

Quell stared. Her shoulders tightened. She searched for a response and was relieved of the obligation when the sound of a fist rapping on the tram car door rang through the cabin. "It's Gravas," a voice called. "We're ready for you."

She pushed off the window, ready to walk away. The droid's voice hitched with urgency. "You have a lead?"

"Probably not. I guess we'll find out."

She was nearly out the door before the droid said: "When you locate Caern Adan, I intend to be with you."

III

Wyl Lark had missed the tranquility and awesome scope of space, and despite the horizon line of asteroid CER952B bisecting the endless blackness, he felt *aloft* in a way he hadn't in the infinite city of Troithe. He watched mountains in the distance resolve into watchtowers and balustrades and castle walls that bled rivers of dust. He tried to recall what little he knew of Cerberon, and recalled the legend of a moon—*the Fortress Moon*—shattered centuries ago, its remnants left to their decaying orbits and eventual demise in the heart of the black hole.

He pitched toward the asteroid's surface, skimming fifteen meters above the rock and pulling up in time to leap above a barbican. He let his eyes slip to his scanners, watching not just for movement but for energy readings, life-forms, heat signatures. He saw nothing, and was satisfied.

Three passes later he allowed the thin atmosphere to slow his vessel and stopped above a crater the size of his birthplace of Cliff. He switched to repulsors and landed gently, attempting (for his own amusement as much as for the mission) to leave no mark in the dust. By the time he strapped on his rebreather and climbed out, his ship was surrounded.

The newcomers were dressed in patchwork combat gear marked haphazardly with the starbird insignia of the Rebel Alliance or the sunrise symbol of the Sixty-First Mobile Infantry. No one wore the symbol of the New Republic. A young man, bronze-skinned and hard-eyed, stepped forward. Wyl recalled that he'd been introduced as *the Captain.*

"You see anything out there?" the man asked, in a colonial accent almost too thick for Wyl to understand—the antithesis of the clipped, enunciated Coruscanti privileged by the Empire.

"Nothing," Wyl said. "Nothing on scanners, nothing on visuals. You should be safe."

The Captain let out a huff of a breath that might have been a laugh. Wyl nearly apologized, instead giving a look of chagrin and bringing up his comlink. "Chass?" he said. "Anything on your end?"

The twang of electronic music crackled through the link before Chass replied: "Wrapping up now. Checked the orbits, we're all clear. Shot down a few rocks just to open the way."

"Understood. Rendezvous at the site." Wyl waited for her acknowledgment then deactivated the comlink and looked back at the Captain. "She says there's nothing that should throw off the orbital path—"

"We heard," the Captain said. "All right. We'll go dark in five hours—need to set some equipment in place, but after that we'll shut down all transmitters, all scanners. We've got scouts watching over the probable landing sites but we won't be looking skyward. If there's any final information you want to deliver, now's a very good time to do it."

"Nothing on our side." Wyl looked at the squads in front of him—

twenty soldiers, perhaps, out of the hundred or more who were hidden away among the rocks of CER952B. They stood at ease, unafraid. Most of them were older than the infantry he'd spent time with on Troithe, and they wore the scars and cybernetics that old soldiers earned. "These people you're going against—" he began, hesitated, then forced himself to continue. "—Shadow Wing is dangerous. You know that, but you haven't fought them."

I had to say it aloud.

The Captain grinned. "In the air? I'm sure they're death on wings. Down here, parked and hiding and waiting for their ride to Troithe? If they step out of their TIEs, we'll slit their throats in their sleep. If not, we'll clip their feathers and offer them a fair fight." Despite the words, there was neither pride nor malice in his tone. "Keep the rest of my company safe on Troithe, and I promise we'll do our part."

Wyl inhaled deeply and felt condensation build in his rebreather. A woman beside the Captain in a retractable armored mask nodded to Wyl as if reaffirming the promise.

"I'll do my very best," Wyl said.

Without a word of farewell, the Captain turned to leave.

This was the final stage of Adan's plan. Troithe was now a prime target for Shadow Wing to retake. The intelligence section of the working group had arranged for word of the planet's plight and details of asteroid CER952B to reach the 204th. Within a matter of days the enemy was expected to slip into the Cerberon system and encamp on the asteroid, believing its orbital path would bring it within striking distance of Troithe.

Instead of preparing the perfect ambush, however, the fighter wing would find itself hiding among New Republic soldiers handpicked for sabotage and assassination. It was a good plan, Wyl thought—Adan had told them, "Shadow Wing is strongest in the air. Why make things difficult?" and he understood the logic. It felt strange to end their units' rivalry without a single shot from Alphabet Squadron, but Quell had approved and General Syndulla had signed off. It would save lives in the end; prevent another Nacronis.

He wondered if he'd ever hear Blink's voice again. He hoped the troops on CER952B somehow allowed the enemy a chance to surrender; yet they didn't seem the sort to risk themselves for the foe.

Wyl couldn't judge them. He couldn't imagine killing face-to-face for as long as they had.

Chass flew on his wing, the asteroid barely a glimmer behind him now and the burning eye of Cerberon staring through the spiraling debris field. He thought about all Adan had done with the working group, everything the man had accomplished bringing them together to stop the threat of the 204th, and he felt a surge of guilt at not having attempted to know Adan better. He'd never especially *liked* Caern Adan; but then, Wyl had never really given him a chance.

The thought of Kairos intruded into his mind next—Kairos, whom he'd had *every* chance to know better. It was far too easy to forget what had happened to her. The silence of her absence was little different from the silence of her presence.

"Sending course adjustment," he said as he plotted a path through the debris. The computer could've transmitted the signal to Chass's B-wing automatically, but he wanted to hear a voice, if only his own.

"Acknowledged," Chass said. She was silent a moment, then asked: "Any word from Quell?"

"Still aiding the analysts, so far as I know." She'd told him little more than that.

"Any word when she'll be back?" Chass asked. Wyl heard a twist in the taut cord of her voice that he was surprised to identify as concern. He hadn't realized how attached Chass had grown to Quell, though he'd seen it happening slowly over the past weeks. He smiled sadly to himself as an old, forgotten pang struck his chest.

"No word," he said. "I'm sure she'll be all right."

"Screw that," Chass said.

Her B-wing was too far out for Wyl to see but he noticed the change in vector on his scanners. "Chass? What are—"

She didn't let him finish. "If Quell isn't going back to the *Lodestar*, I don't see why I should. Meet you there sometime."

Wyl considered chasing her. He could've caught up easily; stayed on her wing, shot out her engines if he had to. But there was no mission waiting for them, and he recalled all the conversations he'd had with Chass about *taking away her choices.*

He stroked the console of his ship, hoping it would give him comfort as he maintained his course for Troithe. But the ship was just a ship, not one of the sur-avkas of his homeworld, and it lacked the power to soothe him.

IV

"So why the hell did you bring *me*?" Nath Tensent asked, leaning back into torn synthleather upholstery as the freighter—an old exhaust-belching Kuati model likely dredged from a junkyard, the sort he'd have pegged as easy prey in his days running protection rackets in a TIE fighter—kicked its way across the void.

"The droid suggested it," Yrica Quell said. Given the deathly disinterest in her voice he was surprised she cast him a *look* as she answered. Then she looked back to the stars.

Nath tightened his harness and pressed one foot against the maintenance panel under the console, attempting to silence its rattling. "So how about it, droid?" he called over his shoulder. "Why the hell'd *you* bring me?"

The voice of the torture droid emerged from the cabin, almost lost in the rumble of the engines. "You are a capable and adaptable individual," it said. "Adaptability is a talent all the more valuable for its rarity."

Nath smirked and translated: *You and Quell don't have a clue how to run a mission like this.* But it would be rude to say so, so instead he replied, "Remember the first time we met, and you stuck a needle in my throat?"

"Yes," the torture droid said, and Nath laughed loud and freely.

He didn't imagine *adaptability* was the full reason he was there, but while he'd never been fond of Caern Adan he'd never been afraid of hard work, either. Others—mostly superior officers and educators—had occasionally called Nath slothful; in truth, Nath simply knew what was worth his time and what wasn't. Rescuing Adan was a gamble with little risk—there were a dozen ways for Nath to come out ahead, and only one possible outcome that was truly unacceptable.

"Check the atmospheric controls," Quell said, and Nath brought his hands to the console. "I don't trust this thing to hold together on entry."

"Just what I like to hear from my pilot." He brought up heat dispersal reports and transferred power into the gravity buffers. "You want me to confirm our landing pad?"

Quell didn't look over this time. "I didn't arrange one."

They were both jolted as the freighter ripped through Catadra's atmosphere. The vast immobility of space, where stars and moons and asteroids appeared locked in place across vast distances, gave way to the tidal rush of clouds. Then the mountains came into view: the uncarved stone peaks, jade-flecked and gray, with crags too narrow to build upon; then the brittle upper reaches, cushioned by pale fungi that lived on the heat of the solar projectors; and finally the slopes, intricately chipped into a band of streets and temples and palaces. Nath couldn't see the craters of the war, but she could picture it. Catadra had been their second target in the Cerberon system, and they had been intimately involved with its ruination.

"You have any plan at all?" he asked. "Any reason to think Adan was taken out here?"

"Two reasons." Quell's voice held steady as the ship rocked. Nath had to strain to hear her. "The analysts dug into the sensor records from Troithe's satellite defense network. The network's patchy but they found indications that a ship slipped through one of the holes two days ago. Unregistered, non-lightspeed-capable."

"Could be anything or anywhere by now. Could be another smuggler."

"That's our second reason. Gravas says there was chatter about an auction happening on Catadra. If it was a gangster who took Adan instead of the Imps, he'd be looking for a way to profit."

Nath thought this over. If he'd been a gangster stuck in Cerberon with a New Republic Intelligence officer in his cargo hold, he might've done the same. "Minimal military presence on Catadra, so it's safer. Who do you sell to here, though? The cults and the war orphans aren't exactly drowning in cash."

"That's what we're here to find out."

"And why you need *adaptability*?"

Turbulence snapped Nath forward in his seat hard enough that the breath was forced from his lungs. Quell barely shifted in her seat.

"Exactly," she said.

Catadra was a maze of a world, still stinking of ash and melted plastoid from the bombing campaign. Throngs of civilians packed stairs and throughways, creeping through bottlenecks to circumvent shattered bridges on their way to—well, wherever it was the Catadran masses went. On Troithe, the spaceport refugee camp had been pitiful but well managed. On Catadra there was anarchy allayed only by (if Nath understood correctly) gangs, cults, and a paltry selection of New Republic emissaries.

Then again, Catadra housed maybe one one-hundredth the population of Troithe's endless city. The locals were lucky they got as much attention as they did.

They left the freighter guarded by the torture droid and a cybered-up Weequay that Nath paid with stim-shots from the freighter's medical supplies. ("We may need those if Adan is wounded," the torture droid had warned, and Nath had rolled his eyes and left a single dose behind.) From there, they made their way to the auction site: a cantina by the name of Father Ambrosia's Glorious Revelation or, as the locals called it, "the Rev."

The Rev was built into the upper levels of a tower constructed of turquoise stone, with ladders against the interior walls and wooden platforms crossing the central gap to provide space for tables. Nath led the way, wondering how many drunks had toppled off the higher platforms as he called, "Catadra's saviors are here! Bring us some swill, quick as you can." He made sure his sidearm was visible and gestured to Quell's exposed squadron tattoo.

He saw Quell suppress a flinch of irritation, but she understood. Her posture was straight-backed and haughty as she surveyed the room, and she made no effort to avoid the thin packs of midafternoon patrons (sad-looking middle-aged males, mostly, from a diverse array of species) as she marched toward a table. The customers parted for her and she and Nath took their seats.

"You do more policing planetside than you let on, back in the day?" he asked.

Quell shrugged stiffly. "They taught us to be careful on leave. Sometimes we docked at planets that weren't fond of the Empire; it was better not to show weakness."

"I hear that," Nath said, and waved at a serving droid.

He'd taught his squadron much the same—outside the Core systems, people feared the Empire or hated it. If you were strutting around a strange city, you wanted fear to win out. Today the point wasn't to intimidate the people of Catadra so much as to get their attention, but the old tricks still worked.

Without saying a word, they both adjusted their wire-frame chairs so that they had a complete view of the room. Nath caught several of the patrons looking their way before feigning a glower to discourage them. He *wanted* them watching, but he had to keep up the show.

"How long do we wait?" Quell murmured after a droid had floated down to deliver their drinks.

"Could take a while for word to spread. Or it could be five minutes, if no one's feeling subtle."

"If we stick around *too* long, it'll look suspicious," Quell said.

Nath raised a tin cup full of something bubbly and steaming that smelled like wet fur and cabbage. "That's okay by me. Settle in, drink slow, and look like you enjoy the company."

Quell grunted. They drank. Nath wasn't surprised to find that Quell had no instinct for conversation. He proffered a handful of harmless subjects (news of the war in the southern galactic quadrant; civilian relief efforts back on Troithe; speculation about Chass's evening activities, when she disappeared and pretended otherwise), but Quell took to none of them. He decided that if she wasn't going to cooperate he might as well get answers to questions he was genuinely interested in, and said, "You know you could've found someone else for this job."

"Instead of you?" Quell asked.

He shook his head. "Instead of you. New Republic Intelligence has gotten fond of Adan. If they *really* believed this was the best way to find him, they could've brought an agent out eventually." He brought the cup to his lips but didn't drink. "Without the general around, you ought to be prepping for Shadow Wing."

Quell's eyes were fixed just above Nath's left shoulder. "The plan is set. The troops are in position. We've got days before Shadow Wing is supposed to arrive. Meantime I thought I'd search."

"Never figured you cared that much for the man."

She scowled and took a swig of her drink—a real swig, Nath noticed, watching the pulse of her throat. "I don't."

He could have pushed the subject, but she'd given up enough and he didn't want to overplay his hand.

Caern Adan knew the truth about Nacronis—that Lieutenant Yrica Quell of the 204th, instead of trying to save the planet from destruction during Operation Cinder, had been a willing participant in the genocide. The New Republic was still in the phase of *talking* about war crimes more than *prosecuting* them, but the day for tribunals was coming and Nath doubted Quell would look much better than the Death Star gunners who'd vaporized Alderaan.

The fact that Quell remained virtually unsupervised suggested Adan hadn't shared that truth with much of anyone. Except maybe Quell herself.

And *Nath* knew what *Adan* knew because Nath had supplied the intel—obtained it above Pandem Nai at Adan's request. Quell surely wasn't aware of that.

Nath had noticed the bond forming between Adan and Quell over the past weeks—there was no fondness in their exchanges, no joy; at most a mutual respect. Still, there was an ease about them as if they'd both accepted the nature of their relationship. Nath had also seen the two together aboard the *Buried Treasure,* however, back when Adan had been threatening to have the woman executed, and Quell didn't seem the type not to hold a grudge. Something had changed, and the truth about Nacronis was the obvious answer.

Maybe, Nath thought, Quell didn't want to find Adan at all. Instead she wanted to convince the world—convince herself—that she was doing everything she could, so she could rest with a salved conscience when Adan was never seen again.

He almost laughed to himself when the simpler answer occurred to him: If Adan had been captured, she didn't want him telling anyone else what he knew.

I don't envy you your troubles, Yrica Quell, he thought, and swirled his drink so that steam spiraled through the air.

It was well after nightfall (or what passed for nightfall in the Cerberon system) when they caught their stalker in the act. Nath was on his fifth drink while Quell had gone through considerably more in her efforts to blend—she'd managed to dilute the noxious concoctions enough to stay sober, but her lips were stained green by whatever it was they'd been served.

Nath had been the one to spot the squat Utai in the corner whose stubby eyestalks strained to look their way without *seeming* to look their way. The puckered mouth chewed samples from a small dish of leafy herbs. Nath guessed the Utai had come to the Rev for the sole purpose of observing them.

Several gestures and minutes later, Nath and Quell agreed to their next move. Nath loudly declared his intention to "check on the thing," and strolled out the door. On the off chance the Utai didn't follow him, he imagined the humanoid would take the opportunity to approach Quell. Either way suited him.

He spotted the Utai's squat shadow as he turned down a staircase and smiled as he headed for the landing. He allowed himself to stumble, missing a step and bowing his body low. When he heard footfalls close by, he grappled the Utai by the legs, sliding his arms up to a solid torso. He ignored the ensuing screeching sound. Within a few moments he had his foe compressed in his arms, and Quell stood a dozen steps above leveling her blaster at the Utai's head.

The Utai stopped wriggling.

"You want to take lead?" Nath asked.

Quell descended. The weapon in her hand stayed perfectly trained on the Utai. There was nothing kind in the woman's eyes. "You know about the auction?" she asked.

The Utai's voice was a high-pitched gurgle. "I'm a stairmason! Just a stairmason. I cut and mortar."

Nath arched his brow and flexed his arms around the Utai. Quell didn't look at him. "I used to be Imperial," she said.

The Utai's breathing quickened. Quell's finger shifted on the trigger of her weapon.

"I am guided by the Force in all my deeds," the Utai whispered, as if chanting a mantra, "and through the teachings of my masters I find harmony in its guidance."

"Wasn't expecting that," Nath admitted. "Force or no Force, we still need an answer."

"Where's Caern Adan?" Quell asked.

The Utai whimpered. "Who?"

"The New Republic Intelligence officer kidnapped off Troithe," Quell said.

Nath elaborated. "The one you sold. We want to know who the buyer was."

"I don't know!" the Utai said. "I don't know. They were Imperial, but I didn't sell him—I was there to buy. My fellowship was outbid."

"Bet you can help us out," Nath said, and the Utai agreed.

CHAPTER 8

THE ILLUMINATING BRILLIANCE OF STARLIGHT

I

S oran Keize considered himself a soldier first and a pilot second, but his purest joy was the melding of those two art forms. It had been too long since he'd flown a combat mission, and even with his cannons offline and their computer-simulated replacements lacking the electric buzz and resonant kick of true weapons, he reveled in the experience. His life aboard the *Edict* and the *Aerie* seemed meaningless as a dream; even his brief, intense existence as the wanderer Devon seemed clouded by gray apathy as his TIE fighter skimmed above the icy ring system of a nameless moon.

"Adjust vector. Prepare for attack run."

He spoke unhurriedly into his comm, though he was sweating under the thick material of his flight suit. He monitored the squadron's reactions as twelve fighters dived together, subdividing into two-TIE elements as they navigated the frozen field. He could have put the pilots through the same maneuvers from the *Aerie,* even recorded it all and reviewed the results at his leisure, but he would soon be flying again himself. He needed to remember his skills.

He needed to restore Shadow Wing's faith that he could lead.

They emerged from the ring, plunging toward the *Edict*. The Star Destroyer was unlit save for a few glimmers on the dagger's port edge—it was too obviously underpowered to fool any enemy, but even now the crew was making modifications to the vessel. The cadets were tearing apart bulkheads, rewiring turbolaser batteries, and chaining targeting computers; when they were finished, a handful of weapons officers would be able to wield the vessel's full ruinous potential. The point-defense stations—the Destroyer's primary counter against starfighter attacks—would remain nonfunctional without the hundreds of individual gunners required to operate them, but that was an acceptable trade-off. The *Edict* would serve well in the assault on Cerberon.

"Move on your assigned targets," Soran declared. "Weapons free."

The TIEs raced across the *Edict*'s hull, simulating dozens of strikes against critical systems. Soran loaded false sensor readings into the squadron's scanners, calling out instructions to evade New Republic X-wings or incoming missiles. He noted Vann Bragheer's aversion to zero-thrust turns and Karli genFries's habit of only firing well after closing range. He admired Ran Chorda's perfect alignment with her flight leader. Palal Seedia showed no sign of the worrisome aggression she had displayed against the New Republic. In the days ahead he would discuss these things with the pilots' commanders; in some cases he would need to make time to advise the pilots themselves.

First, however, he was going to put the squadron through a final test. He punched a new program into the computer and distributed it among the others.

"All pilots: We are beginning another exercise. The *Edict* is no longer in play. Your only goal is to eliminate me."

First he was going to enjoy himself.

When the turbolaser adjustments aboard the *Edict* were complete, Soran's next task for the cadets was the repair and reprogramming of the TIE training drones. The Star Destroyer carried a full squadron rigged for autonomous operation—poorer fliers than even the droid fighters of the Clone Wars, but largely functional and potentially useful for the coming fight. He set the crew an impossible deadline and hoped they would rise to the challenge.

No one questioned his leadership of the unit. If he could balance vision and pragmatism—the iron fist and the comforting hand—along with demonstrating personal competence, he hoped no one would.

It was his pilots to whom he devoted the most attention. The combat-readiness of the squadrons pleased him—in the mock battle, he'd whittled his twelve enemies down to three before a simulated shot had finally disabled his ship. Not his ideal outcome, yet that performance wasn't notably worse than what he'd seen at the 204th's finest hour. His people hadn't dulled their skills while he'd been away, nor had his own abilities atrophied beyond repair.

So when he briefed the wing—not in the ready rooms, as per protocol, but walking among the fighters in the *Aerie*'s hangar—he focused not only on the mundane matters of battle scenarios or the Cerberon system's anomalies, but on the opponents they chose to face. He played back holos of Hera Syndulla in her personal combat-modified freighter, a ship she called the *Ghost*. He analyzed the tactics her battle group had applied at Pandem Nai—the risks she had taken and her willingness to apply all the force at her disposal, nearly leading to the planet's annihilation.

"General Syndulla is not the only individual combatant we've identified from Pandem Nai," he said as he walked among his pilots. The squadron commanders had heard it before, and observed their subordinates. The rest watched Soran. "We believe at least two of the ships at the vanguard of the attack were piloted by the rebels who battled the *Aerie* in the Oridol Cluster.

"The B-wing pilot is unknown, but we've compiled a profile I expect you all to review. He is an able marksman, easily baited into solo flight, and highly capable with his ship. Still . . . *highly capable* only goes so far in a B-wing, so long as we keep in mind our advantages.

"More intriguing is the A-wing pilot, a man who introduced himself over an open channel as Wyl Lark and who attempted to undo the catastrophic damage at Pandem Nai—too late to save many, but we can appreciate that his effort was greater than that of his peers. Based on his flying and his accent, I believe that Lark is one of the Hundred and Twenty—Polynean terrorists, expert pilots all. Study the footage you've been sent."

Soran had encountered a Polynean a year prior to Endor. He recalled the fight now, thirteen minutes that had felt like days weaving through the Cataract of Moons; felt an impossible, lingering soreness in his arms. For the benefit of the pilots before him, knowing he'd yet to secure their loyalty, he did not allow himself to smile.

He tapped a remote and cycled through holograms of the other ships in the vanguard: The U-wing, whose pilot was bold and almost animalistic—a talent whom he suspected had never received formal training. The Y-wing, a modified BTL-A4 model that had been piloted by its astromech for a stretch midway through the Pandem Nai mission; after Soran had pointed out the droid's role, one of the ground crew had taken an interest in the footage and asked permission to examine it more closely. The X-wing had gone down after Pandem Nai's atmosphere had ignited; Soran spent the least time studying its owner, recognizing the idiosyncrasies of a former TIE pilot but focusing his attention elsewhere. Syndulla's people were many, and he was one man.

He attempted to judge his audience as they reviewed the data—he wanted them dedicated, determined, *purposeful,* but if vengeance began to become an all-consuming passion then he would lose them as surely as if they had no purpose at all.

"Lark referred to his unit as *Alphabet,*" he told them. "Given its composition we may safely assume it was assembled by Syndulla to counter the 204th at Pandem Nai, though we cannot confirm whether it remains intact. Its pilots are priority targets due to their knowledge of our operations. However, *every* unit in Syndulla's battle group will be familiar with the 204th.

"Next we have the squadron identifying as *Hail*—"

Lieutenant Seedia rose to her feet. "Sir?" she said. "About Wyl Lark?"

"What is it?" he asked.

"I was in the Oridol Cluster," Seedia said. "I have an idea."

It was Teso Broosh who presented Soran with the rank pins, one evening after dinner with the squadron commanders. The meal had been a spirited one, the lot of them presenting options and debating plans and laughing as much as they sniped. Gablerone was as intolerable as always, and Darita as clever, but they had a common cause now.

Afterward, Broosh had lingered and they'd discussed the well-being of Squadron Five. It was only after Soran had begun stacking meal trays that Broosh said, "The other commanders and I—we decided it was time," and held out the colorful uniform plaque.

"*Colonel* Soran Keize?" Soran asked.

"Special adviser no longer. Whether you earned it or not," Broosh said, "it's the role you have. Even those of us who don't like it know the pilots need to respect you. Live up to it, will you?"

Soran took the pins and slid his finger over the red and blue squares. He laughed softly as he affixed the plaque to his uniform and clasped Broosh's shoulder with one hand. "I will try. I swear it."

They parted, and Soran returned to his quarters feeling lighter than he had in weeks. He sat at his desk and reflected on the woman who had come before him—reflected on Colonel Shakara Nuress, whom he had considered a friend and realized now had been doomed the day the Emperor died.

You could never have survived this galaxy, he thought, and that was the tragedy of it: that a woman as brave and brilliant and loyal as Shakara Nuress could not have adapted to the anarchy now gripping the cosmos; that none of the commanders of the 204th were true Imperials as she had been, because no true Imperial could last. Nuress would have resisted employing guerrilla attacks and seen the gutting and rebuilding of the Star Destroyer *Edict* as a sort of desecration. She would have broken a crew of cadets, not nurtured them. She would have stood against the New Republic fleet like a cliff against the ocean until she finally crumbled.

Soran had so admired her steel certainty.

He was recalling their conversations together—almost all of them focused on military matters, whether reviews of logistical data or discussions of personality clashes among the crew—when his desktop blinked to indicate that a message had been relayed from the bridge.

He expected another desperate Imperial communiqué—some plea for help on obsolete frequencies broadcast to every allied vessel in the sector. Instead a hologram appeared depicting the worn face of Colonel Madrighast of the *Unyielding*. Colonel Nuress, Soran recalled, had always disdained Madrighast; yet Soran had found amusement in his bluster.

There was no bluster in his voice now. Soran strained to understand words through the hiss of distortion.

"—whether you survived Pandem Nai. But if any vessels from the 204th Imperial Fighter Wing remain intact, I offer an invitation."

The image disappeared in a blur of static and did not return. The audio popped and quieted but returned to intelligibility a moment later.

"—that Admiral Rae Sloane has taken command of the fleet. I have no confirmation at this time but we are attempting to rendezvous at the enclosed coordinates. I do not believe this is a rebel trap, but nor do I believe the journey will be easy. We have information about rebel interdiction blockades along the hyperlanes—"

The audio degenerated again until nothing remained but an oscillating warble. Soran waited through twenty seconds of noise before the recording ended.

If he'd been asked to guess which single leader would unite the Imperial fleet, Admiral Rae Sloane would not have made his short list. Her reputation was one of a loyal and competent retainer—at best she was known for a spark of genius she'd rarely had opportunity to stoke. Soran associated her with neither charisma nor political power, but if she had risen above the fray to take the command chair? He harbored no objections.

He did not believe she—or anyone else—could reforge the shards of Empire.

He did not intend to chase rumors with Colonel Madrighast.

His people were committed. They had a task they believed in—one that would test them, challenge them as soldiers sought to be challenged while offering the tangible prize of their tormentors' defeat.

Pursuing dreams of a reborn Empire would destroy them as surely as it had Shakara Nuress. Perhaps his subordinates would disagree; but Colonel Soran Keize was in command of the unit now.

II

Chass na Chadic was drinking a teensy-tiny bit too much, but at least she wasn't doing it alone. She'd made new friends. Friends of varying shapes and sizes, friends committed to seizing her B-wing by hook or crook, but friends nonetheless. "Fifty on blue," she said, slapping her hand down on the table. "And bring me something fizzy."

The establishment was called Winker's—a cantina, gambling den, trading post, and fuel stop rapidly built in the ruins of the garrison-world Verzan on the outer fringes of the Cerberon system. After Syndulla's battle group had obliterated most of Verzan's airless surface, an entrepreneurial pirate named Edineezious Winker had taken advantage of the open real estate. Since Verzan was too small to retain an atmosphere, Winker's magnetic field surrounded the totality of the rock's population—a permanent staff of two dozen ready to service a visitor complement of a hundred or more.

Most of the people enjoying Winker's hospitality were stranded—fuel was in short supply, only a few traders still ran local routes to Troithe and Catadra, and most anyone with access to hyperspace travel was long gone. But the gambling tables were open for business and the guests eager to pass the time.

"Fifty on blue," the computer agreed. Chass swore as the blue mark shifted to gray. She didn't know the game well, but she knew *that* wasn't good.

"Pity, pity, terrible pity," said the Vurk to her right. The reptilian man loomed over her by a full half meter, his crest painted in intricate crimson-and-azure whorls. He enunciated too well for someone with so many teeth. "Your mind is elsewhere tonight."

"Spiraling down the black hole, is what it's doing," Chass said. Another drink had appeared on the table before her. She grasped it in one hand, attempted to play a fresh mark with the other, and was rebuked by the computer. She slapped the button three times before she realized it wasn't her turn. "What was I saying before?"

"Something about *friends.*" The synthesized voice came from the respirator mask of the Kel Dor to her left. "But please focus—"

"I don't need to focus!" Chass spat. She felt her drink splash her wrist as she swung the cup away from her body. "And I'm not here because of my friends. My friends are fine."

The computer indicated a new round had begun. Chass stared at the Kel Dor's respirator and thought of Kairos. The strange woman was floating in a bacta tank somewhere, if she'd been lucky enough to warrant the treatment despite the medicine shortage. Or maybe she was bleeding on a surgical table under a rusty scalpel droid.

"I'm not worried about her," Chass said. She took a swallow of her drink and felt tingling down her throat and into her stomach, where bubbles danced eagerly above her intestines. "Freak doesn't talk much but she's tougher than she looks. So's—" She began laughing. "So's Kairos."

She missed them. Quell and Kairos both. Somehow they made her feel *safe.* It was disgusting, but real.

"Perhaps you should bring your friends here sometime," the Vurk said. "We'd be happy to take their credits."

"They're *working,*" she said. "There's a big project going on. Real big and real nasty—but you can't trick me into talking about it, because it's secret."

"I wouldn't dream of trying," the Vurk said. *Probably lying,* Chass thought. "Bring them here after their project, then. Celebrate together."

She bared her teeth and slammed her cup against the game table, but her voice was soft. "There's not going to be an *after.* They're not going to be my friends *after.* Don't be an idiot."

That was why she was at Winker's, after all. Why she'd progressed from spending her evenings drinking alone to drinking with the infantry and refugees to flying to the fringes of Cerberon: so she didn't *have* to think about what came after Shadow Wing.

Screw Wyl Lark, she thought, suddenly furious. If she'd died in the Oridol Cluster or Pandem Nai, she'd have died a hero. Only losers and fools died now. Losers, fools, ground troops, and Kairos.

She saw that they'd somehow played another three rounds. She wasn't sure what she'd spoken aloud. "The time has come," the Vurk said. He raked his claws gently down her forearm, drawing pale lines and demanding her attention. "The set is complete and payment is required."

Chass stared blankly at the Vurk. "The money's in the pot. Don't mess with me."

"You didn't have the money," the Kel Dor interjected. "You promised your ship instead."

She felt onlookers and other gamblers shuffling behind her. Some were edging away; others were blocking her exit. "That's garbage," she said, emphasizing the words with another slam of her empty cup. "You think I'm *that* out of it? I paid you!"

Doubt crept into her brain. She smashed it back down.

"I will take your ship," the Vurk said. "It is what I am owed and I will not remain here another month—"

Chass felt her knuckles dig into her wrist as her fist hit the immovable wall of the Vurk's body. She followed the first punch with a second, then a third, both equally ineffective. The next moment she was airborne and her ribs hurt, and she realized she'd been hoisted by the Vurk and tossed backward into the crowd.

She braced herself, ready to feel her skull crack against the pocked metal floor. Instead she fell into a cushion of flesh that gave beneath her, then buoyed her as whoever she'd smashed into lifted her upright. "Come on," a voice snapped, and a hand clasped her raked arm.

She didn't want to run. She tried to pull away. When she saw the Vurk barreling toward her, however, she followed her rescuer's lead and they dashed between patrons, out the door of the gambling lounge, and into the narrow alleys that joined the outpost's shanties. She caught a glimpse of a humanoid body dressed in checkered swatches—a style she vaguely remembered seeing on Troithe—and somehow rushed past her rescuer onto the cracked-glass field of the landing pad.

She smelled ozone and heard the electric ripple of three stun shots. She spun on her heel, trying not to fall as she did, and saw her rescuer standing above the body of the Vurk.

"What was *that*?" she asked, pushing past the checkered man to reach the Vurk. "No one asked you to kill him for me!"

"Stunned only," the man said.

"You know how a Vurk's anatomy works? You know what three stun shots will do to one?" She gave the man another glance, confirming her suspicions: *Human.* Late middle-aged, red-faced with burn scars across his cheeks and scalp.

She looked back at the Vurk. He was still breathing. She was almost disappointed, but the human didn't correct her.

"You should leave Winker's," he said. Chass swayed and corrected the imbalance. "I suggest you set your controls to automatic pilot."

Chass snorted and glanced across the nearly empty landing pad to the B-wing. "You don't want anything?"

"In your heart, you're already among us." He spoke like what he was saying made sense. "I've seen you here before. You long for answers. For fellowship."

Chass's brain wasn't working right. She wasn't sure whether she was supposed to understand. "I don't want to sleep with you," she said.

"Nor I with you," the man said. "But if you ever wish to find answers, I invite you to find us. The Children of the Empty Sun welcome anyone prepared to put aside weapons and violence for the will of the Force."

Chass spat on the ground. "You're the local cult?"

"Call us what you like. We provide meaning and sustenance—spiritual and physical—to the people of Catadra and the other worlds of Cerberon. Through the Force and our leader, we—"

She landed one solid punch to his throat and he fell coughing. Chass marched to her starfighter, fumbling her way inside and wishing he'd let the Vurk eat her alive.

For the rest of the flight home, she thought of her mother and all the cults she'd known in her life. She hoped to wake up with the memory of Winker's long gone.

III

Catadra's moon was called Narthex, and though it had once been inhabited it had been left to fast-growing crystalline brambles called dirkweed for the better part of a millennium. The weed's dull, slate-blue hue seemed to tinge the atmosphere, as if the whole world were obscured by campfire smoke.

Finding the hideout where Quell believed Caern Adan was being kept had not been overly difficult. The Utai at the Catadra cantina had led Quell and Nath to a gaunt woman named Sarvada Dream, who was romantically involved with Adan's kidnapper—a nephew of the smuggler flushed out by Alphabet's operation in the Cerberon debris field. Sarvada confirmed that Adan's buyers were Imperials recently returned from some special mission near the system's black hole. After questioning from Nath, she'd pointed the way to an Aleena operating a combination soup stand and illicit comm station; the Aleena admitted to regularly relaying in-system data to an ancient observatory on Catadra's moon.

After a painstaking covert approach, they'd landed half a kilometer from the observatory. IT-O stayed with the freighter, and once Quell and Nath had picked their way up the bramble-ridden slope they were able to see that the structure was little more than a bunker embedded in the crumbling top of a mesa. "Would've been a sorry hiding spot in the worst days of the Rebellion," Tensent observed, peeking above a pair of boulders and avoiding the cutting edges of the dirkweed. "Probably not more than a dozen Imps, if that, but"—he shrugged—"could still be tricky, under the circumstances. Might need to call the working group."

Quell could count exactly how many firefights she'd been in outside a cockpit. She knelt beside Tensent, back aching. "No strike team. I want to do it now, and I want to do it alone."

"You want to get killed?" Tensent asked, as if it were the same to him either way.

"Right now, we need stealth more than firepower. It's better this way."

Because if Adan was inside, they'd been talking to him. If they'd been talking to him, they knew the truth, and truth spread like a virus.

Tensent said nothing and didn't bother to hide his disbelief.

"We have to get him out before he tells them about the trap. About Shadow Wing," she said, which was very nearly true.

Tensent cast a glance behind him and down the slope toward the freighter. He lowered his voice, but his tone remained casual. "If he's in there, no guarantee he's intact. Or if he's intact, no guarantee he comes back out."

Quell furrowed her brow, watching Tensent and trying to decipher what he was saying.

"If we bring Adan's corpse back to Troithe," Tensent said, now smiling tightly, "who's to say when or how it happened? But you *will* get killed if you go in solo."

She felt cold sweat trickle down her aching back.

Tensent knew. He knew *something*, and he'd given her permission to cover up the crime.

"I'm getting him out," she said, and looked to the observatory. "You can watch my back."

She wouldn't murder Caern Adan, but she was ready to be a murderer.

She'd borrowed more than just the freighter from New Republic Intelligence and more than a sidearm from the *Lodestar*'s armory. A handheld scanner revealed the presence of civilian-grade perimeter alarms arrayed outside the observatory; she disabled two by hand, stabbing dirkweed through cracks in the plastoid casing and slicing open her left forefinger in the process. She stanched the bleeding with a sleeve and waved Tensent forward.

They'd spied the single stormtrooper patrolling outside and agreed to a plan: Quell would ready the portable communications jammer, thumb hovering over the activation trigger, while Tensent neutralized the threat. "You want to be first through the door," he'd said, "that's fine with me—but can you swear you can take one in the open?"

She couldn't. She watched as Tensent swaggered toward the trooper while the Imperial's back was turned, somehow making not a noise on the gravel-strewn terrain. She nearly forgot to squeeze the jammer as Tensent casually opened a vibroknife and swung it upward, blade sliding between the stormtrooper's helmet and chest plate. He did it so carelessly, she was sure he'd done it before.

She scurried to the corpse and saw the grime on the trooper's once-pristine armor. Whatever unit she faced was as run-down and ragged as the rest of the Empire.

Tensent shrugged and gestured her to go next.

A spectrum-scope suggested no one immediately inside the observatory entrance. Quell guessed the building contained a single main room and a few closet-sized alcoves. She attached an explosive to the front door and cleared a trail through the dirkweed to the back of the structure, where she sought a ventilation shaft. She found none, waved an increasingly impatient Tensent over, and allowed him to hoist her to the low roof where she clambered to the telescope. The lens, she was pleased to see, was broken.

She withdrew a gas canister from her satchel. She didn't expect it to do much good—cyclo-dioxis was invisible, nonlethal, and efficiently neutralized by a stormtrooper's helmet filters—but she dropped the canister into the telescope anyway and listened to it bounce and rattle and smash through the far lens. Then she donned her own respirator and activated the release switch, listening to the calming aerosol hiss.

Moments later someone attempted to open the door. The explosive activated automatically and the second stormtrooper died with a face full of shrapnel and a charred torso.

Tensent was firing as Quell slid off the roof to the side of the door.

She spun, aimed her weapon, and shot two unarmed stormtroopers still attempting to secure their helmets. The remaining soldiers were clad in nightshirts, crawling toward the ruined doorway through the cyclo-dioxis haze if they were moving at all. Quell looked into their bloodshot eyes, their cheeks gaunt with malnutrition, and executed them one by one. She found two more asleep on cots in the first alcove, bandaged skin stinking of rot and unguents. She shot these, too, ignoring the shaking in her hands and knowing that General Syndulla and Wyl Lark and maybe even Chass na Chadic would have done otherwise.

They didn't have the secrets she did.

When she sensed a presence behind her she barely thought to move. Instinct saved her from a rifle smashing her scalp; instead the heavy barrel smacked her shoulder, pumped her arm full of pain, and she dropped to her knees. She pivoted as fast as she could, hoping to catch her foe by the knees, but she barely tapped white-clad shins.

Above her was a stormtrooper—unhelmeted, but wearing a respirator mask. The woman was aiming her rifle at Quell; Quell fell back and fired as her enemy did. She felt heat and smelled her own burning hair as a particle bolt impacted to the right of her head. Her pistol pulsed in her hands as she fired wildly. In another instant the stormtrooper fell forward onto Quell, and Quell lay beneath the corpse, breathing heavily.

When she managed to stand, she found Adan unconscious on a cot in the second alcove. His lips were crusted with blood, and a bruise rendered the left side of his face almost unrecognizable. One of his antenna-stalks was extended farther than the other and was bent crookedly. Quell found her eyes growing wet and wiped the moisture away, fearing its interaction with the cyclo-dioxis gas.

She left Adan where he was and checked the portable computers in the main room. She could access only one—the others were locked or damaged—but all she found were maps of the innermost sections of the Cerberon debris field. She recognized none of it, could make no connection to the CER952B asteroid or the trap set for Shadow Wing.

She laughed, nearly choked, when her first instinct after reviewing the files was to shoot the computer screen. She wondered if that was the way of all troops on the ground, or only the amateur murderers.

The droid arrived five minutes after the shooting stopped. It hovered over Adan attentively as the gas cleared and Nath Tensent flew the freighter closer to the observatory. Between Quell and Tensent they managed to carry Adan without much jostling. They set him gently in one of the bunks in the freighter's crew quarters.

Tensent had said nothing about the bloodshed in the observatory and now said only, "I'll get us moving. Man probably needs more attention than we can give here."

"I can identify no internal injuries," the droid said. "I believe his interrogators saw value in preserving his life."

"You'd know," Quell said.

Tensent shrugged and sauntered into the access corridor, heading for the cockpit.

She knelt by Adan's side as the deck shuddered and the freighter lifted off. The droid injected him with a series of watery mixtures and subjected him to sonic pulses that had no obvious use but caused the intelligence officer to groan in his sleep. "His bioreadings are stable," the droid eventually announced. "He is malnourished and dehydrated but his injuries are not life threatening."

"I think they were all malnourished and dehydrated," Quell said. She wondered how long the Imperial unit had been on the run. Certainly the moon hadn't had much to offer in the way of supplies.

The droid did not speak. Quell felt the freighter exit Narthex's atmosphere—felt its trembling even out and heard the engine whine downshift to a groaning pulse as the vessel diverted power from heat shields to thrusters. Somewhere, a sealing bolt dropped onto deck plating.

Even in its native era, the freighter had been nothing worth flying— a low-cost model for in-system hauls, barely cheaper than the more sophisticated models it had been built to imitate. It was a machine reliant on the ignorant and the desperate to earn its keep. She felt a certain kinship with it.

Adan made a sound not quite like words. She saw he was turning his head and she fetched a pouch of water. She held it to his lips, started to tip it back, but he took it from her with shaking hands and managed to drink on his own.

"Quell," he pronounced, as if testing the name.

She wondered if he was aware of IT-O hovering three meters away.

"Yes," she said. Then a moment later: "You're safe."

He didn't seem able to hold himself upright. He lay rigidly on the bunk's thin padding, voice ragged as he asked: "What happened to Kairos?"

Her shoulders stiffened. It wasn't what she'd wanted to hear, though she couldn't have said what she *did* want. "She's alive. She's with the medics, but not awake."

IT-O floated behind her. Adan's whole body began to tremble, as if in harmony with the droid's low humming. Then he stilled and whispered, eyes closed: "I didn't tell them. I didn't tell them about the mission. I told them about the *Lodestar* and the squadrons but they never asked the right questions—"

"The particulars can wait," IT-O said. "Rest."

Adan looked as if he wanted to protest, but did not.

They flew on. Quell remained at Adan's side, watching him breathe, watching his antenna-stalks gradually uncurl like arthritic limbs finally relaxing. She absently drank the rest of the water pouch and remembered to replenish it afterward. Eventually Tensent emerged from the cockpit, surveyed the room, and seemed satisfied, returning without any questions.

Quell was surprised when she heard Adan utter her name again. She'd thought he'd fallen asleep. "I'm here," she said.

Adan moistened his lips several times before he asked, clearer than anything else he'd said since his rescue: "How long has it been? Since they took me?"

She gave it thought. "A week now. A week exactly."

Adan exhaled rapidly in either a cough or a laugh. "I'm sorry," he said. "I'm sorry."

Quell had no idea what he meant, and he didn't speak again.

IV

Two men escorted the black cylinder, one in front to guide its path and one in back steering the repulsorlift controls. Within the antigravity frame the cylinder itself was unmarked, its surface flat save a single panel the size of a human palm. Its edges gleamed like glass, but its surface was unreflective. It reminded Wyl Lark of images he'd seen of pallbearers ushering coffins into graves—the burial rites of strange cultures.

The men were not pallbearers, however. They were healers, medics of the New Republic, and they deserved better than his cynicism.

Go to them, he thought. *Tell them of the cures of the Sun-Lamas—* But he banished that thought. He had nothing to share that would be of use.

He hoped the specialists aboard the medical transport *Bright Vigil* would serve Kairos better when they arrived. The droids would tell Wyl nothing of her condition other than that applying bacta—the miracle fluid, capable of everything short of resurrection in a hundred species—had failed, and that keener minds were required. The black cylinder was a suspension tube meant to arrest Kairos's decay until she could be examined on Chandrila, where the *Bright Vigil* was bound.

"May the Force be with you," Wyl whispered as the cylinder disappeared past a row of airspeeders. "May your breath be the breath of the wind."

He glanced about one last time, distantly hoping to spot Nath or Quell or Chass hurrying down the tarmac. But Nath and Quell were hunting for Adan and Chass was . . . somewhere.

Wyl was late. He heard an engine loud enough to shake the tarmac and ran until his breath felt like shrapnel and his underarms were soaked with sweat. He leapt onto the *Lodestar*'s loading ramp moments before it began to retract. One of the engineers cursed at him in disapproval. Sergeant Borys, chief of the ground crews while Ragnell was on Troithe prepping the newly assigned fighter garrison, laughed uproariously.

"You know we're just moving into orbit?" Borys called from across the bay. "We're running shuttles to the planet three times daily."

"If they catch me riding a shuttle, my squadron'll never let me live it down," Wyl said. He spared a smile for Borys, then turned to the boxy olive droid rolling his way. T5 belonged to Nath, but the churlish astromech rarely let Wyl pass without a friendly greeting.

He let T5 babble awhile, and stopped to chat with Sergeant Yava-Thine and her nestmate P'i on his way out; he ran into three members of the *Lodestar*'s bridge crew with whom he exchanged good wishes and news of the war. By the time he made it to his billet he hadn't forgotten Kairos but his mood had lifted considerably. The galaxy had reminded him that, even without his squadron, he wasn't entirely alone.

As he sat on his cot he saw that the message light on the console beside his bunk was blinking. He hit a key and checked the display and was surprised to see the sender designated as Caern Adan. The message proper was prefaced with a lengthy set of technical headers:

SECURE (MULTISYNC TYPE 7) ENCRYPTION / TIME-DELAY TRIGGER (SYSTEM LOGIN OVERRIDE / 170 STD HOURS / AUTH LEVEL 5 TO DISABLE) / RECIPIENT LIST HIDDEN

Wyl puzzled over the codes and moved on to the opening text:

TO BE DISTRIBUTED IN THE EVENT OF THE DEATH OR DISAPPEARANCE OF CAERN ADAN, CONCERNING NEW REPUBLIC INTELLIGENCE ASSET YRICA QUELL.

He read on, feeling somehow that he should not.

CHAPTER 9

HIGH-VELOCITY IMPACTS ON
A PITTED SURFACE

I

The freighter took two hours to reach Troithe on its voyage from Narthex, moving at a fraction of its top speed in order to avoid straining the wounded Caern Adan. Tensent had argued briefly with IT-O about just how carefully they needed to fly, but Quell recalled being moved to nausea by the shuddering deck plating and agreed that reducing velocity was wise.

She had taken the copilot's seat by the time they approached planetary orbit and was surprised to see a capital ship register on the sensors. Then she recalled the *Lodestar*'s scheduled departure from the planet surface. "Hope you remembered to say goodbye to our friends below," Tensent murmured.

"Why say goodbye when we'll always stay in touch?" Quell asked. Her mother would have scolded her for the sarcasm but Tensent only laughed.

She contacted the *Lodestar* and arranged for landing clearance. The flight officer hesitated when she gave her codes—Quell surmised that no one had registered the freighter with the battleship's crew—but hastened to grant permission once Tensent chimed in and mentioned Adan's presence. "Sorry for the delay," the officer said after another pause. "Mister Lark asked to be notified as soon as you returned."

"*Mister Lark,*" Tensent echoed. He shook his head as they brought the freighter in. When the vessel had alighted, Quell led the way to the boarding ramp. IT-O remained with Adan, who still slept in the darkened crew quarters.

The hangar was largely empty of *Lodestar* personnel, except for a ground crew refueling one of the Meteor Squadron X-wings remaining after Syndulla's departure. Waiting at the base of the freighter's ramp, however, were Wyl Lark and Chass na Chadic. Both wore civilian attire, which suggested to Quell that whatever was going on lacked real urgency. But Lark's expression was guarded—almost unthinkably so for the normally animated boy—while Chadic stared toward Quell and Tensent with fatigued eyes, drawing breaths that caused her chest to visibly rise and fall.

"What's the word?" Quell asked. She saw the tension. She didn't understand it.

"How's Adan?" Lark asked.

"Stable," Quell said. "He'll need a medical team, but Ito thinks he'll recover."

Tensent jutted a thumb toward the ship. "It was exactly what you'd figure—Imps nabbed him. Says the plan's still on, though."

"Good," Lark said. "Good."

Neither Lark nor Chadic stepped aside when Quell reached the bottom of the boarding ramp. Quell glanced back at Tensent, who shrugged and remained a meter behind her. She looked at Lark and waited.

Chadic uttered a syllable that Lark spoke over. "We know about Operation Cinder," he said.

"Forget that," Chadic spat. "We know about Nacronis."

Quell flattened her expression, burying whatever reaction she'd begun to show. Her field of vision seemed to narrow, darkness encroaching around the edges. "What about Nacronis?" she asked.

"I'm with her," Tensent said. She heard his feet impact the deck as he hopped off the boarding ramp and stepped to one side, outside the field between Quell and the other two. "What about Nacronis?"

Lark seemed to struggle to look away from Quell. He did so only for an instant, glancing at Tensent in acknowledgment before focusing on Quell again. "She destroyed it," he said.

"Way I recall," Tensent replied, casual as a promise, "she tried to stop it."

Chadic snorted. "Check your messages. Adan rigged a file to go out in case he disappeared—probably because he was afraid she'd shoot him in the head. She wiped out the whole damn planet and lied to us about it."

"Unless she didn't," Lark said. "Unless there's another explanation."

All of them fell silent. Quell perceived an opportunity to answer—to explain away her crimes, to use words to suture the weeping wound in her squadron. She searched and found nothing. The opportunity was real, yet she lacked the spirit or mind to take advantage of it.

The moment passed. She said nothing.

Chadic yelled: "She did what the *Death Star* did—she killed a planet!"

Quell flinched and rocked on her heels. She didn't step back. Chadic kept talking, her voice hoarser than usual, the hint of a lisp in her inflections. "She smothered whatever-million people in silt, crashed her ship, then pretended to be a defector. She offered to go after her old unit because she thought it would let her *get away with it*. She should be in prison." Chadic's head twitched, like she was impaling an insect on her horns. "So should Adan, probably. So should anyone who signed off on her running a squadron."

"Adan didn't know." The voice was Quell's, and it took her by surprise; she comprehended the idiocy of her statement. "General Syndulla didn't know."

Though maybe she does now.

"Adan should rot," Chadic cried. "The whole corrupt New Republic can rot if this is how it treats mass murderers."

The Meteor Squadron ground crew was watching them now, no longer even feigning interest in the refueling operation. If Quell's shame hadn't been broadcast to the entire ship yet, there would be no stopping it now. She sought words and seemed to choke on her breath, managing only: "I left, though. I did leave."

That, too, was a lie by omission.

Lark's expression remained frozen. "Are you still loyal to them?" he asked. "To Shadow Wing?"

"No," Quell said. It sounded weak and confused.

"What about at Pandem Nai? When we almost burned away the planet? Did that have anything to do with—"

"No," she said again, not understanding what he meant, where the question had come from.

"Did that have anything to do with Nacronis?" Lark tried again. "Or with the lies, or with Adan?"

"No," she said for a third time. "No." The darkness at the edges of her vision was creeping inward. She thought about Pandem Nai, cringed at the memory, and found the confession she hoped Lark wanted. "It was just a stupid mistake. All of it was a stupid mistake."

Chadic loosed a sound between a snarl and a laugh, twisting her head away. Lark breathed deeply and asked, "Including Nacronis?"

"Yes," Quell said.

She heard Tensent murmur Lark's name, but the boy didn't seem to hear. His voice broke as he asked, "What if it hadn't been Nacronis? What if it had been Troithe? Or *your* homeworld?"

I don't have a homeworld. I grew up on Gavana Orbital. You know that, she thought, though she recalled their dinner when Lark had claimed she had never talked about her family.

He didn't wait for an answer. Quell barely heard him as he asked: "What if it had been Polyneus?"

His homeworld.

"Nacronis was the only target," she said. "No one had even heard of it before the orders came."

"Maybe," Tensent said, steadier than Lark or Chadic or Quell, "you should tell us something about why you finally *did* defect. Adan must've trusted your reasons. Or at least the torture droid did."

Chadic shot a glare in Tensent's direction. Lark nodded slowly.

"Hell," Tensent continued, "your motive for jumping ship might've been purer than mine. We've all got our stories."

Quell recognized what he was attempting. He'd stepped in to save her once before, long ago, when Adan had threatened to throw her out an air lock. Yet whatever Tensent had learned about her, he didn't understand how abominably flawed her motives really had been. How it was Major Keize's decision, not her own, that had saved her from living and dying in Shadow Wing. How she hadn't been strong enough to continue killing or to walk away.

She gave her head a small shake. Tensent stood watching, prompting her with a stare that became increasingly less subtle until he finally sighed and stepped around Lark and Chadic, taking a place behind and between them.

"Nothing to say, then." Tensent looked between his two companions. "Sorry, Lieutenant. Silent isn't guilty but it sure doesn't look good."

"You should probably go to the brig," Lark said softly.

"Why?" Chadic asked. "The New Republic is *fine* with it all. They'll probably have us arrested for reading Adan's message."

Quell idly wondered about the recipients of Adan's communiqué. Had he included Syndulla? Would the general come riding back from the Bormea sector, ready to take Quell away to face justice while expressing grave disappointment? More likely, Quell thought, she'd never see Syndulla again—the general would write her off as a mistake and abandon her like garbage jettisoned prior to a lightspeed jump.

"You can summon security if you want," she said. She reached for the blaster on her hip and spotted Lark tensing as her fingers curled around the grip. She lifted the weapon without bringing it into her palm and tossed it onto the deck, where it clattered loudly. "Not much point in fighting, is there?"

"Probably not," Tensent agreed. "We'll sort it all out and see how it looks tomorrow."

Quell was confident she knew how it would look. Her sins had caught up with her and her life in the New Republic was over. The only question was whether anyone was so horrified by her actions, felt so personally aggrieved, that she could expect to be assassinated while in custody.

She might well die in prison. She decided she wouldn't go down easily.

She looked from Chadic to Lark to Tensent. She wondered how they would react if she said: *I'm sorry.*

"The plan will still work," Quell said instead.

Then sirens began to wail, and no one was paying attention to Quell any longer.

▐▐

Colonel Soran Keize of the 204th Imperial Fighter Wing stood aboard the bridge of the Star Destroyer *Edict* and watched the whirling cerulean funnel of hyperspace rip away as reality re-formed. The stars that fell into place beyond the viewport seemed strangely bright—he realized they were *closer* than he was accustomed to, thanks to the remarkable stellar density of the galactic Deep Core—and the experience as a whole was the opposite of what he had anticipated. The dark heart of Cerberon, the singularity at the center of the system, was visible even from the *Edict*'s position; but it was not the most magnificent sight in the heavens.

"Scanners have locked onto the *Aerie*," Styll declared. The former captain of the *Allegiance* stood proud beside Soran, as if command of the *Edict* were an honor—as if the Star Destroyer hadn't cannibalized his beloved vessel and as if his crew were proven warriors instead of cadets. Soran admired Styll's spirit and hoped his officers felt the same. "Arrival coordinates are within tolerances. We are thirty seconds behind them."

"Good," Soran said. "Proceed with the plan. I'll expect updates beamed to my ship as long as possible."

"Understood," Styll said.

Soran surveyed the bridge once—observed the cadets intent upon their consoles and Nenvez, their instructor, pacing and barking commands; observed Styll fixed in the center, like a mass around which all else orbited; observed the bright stars and the glimmer of planets and the *Aerie*'s burning ion trail.

Not many days before, he would have heard muttering or been sneered at as a mere *adviser* to the people he loved.

Godspeed, he thought, and did not say it aloud. He had given his people their mission. He had prepared them. For now, he could give nothing more.

He marched into the turbolift, counting down the seconds. He'd need to maintain a brisk pace to launch on schedule—there were three hundred meters of unpowered, airless deck sections for him to traverse between the Star Destroyer's bridge and hangar—but he was already in his flight suit and the rest of his squadron was in place. He adjusted his comm system and locked his helmet. "Lieutenant Seedia?" he said. "Is everything set?"

"Yes, Colonel," the voice replied. "Lieutenant Bragheer is with me. The programs have been loaded."

"I'm pleased." Soran had chosen Seedia for the mission out of inspired boldness; he had chosen Bragheer as a counterweight. Seedia was new to him, a brilliant and dangerous pilot who had the potential for greatness with proper tutelage; Bragheer was a mainstay of the 204th and utterly reliable. They would serve well as a pair. "Await my arrival."

The lift doors opened, and he trotted along corridors lit by emergency lamps. He wondered for a moment whether his plan was the right one.

If the calculations they'd received were accurate, an asteroid was whipping toward Troithe even now, unnoticed by the New Republic battle group. That asteroid had room enough to house the 204th's entire fighter complement—it could have permitted the wing to strike at Troithe from hiding, giving no time for alarms to be sounded or shields to be raised.

He'd developed an entire strategy around asteroid CER952B. It had been a good plan. But it had left too much to uncertainty, and it was a plan for a commander more dedicated to the fallen Empire than to his unit.

Soran Keize hadn't come to Cerberon to reclaim it for the Galactic Emperor or for Admiral Sloane's fleet or out of some concept of ideological purity. He would plant no flags. He had come to strike a fatal blow to General Hera Syndulla, and to give Shadow Wing the victory its pilots so dearly needed.

CHAPTER 10

STARFIGHTERS LIKE MOTES OF DUST

I

Quell stood frozen as the hangar, no longer empty, was flooded by a stream of pilots racing to their starfighters; engineers disconnecting cables; astromechs loading into X-wings. The sirens still screamed, though the piercing sound had been dulled by repetition.

Lark had run to intercept one of the Meteor Squadron pilots. Chadic stood in front of Quell, playing guard as if oblivious to the chaos around them. Quell's blaster still lay on the floor, abandoned. Quell wondered what the two of them looked like to everyone running about, silent and motionless as they were.

Tensent was several meters away, crouched in front of T5 and cupping his ear to hear his battered astromech's whistles. Presently he cursed, spat on the deck, and turned to Quell and Chadic. "Two Imperial ships just entered Cerberon space," he said. "Star Destroyer and a cruiser-carrier."

"Blast," Chadic muttered. She didn't turn away from Quell.

Quell grasped at the tactical situation through the fog in her mind, as if doing so could distract her from the horror caressing her soul. Her thoughts were slow and confused, but one by one she envisioned the dots of warships and fighters on a system chart. Even with Vanguard Squadron and Syndulla's detachment gone, the New Republic had the advantage in a defensive battle.

"We can hold Troithe," Quell said.

Lark returned to the group, eyes showing an alarm that his expression concealed. "Two ships," he said, "a Star Destroyer and—"

"Old news!" Chadic snapped.

T5 chirruped over the sirens again. Tensent translated, "Star Destroyer just launched a TIE squadron. TIEs are escorting the cruiser-carrier, heading for Catadra. Destroyer's coming our way."

Quell stumbled toward shadows in the fog, attempting to register what she was hearing and update her mental map. Her brain spat an error message: *It's over. You should've stayed at Traitor's Remorse.*

"They'll hit Catadra hard," she said. "But even a Star Destroyer won't get through Troithe's shields."

"Shut up," Chadic said.

Lark glanced toward the hangar doors and the invisible magnetic field as the first X-wing roared free, its thrusters filling the chamber with the scent of burnt fuel. "We need to get out there," he said. "If she's—Catadra's exposed. Imagine the damage those TIEs could do on a bombing run."

"*She* stays," Chadic said. Her boot heel stomped on the blaster, pulling it skittering away from Quell.

"Agreed," Lark replied. "That brings us to three, though, so we'll defer to Meteor Squadron for command."

"Fair enough." Tensent gestured at the astromech, which began rolling toward his Y-wing. He hesitated a moment, then followed at a trot.

"I can help," Quell said. She didn't know why. Maybe she wasn't ready to see her squadron die without her. Maybe after Kairos that possibility seemed real.

Chadic wrinkled her nose and showed teeth. "I will shoot your skull hollow before I fly with you again."

Lark winced. Another starfighter exited the hangar, its wash rippling his hair. "You can't fly," he said. "You'd only be a distraction."

He stared at Quell until she reluctantly nodded. Then he placed a hand on Chadic's shoulder to guide her away. "She won't go anywhere," he murmured to the Theelin. "We'll finish when we get back."

Chadic swore softly but followed Lark across the deck.

Quell didn't move, didn't even think, as the last Meteor Squadron starfighters exited the hangar. A-, Y-, and B-wing went next. She felt the wake of hot air and blinked toxic particles from her eyes. Soon she could see straight across the nearly empty bay, over a floor littered with cabling and ladders and diagnostic tools. Her eyes fixed on the lone starfighter remaining: an X-wing with the crest of Alphabet Squadron painted on its nose. It was the second ship she'd flown with that design, after the first had gone down with D6-L.

D6 also hadn't known about her crimes. She felt its memory chip on her breast.

She saw the round dome of CB-9 protruding from the top of her X-wing. She took long strides, moving as if on a conveyor beyond her control, and was beside the vessel in moments. "Open the canopy," she ordered. "They need us out there."

The astromech buzzed.

"There's a Star Destroyer headed this way." She heard impatience in her voice and tamped it down. "The *Lodestar* is undercrewed and most of its defenders are heading to Catadra. This ship could use the extra help—even one fighter could make a difference."

The droid buzzed again, low and angry like a locked door or a computer socket rejecting an incompatible plug.

Quell slammed her palm against the side of her starfighter. "Open it!"

The droid did not open the cockpit.

She put her back against the vessel, watching the lights of Meteor and Alphabet Squadron recede into the distance, away from the *Lodestar* and off to war.

II

Alphabet Squadron—what remained of Alphabet Squadron—flew in a three-fighter wedge with Wyl Lark at the spearpoint, pursuing Meteor Squadron en route to Catadra. Wyl could've easily caught up with the X-wings, but he would've needed to leave Nath and Chass behind.

"Deceleration in four minutes, ten seconds," Meteor Leader called through the comm. "If the droids are right, we'll enter Catadra space about thirty seconds before that cruiser-carrier shows up. It'll give us time to arrive and form up, but there's not much room for error."

"Copy that," Wyl said. "Has the carrier deployed its TIEs yet?"

"Just that escort from the Star Destroyer right now. Not a lot of weapons aboard a *Quasar Fire*-class carrier, either."

"This attack could be a distraction," Tensent offered. "TIEs hit civilian targets on Catadra while that Star Destroyer tries to crack Troithe."

Wyl knew the next voice well—Meteor Four, a Rodian named Neihero he'd enjoyed a hallway flirtation with for the past month. "One Star Destroyer won't do much against Troithe's shields. More likely to get torn apart by the orbital defenses."

"You're all in the running for admiral, all right?" Meteor Leader again. "Cut the chatter, though, or go to private channels. *Lodestar* knows what it's doing, and we've got a fight ahead."

The comm emitted the soft hiss of a dead frequency. Wyl adjusted his helmet—he'd been too rushed and distracted to switch to a proper flight suit, which meant he couldn't form an airtight seal and he'd be in trouble if he ran into oxygen problems—and tried to shut the image of Yrica Quell standing dead-eyed and defiant out of his mind.

Why hadn't she spoken up for herself? Why not confess her guilt or apologize for the lies? She'd simply stood there: the woman who'd destroyed Nacronis and led Alphabet against her former comrades.

Wyl had half hoped to hear her growl and rant and defend all she'd done as *necessary for the preservation of order in the galaxy.* That would've made things clearer. Or if not, if she could've asked for forgiveness—

No, he thought. He didn't know if he could offer that.

He'd never longed to be Home more badly.

He busied himself with procedure. He checked A-wing subsystems he should've checked before departure; linked targeting systems with Chass and Nath in case they made a joint run against the cruiser-carrier; adjusted power distribution between thrusters and deflectors and weapons and thrusters once again. He should've been thinking tactically, assessing ways that Alphabet could assist Meteor in the defense of Catadra, but there was too much going on. He wasn't in command anyway.

The Deep Core sky blazed above and around him. The dimmer streak of the debris field swept across darkness on his port side, a river whorl with its ultimate terminus inside the burning eye of the black hole. Wyl shifted in his harness, leaning forward and craning his neck so that he saw nothing of his console or the canopy frame. The infinite expanse of space calmed him. Eventually, however, his back grew stiff and he fell back into his seat.

Meteor Squadron began decelerating as it approached Catadra. Wyl waited forty seconds, closing a portion of the distance between Alphabet and Meteor before signaling his comrades to do the same. They were two minutes out from Catadran orbit when his comm activated again.

"Wyl Lark?"

The transmission was badly distorted, full of digital stuttering and static. Wyl couldn't determine whether the voice was male or female, let alone if he knew the speaker. The A-wing's computer failed to identify a source, but it wasn't a general broadcast—someone was wide-beaming a signal using Wyl's transponder codes.

"Hello?" he said.

"Wyl Lark," the comm said again. "We've met before. We spoke in the Oridol Cluster, and again over Pandem Nai. You understand?"

He did understand, and suddenly the galaxy seemed to compress around him.

He was speaking to *Blink.*

"I understand. What's going on?" *What is this?*

"I don't have much time. You need to turn around and get back to Troithe. Do you hear me?"

If Blink was communicating with him, that meant Shadow Wing was in Cerberon. It suggested that the cruiser-carrier powering toward Catadra was the same cruiser-carrier he'd encountered in Oridol. It meant Blink had received his messages, had heard his secret confessions—

You never sent those messages.

None of it made sense.

"I hear you—" he began, and then a shock of pops and stutters erupted from his speakers. He recognized the familiar static of a jamming signal but looked to his console to confirm. His scanner showed a flickering field of a hundred marks, and his comm rig was flooded across the full frequency spectrum. He surveyed the darkness, saw the stars and debris and the black hole; saw the faint tails of Meteor Squadron approaching the bright thumbnail orb of Catadra. Nothing about the battlefield had changed, so far as he could tell—there was no hidden fleet sweeping into view.

It was likely the Star Destroyer was sending the jamming signal, then—the cruiser-carrier wouldn't have the power to blanket so much of the system, but the massive battleship might. For whatever reason *(Is it just because of Blink?)*, the Empire had chosen to isolate and silence Catadra and Troithe—the Imperial and New Republic forces would fight over the two worlds in parallel, each set of combatants unable to contact comrades elsewhere.

Wyl adjusted his comm settings. "Lark to all New Republic ships: Shadow Wing is here. Repeat, Shadow Wing is *here*. The enemy is the 204th Imperial Fighter Wing." He had no illusions that the transmission would break through.

Blink had told him to return to Troithe. Wyl didn't know why—couldn't know whether it indicated a respect born at Pandem Nai for Wyl personally, a desire to avert a disaster, an intention to defect, or something more foul. He imagined the outcomes, tried to remember the details of his prior exchange with Blink and what he knew about the pilot.

Maybe it didn't matter if all his instincts told him to do something foolish. Meteor Squadron didn't need him. Troithe might.

The Alphabet fighters had fallen out of computer-assisted formation when the jamming signal had severed their link. As Wyl put pressure on a rudder pedal and swung his ship around, he made a wide arc and lit his thrusters as bright as he could. The pressure crushed him against his seat, but with a lot of luck Nath and Chass would see him against the dark—recognize that he was returning to Troithe and follow.

Wyl didn't believe in luck, but if such a thing existed? He was surely due his share.

III

Chass na Chadic felt sick.

Her mouth was dry, moistened only by the occasional surge of bile. She'd managed to grab an emergency flight suit but it was too loose and her whole body was covered in goosebumps from the cockpit's aggressive cooling systems. Her head throbbed. She hadn't slept more than forty minutes in the past day.

Then there was Yrica Quell, the woman who'd betrayed her.

Chass should've expected it would happen sometime, somehow—Quell had never *really* given her a reason to trust. So Chass had let herself be won over by the fact that Quell obviously liked her, ignoring all the warning signs and never questioning whether someday payment would come due.

She'd slept in the woman's bunk and this is what she got.

Chass wasn't drunk anymore. But as she sat in her cockpit breathing through her teeth and wincing at every jolt, she doubted she was fit to fly.

The jamming signal hit as she decelerated toward Catadra. She muted the static screech and squinted at the chaos on her scanner. She was tempted to find something to cover the garbled and irritatingly bright screen, but she knew the difference between stupid and *stupid*. While her head was down something flashed in the distance outside the canopy bubble, but whatever it was was gone by the time she looked—possibly the first volley of weapons fire, more likely some Cerberon debris floating past.

"How long till cruiser-carrier intercept?" she mumbled. *"Ninety seconds, sir. Get ready to attack!"*

Who needed a comm signal to know what Meteor Squadron would've been saying?

She went halfheartedly digging for her music chips, wondering if there was anything in her repertoire that wouldn't make her feel sicker, and spotted a warning indicator. She furrowed her brow and confirmed the problem with the computer. *How'd I end up low on fuel?*

But she knew the answer and she began laughing softly. She'd returned from her jaunt to Winker's barely four hours earlier and had drained the B-wing's reserves flying around the Cerberon system and back. She vaguely recalled a conversation in which she'd promised half her fuel supplies to pay off a bet, though that might have been a figment of her imagination. Either way, it didn't surprise her that the understaffed ground crew hadn't topped her off yet.

It was just like being in the Rebellion again instead of the New Republic.

Chass smiled crookedly, wearily, and flew on. She had enough fuel to make it to Catadra and she had enough weapons to take down a cruiser-carrier. She could win the whole battle herself if she had to.

IV

Quell strolled through the *Lodestar*, past crew members hurrying to battle stations and droids locking down maintenance panels, feeling the shudder of the battleship as its engines surged in power and its thrusters maneuvered the vessel over Troithe. No one had come to arrest her. No one seemed to notice her. Those who'd learned of her betrayal first had already written her off as another Imperial prisoner. Others, she assumed, had yet to be informed.

For the moment, she still had skills to offer. For reasons she couldn't fully understand, she wanted to do her part in the battle.

When she reached the bridge, she stepped out of the lift and out of the way, observing from beside one of the rear vehicular deployment stations (unused, she suspected, since the Clone Wars). The crew chatter was almost deafening, loose and undisciplined to her sensibilities, and the narrow lanes and control pits were crowded with junior officers. When she sought information from the main displays, she found only blank tactical maps and images of Troithe. It wasn't until she saw a young ensign sketching approach vectors with a droid that she realized what was going on and the indecipherable chatter began to make sense.

The Star Destroyer was jamming scanners and communications, which left the *Lodestar* reliant on visual sensors only. The crowd was made up of comscan experts and runners and junior officers relaying information to the tactical center, all trying to plot enemy positions based on best guesses and estimated trajectories.

Someone shot a hand up near the weapons station. "Destroyer is five minutes out!" the hand called.

"Have they deployed their fighters yet?" The crowd shifted at the voice, opening a passage from the weapons station to the center of the bridge where Captain Giginivek—a frail Ociock whose feathers had thinned to downy patches with advanced age—stood. His voice was thin and reedy yet somehow still carried.

"Not yet, except the Catadran contingent," another officer called. "It's possible they're concerned about the Destroyer outpacing the squadrons. They'll deploy fast once they begin."

One hundred forty seconds to release the entire wing, minus the time for the squadron escorting the cruiser-carrier. She mouthed the words but didn't say them aloud. There was no guarantee of a full complement, either—everything had changed after Endor—and the presence of bombers and interceptors would alter the timing, too.

"Shall we attempt to close, sir?" This from a woman at the nav station. "If we intercept before they reach Troithe, we can prevent the TIEs from moving against the planet."

"We would also be out of range of Troithe's defenses," Captain Giginivek said. He scratched his gullet with short, chipped talons. "Better to sit and wait? Better to sit and wait and fight?"

Quell didn't know the captain well—General Syndulla had expressed her fondness for him to Quell, but Quell had never spoken to him directly. She wasn't entirely sure he would recognize her on sight—which would be to her advantage if Adan's revelations had reached him, and an impediment otherwise.

"Whoever's commanding that Destroyer isn't a fool," she said. She stepped out of her corner, shouldering her way through the crowd with sharp, brittle joints. "He's got to know about Troithe's defenses, which means if he's closing he's doing it for a reason."

The captain twisted his neck ninety degrees without rotating his body. One pupil contracted as he focused on Quell. "How do we know he's not a fool? Hmm?"

She heard one of the bridge crew muttering her name into a comlink. Someone who had been informed about her? She remembered Lark's request to the bridge that he be notified when she landed and wondered if he'd said anything more. "He's survived all these months since Endor. He *can't* be a fool," she said. She smiled mirthlessly. "He could be suicidal, but not a fool. The longer we wait, the more we allow him to set the terms of approach."

"I—" The captain twisted his neck to face the nav station again. His beak opened and closed several times before he finished. "—agree. Take us out, Lieutenant. I doubt Troithe's shields will collapse easily, but I'd rather not risk the Destroyer concentrating fire and punching through to the city. One block destroyed could mean millions lost."

That, too, Quell thought, and shrugged away the shame that crept over her.

The deck juddered more fiercely as the *Lodestar* left orbit. "To these coordinates," the captain said, gesturing at one of the tactical maps. "If required, we can retreat back to Troithe and gain the assistance of the planetary defenses."

It was a good plan, Quell thought. A prudent plan. Though there were no guarantees in war.

The crew resumed plotting, now attempting to calculate an intercept course to reach an enemy whose trajectory they couldn't map with certainty. With scanners still down, point-defense turrets were repurposed as scopes to watch in all directions for approaching ships. Someone announced that, if previous estimates held true, the cruiser-carrier had engaged Meteor Squadron over Catadra.

A few seconds later, another crew member called: "Troithe starfighters are in the air, coming our way—" Quell frowned, trying to remember how many fighters Syndulla had left behind as a planetary garrison. Certainly not many. "—and two allied ships incoming from Catadra. An A-wing and a Y-wing."

The captain snuffled in curiosity but asked no questions.

Nath Tensent and Wyl Lark, Quell thought. She parted her lips to speak to the captain, but wasn't sure what to say.

Something about the battle was strange. *Everything* about the battle was strange.

What was she missing?

V

Everything goes according to plan, Soran thought. *But then, everything always does at the beginning.*

His TIE fighter led the squadron through the *Aerie*'s wake, his engines' comforting scream resonating through the craft's frame. Cold air circulated through his helmet's oxygen dispenser and condensed moisture in his nostrils. He smelled a faint odor of mildew—he'd forgotten to sanitize the tubes after his last flight.

Before Devon, he'd never forgotten anything so routine.

Then again, maybe Devon didn't deserve the blame. It was *Colonel* Soran Keize who'd become distracted.

With the *Edict*'s jammers at full power, he was limited to optical communications. The nine training drones operating in sync behind him were programmed to follow his engine trail and receive orders by blaster cannon burst pattern. Once the battle began, there was a risk they would become separated as their combat programming took precedence—the computers would still be able to identify Soran as the squadron commander, but only if his ship moved through their field of vision. Lieutenants Seedia and Bragheer, on loan from their respective squadrons, would be necessary to herd the machines into position once the chaos began.

They were good soldiers, both of them. Bragheer hadn't hesitated when Soran had warned him that the mission was very likely to end in his death. Seedia had paused, but had asked no questions. She reminded him of Yrica Quell, that way.

The pale orb of Catadra grew large past the wedge of the *Aerie*. He scanned the darkness encircling the planet, trying to pick out the glimmer of New Republic reinforcements en route from Troithe. Before activating the jamming signal, the *Aerie* crew had transmitted estimated enemy arrival time and vector, and Soran processed the data through his targeting computer to narrow his search. He recalled stories from his childhood about ancient astronomers marking off sections of sky with their telescopes as they hunted planets and stars and comets.

Enjoy flying without scanners or comms, he told himself. *Enjoy the peace before the battle. This is the only reprieve you'll get.*

He almost laughed. The idea appealed, but meditative reflection wasn't easy to come by.

He spotted the flash he was looking for—a faint glimmer in the target sector—and gently steered his TIE toward it while the *Aerie* made for Catadra. He brought up the view from the rear recorder cam on his console, noted with approval that the drones were maintaining formation, and increased speed. It had been some time since he'd needed to calculate distance visually, but he guessed he had half a minute before reaching the enemy position.

There was a great deal at stake. Yet Soran Keize, ace of aces, had learned after many years how to let the fear of death and failure and responsibility wash off his body and atomize in the stellar radiation of deep space—a lesson he'd often tried to impart to his officers, with varying degrees of success. Gradually he relaxed in his seat. He gripped his control yoke in one hand while the other rested at his side.

The orders have all been given. You are no longer a commander. You're merely a soldier, and you know how to fight.

The thought was unexpectedly pleasing.

The enemy came into view—not even a full squadron, which was unexpected and suggested three possibilities: The enemy was lying in wait, preparing an ambush somewhere; General Syndulla's battle group had reduced the size of its fighter complement since Pandem Nai; or the general had retained more resources to protect Troithe than anticipated.

The last could pose a problem. But if adjustments needed to be made, he would adjust.

The specks of enemy starfighters became burning sparks, then grew rapidly until he could make out the familiar profiles of X-wings, strike foils spread. They'd seen him and were preparing to break and flank his squadron. He angled to starboard, trusting that the drones would follow, and set course to pass the enemy X-wings at a tangent.

Had his foes possessed functional scanners or communications, he might have chosen otherwise. But their reactions were uncoordinated— not clumsy, not undisciplined, but imperfect and imprecise. As Soran skirted the enemy formation he saw the lightspeed-swift indecision of the nearest fighter as the pilot debated whether to move against Soran or split away. Soran recognized his opportunity. He ignited thrusters, powered up repulsors, and he felt the crush of g forces as his TIE turned ninety degrees. He squeezed his cannon trigger, releasing a burst that tore into the enemy X-wing; the nova that followed—that burned a cyan splotch into his vision—assured him that the foe had been destroyed even as he dived.

The battle was joined.

Four seconds later he earned his second kill.

For the first time in months, he had truly returned to the fray.

CHAPTER 11

BEHEMOTHS DANCING LIKE PLANETS

I

Nath Tensent watched the two battleships arc toward one point, each vessel the shape of a dagger and each powerful enough to polish the surface of a moon. Space distorted all scale, and the *Lodestar*—positioned so that Nath could see only its narrow edge—seemed little smaller than the massive Star Destroyer stacked with command modules and deflector globes; yet only one of the ships could be numbered among the most technologically advanced weapons in the galaxy. Nath watched the faraway exhaust trails of missiles tearing out of the Destroyer, moving at incomprehensible speeds across the gap between the vessels. He worried the fight would be a lopsided one.

But that wasn't his biggest concern. He was thinking about Wyl's last message.

T5 had somehow picked up Wyl's signal through the jamming field (the droid was more talented than Nath liked to give it credit for), and after Nath had spotted the boy's course change and followed him away from Catadra, T5 had worked furiously to decipher the garbled transmission. Halfway back to the *Lodestar*, Nath had heard the words:

Shadow Wing is here.

They didn't explain what Wyl was planning—if Wyl was planning anything—or why the boy had decided to leave Meteor Squadron and Chass to return to Troithe. Nath didn't understand how Wyl knew or what the implications were.

Shadow Wing wasn't supposed to arrive for days. So had Adan spilled his guts and revealed the trap after all? Had Shadow Wing come, taken a look at asteroid CER952B, and decided *This looks suspicious, let's just fight*? The whole idea had been to *avoid* facing Shadow Wing in ship-to-ship combat.

Alphabet had held its own at Pandem Nai. But this felt too much like the *first* time Nath had encountered the 204th, at Trenchenovu. The time they'd ambushed him and slaughtered Reeka and Mordeaux and Piter and the rest of his squadron.

It wasn't an outcome he cared to see twice.

The *Lodestar* and the Star Destroyer now dominated his field of vision, each ship loosing turbolaser salvos as it passed alongside the other. The battleships hadn't reached optimal firing range—the emerald laser streams did little damage through the vessels' screens and neither ship had brought point-defense weaponry into play—but that wouldn't matter if Nath and Wyl got between the behemoths. What an *Acclamator*-class could shrug off could disintegrate a starfighter.

He shouldn't have been surprised: Wyl was heading straight into the cataclysm.

Nath cursed, slammed a fist against a panel slowly rattling itself loose, and considered his options. Whatever was going on, he didn't have enough information to make a plan. Even loaded with ordnance, he didn't have enough *ship* to make a difference in battle. T5 was shouting warnings and the jamming field was still active.

"Tensent to *Lodestar*!" he called anyway, thumbing the comm. "Shadow Wing is here. Repeat, Shadow Wing is part of the enemy force."

But T5 had been lucky to catch Wyl's signal from half a klick away in a noncombat situation. With radiation flooding the area from the particle blasts and active deflectors, there wasn't a blasted hope that the *Lodestar* would catch his message.

And though Nath was loath to admit it, Quell was the person he trusted most to figure what Shadow Wing was up to. He wasn't sure where her brain was at after she'd had her secret exposed, but he needed a way to contact her.

"All right," he said, and growled as his aging ship shuddered under his aging bottom. "Get ready, droid. We're going to try something idiotic."

II

"What the blazes is he *doing*?"

Quell wasn't sure which of the two dozen officers crowding the bridge had spoken, but whoever it was spoke for them all.

Shortly after the *Lodestar* had exchanged its first volley with the Star Destroyer, Lark and Tensent's approaching vessels had veered onto different trajectories. While Lark had gone weaving between particle blasts and begun shooting down enemy missiles, Tensent had closed distance with the *Lodestar* and was now skirting the battleship's surface with barely two meters of clearance. The scanners were still inoperable but the cams had tracked him until he'd swept dramatically over the bridge viewport, firing his dual laser cannons three times into the void.

It was a stunt, and a dangerous one. Tensent was staying well away from the incoming particle fire, but if the *Lodestar* shifted unpredictably Tensent's Y-wing would be dashed against the hull. And for all his bluster Tensent wasn't a man prone to pointless stunts. He had a very good reason for what he was doing.

So what was it?

Captain Giginivek was crying out orders as the *Lodestar* completed one pass and began another, sweeping closer to the Star Destroyer.

He'd ordered his comscan officer to find a way to cut through the jamming and contact the Y-wing, but Quell had been among the rebels long enough to recognize rebel thinking—always attempt the impossible, hoping you would somehow succeed. It was a fine ideal but a wasteful plan.

She edged over to one of the monitor stations and adjusted the controls. A panel barely the size of her palm, intended for internal security monitoring or hull temperature readings, flickered and showed Tensent's Y-wing as he continued racing across the *Lodestar*. Again, he fired into nothingness, this time as he passed the forward observation deck. Again, it was three shots—a burst from both cannons, a pause, then two more bursts.

It was the same timing as the first shots, down to the second.

The cannon fire was the message, then. Quell dredged the depths of her mind for Imperial codes, rebel codes, means of translating ones and twos into letters or signals. She thought about the system she'd created for Kairos to communicate with the rest of the squadron. (She tried not to think about Kairos.) She concocted a dozen possible interpretations of the message and none of them rang true.

Tensent moved away from the *Lodestar* and out of the field of fire. Quell replayed the recording.

Then she saw it.

Not one blast followed by two—*two* particle bolts, one from each of two cannons; then a pause; then *four* bolts.

Two-zero-four.

She straightened, bracing herself on the console as vertigo sought to send her tumbling. The reprieve she'd found from the day's nightmare in tactical analysis and amateur cryptography was past, and the turn of events that had begun in the hangar seemed to crush her ribs, force out her breath. She drifted through the bridge anyway, crossing toward the captain. "It's Shadow Wing," she called. "Tensent is telling us it's Shadow Wing."

Captain Giginivek peered at her, beak hanging open dumbly. She stared back, waiting for a question: *What does that mean?* or *How do you know?* or even *How do we fight them?*

Instead he said, "If that's Shadow Wing out there? Then where are the TIE fighters?"

Quell had no answer.

III

What does Blink want?

The thought echoed in Wyl's mind, recurring like the chorus of one of Chass's songs. His A-wing dipped and looped around turbolaser volleys bright as suns; he spun and raced between the land that was the *Lodestar* and the sky that was the Destroyer; he channeled power from deflectors to thrusters until he felt light-headed from the g forces. He watched the telltale exhaust trails of the Destroyer's missiles and followed them, squeezing his trigger despite the numbness in his fingers and pulling up, fast as he could, when the warheads detonated beneath him.

Through it all, he thought of Blink and the Shadow Wing pilot's message: *You need to turn around and get back to Troithe.*

What did Shadow Wing intend? Whose side was Blink on? *What does Blink want?*

He'd chosen to defend the *Lodestar* because he had nothing else to do. There were no orders forthcoming through the jamming field, but protecting lives was never a mistake; he could do that much.

And when the missiles stopped coming, as they would soon? When the *Lodestar* and the Star Destroyer clashed with energy weapons alone, or when the Destroyer finally unleashed its TIEs? Would he know what to do then?

What does Blink want? Was Blink aboard the Destroyer?

The brilliance of the turbolaser volleys faded as the two battleships completed one pass and reoriented for another. Wyl steadied his breathing, tensed and relaxed his muscles, then stroked the console as he scanned the darkness. He spotted a glimmer he expected was Nath, but then saw another glimmer behind it, and a third, all coming from the direction of Troithe. The planetary garrison had arrived.

Wyl swung his ship wide and spotted the crisper profile of Nath's Y-wing, intact and unscarred. Wyl took comfort in the man's survival—but most likely, Nath was looking to Wyl for direction.

"All right," Wyl murmured. "All right. We're going back in. We promised to protect them, to see the war through to the end. And we'll do it."

He opened his throttle and pitched upward, flipping and spinning until the Star Destroyer was centered in his view.

IV

The TIE pilots weren't good but they were smarter than most. It wasn't just the pounding in Chass's head that made them seem competent, either—even outnumbered, they were putting up a decent fight against the X-wings of Meteor Squadron, using superior speed and maneuverability to break apart New Republic flights and isolate individual opponents. For every TIE that went down (and Chass had taken out two herself—assisted with two, anyway, by strafing the battlefield with all guns alight), an X-wing was torn up alongside.

She swore as the TIE wave crested again, filling the gaps between her ship and the nearest Meteor craft. She squeezed off a shot then loosened her grip on her trigger—without scanners, deep in the melee, she was as likely to hit friend as foe. One TIE nearly sheared off her port ion cannon as it passed; another seemed to defy all laws of inertia, making lateral leaps to blast at one X-wing, then another. Particle bolts splashed against Chass's nearly extinguished deflectors. With a groan, she rotated her foils to try to throw off enemy targeting and dived out of the worst of the fracas, hoping she didn't pull a TIE on her tail.

A lilting, unaccompanied voice sang discovery and delight through her speakers. Chass growled and kicked her console; she wasn't in the mood. Light spilled over her shoulders as a fighter exploded behind her.

Probably a TIE. Maybe a TIE.

She wished for once that she could talk to Wyl or Nath, or even Quell. The TIE pilots were mostly rotten technical fliers yet still made the right moves. She'd spotted one of the enemy ships claim multiple kills and wondered if that was the foe's weak point—if one pilot was carrying a unit full of morons—but she couldn't track any single ship through the jamming field to be sure.

Three warning indicators lit on her console. One immediately winked out (rear deflector screens were trashed), one stayed steady (fuel reserves creeping toward zero), and one Chass scrambled to fix (starboard foil distributor was running alarmingly hot). Her ship had seen better days.

Maybe none of it mattered. Troithe and the *Lodestar* would take down the Star Destroyer, and Catadra—

Maybe Catadra was where Wyl and Nath had gone.

She was pulling up, orienting herself to return to the battle and swallowing bile, when she spotted the cruiser-carrier. It had continued on its course toward Catadra when the fighters had split off to intercept Meteor, but it appeared in no danger of entering atmosphere. Instead, its thrusters burned bright and its path would take it past the planet toward the Cerberon debris field.

Chass looked above her and saw the ongoing explosive furball like a fireworks display. "You all have fun—you don't need a bomber to protect, so I'm taking the carrier," she said, realizing a moment later that she'd failed to thumb the comm controls.

You really are too much of a mess to fly, she thought.

But it didn't matter.

She settled back, diverted power to her thrusters, and pushed the B-wing in pursuit of the cruiser-carrier. Starlight reflected faintly off Catadra, gently caressing her cockpit with blues and greens. The music changed to a cryptosymphonic house jam using an old Corellian folk tune as a bass line. Chass grudgingly approved and rocked to the beat as she leaned forward in her harness, trying to get a better look at her target.

A sense of familiarity hit her, as if she'd lived through the fight before—rocketed after the same cruiser-carrier and blasted it in a dream. She swiveled her head, reassessed the situation in confusion, then allowed her eyes to alight again on the carrier.

She recognized the shattered hull plates over its engines. She recognized the missing turrets and the heat-accelerated discoloration.

She knew this ship. She'd bombed it in the Oridol Cluster and found it again over Pandem Nai.

Her jaw ached and she realized she was grinding her teeth. She ignored the fuel warning and boosted thruster power further as the cruiser-carrier sped away. Nothing that was happening seemed right— none of the tactics made sense, none of her enemies seemed real, and Shadow Wing's carrier shouldn't have been there at all.

But though she was short on fuel and shields she hadn't fired a torpedo today. Sometimes simple answers were best.

V

The dance went on. The *Lodestar* crept closer to the Destroyer with each pass, bringing its point-defense cannons online and loosing sparkling trails of ion light beside denser turbolaser beams. The bridge shook steadily under unrelenting enemy fire, and many of the crew had departed for battle stations elsewhere or harnessed themselves to their stations. Occasionally a New Republic starfighter would flash across the main viewport, navigating the particle storm on its way to target the Star Destroyer's weaponry.

The enemy still had not deployed its TIE fighters. Had not deployed Shadow Wing.

"Divert all shield power to our port screens," the captain cried. "We can't sustain this hammering for long."

"Sir, if another ship appears or they launch homing missiles—" This from the woman at the nav station. *Not your place to speak up*, a dull voice in Quell's mind scolded.

"If either of those things happens we'll shift the power right back, hm?" Captain Giginivek waved a talon in the air and stuck his head toward the viewport.

The captain didn't care about Shadow Wing. No one but Quell seemed to realize that the battle they were fighting wasn't the battle they needed to win. If Tensent was right, if the 204th was involved, what they were seeing from the Destroyer was nonsensical—a waste of resources, unless it was something more sinister.

There were questions in her mind: Why had Shadow Wing come? How had Tensent known? Where were the fighters? But those questions, like the voice that had rebuked the nav officer, were passionless when they should have been insistent.

Instead, thoughts of Shadow Wing led to the irrational certainty that they had come for her. That her comrades had come to retrieve her now that her secret was revealed and she had no place in the New Republic outside a prison or a tribunal courtroom. Shadow Wing would take her away, return her to the life of duty and family and horror she had escaped, and—

It even made a sort of sense, if Adan had told them everything.

—and she would fight with them for the rest of her days, engaged in pointless slaughter until she met her doom.

"If you're not going to help, get off the bridge!" someone snarled, shouldering her aside. The metal of the *Lodestar* groaned and the deck tilted. She fell to her knees and her fingers smashed against a control panel.

"We may be smaller, but our targeting systems appear superior— they must have sustained damage before the fight," the captain said. "However, they will still outlast us. Sooner or later we'll need our fighters back from Catadra or we'll have to withdraw to Troithe."

The pain in her hand drove away the worst of the self-indulgent thoughts. She managed to suppress the rest, and thoughts of Shadow Wing's plan rose up. "What is happening at Catadra?" she asked. "Do we have any information? Can we get a scope—"

"Star Destroyer is struggling to hit the X-wings from the Troithe garrison, along with the A- and Y-wing." The speaker held one ear to his headset; he was linked into the tactical center but ignoring Quell. "If we can give the fighters an opening, they might be able to concentrate fire. Do some real damage."

You're fighting the wrong battle, Quell wanted to tell them, but the captain was replying to the tac center relay and she realized she couldn't blame him. Her insistence that Shadow Wing was manipulating the situation had little credibility and, worse, little obvious relevance. The Star Destroyer had to be the *Lodestar's* focus, because—with all sensors flooded by jamming signals—there was no other focus to be found.

Unless she could find it.

She nursed her hand and looked from monitors to system charts to the captain. No one seemed to notice as she hurried off the bridge and headed back toward the hangar.

VI

"Congratulations," Nath Tensent called as two torpedoes struck the Star Destroyer. The destructive cascade of flame that followed lapped at the hull and broke against the command module like waves against a lighthouse. "You win—shields were breaking there after all."

The droid squealed in reply. Nath didn't smile as he dipped his starboard side and surveyed the devastation. He'd done a lot of damage, sure, but a Star Destroyer was a lot of ship and *this* Destroyer was in no danger of going down. "We'll make another pass when you find me another weak point," he said. "And the kid should be watching out for *us,* not the other way around."

He put his strength into the control yoke, coaxing the obstinate Y-wing away from the enemy vessel. A point-defense cannon flashed and left a trail across his vision, but it was so far off the mark that it seemed impossible he was the target. The enemy's gunnery was another aspect of the fight that wasn't quite right—one of too many to add up.

The droid stuttered an alert. Nath looked above and saw Wyl's

A-wing gliding into a protective position. "See?" he said. "Wyl's off his game but he still knows his job."

Another point-defense beam tore through ether nearer his ship. He winced and swung the Y-wing drunkenly from side to side, attempting to prevent the Destroyer from locking on and obliterating him in a clean burst. The strangeness of the battle wouldn't save him from a well-timed shot.

He considered his next destination. He'd done his part communicating with the *Lodestar*, though he couldn't be sure his message had reached Quell. He'd stayed with Wyl all the way back from Catadra. He could flee now with a clear conscience, and it didn't seem a bad idea—he could fake a malfunction, get somewhere safe, and let the rest of the battle play out as it would.

Grandmother was dead. The people who'd slaughtered his old squadron were dead. If he stuck around for more Shadow Wing, he'd be likely to join Reeka and Piter and the others.

He had a course back to Troithe plotted and had decided what subsystems to ask T5 to "mysteriously" disable when he saw Wyl's A-wing dip a wing in his direction and begin turning back toward the Destroyer. The boy was moving slowly—slow enough to make him an easy target but also slow enough for Nath to follow.

The Y-wing was over a decade old, with half its parts dating to the Clone Wars and the other half salvaged from airspeeders and junkyard freighters, modified by Nath's own hand. No one would find it implausible that a cooling leak took Nath out of the battle. Even Adan wouldn't dock his pay for that.

"One more round," he muttered and turned to pursue Wyl. "Then we'll see."

VII

She'd left Meteor Squadron behind. The starfighters had become sparks leaping and spiraling in the distance; then the sparks had faded, with only the occasional flash to suggest at least one combatant on each side remained.

Then the flashes stopped altogether.

Chass na Chadic should've cared what that meant, but all that seemed to matter was that she could quit checking her aft cam and focus on pursuing Shadow Wing's cruiser-carrier.

The enemy vessel's thruster burn was enough to navigate by, though the craft gained distance from the B-wing with every moment that passed. Truth was, a lumbering assault fighter's engines weren't equal to a cruiser-carrier's. Chass had already closed her strike foils to conserve power and ameliorate heat buildup. She'd shut down the safety warnings on her console. She'd even considered ejecting ordnance to reduce the ship's mass—rejecting the plan only because, in some dusty corner of her mind, she had a memory of long-dead Fadime telling her in similar circumstances that the math wouldn't add up.

Nath had accused her of not wanting to face Shadow Wing. Maybe that was true—she wasn't ready for Alphabet to win the war and be forgotten like everyone else—but she was *absolutely* ready to catch her target and spit out enough firepower to smash a small moon.

She'd had a rotten day. She'd lost what few credits she'd scraped together at Winker's. She'd been abandoned by her own squadron midbattle and she still didn't know why. And Quell—

Screw Quell. Pretend she's on that carrier with the rest of the Death Star brigade.

She increased the volume on her sound system as a Weequay screamed a ballad about living as a Hutt laborer. She'd heard a rumor that the song was a true story, and the Weequay's last act before his own execution had been to record the tale. Part of her preferred to think of it as a lie.

The thrusters of the cruiser-carrier were getting brighter again. Somehow she was closing the distance.

She leaned into the pressure of acceleration, scanning her console for anything that might tell her *how* she'd managed that particular miracle. Her engine output hadn't changed. Jammed scanners still showed nothing about her foe. She squinted and tried to make out the shape of the enemy ship beyond the thrusters themselves, and tasted her lip with her tongue as she realized what was happening. She fell back into her seat and gripped her control yoke.

The cruiser-carrier had hit Cerberon's debris field and had decelerated in order to maneuver among the asteroids and lost comets and shattered worlds. All Chass had to do now was *not slow down.*

Thirty seconds later she was speeding beneath a jagged hunk of metallic rock that reflected the radiance of the Cerberon black hole. Chass shielded her eyes and didn't stop, didn't adjust her course as the asteroid flashed past. Her deflectors flickered as she passed through a dust band, microscopic particles bouncing off her screens or converted into crackling plasma. She barely rotated her airfoil in time to avoid scraping a hunk of yellow ice barely larger than her ship; steering out of the way properly would have cost precious seconds.

The cruiser-carrier blossomed against the darkness until its thrusters became her sun. Without scanners she had no way to know for sure when she was in firing range, but she armed her warheads and respread her strike foils in preparation. She tried to remember the optimal range of a *Quasar Fire*-class vessel's turbolasers—not too much farther than the B-wing's proton torpedoes, she thought.

Her breath quickened when the first flash of emerald ripped across her vision. The Weequay was singing the final verse of his story. The carrier's rear guns fired again, releasing enough energy to vaporize her through her soap bubble shields. She didn't die. *Close enough,* she decided. *Close enough.*

The B-wing jolted as she loosed her torpedoes, the kick from the launch battling its continued acceleration. She fired a second volley and her head whipped hard enough to lash pain down her spine. As she fired a third time she pulsed her ion cannons and watched the radiant energy clusters speed toward the cruiser-carrier.

She was drifting aport from the off-center recoil and she strained against her harness, looking out the canopy, waiting to see the carrier ignite and its thrusters go dark.

Her console screeched at her. She smelled smoke and grease as her acceleration dropped to zero.

The torpedoes and ion blasts sailed beneath the cruiser-carrier and did no damage.

Out of fuel and out of chances, Chass na Chadic stared into the debris field as her B-wing floated uncontrolled among the junk of the Cerberon system. She screamed louder than her music and pounded her fist against the canopy as a TIE fighter raced by on its way to rejoin its mother ship, too busy to put a lone New Republic pilot out of her misery.

CHAPTER 12

LONG SHADOWS OF ASTRONOMICAL OBJECTS

I

Quell took long strides through the hangar but didn't run. If she ran, she would be noticed. If she ran she would tumble onto the deck, skidding and bleeding as the *Lodestar* shook from turbolaser blasts. She circumvented loadlifters and fuel pumps, remembering a boy she'd once seen crushed in an accident aboard the Star Destroyer *Pursuer* after rebels had blown a passing asteroid, launching fire and debris into the hull. If she was going to die today—and the odds of that were increasing steadily—she hoped to die a pilot.

She mounted the boarding ramp of the rusty freighter, hurried through the access corridor to the cockpit, and performed a cursory preflight check before igniting the engine and activating repulsors. With its squadrons already in flight the *Lodestar*'s hangar doors had been closed for combat, but as a squadron commander Quell had the codes to open them. She inputted the sequence and watched with satisfaction as the armored gates slid away to expose the void of space.

In the Empire no one would have waited to nullify her clearance after an accusation like the one Adan had delivered. But for all the New Republic Navy's official embrace of rules and protocol, the *Lodestar* was crewed by the same rebels as always. For once, that fact was in her favor.

The battleship quaked. The freighter jerked in response, its repulsors whining as Quell attempted to keep it from smashing directly into a bulkhead or, worse, something liable to explode. She smelled ozone—power cells overloading—and ignored the odor, ignited a single thruster and maneuvered the vessel through the aperture and into open space.

The bay doors were shutting behind her as she set a course away from the *Lodestar* under the sickly light of turbolaser fire. She was intent enough on her task that she started when a voice asked, "Where are you taking us, exactly?"

The interrogation droid floated through the cockpit doorway. She'd forgotten about the machine—she'd assumed that it had accompanied Adan to the *Lodestar*'s medbay. "I have a mission," she said, which was neither true nor an answer to the question. "Why are you still here?"

She banked hard, attempting to elude any enemy targeting sensors operating on visual input. The freighter had exited the *Lodestar* outside the Star Destroyer's primary field of fire but an eager gunner might still find it. She heard the droid's servos whirring in midair, then a thud and a harsh, low cry of pain.

"We're still here because I was told I shouldn't walk to the medbay," Caern Adan hissed.

Quell swiveled her neck and saw the intelligence officer leaning heavily against the doorframe behind IT-O. He looked as bruised and gaunt as the last time she'd seen him, but his expression was focused and alert. "You were supposed to be gone," she said, and her voice sounded like a child's.

"I'm not," Adan said. "Tell me what's happening."

She delayed answering long enough to bring the ship around, attempting to position the *Lodestar* between herself and the Star Destroyer. Replies flashed through her brain and she struck them down one by one. Adan didn't need to know about Lark and Chadic and Tensent confronting her in the hangar. He didn't *care* about her, or what was going to happen to her in the New Republic.

"It's Shadow Wing," she said, eyes on the viewport. "I'm not sure how or why, but they're attacking Cerberon. They ignored the trap. I think I can find their weak point."

She wondered if he would ask more. It told her something about the severity of his pain when he didn't. "Fine," he said. "Do what you have to. I'll see if I can get an escape pod working."

I doubt it, Quell thought. She considered arguing, asking if he wanted to return to the *Lodestar,* but Caern Adan had never been shy about demanding what he felt he deserved. Half delirious or not, he'd made his choice.

She heard him shuffle back into the access corridor. The hum of the interrogation droid remained. "If you want to help me, then help," Quell snapped. She thumbed a switch on the console, flipping it up and down until the secondary display came to life. "Otherwise, go."

The interrogation droid went.

Quell brought up a system chart and adjusted her heading again, accelerating until she was en route to the debris field and away from the clashing battleships. Warning lights appeared periodically, but they were nothing she hadn't seen during the flight to Catadra.

Two minutes later she glimpsed TIE squadrons heading her way from the debris field. She wasn't surprised at all.

II

Chass na Chadic stared into the burning eye of Cerberon as high-pitched scatterbop played and her B-wing drifted through the debris field. (*No,* she corrected herself, *not through the debris field. We* are *the debris now.*) She fingered her weapons trigger, waiting for the battle to return to her; for a TIE fighter to fly into her field of view.

No TIE fighter came. Her fuel meter did not change.

Her breathing quickened. She began to wonder what would happen if the New Republic lost and no one came to find her.

III

The TIEs swept in without a battle cry or a cold wind to herald their approach. They were dozens strong, turning the *Lodestar* like it was a sailing ship caught in a current, forcing it to expose its weakened screens to the full fury of the Star Destroyer lest it be vivisected by the Imperial squadrons. The TIEs cut down X-wings and chased Wyl Lark through the battleships' killing field, forcing him to abandon Nath Tensent in order to buy a few more seconds of life. Shadow Wing had finally shown itself and the fight that had seemed bound for a straight-forward New Republic victory was now a desperate struggle for survival.

"Nath!" Wyl cried. "Can you hear me?"

The enemy had dropped the jamming field seconds after the TIEs' arrival. With the Shadow Wing squadrons active there were no more secrets to hide.

"I can hear you," Nath answered. Wyl felt the strain and irritation in his voice. "Got your last message. Guess they didn't take the bait, huh?"

"No," Wyl said. A cannon volley flashed across his canopy, close enough to send his deflectors cascading through the visible light spectrum. Two TIEs pursued him and he raced toward the beams of the Star Destroyer in the hope of forcing them to fall back. "I don't know if they realized the asteroid was a trap, or—"

He cut himself off as overlapping voices crackled through the comm speaker—a desperate plea for help from one of the X-wings overlaid with a message to stand by from the *Lodestar*. Wyl listened to the din and added to it: "New Republic forces, this is Wyl Lark of Alphabet Squadron. The enemy fighters are from an elite unit and should be treated with—"

He broke off for the second time as he was forced to navigate the gap between turbolaser beams—one from the *Lodestar,* one from the Destroyer. Sweat crept around his left eye and slipped under the lid, stinging, but he didn't dare blink it away. His pursuers fell back.

"They're not listening to you, brother," Nath said. "You got a plan, though, I'd love to hear it."

"Not a *plan,* exactly." Wyl spared his scanner a glance, saw a gap in the swarm of TIEs, and rushed into the blackness. He'd lost track of whether the Star Destroyer was *above* and the *Lodestar* was *below* or vice versa. "That Destroyer—you seen it hit anything but the *Lodestar* yet?"

"Don't think so. Why?"

Wyl cleared the corridor between the two ships and spotted a trio of TIEs harrying an X-wing. He loosed a flurry of particle bolts, none of which he expected to hit their targets at such a distance. But the shots bought the X-wing room to maneuver, and he wished the pilot well before veering to port, trying to shake a missile lock.

"Enemy point-defense weapons," he managed to breathe. The *Lodestar* suddenly filled his view and he pulled up. The missile behind him detonated against the battleship's hull, and he forced down an apology. *The armor should hold,* he told himself. "The Star Destroyer's targeting is way off, and I don't think it was the jamming."

"Could be. Let's say only its turbolasers are fully functional. What do we do about that when we've got fifty TIEs on our tails?"

Wyl tried to focus, thinking back to fights over Pandem Nai and in the Oridol Cluster. Thinking of Endor, when the rebel fleet had tangled with Imperial Star Destroyers rather than face the firepower of the Death Star. "Close distance, near as we can get, and concentrate on pummeling that Destroyer. Maybe the TIEs will go a little easier on us when they risk blasting their own ship."

He heard Nath's laugh overlap with another panicked cry from an X-wing. "Or maybe the TIEs will switch focus to the *Lodestar,*" Nath said. "Or maybe the Destroyer's point defenses are just fine after all."

"Maybe," Wyl agreed. "Are you with me?"

He finally located the Y-wing on his scanner. Nath was skimming the surface of the *Lodestar*, adjusting course to return to Wyl's side.

"I'm with you," Nath said. "Let's grab some friends and blow that monster."

IV

Quell had passed through the outermost edge of the debris field, penetrating thousands of kilometers into the vast cloud band spiraling into the Cerberon black hole. But her freighter's scanners were active again, and despite the chaos of the field and the poor calibration of her instruments she was able to identify her target. She'd already traced back the relevant trajectories and knew where to look.

The cruiser-carrier was keeping its distance from the battle, but it wasn't hiding.

She'd pieced Shadow Wing's attack plan together en route, for all the good it would do her now. The Star Destroyer was a decoy—barely armed, most likely, certainly undercrewed, and probably rescued from New Republic forces in a battle somewhere along the galactic Outer Rim. (Quell wasn't privy to every intelligence communiqué that made it to Cerberon, but she'd have heard if a captured Destroyer had been retaken from a New Republic shipyard—*that* would've raised alarms.) The Destroyer had been sent against Troithe to busy that planet's defenders while the cruiser-carrier took the long way around the system, picking off divided New Republic forces and approaching from a position of strength to unleash its fighters upon a weakened *Lodestar*.

That much was obvious now. The fighters had ignored her as they'd sailed past, rightly prioritizing Troithe over her sputtering freighter. What the 204th intended to do after the *Lodestar* was obliterated, however, was beyond Quell. The fighter wing didn't have the firepower to take down Troithe's defenses, though a second wave of Imperial attackers wasn't out of the question. If Shadow Wing was able to sabotage Cerberon's remaining long-range comm stations, that second wave wouldn't even need to hurry; Cerberon would remain vulnerable indefinitely.

Or maybe Shadow Wing had come for revenge, to wreck the *Lodestar* and return home. That wasn't a plan Grandmother would have approved—Quell doubted it would have occurred to the woman, so utterly practical in her devotion to the Empire—but she didn't know who was in command nowadays. The attack on Cerberon was the sort of aggressive, wild ploy she'd have expected from rebels during the worst days before Endor; it was hard to imagine Major Rassus or the other command candidates concocting it. It was hard to imagine any Shadow Wing pilot *agreeing* to it.

Quell laughed breathlessly. Earlier, she'd thought that the unit had come to reclaim her. To take her home. But even Shadow Wing had changed beyond recognition.

She refocused on her flight as the cruiser-carrier drew nearer on her scanners. The Star Destroyer was a decoy, undercrewed and damaged. The *Lodestar* and the remaining fighters were strong enough to take it down, and Shadow Wing was willing to sacrifice it. That meant the cruiser-carrier was the 204th's escape plan—the only way the TIE fighters could jump to lightspeed and depart the system.

It meant the carrier was a vulnerability. According to her readings, the vessel was undefended.

She attempted to send an encrypted transmission back to the *Lodestar* with coordinates and full data on the cruiser-carrier. She wasn't certain whether it would get through, given interference from the debris field and the battle itself—or, assuming it did get through, whether the bridge crew would even listen. At best, reinforcements were minutes out; enough time for the carrier to adjust its strategy once it spotted Quell.

All right, she thought. *What does this junk heap have for weapons?*

She powered down the ship's noncritical systems as she studied the displays. The cruiser-carrier was massive enough to be easily distinguished from the asteroids, but the freighter might float well inside the enemy's sensor range disguised as space junk. Yet if Quell got close, what then? A rotating single-cannon turret topped the freighter and appeared to function. Two forward guns were listed as inactive, which might indicate a connection fault or might mean the barrels had been sold off for scrap a decade ago. The freighter had no missiles and its shields were built to protect against radiation bombardment in high-energy star systems, not particle bolts. As a combat vehicle it was sub-optimal.

A red line at the bottom of one of the system readouts caught her eye. She flipped a pair of switches on the console's underside and redistributed power until the red line turned green.

The tractor beam was now operational.

Quell allowed herself a smile. *You're a disaster as a combat vessel,* she thought. *As a freighter, though? You're better than you look.*

She activated the internal comms. "Adan?" she said. "If you want to try an escape pod, you've got thirty seconds before I start my run."

She ignited the freighter's thrusters in short bursts, maneuvering toward a chunk of spaceborne ice twice the size of the ship. Scanners indicated the meteoroid had a metallic core—ideal for what she had planned.

Quell had the tractor beam powered by the time Adan replied: "The escape pod doesn't even have a door. We're staying."

The freighter jerked as she activated the beam and sought to capture the meteoroid without being dragged in its wake. "You're sure?" she asked. She spoke softly enough that she barely heard the question herself, but there was no softness in her tone.

"Are you planning to die?" Adan asked.

"No."

The comm went silent.

Not that I have a plan to survive, exactly.

She became acutely aware of the tension in her shoulders and arms, the pressure with which she gripped the freighter controls, and how her hips dug into the metal of her seat. She lit her thrusters again and tugged the meteoroid through the debris field until she had a direct path to the underside of the cruiser-carrier. The Imperial vessel made no adjustments to its course and did nothing to bring its weapons to bear.

"Check your harness," she said into the comm. "Ito, make sure you're secure."

The freighter juddered and lurched as she increased power to the thrusters. Her instinct was to accelerate rapidly but she couldn't risk letting the tractor beam tear the freighter apart. Instead she focused on keeping the ship steady, adjusting energy distribution with one hand as she steered with the other.

A *Quasar Fire*-class cruiser-carrier incorporated four starfighter hangars into its undercarriage below its main reactor. Quell could see the ship's interior lighting past the hangars' magnetic fields—removed from the battle near Troithe, ready to take the TIE squadrons aboard in case of emergency or retreat, the crew had chosen not to shut the bay doors. Under ordinary operating conditions, the decision would have been reasonable.

As the freighter surged forward, Quell redirected the ship's power from thrusters into deflectors. Inertia would carry her most of the way to her destination. She toggled off port, aft, and rear screens until her forward shields channeled every erg of power the engine could provide.

She wondered if that would suffice. She thought of her squadron: Lark, Tensent, and Chadic battling an enemy they'd never beaten in a fair fight; Kairos in a suspension tube. Quell's relationship with the lot of them was over, all ties severed by the blade that had hovered at her throat since Traitor's Remorse.

Still, she had been their commander. They deserved a chance more than she did.

The sky became the gray of Imperial hull plating—or the gray of storm clouds on Nacronis. The glow of the open hangar bays was Quell's guide beacon, and she wrestled with antique controls—attempting to correct miscalculations without overshooting her target, tapping analog levers and wrenching the control yoke. She returned her right hand to the tractor beam interface every two seconds, correcting for a power imbalance caused by an obvious malfunction she had no time to fix. Delicate adjustments became impossible as the ship bucked wildly, yet she had no choice but to try.

She saw a flash of weapons fire. But it was too late for the cruiser-carrier to stop the hangar bay from filling her vision, consuming her like the maw of a titanic beast.

The freighter struck the magnetic screen. It was more like slamming into water from a ten-kilometer fall than like ramming durasteel—there was *give* to the field, yet at high velocities that fact barely mattered. The sound was overwhelming, a low boom of pounding metal combined with higher shrieks and the crackle of energy across the hull—the electric popping of overstressed power conduits and shield oscillations. The console showed nothing but alerts and warnings. Convulsing in her harness, Quell couldn't see the status indicators for her deflector but she knew it remained intact—it was the needle she used to penetrate the magnetic field, an energy weapon that served as well as any particle cannon.

She clutched the controls, the tactile sensations barely reaching her brain as her head whipped forward and back. In another second she'd know whether the freighter would survive the initial impact, but by then further course adjustments would come too late. She had to match the level of the hangar bay or she'd slam into a bulkhead, and she looked out onto the polished black floor and past the TIE deployment racks to judge her next move. She deactivated the tractor beam and struggled to correct her pitch.

The sound of coruscating energy ceased. A gale buffeted her ship. The magnetic field had broken and the air of the cruiser-carrier was escaping into vacuum.

The next part, she thought with the lightspeed efficiency of neural connections, *will be difficult.*

The magnetic field and the gale had cut her velocity to near-manageable levels. She swung ninety degrees, skimming the deck of the hangar with one wing—using it as a brake to slow her further. Pounding metal was joined by a grinding noise and she spotted sparks out her viewport as she slid toward the hangar's rear wall. She risked taking a moment to slam a palm against the weapons controls, sending the freighter's gun turret spinning. It strafed the hangar, pumping particle bolts into bulkheads and heavy equipment at random. The console no longer displayed readings from most of the ship and she was sure she'd torn off part of her sensor array, but that didn't impede her from completing her turn, orienting the freighter toward the open bay doors just as the meteoroid she'd been tugging came into view, following her like a bullet from a slingshot.

She ignited her thrusters.

The bedlam that followed made her crash through the magnetic field seem orchestrated as a symphony. She heard only a roar. She saw only darkness pierced by flashes of light. As much as she could, she steered to favor the dark, hoping that it would resolve into the comforting emptiness of space rather than the claustrophobic blackness of matter. Her body went numb from the ship's trembling.

She'd done well. She'd completed the mission. Anything else was optional.

She thought of her squadron: of Lark and Tensent and Chadic and Tonas and Barath and Xion. She closed her eyes.

The freighter's convulsions settled.

When she looked out the viewport again, she was free of the cruiser-carrier. Firelight shone from above where explosions racked the enemy vessel. She couldn't tell how much harm she'd done—she doubted she'd inflicted fatal damage but, as she brought the freighter around in a wide arc and peered upward at the ruin of the hangars, she felt confident that the cruiser-carrier was in no condition to jump to hyperspace.

She hadn't saved the fighters over Troithe and Catadra, but she'd disrupted the enemy's plan. That was worth something.

The cruiser-carrier made no attempt to fire as she gained distance. She suspected the crew no longer considered her a priority. The portions of her console still functioning displayed nothing but red yet miraculously, nothing aboard the freighter appeared catastrophically damaged—the engine was intact and her life-support systems were functional, albeit unlikely to remain so forever.

"Adan?" she said into the comm. "We're clear."

She was urging the freighter to reenter the labyrinth of asteroids when a new alarm rang. Her scanner showed a ship in pursuit—based on its size, a single TIE fighter.

She breathed through parted lips as she reactivated the turret gun. She briefly wondered if the carrier had launched a full squadron, but more likely the TIE was a stray, following its mother ship from Catadra and arriving late.

Her forward deflector was dead but she diverted enough power to her rear screens to spark them back into existence. The freighter wouldn't be able to outmaneuver the TIE in the best of circumstances yet she had enough thruster control to make a nuisance of herself. She tapped a button until the turret's targeting screen flickered online and gave her a view of the attacker.

One shot was all she needed. She didn't have to destroy the TIE— just clip its wings and persuade it to return to the carrier.

The range indicator counted down. Her hand felt slick with sweat around the control stick. She split her focus between the debris ahead and the TIE fighter behind, aware that either could kill her in an instant. For all her disdain of Tensent, he would've been a useful copilot.

The targeting computer chimed and she squeezed the turret trigger as she banked to port. She expected the TIE to drop away or detonate in a cloud of burning gas and metal. Instead it spun laterally, one way and then the next, using impossibly precise thruster blasts and repulsor emanations to weave a chaotic web. Quell had no chance to compensate before the freighter screamed, particle bolts ripping apart its surviving wing and one of its maneuvering thrusters. Sirens went off as metal cracked open and exposed the interior to the vacuum of space.

As the freighter spiraled through the debris field, the TIE flashed past. The pilot didn't pause to finish his kill; he redirected his ship toward Troithe and left Quell and the freighter behind.

She stared after him, replaying the TIE's maneuvers in her mind. She *knew* the technique, had seen it played out hundreds of times. She'd studied videos and spoken to the pilot responsible, but she didn't comprehend how she was seeing him here and now.

Major Soran Keize, her mentor, was alive.

He'd broken his promise to leave Shadow Wing.

He'd broken his promise to Quell, and now he'd left her behind for a second time.

V

Soran Keize sped through the debris field, leaving the crippled freighter to career among the rocks until it met its end. That enemy pilot would do no more damage. The casualties aboard the *Aerie* consumed a greater portion of his thoughts, but they could be mourned at another time along with Seedia and Bragheer. His wingmates had fallen with the drones over Catadra; he would weep when no other member of the 204th was at risk.

With the *Aerie* grievously damaged, Shadow Wing would be trapped in Cerberon unless Soran could find another way out. The responsibility enveloped him, clinging tighter than his flight suit. He wondered if he'd led his people to their doom and forced the thought from his mind.

"Colonel?" The comm unit inside his helmet buzzed. Soran recognized the voice of Major Rassus, stoic as always.

"Report," Soran said. "Status of the *Aerie*?"

"Reactor meltdown has been averted, but engineering reports that the hull damage cannot be patched with the materials at hand. We're going to rapidly lose air over the next hour."

Soran frowned, checked his scanners, and adjusted his heading to circumnavigate a shard of broken moon covered in primitive vegetation. "How is that possible?" he asked.

He knew it was a foolish question, particularly when time was short and the transmission was already growing distorted with distance. But losing oxygen aboard a ship the size of the cruiser-carrier was such an archaic concern it left him as stunned as if Rassus had worried about a tattered sail or a broken wheel.

Rassus didn't hide his own distaste. "The primary magnetic field has been badly breached, as you know, and we're unable to seal off the damaged compartments. Insulation foam should be pumped into all gaps to compensate automatically, but we've been running short since the Oridol Cluster. We don't have enough for more than seventy percent coverage."

Damnation, Soran thought, and was grateful he didn't say it aloud.

"Escape pods and sublight drive systems?" he asked.

"Ready and functional, respectively. We can limp most of the way to Troithe, but we can't join the battle."

"Understood," Soran said. "Get as far as you can before evacuating. After that—" *What?* He'd led Shadow Wing to Cerberon for revenge. Instead, the *Aerie*'s escape pods would fall into New Republic hands; the soldiers he'd worked to win over, to *inspire,* would all rot in the new government's prison camps. "—await orders as long as possible. If the worst comes to pass, remember that the first responsibility of a prisoner is to escape."

There was no use obfuscating the truth.

Rassus signed off. Soran was approaching the edge of the debris field now and he peered at his scanners as the *Edict,* the *Lodestar,* and the starfighters blinked onto his screen. He studied the patterns, watched the tactics used by friend and foe, and even before he had accessed the squadrons' comm frequency he was confident that the battle was playing out as designed. Broosh, Gablerone, and the other squadron leaders were operating conservatively, protecting their own against the enemy fighters and focusing their attacks on the *Lodestar*'s point-defense systems. The New Republic, meanwhile, had realized that the *Edict* was vulnerable to concentrated attacks and was focusing its efforts there.

For the moment the *Edict* was still intact. Soran had the option of ordering a retreat—sending the fighters aboard the Star Destroyer and hoping it could extract itself from the battle long enough to jump to lightspeed. It wasn't an impossible task, but the crew of cadets didn't give Soran confidence. Even if the ploy proved successful, it would mean a total failure of the mission: The *Lodestar* would be left unbroken, General Syndulla would be left alive, and Soran would have abandoned the crew of the *Aerie* and sacrificed at least two soldiers for naught.

There's no purpose in fighting an unwinnable battle, he reminded himself. *Don't fall prey to the same desperation that brought the Empire to this point. Don't become Colonel Nuress and lead your people into fire because you can't accept that the war is over.*

He could see the gleaming streams of turbolasers when he realized that one alternative remained.

"Colonel Keize to all forces." He heard none of his anxiety reach his words; a decade of combat experience had given him that much. "Redouble your efforts against the *Lodestar* but give it a clear line of retreat. When it begins to move toward Troithe, stay with it. Stay close.

"I will join you presently."

VI

Waves of ion energy rippled across the Star Destroyer's hull where Nath's torpedoes had impacted. Wyl admired the sight—*like cloud formations,* he thought, even as he recognized that the Destroyer was nearly finished, smoking and sparking from a dozen sections. Most of all, he focused on drawing the TIE fighters' fire away from Nath's Y-wing as the bomber completed its pass.

Yet as he whipped over and around and above the Y-wing, he was surprised that no particle bolts crossed his field of vision. He glanced toward his scanner and saw the nearest TIEs retreating toward the *Lodestar.*

The *Acclamator*-class battleship had stopped broadcasting minutes earlier after its comm array had been damaged, but it was obvious at a glance what was going on. Hard-pressed by the enemy fighters, the *Lodestar* was moving toward Troithe and would arrive in orbit in under a minute. "Keep those TIEs off the *Lodestar*," Wyl called. "Orbital defenses will take care of the Destroyer, but our friends are done for if we don't help them."

One of the surviving X-wing pilots signaled an affirmative. Another asked, "Any word from Meteor over Catadra?"

"If they were coming," Nath answered, "they'd have gotten here by now. Listen to Lark and form a defensive globe around the *Lodestar*!"

For tantalizing moments, Wyl flew through open space without fearing for his life. The Star Destroyer had almost entirely ceased its volleys, reluctant to unleash its turbolaser blasts while the TIE fighters swarmed the *Lodestar;* its role was one of stalking predator, chasing the enemy to Troithe's shelter. The TIEs had already left Wyl's vicinity. He breathed deep and let the void of space stream around him, reveled in the directionless nothing surrounding him and his ship.

Then he plunged back into the fight.

If not for the shining orb of Troithe below, he would have believed himself back in the Oridol Cluster. He remembered the last battle against Shadow Wing there—TIE fighters swarming around a New Republic carrier ship (the *Hellion's Dare* then, the *Lodestar* now), spiraling around it from head to tail and raking its hull while picking off the remaining New Republic starfighters. Wyl hadn't been able to mount a defense of his mother ship then and he wasn't sure this time would be any different. Already another pair of TIEs had locked onto him, chasing him across the *Lodestar's* wedge-shaped body.

The other New Republic pilots—Wyl counted six of them, including himself and Nath—called out updates and targets and damage reports. This, too, was a difference from Oridol: There he had known each and every pilot and held back tears as they'd died. Now he was among strangers. He'd barely bothered to get to know Meteor or the pilots assigned to Troithe. Chass and Quell and Kairos, all of whom should have been with him, were gone.

"Star Destroyer's not stopping!" Nath's voice boomed through the comm. "Got to be coming into range of the satellite defenses by now!"

The hull of the *Lodestar* sped above Wyl and particle bolts splashed against plating as his pursuers narrowly missed him. He could've raced toward the planet but that would've left the TIEs free to molest the battleship. If he slowed to allow Nath a chance to intercept, the TIEs would flank him and catch him in their crossfire. He scanned the horizon and spotted a billowing inferno spilling from the *Lodestar's* ventral power distributor—a poor omen for the battle but his best hope. He braced against the g forces and made for the flames.

The inferno burned blue-white, fed by gases from the battleship's interior and hot enough to turn hull plating molten. Wyl didn't know how his shields would fare but he was confident the TIEs would suffer worse. The light blinded him as he plunged in and he felt his canopy grow warm; still, he dropped his speed, staying within the chemical furnace and praying the TIEs would outpace him—that if he survived the fires he'd find the enemy waiting on the other side, perfectly positioned ahead of him as targets.

He hoped neither of them was Blink.

He burst out of the fire, spotted the TIEs, and squeezed his trigger. His shot went wide—wide enough that he wondered if he'd damaged his cannons in the flames—but his foes veered off in response. He had time to feel half a second's worth of hope.

Then the *Lodestar's* hull erupted in three places, shards of metal ripping free and expanding like halos around shafts of emerald light—turbolaser beams that had pierced the great battleship and washed the galaxy in their sickly hue. A shock wave of oxygen and debris struck Wyl's A-wing, and he attempted to wrest control as he tumbled away. He heard oaths and curses over the comm and heard a woman cry, "*Lodestar* down! *Lodestar* down!"

He knew it was true.

The Star Destroyer was out of sight above the battleship. The combatants had crossed into Troithe's upper atmosphere during the fight, and the etched patterns of cities decorated the continent far below. The tug of gravity was weak but it was enough to cause the broken *Lodestar* to dip, coaxing the massive vessel toward the planet.

Wyl fought away a haze of uncertainty. He didn't know what to do but Nath was still alive, fighters were still active; he picked the nearest target on his scanner and swept in to engage. The TIEs were staying close to the *Lodestar* as it fell, and he didn't understand why; nor did he understand the bright flares far above him, past the *Lodestar,* too brilliant to be starfighter weaponry.

"She's been avenged," Nath said, steady through the comm.

"What?" Wyl asked.

"Orbital defenses hit the Star Destroyer. Got too close while dealing the coup de grâce to the *Lodestar.* Going down."

Wyl mindlessly shot at a TIE and imagined the two warships plummeting to the surface of Troithe. *It's happening again,* he thought, and felt as much as remembered the gas mining stations dropping to Pandem Nai; the cities endangered because of the squadron's vendetta against Shadow Wing. He envisioned *Lodestar* and Star Destroyer burning through the atmosphere and demolishing kilometers of skyscrapers and housing blocks and cultural centers.

Next, he remembered the shields.

Troithe was *not* Pandem Nai. It was built to repel orbital bombardments. Adan's whole plan had relied on it.

Wyl didn't know if that meant the shields could survive the fall of two capital ships. But he could hope.

VII

The TIE fighters had entered atmosphere, and a steady rain of trailing embers and smoking metal fell from above. Soran had flown through worse conditions but not often, and he had to grip his control yoke tighter than he'd like against the violent shaking of his vessel. A TIE/ln's hull plating and viewport were less a barrier to open space and more a membrane surrounding their pilot—that was the beauty of the ship that no rebel starfighter could match, and as good a reason as any why Soran had never accepted permanent assignment to a more powerful TIE interceptor. The standard-model TIE was a weapon a pilot wielded as he soared through the sky. Yet there was no escaping the disadvantages when an environment became hostile.

"Keep your fighters steady," he said, and suppressed a groan as his vessel bounced and he nearly bit off the tip of his tongue. "Remain in position relative to the warships."

The squadron commanders acknowledged one by one. The voices of Broosh and Gablerone, Darita and Phesh, Hussor and Wisp came through, each giving Soran strength to continue; a cause worth hoping for. Each voice deepened his fear that he was only digging their graves.

The *Edict* burned above him, the Star Destroyer's thrusters failing and its repulsors struggling to keep it aloft in atmosphere. Styll had led Nenvez and his cadets through the battle and performed better than Soran had ever expected, but heroic efforts couldn't save the vessel now. As its deflectors and heat shields failed and hull plating tore free to expose internal machinery, its decay accelerated to unthinkable speeds. Soran had authorized the crew to evacuate, though he suspected Styll—who had sacrificed the cruiser-carrier *Allegiance* to permit the *Edict*'s rebirth and who would have no role to play if they survived Cerberon—might insist on staying till the end. He hoped the man did not.

Below Soran was the *Lodestar,* launching escape pods like missiles as it, too, burned. The *Acclamator*-class battleship had not only suffered thruster failure but lost one of its drive modules as the vessel crumbled to pieces. Soran did not imagine that General Syndulla would go down with her ship as Styll might with his. Maybe during her rebel days, he thought, but not when she could find a command anywhere in the New Republic fleet.

Between *Lodestar* and *Edict* was the TIE swarm, still under periodic and futile attack by the New Republic starfighters. Those enemy craft were an inconvenience more than a serious threat, but even an inconvenience could prove fatal in trying circumstances.

"*Lodestar* approaching planetary shield, sir!" Hussor called through the comm.

Soran checked his altitude before peering out the viewport. He could see a faint shimmer of distortion extending across the glittering darkness of the cityscape. He tried to recall the technical specifications of the Troithe shields—he'd spent hours culling through reports and manuals as they'd planned the mission, learned exactly what sort of bombardment they could sustain. But he was guessing now at the payload: the mass of the *Lodestar,* multiplied by its velocity as derived from Troithe's gravity and the counterforce of the repulsors and the distance it had already fallen . . .

Someone could have run the numbers. Soran couldn't. Not in the moment.

An X-wing flashed toward him, firing its four cannons as its bulk spun and hopped in the gale-wake of the *Lodestar.* With a grimace of annoyance Soran opened his throttle, fought inertia and atmosphere to rotate the TIE toward his foe, and dispatched the enemy.

Add the X-wing to the payload.

When the *Lodestar* hit the shield seconds later, Soran felt the sonic shock wave through the membrane of his ship, through flight suit and flesh. His TIE was forced upward as a caldera of flame and smoke and metal (and, a part of Soran's mind reminded him, organic matter) rose and expanded with the liquid motion of a raindrop striking a cockpit canopy and the destructive might of a plasma bomb. He spared a glance down as his ship tumbled and saw the flames washing across air; the dark central mass of the battleship fixed in place while smaller sections skittered across the dome of the planetary deflector.

It's holding.

"Now," he cried, no longer concealing the urgency or desperation in his voice. "Go!"

The sky fell as the TIEs scattered. In the eternal night of Cerberon, the plunging *Edict* cast no shadow. Instead the fiery light from below reflected off the Destroyer's hull, bathing the world in infernal radiance. *Was this what Pandem Nai was like?* Soran wondered as he sped after his comrades, clearing the area for the second impact.

The shock wave was stronger this time, and the tidal wave of fire rose over the fighters as they tumbled fifty meters above the planetary shield. Soran saw one of his pilots dip and skirt the energy barrier, one of the TIE's wings shredding before the vessel erupted in a flash. A second TIE whirled through the air and was blasted by a Y-wing— a *Y-wing,* clumsiest of all the rebel fighters—as it attempted to regain control. He held his breath as he glanced behind him at the widespread wreckage of the two battleships and strained to see the flickering of the shield.

For a moment the central remains of the two warships seemed to sink, as though they'd found rest in the silt marshes of Nacronis. It might have been an optical illusion—Soran's desperate hope combined with the heat-shimmer of the air—but it gave him solace. What oc- curred next was unmistakable: a clap like thunder rent the air and the planetary shield rippled back in an expanding circle, seeming to sub- lime. The ruins of the *Lodestar* and the *Edict,* now spread in a two- kilometer radius, dropped toward the city.

"Down!" Soran called. "Down!"

He switched off thrusters and repulsors and felt buoyant as the TIE fell. He forced himself to keep his attention on the console rather than the world outside the cockpit and saw his squadrons changing altitude as he did. Two seconds later he reactivated his equipment and took the jolt as the fighter leveled out. Above him, the sky was rippling again as the planetary shield re-formed.

"All squadrons, descend to the city and begin your attack runs. Keep the enemy on the defensive—do not let them coordinate a counterof- fensive and do not hold position longer than necessary." The TIEs were already fanning out, scattering across the urban expanse. Soran paused before adding, "The next several hours—maybe the next days or weeks—will be trying. But you are the best the Empire ever produced. You are the 204th Fighter Wing. You will survive and you will tri- umph."

The squadrons raced through the steel canyons. Trapped beneath the re-formed shield barrier, it was the only real choice they had—but that was part of the plan. Soran wasn't certain what would become of the *Edict* and the *Aerie*'s escape pods, but their navigation systems were smart enough to avoid smashing directly into the shield; the crews had a *chance* at survival, and a slim chance was better than none.

Shadow Wing could not leave Troithe. Shadow Wing could not leave the system. But General Syndulla's flagship was gone. The forces protecting Cerberon had been devastated. Retribution had been exacted for the pilots who lived and for those who had died above Pandem Nai.

There would still be time to escape.

Soran Keize could still redeem himself.

PART TWO

OVER THE ABYSS

CHAPTER 13

SHADOWS AT DUSK

I

The TIEs had vanished like a flock of grazing birds disturbed by a passing landspeeder. The surviving New Republic pilots—and there were barely a handful—tore after the enemy squadrons, aware that they were outmatched but determined to track the foe before they disappeared into the city.

Wyl stayed at Nath's side as the Y-wing skirted the rooftops of unlit towers, damaged repulsors flickering online and off. He was concerned about T5—if the ship had taken a hit, was the astromech damaged, too?—but he knew better than to distract Nath with questions while they were struggling for survival.

Instead he listened to calls coming through on the New Republic military comm channel: Emergency signals from shield generator stations and makeshift military bunkers. Urgent requests from the spaceport for a status report on the *Lodestar*. "*Lodestar* is down," Wyl replied, when no one else spoke. "We've got a few fighters left. Who's in charge of the ground defenses?"

The woman on the other end of the comm laughed. "*What* ground defenses? We blew up the anti-air weapons on the way to the capital. Unless you want the infantry to shoot TIEs with their rifles—"

Nath's voice broke in. "Got it!" he called. "Damn piece of shrapnel's still sticking out the side of my ship but we rerouted the power."

"What do you need?" Wyl asked. Maybe to the woman at the spaceport; maybe to both of them.

The woman didn't hesitate. "Give me a point of contact. If we lost the *Lodestar,* Meteor Leader should be in charge—"

"Gone," Nath said.

"Maybe Alphabet Leader? Lieutenant Quell—"

"Gone," Nath repeated.

Wyl winced at the callousness of Nath's tone. Quell could be alive— enough escape pods had launched that it was possible. Chass and Meteor Squadron, as well. He swung the A-wing in sight of Nath and set course after the largest cluster of TIEs. He tried to listen to the conversation while scanning other distress calls, pulling up maps of Troithe and estimating flight times. He tuned out Nath and the spaceport operator altogether as he caught a fragment of transmission—a cry for help from Thannerhouse, where the New Republic had established a supply depot for the infantry invasion of the capital.

"Take a look at these coordinates," Wyl said, and sent the particulars to Nath. "TIEs are en route there. I'd say it's our priority."

"Sister in the spaceport just said to protect the shield generators in case of a follow-up attack." It didn't sound like an argument so much as a statement of fact.

"You've seen Thannerhouse," Wyl answered. "It's still densely populated even after the flooding. If you want to split off we can cover more ground—"

"Not an issue. You say Thannerhouse, I'm with you."

Wyl cycled through transmissions again. Shadow Wing was hitting six targets already and moving toward four more. One New Republic fighter per target wasn't enough to make a stand.

"I'm accelerating to top speed," he said. "Catch up as soon as you can."

Wyl listened to the reports from the Thannerhouse District as he flew.

"Three of them on the scanner, now. We're trying to evacuate the civilians."

"They're firing on the dams! They're trying to flood us out!"

"Rebel—New Republic—screw it, rebel ground team is trying to get a bead on them. We've got one Plex missile but we'll do what we can."

He saw the flare of cannon fire reflected on the water as he approached. Nath was minutes behind him but Wyl centered a blip on his scanner and raced toward his target, firing long before he had any chance of scoring a hit. Destroying the enemy was secondary to stopping their attacks, and he knew they would come for him.

They did. All three TIEs abandoned their objectives and, as one, spread out to force him into their field of fire. Any TIE he locked onto would flee, he knew; if he attempted to pursue, the others would chase him and position themselves for a killing shot. His A-wing had no meaningful edge when it came to speed or maneuverability in a close-quarters melee, and his shields would fall rapidly against a barrage from multiple opponents.

So instead of fighting, Wyl dived for shelter, skirting between buildings and skimming the water, limiting the angles from which the TIEs could attack. They shot at him anyway and he panted in dismay as their particle bolts tore through squat cantinas and makeshift canal locks built of sandbags and energy field projectors. He led the TIEs through narrow corridors and skipped across the surface of the lake, battering his body against his cockpit and leaving a trail of steam and froth behind him. When he saw water churned by particle volleys overturn a distant raft with the stick-figure of a man aboard, he cried out and pitched toward the sky again.

Quell would have told him to deactivate his thrusters, to drop and reposition and fire at the TIEs from below; or to shoot one of his two remaining missiles into the lake and take advantage of the resulting wave. But Wyl had learned to fly from the sur-avkas of Home and he was too worn and weary to concoct some technical trick. He flew upward, straining his bones as particle bolts flashed around him. His console flared and whined as his shields collapsed.

From a position of perfect vertical ascent he jerked at his controls and tilted the nose of the A-wing backward, flipped the vessel over, and hurtled down toward the TIEs and the lake. Blood rushed to his head and he fired wildly as blasts tore into his wings, felt the agony as though sharing sensation with his ship, and tried to laugh as the TIEs scattered.

He was certain he'd hit one. Not full-on. Not enough to destroy it. But he'd done *something*.

Sparks rained onto his canopy as he pulled up to avoid slamming into the lake. He heard the screams of the TIEs' engines change pitch as a deeper rumble joined the cacophony. He was too dizzy to see as he ascended gently, attempting to keep the wounded A-wing from veering to one side.

But the voice came through clearly: "You make moves like that, I'll keep hammering while they stare."

Wyl risked blinking and let his eyes focus on his scanner as he flew in a broad spiral toward the sky. "Where'd they go?" he asked.

Nath answered almost before Wyl finished speaking. "They went away. Take a breather. No one died, so call it a victory."

The A-wing bobbed in the air, repulsors active but thrusters cool, the whole ship askew by ten degrees and forcing Wyl to shift uncomfortably in his seat. There was a tangible silence he attributed at first to the stillness of his vessel. Then he realized that sometime during the battle all comm chatter had stopped.

The sweat soaking his clothes stank faintly of iron. He searched through frequencies for anything but static. "Nath? I'm not getting any signals."

"And you're not going to."

"We have to get to the next target," Wyl said. He assumed he'd heard Nath wrong. "We need the coordinates of—"

"Pretty sure global comm rigs are down, brother. Enemy squadrons must've hit them first thing. So long as we're planetside, it's short range only, unless you've got one impressive transmitter tucked under your chair."

Wyl shivered, pulled himself up the slant of his seat and tightened his harness. "So we work from last known enemy destinations. Spaceport, shield generators, bunkers." He tapped at his console and pulled up a set of low-resolution maps. Without data from the *Lodestar* or a New Republic ground base he'd be limited to whatever was stored aboard the A-wing—enough to navigate by, with classified data limited in case of capture. "Flying at low altitude, we're maybe twenty minutes from one of the secondary spaceports. Could be a target."

"Could be," Nath agreed, with the phlegmatic tone of a tutor humoring a student.

"Unless you want to return to the primary?" Wyl asked. "The whole refugee camp is probably in crisis. Most of the military personnel moved out a few days back, but Adan's analysts were staying in the tower . . ."

"Don't think that's a good idea."

"Nath—"

"Wyl." The bass of his voice was cut with static. "You think this is all real urgent, I know, but you're panicking."

I am, Wyl thought, *but it doesn't matter.* He tried to speak. Nath kept talking.

"Give me sixty seconds to make my case," Nath said. "It's all I need."

Wyl nodded briskly, as if Nath could see him.

"Basics first: We're outnumbered and outgunned. Meteor Squadron hasn't made it back from Catadra and I'm doubting they will. Syndulla and Vanguard Squadron could be gone for weeks. And the ground situation's about to get worse.

"Troithe's Imperial holdouts don't have much in the way of air power but we left a lot of stormtroopers out there after taking down Governor Hastemoor; they're going to use this chance to act. They're also going to be backed by whatever two, ten, forty percent of the population still supports the Empire. There's going to be rioting and chaos and any New Republic allies on the ground will have their hands full."

Wyl listened to Nath's voice, grave and easygoing at once, and noticed how cold his wet outfit really was. His flight suit had been designed to absorb sweat as little as possible; but he was still in civvies.

Nath went on: "Now, we can keep flitting around, but we've both taken damage and I don't think we'd last an hour. My suggestion is we fly real low to avoid detection and try to pick up local comm signals. Find support where we can, make a plan after there's more than two of us."

The idea was repulsive. Shadow Wing was attacking, and if Alphabet did as Nath suggested they'd be abandoning the Empire's victims.

"I hate it," Wyl said.

"I bet."

Wyl laughed hoarsely.

"All right," he answered. "All right."

He wanted to tear his helmet off and toss it into the lake. He wanted to stare into a sun that didn't exist in Cerberon and warm himself and dry his sweat. If he couldn't fight, he wanted that.

He hoped Chass was faring better than he was.

He forced himself not to think of Quell at all.

II

Chass na Chadic floated with the rest of the Cerberon system's garbage. She was sprawled across the B-wing's console with her face pressed to the canopy bubble and her legs and feet tangled loosely in her seat harness. The transparent metal felt solid and cool against her cheek as she took in the glittering darkness, and she occasionally thumbed her audio system, restlessly switching from one song to the next but never really listening.

She had survived again. She'd survived a battle no one else had. By now, she should have been used to it.

It was over three hours since the battle above Catadra, and no ships had appeared on her scanners. She'd picked up no transmissions. However the fight had ended it hadn't been good for the New Republic—maybe hadn't been good for Shadow Wing, either, though she had no way to guess. As the minutes had ticked by she'd gone from frustration to rage to despair, and then—after she'd slammed her head against the canopy—gone into a state of boneless dispassion.

She thought about Wyl and Nath and Quell, all of whom were likely dead (except Quell, maybe, the only one whose death Chass might actually enjoy). The thought was a stone in her throat but she knew the hurt wouldn't last. She'd put Wyl and Nath away the same way she had Fadime and Yeprexi and Quaysail, the dead of Hound Squadron whom she rarely thought of anymore; or even Batriok and Snivel, of the Cavern Angels.

You loved Snivel. You loved Snivel. When's the last time you thought of him?

It would be the same with Alphabet Squadron.

She smashed her forehead into the canopy again to drive sensation into her skull. Her mouth hung open as she tried to breathe and she heard herself laughing. Little dancing blotches of light orbited the asteroids outside.

She thought about Jyn Erso, the woman who'd given her life to stop the Emperor's first Death Star. The woman whose sacrifice had inspired Chass to follow in her footsteps to ruined Jedha; inspired her to join the Cavern Angels. Chass had heard more than her share of martyr tales as a child, been lectured over and over about the reincarnation of Howeth Zaubra and Father Kashevon's Day of Atonement, but those had been lies meant to manipulate the credulous. Jyn had been *real*.

Chass was the antithesis of everything Jyn Erso was. Where Jyn died, Chass lived. Where Jyn brought life, Chass left the burnt corpses of friends in her wake.

Jyn had fought an impossible war against an overwhelming enemy. Chass was finishing an easy war from a position of strength—even if the New Republic was having a bad day.

She heard a buzzing sound over the soft music and, in her haze of pain and self-pity, thought it was an insect. She slapped at the console expecting to feel the chitinous shell of something beneath her palm. When she realized the sound was one of the ship's alarms, she slithered back into her seat and scanned her readouts.

Her oxygen gauge showed a malfunction. Might have been a leaking tank. Might have been a damaged sensor.

She swore softly and sucked in a long breath. *Tastes fine to me,* she thought, but the indicator didn't stop flashing. Two minutes later it still hadn't stopped.

You want to wait around? Suffocation's slow but it'll put you to sleep before the end.

The idea wasn't appealing.

She reached under her seat to where she'd stowed her sidearm—the custom KD-30 with its acid-packed rounds—and nudged the barrel with her fingertip. It was there if she needed it, but the thought of her brain dissolving into organic mush was no more appealing than suffocation. Possibly more painful, too.

"Going out there, then," she muttered, and began rummaging through the emergency supplies. She hoped someone from the ground crew had replenished those recently, even if they hadn't refueled her in time.

A B-wing's oxygen tanks were accessible from an exterior maintenance panel to the rear of the cockpit pod. Theoretically the tanks could also be accessed by dismantling the bulkhead behind the pilot's seat but, Chass thought, what was the point? If she was going to find damage it would be outside.

She didn't pull up the ship's schematics or search for the emergency manual. Chass knew her B-wing from bones to bolts—knew her fighter as well as Nath knew his, and better than Quell had ever figured out her X-wing. The Cavern Angels had forced that discipline onto her, even if she'd resented the hours reading technical sheets and reassembling model engines. Nonetheless, she mentally reviewed the diagnostic process and repair sequences twice before strapping on her rebreather, sealing her oversized flight suit, securing the cockpit's stray objects, and overriding the safety controls to shut down life support. When the air in the cockpit had been extracted and stored and gravity had dissipated like an unwelcome odor, she slid open the canopy and let darkness inside.

Space engulfed her. The last remnants of oxygen hissed away as Chass gripped her control yoke and floated free. She instinctively breathed faster; then she forced her respiration back to a steady rate and let go of the yoke with one hand, wrapping gloved fingers around the canopy's empty channel.

Slowly. Slowly.

Hand-over-hand, she pulled herself out of the cockpit proper and over the edge. Her legs swung away from the ship, and she twisted and kicked, using her grip on the hull for leverage until her feet awkwardly hugged her primary airfoil beneath the cockpit pod. She wouldn't be able to cling to it all the way, but momentary security was better than none at all.

She'd seen comrades sucked into space through holes blown in battleships. Some spacers developed phobias after sights like that, but Chass had only found it *ugly*.

Maybe that's what happened to Quell when the Destroyer met the Lodestar.

She crept along the exterior of the pod, reaching out her left arm half a meter, finding a hold, pulling partway, and crossing over with the right arm. Grips weren't difficult to find near the canopy but soon she was forced to stretch, to cling to jutting metal knobs or squeeze airfoil ridges with her knees. If her neck tilted back too far she was confronted with the infinite darkness that made stillness feel like falling. When she caught a glimpse of the burning eye of the Cerberon singularity, its gaze was almost a relief. If it was *down*, the rest of the universe was *up*.

Slowly. Slowly.

It couldn't have taken more than five minutes to reach the rear of the ship but it felt like an hour. She gripped the gyrostabilizers with one hand as she eyed a scorched and cratered hull panel. She'd tucked a multitool into her flight suit but she didn't think she'd need it now—she reached into the burnt hole and tugged, working the whole plate free. The metal was still warm beneath her fingers.

She let go of the plate and allowed it to float away. Inside the compartment, wires and tubing packed every centimeter not occupied by the two rust-colored liquid oxygen tanks. The tanks appeared unharmed; when she ran her hand over the metal, she felt no seepage or fractures.

Sensor fault. Has to be.

She let out a breath and felt moisture accumulate around her lips inside the rebreather tube. If she died today it wouldn't be by suffocation after all.

Then the wires flashed silently. A spark burst from the compartment. Unthinking and surprised, she pushed away from the ship and the danger.

She realized her mistake almost in time to correct it, but the B-wing was out of reach in an instant and she was languidly drifting backward. She glanced about as if she might find a convenient tree branch or scaffold to catch, but there was nothing. She kicked against vacuum, tried to stretch out her arms as her ship and her life pulled steadily away. She'd been taught about zero-gravity maneuvering but that had been ages ago and panic flooded her brain.

Start simple: If nothing stops you, you'll float in the same direction forever.

She remembered the multitool. *Throw it!* she thought. If she hurled it away from the ship it would push her back toward the B-wing. She managed to fumble it out of her suit but she struggled to spin around. When she finally tossed the tool away it barely slowed her.

Meter by meter, the distance between Chass and the B-wing increased.

If she'd brought her sidearm she could have fired it—*that* would've been enough kick to carry her back. She checked her suit pockets but the weapon was still in the cockpit. If she'd been in an X-wing or a Y-wing—a starfighter with an astromech—she could've asked her droid to pilot the ship to her. She ran through scenarios as her mind screamed: *Think faster!*

She only had a few minutes of oxygen in the rebreather. Maybe she'd be suffocating after all.

The B-wing wasn't far. On the ground she could've reached the cockpit in seconds. She almost wished it would disappear into the distance; it would've felt like less of a mockery.

If your death had to be pointless, you could've at least died in battle.

She drifted and breathed and was surprised to feel her eyes water. This wasn't how she'd ever wanted to go—not in her darkest moments, not when Shadow Wing had taken everything from her or when she'd been lost on Uchinao or when she'd first broken free of the wretched life her mother had given her.

She wondered how long it would be before her corpse joined the debris and fell, burning forever, into the eye of Cerberon.

As her vision shivered and oxygen deprivation ate her brain like an acid-packed bullet, she thought she saw lights.

III

The freighter cockpit was cold but Quell was sweating. Every muscle had begun to cramp, and her fingers and wrists had settled into the liminal space between numbness and agony. For five hours she'd sat hunched in her seat, metal frame digging into her back and bottom through threadbare padding, attempting to navigate the debris field with a single maneuvering thruster.

She had no repulsors. No primary jets. She could nudge the vessel to port and she'd done so repeatedly as the ship had drifted into ever-denser rock clusters. Now whirling stones spun around moon-sized asteroids and she rationed her thruster usage in concession to the screaming red warnings that appeared with every ignition. She couldn't turn around, and the tides of gravity had put her on a course for the black hole at the heart of the system.

She should have been worried about that. But every minute she avoided a fatal collision was a victory, and exhaustion guaranteed that she would make a mistake long before the black hole became a problem.

During the brief, unnerving periods when no rocks hurtled toward her, Quell thought about Major Soran Keize. The freighter's flight recorders were damaged beyond repair and she had no way of reviewing the footage of the TIE fighter that had crippled her. Yet she had an excellent memory and she replayed the TIE's maneuvers in her mind, finding no other conclusion than that her mentor had rejoined Shadow Wing.

It was Keize who had told her to leave after Nacronis—*ordered* her to leave, and he'd promised he would follow. Had he betrayed her? Had he lied to her to ensure that she did as commanded? Did it even matter anymore?

Had *she* betrayed him?

A scream came from the access corridor, hoarse and short-lived. The interrogation droid had taken to injecting its patient with stimulants to keep him alert. Quell was growing used to the sounds.

She'd asked the droid to make repairs to the vessel; to calculate some escape from the debris field; to take a fraction of the burden of rescue from her. But neither the droid nor Adan had any skills she could use. They'd applied emergency sealant to two gaping holes in the hull but the droid knew less about fixing drive systems than Quell did. Even if Adan had been healthy she doubted he'd be any better equipped.

She looked between the viewport and her sensors as the ship approached another asteroid. She gave the maneuvering thruster a two-second burst of power and sidestepped death. No new warning lights flared; the ignition jets would last her a little longer yet.

As she scanned for the next obstacle a sensor readout caught her attention. "Ito?" she called. "Get in here if you can leave your patient."

A minute later the droid's soft hum joined the uneven throbbing of the engine. She didn't dare turn around but she flapped a hand at the console. "There's an energy reading. Looks like it's coming from a planetoid, faint but steady. You recognize it?"

The droid floated over the console, edging into Quell's peripheral vision. "I do not," it said. "But I recognize the region."

"So do I." Quell forced herself not to look over—she couldn't read the droid's expression anyway and she wouldn't allow herself to be distracted. "Adan's captors were charting this area of the debris field. Or they'd been here. Or were planning to."

"I agree it has some significance, given the energy reading. But we are too far outside my specialization for me to speculate further."

"It's something, though," she said, almost whispering. "It's something."

"Adan is awake." The droid's hum fell in pitch. Quell wondered if it was trying to calm her. "Given what he's said, I find it unlikely that he has any information about his captors' interest in this region. However, I will inquire if you wish."

Quell tapped at the console, calculating potential approach vectors and liking none of them. "No point. If I'm going to get us there, I need to adjust our angle *now*."

"You intend to land on the planetoid?"

She laughed through dry lips. "It's that or keep floating until we hit something. But I'm not sure I'd call what we're about to do *landing*."

The droid floated in the direction of the access corridor. "I'll secure Adan and myself. What do you expect to find?"

Quell shrugged. "I don't expect anything. A ship if we're lucky. A fading nav beacon if we're not."

If the droid replied she didn't hear it. She ignited the maneuvering thruster, watching heat and power readings spike and course projections alter on her flickering display. The freighter roared in protest and Quell bounced in her seat. But this wasn't the challenging part—if she timed the ignition burst perfectly, aligned the ship's vector with what she'd plotted on the computer without destroying her drive system entirely, she'd go racing directly for the planetoid with no way to stop, no way to slow down except whatever atmospheric friction she might encounter.

She checked her harness and leaned back in her seat for the first time in hours.

Relax, she told herself. *It'll probably be over soon.*

CHAPTER 14

THE JOYOUS TOGETHERNESS OF SHARED SUFFERING

I

Colonel Soran Keize walked through the dim corridors of Raddak-kia Plaza communications center with his flight helmet under his left arm and his blaster comfortably gripped in his right hand. Through the floor plating—the dark, burnished durasteel common to Imperial facilities everywhere, unable to entirely cover the stained wooden floorboards prized by aristocrats from an earlier era—he felt the rumble of proton bombs detonating kilometers away. As he walked, he hummed; then, prompted by his own humming, he began to sing softly.

Tack into the danger, boys
Onward through the night
Upon the morrow we'll hoist our flag
And set Queen Gann alight

It was a Corellian traders' song, one that went back centuries and whose lyrics were full of nonsense words—references to mizzens and marlinspikes and anchor rodes. The song recounted a perilous voyage, and when Soran realized why he was singing it he stopped abruptly.

It had been Captain Gablerone's favored drinking song.

Soran had never liked Gablerone, but they had been comrades for an eternity. Now Gablerone was dead, incinerated at some point during the final battle above Troithe—when and how, Soran had yet to learn. Gablerone was not the first casualty of the assault on Cerberon; nor, Soran was sure, would he be the last.

He resisted the urge to kick the door panel as he arrived at the entrance to the control chamber. He smoothed out his breathing, tapped the trigger, and stepped inside to join his people.

He'd chosen Raddakkia Plaza as a landing zone and temporary operations hub based on what he recalled from his studies of Troithe prior to the attack. (Soran had never considered himself studious or possessed of a particularly keen intellect—he thought of Lieutenant Quell's obsessiveness—but a soldier survived by preparing for contingencies.) The comm center had been abandoned soon after Endor when the governor had ordered the redeployment of all planetside troops; yet it was deep within territory historically friendly to Imperial rule.

It was not *safe*—only a fool would call it safe—but it was a better location than most to regroup.

The pilots already inside came from every squadron in the 204th. Their TIEs had been damaged or required refueling and repair; while their comrades continued bombing runs over the city and harried New Republic forces, those who were grounded took on the tasks of the *Edict* and *Aerie* crew whose escape pods had yet to be located. Six young women and men moved among the control room terminals, trying to bring neglected systems back online. Three more stood guard over the TIEs in the plaza while another two attempted to patch simple damage to the ships. All of them sweated in their flight suits as they worked, though many had stripped off helmets and gloves as they rewired connections and called to one another over the holographic display table.

None of them were meant for the work before them, but a TIE pilot was trained to be able to reassemble an ion engine, reprogram a targeting computer, or build a distress signal from the wreckage of a skyhopper. Pilots couldn't replace the command staff or ground crew of their carrier ships, but they were far from helpless.

"Do we have a data feed yet?" Soran asked.

Lieutenant Nord Kandende—Gablerone's troubled officer, whom Soran had caught offering blood to the Emperor's Messenger aboard the *Aerie*—rose from his station and waved the others back to their tasks. "We have a feed," Kandende said. "Not a lot of data. We're merging sensor readings from all units in communications distance—they're chaining transmissions for extra range, though Squadron Three keeps straying too far out."

"Good enough for now," Soran said. He moved to the holotable's edge and adjusted controls until the display flashed into life. "But I want the plaza's main transmitter operational by sunset."

Kandende hesitated then hurried back to work. Soran had no idea whether a sunset deadline was remotely achievable, but he guessed Kandende didn't either. Sometimes that was motivation enough.

He stared into the shimmering holographic cityscape for over an hour, watching the firefly glow of TIEs crossing the map of Troithe. There were few non–Shadow Wing ships in flight when he began his vigil; by the end, there were none. Virtually no civilian vessels remained in Cerberon, and the governor's forces had been decimated over the previous months. That left only the survivors of General Syndulla's battle group, and they had gone into hiding at low altitude or left the range of the TIEs' patrol patterns.

For the moment, then, Shadow Wing was Cerberon's predominant air and space force. For the moment, its advantage was overwhelming. Even taking into consideration Syndulla's ground troops and assuming negligible aid from local Imperial loyalists, the 204th could lock down Troithe. As the situation became clear, Soran designated targets and spoke tersely over a comm frequency that made all his pilots sound like droids; and when the immediate threats had been destroyed—when the best-fortified New Republic outposts had been hammered by TIE bombers and the scattered anti-air cannons obliterated—he recalled two squadrons and organized a unit rotation to allow his fatigued people short rests.

That was the greatest reprieve he was comfortable offering. Ending the patrols altogether wasn't an option, given how rapidly enemy ground forces could potentially regroup. Troithe was a planet already exhausted by war, but exhaustion could resemble fortitude in extreme circumstances; Shadow Wing could not afford to become complacent.

A proper casualty report was assembled at last and Soran learned of three more pilots killed in the fighting. Two he had known: Thrail Le-Norra, a serious young recruit from an agriworld who'd joined the wing shortly before Endor, whom Soran had needed to coax into asking advice when required ("Inexperience is not failure," he'd coached the boy while trying not to smile); and Wilhona Breathe, the gentle patriot whose infant nervous system had been afflicted by Separatist toxins in the Clone Wars, guaranteeing her a protracted death by the age of forty (they'd never spoken directly of this—the note was in her medical file and Soran had said nothing, taking quiet pleasure as she bonded with her squadron mates and confessed her secret to one after the next). The third casualty was Bangroft Casas, an ensign from Pandem Nai who had served as Grandmother's shuttle pilot and been promoted to TIE duty after her death; Soran had meant to meet with every new addition to the wing since his departure, but time had slipped away—

Make no excuses. Focus on the question at hand.

What do you do now?

He had no way out of Cerberon without a carrier ship. He'd never intended to risk his people's lives capturing the planet. His mind oscillated between self-recriminations and a need for movement—a need to march out of the communications center, take off in his TIE fighter, and rush to the defense of those pilots still on patrol.

You're falling apart, Soran. This would never have happened before Devon.

"Sir?" a voice asked.

He whirled and heard himself say in a harsh voice that inspired neither calm nor confidence, "What is it?"

He stared across at a young woman with fresh burn scars covering her face and one arm in a makeshift sling. She still wore her pilot's uniform. He dredged a name from the depths of his memory: Lieutenant Falshoi. She didn't flinch at his unearned anger; she looked too weary and broken to flinch.

"Broosh and his people are back from the supply run," she said. "They've got a makeshift galley in one of the conference rooms. You should eat—I can bring you something."

"Of course," he said. "Thank you."

He returned his gaze to the hologram and counted up the dead. He'd lost more people in a day than he had in a month prior to Endor, and the war for Troithe was only beginning. The melody of Gablerone's drinking song came back to him, and Soran imagined the captain looking at him with a mix of disdain and good humor.

You wanted command of the unit, Gablerone's ghost told him. *You sought the responsibility. What are you going to do with it?*

Food did nothing to calm him, but he ate. Reports from the front of scattered anti-air fire and riots on the ground—some pro-Republic, some pro-Imperial, each hard to differentiate from the other—did nothing to quell his desire to join his squadrons, but he listened.

Soran Keize eventually turned from the hologram of Troithe to charts of the Cerberon system. He assigned three flights to search for escape pods from the *Edict* and the *Aerie* and see if they'd made planetfall beyond the reach of Troithe's shields—in the planet's oceans or across the scarred continent. He chose other flights to leave Troithe, to patrol Cerberon and watch for vessels attempting to escape. The moment the New Republic received word of the system's fall, a countdown would begin ending in Shadow Wing's defeat; no one could be allowed to depart Cerberon carrying a plea for reinforcements.

He still didn't know what to do, though.

It wasn't yet midnight when Kandende reported an encrypted Imperial transmission coming in from one of the aging refinery districts at the north end of the continent. One of the TIE patrols had picked it up during its third pass over the region—either the signal had just been activated, or it was weak enough to be nearly undetectable.

"Let's see it," Soran said.

The display table flickered again. Ribbons of light coalesced and sculpted the head of a woman whose dark, youthful face was crowned by elaborate braids and gemstone studs. Her expression conveyed the formal dignity of someone for whom formality and dignity were all she had left. Creases under her eyes suggested the scars of exhaustion. "—someone receiving? Channel nine-two-alpha utilizing military clearance code six-three-delta-delta—"

The woman went on, each syllable enunciated with marked determination. Soran didn't recognize the code and, without the *Aerie* or the *Edict,* had no way to confirm its authority. But he decided the risk of replying was minimal, and he adjusted the table's comm controls. "This is Colonel Soran Keize of the 204th Imperial Fighter Wing," he said. "To whom am I speaking?"

If the woman was surprised, she didn't show it. "This is Acting Governor Fara Yadeez. It is a privilege to speak to you, Colonel."

"Acting governor?" Soran asked. Stress and weariness scraped at his brain as he attempted to recall facts he'd never expected to need. "What's become of Governor Hastemoor?"

"Killed by the rebels in the attack on the capital," Yadeez replied. There was bitterness in her tone but no sorrow. "The cabinet and advisory council were hard hit over the past months. I don't know if you received our dispatches following Endor—"

"Only in part."

"Then suffice it to say that the line of succession ends with me, Colonel. I *am* the rightful ruler of this planet, until such time as I am replaced by sector command or a higher authority."

Soran wondered just how far Fara Yadeez had climbed. But he heard the implied question and said, "I am not here to replace you, Governor. The Empire is grateful for your service in this chaotic time." It was a lie, but the polite sort of lie he imagined Yadeez might appreciate for what it was—or if not, simply accept as flattery. "We have very little information about the loyalist forces on Troithe. Can you tell me your status?"

"I don't have a hidden army waiting to strike, if that's what you're wondering. We've mapped pockets of resistance but haven't opened communications with the guerrilla fighters or the district leaders still loyal. The New Republic has been *aggressive* in containing us. I accept full responsibility for the state of things—" She forced the words out with obvious difficulty; Soran admired the effort. "—and would welcome whatever guidance you can provide."

Yadeez paused. Soran watched her as her expression softened. For an instant the formality and dignity dropped away and were replaced by a profound humanity.

"Thank you for coming," she said. "I'm not deluded enough to think that Cerberon was ever the Empire's top priority and I don't know what made you decide to come now, but—we've been dreaming of this day. Now we have a chance. Now we have hope."

She waited.

We're not here to rescue your world, Soran thought.

He said nothing, and Fara Yadeez transformed back into the acting governor of Troithe.

"Send me your location," Soran said after another moment. "We should meet face-to-face. We have a great deal to discuss."

II

They sat on the lowest level of a three-story speeder garage and repair shop in the decaying Highgarden District. The district was neither tall nor verdant, though Wyl had seen a handful of electro-fenced lots that might have been parkland in a different era. The garage itself had been built for maintenance droids and meter-high Ugnaught workers, and as a result Wyl, Nath, and the two dozen soldiers, pilots, and support crew present had to take care not to smash their heads against the pipes and deactivated light fixtures above their scalps.

The entire building buzzed with each distant explosion—every ion bomb bursting or mortar round hitting home. If there had been rain, Wyl could've pretended he was riding out a storm.

"Fighting's getting worse on the east side," an infantry soldier called out. He was crouched at the metal bars enclosing the garage, peering out with a pair of electrobinoculars. "Lots of blaster flash. Handhelds, no cannons. Probably mostly pistols. Could be close enough for us to join them."

Wyl shifted on the duracrete floor. Nath reached out beside him, gesturing as if ready to hold him back. But it was Sergeant Carver who spoke, rising slowly from where he'd been lying down. "No," the burly man called. "No one's going anywhere."

"What's your thinking?" Nath asked.

The other troops looked between Nath and Carver. Wyl recognized Nath's tone. The older pilot knew exactly what Carver would say and wanted to make sure he had the opportunity to say it.

"First? This is our rendezvous point, and we've got twenty, thirty stragglers who could still show. I want to be here to meet them if they do." Carver scratched at his calves, then swept his gaze across the assembly as if looking for anyone ready to argue. "Second? We walk into that mess, we've got a real good chance of losing. We don't know who's fighting. We don't know the terrain. If the locals are slaughtering one another our odds of doing *good* by getting in the middle are piss poor. Remember Switchmount?"

The man with the electrobinoculars nodded slowly.

"Or Mardona," a woman's muffled voice called. Wyl had trouble locating her until he noticed the bundle of torn blankets covering a lump in the corner.

"Thank you, Twitch," Carver said. "Besides, you know how a good riot goes. Always blows over by morning."

The sergeant grinned broadly like it was a joke. Wyl didn't get it, but Nath snickered beside him and several of the other soldiers began laughing. It was Vitale who called out, "We'll just wait till daylight, then," and the meaning finally struck home.

Wyl still didn't find it funny, yet he made himself smile. He'd heard worse among Riot Squadron and he could've let it pass if it had ended there; instead the joke and the laughter seemed to rouse the troops' spirits and they began speaking to one another about past battles, past incidents where local populations had been caught between the company and the Empire. Past fights where the Sixty-First Mobile Infantry had been left for dead by the Rebel Alliance at large. Zab, the sergeant Wyl had met on the night Yrica Quell had joined them for dinner in the refugee camp, spoke of the company's battle on the planet Sullust. "Lost our troop carrier that time. *Lodestar* was prettier, but nothing beat the—"

This, in turn, set off a round of debate about the merits of the *Lodestar*. Wyl thought of the battleship falling toward Troithe, torn to pieces by the TIEs as it burst against the shield; he thought of the escape pods and wondered whether Quell had been among those lucky enough to depart. He didn't blame the infantry troops for their callousness—they hadn't been aboard the *Lodestar* long, nor had they witnessed its demise.

"Excuse me," he murmured to Nath, and he wobbled as he moved through the garage with his head bent forward, hands touching the ceiling to keep him balanced.

Wyl spent the next hour on the garage's top floor, where the two fighters were stowed between industrial meat processors stinking of ammonia and splashed with green stains. The ceiling was tall enough for Wyl to stand erect, but the scent sufficed to drive the troops below.

He was helping T5 weld a section of the Y-wing's landing gear when heavy footsteps rang out on the grating and he recognized Nath's bellow behind him. "Not in the mood for conversation?" he called.

"Too soon to laugh about the *Lodestar*, is all," Wyl said, and shrugged.

"You don't like the infantry much, do you?"

Wyl turned about and rose, gently leaning against T5 as he did so.

The droid squawked happily, apparently taking the gesture as a sign of affection. "What makes you say that?" Wyl asked. "They seem like good people."

"You think that about Shadow Wing, too," Nath replied, and Wyl would've argued but his mind went to Blink. "It's nothing to be ashamed of, but you'll spend half a day listening to the ground crew talk about their mothers and you won't spare an hour for this sort."

"We don't have much in common—"

"You don't much like fighting face-to-face, and you don't like being reminded that it happens."

Again, Wyl wanted to argue. "Maybe," he said. "If I insulted anyone down there, I'm sorry. I'll swing by after—"

"No one cares, brother. Just figure since we're stuck with them, you may as well be honest with yourself."

Nath inspected the welding job with a skeptical eye, but he didn't object to the results. They worked side by side until the heat of T5's arc welder left them sweating and they climbed onto a ledge overlooking the streets of the Highgarden District. The wind was cold and the sky was dark, save for the eternally bright stars and the burning eye.

"Adan didn't want us fighting them at all," Wyl said.

"No one wanted us fighting them. That's why half the infantry company is sitting on an asteroid somewhere, waiting to spring the trap and cut down the Empire's favorite pilots while they're *not* flying. But it looks like that didn't happen."

Wyl nodded carefully and let his legs dangle into the chill void. In the distance he saw flashes of crimson light. The bombs had stopped falling.

"It's our responsibility now," he said.

"Only if you want it."

Nath was watching him, uncharacteristically somber.

"It's our responsibility," Wyl said. "We brought Shadow Wing here. We clean it up."

They sat in silence a long while. There were no sounds of city life.

No humming speeders or laughter in the distance. Nath finally pushed back away from the edge of the ledge.

"Get some sleep," Nath said. "Infantry commanders are meeting in the morning. I got myself an invite, but I think you should be there."

The solar projectors did not ignite when morning came. Whether intentionally sabotaged or damaged in the fighting, no one knew. Either way, the city remained lit by starlight and the black hole—enough to see by, enough to breakfast by, but an ever-present reminder that the skies belonged to shadows.

More soldiers—no pilots among them—had trickled in during the night but the complement from General Syndulla's battle group still numbered fewer than fifty, mostly combat personnel with a smattering of support units. Perhaps another twenty volunteers had shown up representing local Troithe forces. Wyl wasn't sure how the qualifications for leadership had been determined, but the combined unit's six representatives sat with Wyl and Nath in a cramped, low-ceilinged office on the second floor of the garage. Someone had connected an emergency generator to the computer system, and one cluster of soldiers sat muttering softly and staring at holos of Troithe.

Carver was among the infantry squad commanders, as was the middle-aged woman called Twitch who'd been hidden by blankets the night before. A bone-crested Houk filled most of one corner with his silent bulk. A human named Vifra represented the surviving engineers, and was so encrusted with ash (save for a few stripes down her face where she'd clearly wiped a sanitation cloth) that Wyl wondered if she'd spent the past few hours escaping a bombed building. An elderly human male called Junior stared blankly at the computer images and fiddled with a holographic toy. Finally, a slender female Sullustan announced that she'd been liaising with the local forces and would represent them at the meeting; Wyl hadn't caught her name.

Carver raised his voice when they'd all assembled. "Basically, we're up to our necks again. Captain's floating on an asteroid somewhere wondering why Shadow Wing hasn't shown up, which means officially command of the Sixty-First Mobile Infantry passes to me." Several of the others protested. Carver cut them off. "However, since we're *guests* of the locals and our starfighter corps friends officially outrank us all, I figure we ought to chat as a group."

Wyl and Nath exchanged a glance. If the man didn't realize that Alphabet Squadron was part of New Republic Intelligence and not officially military, now wasn't the time to bring it up.

"If no one objects," Carver continued in a tone that made it clear objections weren't welcome, "let's go around and run down what we've got to work with. After that, we look at the state of the planet. Then we talk options."

They did as Carver suggested, and it became apparent that conditions were worse than Wyl had expected. The company was not only understaffed but also underequipped: Most of the squads had been routed by Shadow Wing bombing runs and fled their positions unprepared. Twitch reported that one of her squad was armed only with a combat knife. Vifra wasn't encouraging about the prospect of contacting other scattered infantry units—any signal likely to get through, she said, was also likely to be traced by the Empire. By comparison, Alphabet's munitions-depleted A-wing and aging Y-wing were shining beacons of New Republic combat-readiness.

They moved on to the tactical situation next. The Sullustan had pieced together reports regarding the riots and enemy bombing campaign. The districts Syndulla's battle group had left untouched en route to the capital were in chaos, with small numbers of heavily armed Imperial guerrillas attempting to lock down territory. Shadow Wing patrol patterns had shifted, prioritizing oversight of territories sympathetic to the New Republic. Bombing runs had decreased in frequency over the past twelve hours, but the 204th remained quick to obliterate whole city blocks whenever an uprising began.

"We have one report of TIEs heading offworld," the Sullustan finished. "We couldn't confirm it. Still, it's possible they're spreading through the whole system."

"Who cares?" Twitch asked. "We're grounded. Unless you're going somewhere?" She jutted a thumb at Wyl and Nath and smiled nastily. Wyl simply shook his head.

"Way I see it," Carver said, "our best bet is to reestablish a base of operations. Probably by taking it from the enemy. We hit hard and fast, we bring up anti-air defenses, and we become a rallying point for the rest of our forces. From there we figure out where the enemy fighters are based—"

A fresh chorus of arguments began. Wyl didn't participate. He felt unqualified to judge the plan—though he recognized its flaws as well as anyone, he had no confidence in any alternatives he could propose. He listened as the others debated the company's anti-air capabilities and traveling speed; he readied himself to speak up and describe Shadow Wing's capabilities, the damage that a proton bomb could do, but no elaboration was required. The commanders were debating how to *survive* the foe long enough to receive reinforcements or assemble a superior plan—not how to destroy it.

Wyl watched their expressions. If he'd known the commanders better he could have dug deeper, drawn out hidden reservations. If they'd been at odds he could have played peacemaker. But his skills were useless here.

"Not to state the obvious," Nath said after Junior began to cough and the others made the error of pausing, "but the governor didn't have the anti-air guns to take out our fighters. We've got a total of six or seven surface-to-air missiles, which won't put a dent in Shadow Wing. Without a way to keep those TIEs grounded, there's no point getting clever."

"Big enough ion pulse could knock them all out of the sky," Vifra muttered.

Carver didn't hide his irritation. "If we had those kinds of warheads, we wouldn't be debating what to do."

The rumble of bombings resumed. Wyl looked at the ash on Vifra's cheeks and tried to imagine how far Shadow Wing would go to destroy what was left of the New Republic military. He thought of walkers toppling skyscrapers and the burning skies of Pandem Nai.

He looked at the map of the city and the planet, staring into the hologram until the light burned his eyes.

"We should retreat," he said. Too soft at first, but when he repeated himself the others looked to him. "We should retreat."

"Nowhere to run, boy," Twitch said. She snickered. No one else did.

"The 204th has destroyed planets before," Wyl said. "So long as we're in the city they won't hesitate to raze whole districts, kill—" He glanced at the Sullustan, ready for her to correct his numbers. "—millions? Billions? The governor was invested in the world in a way Shadow Wing isn't. This conflict will be different.

"We can't afford to fight here. Every minute we stay, every minute they hunt us, we're putting the civilian population in danger."

"Then we disband." Vifra looked among the others, searching for agreement. "If we can't do much damage anyway, we go underground. Become rebels again. Spread out and hold on until something changes."

"What if that *something* is Imperial reinforcements instead of New Republic ones?" Carver asked. "There's a reason we never scatter without a plan to reunite. We wouldn't be in this mess if half the company weren't in space."

The Houk shifted, glowering at Carver and cracking open his massive jaw before being interrupted by Junior. The human had set his toy aside and was manipulating the hologram. "What about the other side?" Junior asked.

The holoimage of the planet spun fast enough to render the image a blur before re-forming on the Scar of Troithe—the lifeless, mined-out continent that had provided the raw materials for the city.

"No civilians to worry about," Carver conceded. "But what are we supposed to do out there?"

The Sullustan squatted beside Junior at the holo display, rapidly adjusting settings and magnifying the desolation. Something blinked among the rocky plains and chasms. "The last of the mining megafacilities was never scrapped. The shaft goes kilometers underground—it was used for core drilling and bulk freighter launches decades back."

"Is it deep enough to take hits from a TIE bomber and stay intact?" Vifra asked.

"Take a look." The Sullustan shrugged.

The arguing resumed as the Sullustan pulled up what outdated technical readouts were available on the public network. Carver suggested that retreat was neither wise nor necessary but couldn't address Wyl's concerns regarding civilian casualties. Twitch appeared disinterested until Junior raised the question of transporting the company across such a long distance, at which point she became viciously opposed to the "death march" she anticipated would destroy her squad. But the mining facility appeared defensible. "Maybe we can get there without anyone noticing," Junior said. "Maybe we can launch attacks from there."

"Hit-and-run strikes from a safe position could open things up," Carver conceded. "Buy time, give the locals room to maneuver. If we give you flyboys a secure fallback position, you think you can take on the foe?"

Wyl looked to Nath, but Nath waited for him. Cautiously, Wyl worked through the logic aloud. "Every time we've been beaten by Shadow Wing, it's because they chose the terms of engagement. They're good at what they do, but they're not invincible. Even so"—he spoke without flinching—"we've only got two starfighters."

Carver sighed loudly. He'd begun to speak when Nath interrupted: "We don't need starfighters. We just need airpower. Maybe it's time to lower our standards."

"Meaning what?" Carver asked.

"Mister Lark here used to fly birds on his homeworld," Nath said. "Big city–world like Troithe, you going to tell me there's nothing that'll lift off?"

The Sullustan and Vifra spoke almost simultaneously. "Civilian airspeeders," the Sullustan said, "or maybe some rusting police cruisers from before the Empire, but—"

"We've got portable cannons, heavy rifles." Vifra screwed up her face. "I can weld and wire. We're still talking about vehicles that can't match TIEs for speed or firepower."

Nath grinned, showing white teeth. "TIEs aren't much match for an X-wing, either. Like Wyl said, we choose the terms of engagement. We make sure we've got a clear line of retreat. We build an air unit of our own, we operate from the megafacility, we make a difference."

"Say we get you a unit." Everyone looked to Carver now. "You can lead it?"

"Hell no." Nath leaned back and kicked out his legs before jutting a thumb at Wyl. "That's what he's here for."

They didn't speak in private again until late afternoon, when Wyl caught up to Nath as the older man readied the Y-wing for flight. "Tell me why," Wyl said.

Nath squatted on the vessel's hull, roughly jiggling T5 back and forth until the droid locked into the socket. He didn't pretend not to understand. "Maybe I didn't want to spend the day looking over personnel reports, deciding who among the ground-pounders is qualified to fly."

"You'd be better at it than me." Wyl craned his neck, trying to make out Nath's expression in the dim light. "I've handled field command before, when I had to. You've run a proper squadron. And you know these people better than I do; they love you. They'll be glad to follow you."

"They do love me," Nath said, "because I've put in more hours than you have. But they respect you already—not just because we've saved their butts, but because you're 'the Polynean.' Turns out Meteor Squadron's been sharing your legend."

Wyl laughed. Nath didn't. The Y-wing emitted a metallic grinding noise and began to hum. "I'd believe that *you've* been sharing my legend. Again, the question is *why*?"

"Put it this way: I don't *want* command of these people. If you don't take it, no one does."

Wyl tried to read the man. He couldn't see the reasoning but he recognized the inflexibility. "All right," he said. Whatever the full truth was, Nath wasn't wrong. "That mean you're taking my orders, too?"

"That's the plan." In an instant the charming pirate, the con man, returned. "I'll see you in a while, with ships in tow. Unless Shadow Wing finds me first."

III

Quell woke unable to breathe or feel her limbs. There was pressure on her chest and pressure on her back, and her attempts to escape whatever squeezed her were rebuked with sharp pain down her spine. She realized she was lying facedown and centimeter by centimeter she rose, forcing bruised fingers—she could see her hands, if not fully sense them—against unstable metal paneling until the pressure alleviated and she could suck in lungfuls of thin air.

When oxygen had returned to her brain, she saw that she was still on the bridge of the freighter. The pilot's seat had uprooted from the deck and lodged her body between itself and the main console—perhaps a stroke of luck, since the transparent metal of the viewport had torn open in three places, leaving jagged halos that could have easily impaled a body. Sand the color of blood had poured inside through the gaps, and a cold, high-pitched wind whistled and fondled Quell's torso and head.

The breeze alerted her to a sore spot on her temple where her hair felt glued in place. She didn't need to touch her face to know that the locks were matted and sticky with gore. Her memory-chip necklace, meanwhile, had cut into her chest and left a stinging gash.

She was alive. This was the most surprising of her findings.

She attempted to pull away from seat and console, discovered she was still constrained by the safety harness, and spent several minutes disentangling herself after concluding that the automatic release didn't function. The process dizzied her but allowed her to confirm that all of her limbs were operative and her blood loss was under control. If she had broken bones—and she suspected she did, given she broke more easily than she bruised—they were bones that weren't supporting anything vital: Fractures in ribs or fingers. Maybe a shoulder.

She hoped not a shoulder this time.

She eased out of the cockpit and into the access corridor. The entire vessel was canted ten degrees or more, which forced her to find footholds for every step. She was intent enough on maintaining her balance and fighting down bile that she was two meters along the hallway before she realized the entire port side of the ship was gone—bulkheads and compartments torn away, interior exposed to the same sand and darkness as the cockpit.

She considered the implications—*irreparable damage to the freighter,* to start with—and filed the facts away.

Her next stop was the starboard cabin where she'd left Adan and IT-O. She might have called out if she'd been feeling up to speech, but her jaw ached and the bile was still attempting to rise. With no working lighting and no starlight penetrating the ship's depths, she had to feel her way around the last bend and wait for her eyes to adjust upon reaching the room.

A jumble of geometric lines resolved into ruins. The bunks had toppled and a mass of tubing had ripped free from the wall, burying most of the floor. Quell spotted Caern Adan's hand and traced it to his body. The intelligence officer's form was covered by one of the bunks but appeared intact. Quell couldn't tell if he was breathing; she knelt to rest as much as to take a pulse.

Adan's hand was warm. Quell felt the rhythm of his heartbeat.

You could leave him.

The thought surprised her, but she followed its course. He had betrayed her. Exposed her crimes to her squadron. Ensured she would have no future in the New Republic or anywhere else. She'd chosen to let him live when she'd rescued him from his captors, but now?

Now she had a second chance.

She groaned in misery as she raised the bunk, wedging her knee to prop it in position and gripping Adan under his shoulders. She pulled, knowing she was liable to exacerbate any injuries he might have; but leaving him buried couldn't be any better. She rested and caught her breath once she'd freed him, then felt the body sliding on the canted floor and heard creaking metal. *All the way, then,* she thought, and dragged him out into the access corridor and onto the red sand.

The wreckage of the freighter provided shelter against the wind; a strong breeze raised plumes that crossed the arid plane like phantoms. The bright starlight was filtered through the clouds of the debris field, but the fiery iris of Cerberon's eye crested the horizon like an obscene rainbow, fierce enough to see by. Past the crater wall created by the ship's crash the red desert appeared endless, rolling into low dunes no taller than Quell's knees. It was as if a sea of blood had been locked in stasis, its waves paralyzed and left to dry until all that was water was now dust.

Quell sat beside Adan and realized she was breathing heavily from the effort of moving him. She reassessed her condition: Her garments were torn, and cuts and abrasions covered the backs of her hands. She'd instinctively stretched one leg out and tucked the other beneath her, contorting her body to reduce the worst of the pain in her spine.

She was gathering the strength to return to the ship when Adan shifted beside her. He lay on his back and rolled onto a shoulder before dropping again.

"Where?" he breathed.

"We're still in the debris field," Quell said. She coughed upon finishing the sentence, smelled a foulness in her breath, and spat a few grains of sand. "It was land here or nowhere."

Adan squeezed his eyes shut, reopened them, and carefully turned his head. "Ito?"

Quell was surprised to realize how little she'd thought about the droid since waking. "I don't know," she said.

She mentally retraced her path through the ship. With most of the freighter gone there weren't many places for the droid to hide. She searched memories of the rubble for the black sphere or the light of the droid's photoreceptor. She found nothing.

"The ship came apart on descent," Quell added. She looked to the horizon again. "I don't think Ito is with us."

Adan shuffled backward, propping himself on his elbows and then his palms. "We need to find it," he snapped, though his voice was too weak to carry. "Figure out where Ito's gone immediately!"

She recognized the tone and flinched. She was in Traitor's Remorse again; aboard the *Buried Treasure* again; in the ready room of the *Lodestar* being put down by a man who saw every failure as rebellion.

The Adan whose company she'd grown fond of—the man she'd shared meals with on Troithe, worked with to sway the general, and laughed with on cold mornings while her squadron was flying—was suddenly gone.

Quell stared into white eyes in a dark face.

"Not now," she said, but she kept her voice soft and lowered her gaze to the sand. "We're not in any condition to go out there."

Adan's breath came quickly as the strain of staying upright appeared to settle into his bones. "I won't abandon my droid."

"If the droid is offline, leaving it alone a few hours more won't make any difference." She rose onto her knees, squatting beside Adan. "We should salvage anything we can use to survive—food, water, maybe a tarp, anything resembling a medkit—then make camp and see to our injuries. There'll be time to look for the torture unit tomorrow."

There was no force in her words. She doubted she had the strength for defiance. Yet she saw the panic burn off Adan's face and be replaced by something colder and calmer and just as bitter.

"Tomorrow," he agreed.

"I like Ito, too," she murmured as she rose to her feet.

They spent the next hour searching the wreckage in silence. Quell moved more swiftly than Adan but she noticed him doing what he was able—albeit usually from a seated position. They found little worth having, with Quell's prize being a mini vaporator—enough to supply water for one person each day in an ideal planetary atmosphere (less if Quell's luck held steady). The crushed but in-the-wrapper mealpacks Adan located in the cockpit would provide a solid week of sustenance if rationed carefully, and would potentially offer additional hydration. The arsenal Quell had taken from the *Lodestar* had disappeared; she suspected the hole in the cockpit viewport might be connected.

They made camp around the side of the ship, as far from the wind as they could get, and hung sheets to form a thin and ineffective tent. They lay on a tarp beside each other, close enough to share body heat but turned so that Adan stared at the freighter's broken hull and Quell looked at rippling fabric. She was tired but she doubted she could sleep.

"What happened to Kairos?" Adan asked in barely more than a whisper.

You asked that already, she wanted to say. *That was the first thing you asked when I saved your life.*

"She was with the medics. She's alive now. Unless something happened."

Unless Shadow Wing had obliterated her. Unless Quell's efforts to give her squadron a chance had failed.

She began to think about what might have occurred after Soran Keize had savaged her freighter and flown on to the battle over Troithe. But wondering whether Lark and Tensent and Chadic were still breathing wouldn't help her now. Speculating whether the *Lodestar* was intact wouldn't help, either.

"Yrica," Adan said.

She grunted in acknowledgment, then thought to say: "What?"

"The mission was yours. If anything happens to her—if anything happens to Kairos—I will hold you responsible."

Adan said nothing after that, and Quell shifted, digging her head into the sand through the tarp.

She wasn't concerned. What more could Adan do to her?

CHAPTER 15

FANTASIES OF GRANDER DAYS

I

In the shrouded lands between sleep and waking, Chass na Chadic found she was young again. The faraway singing that reached her ears was the singing she'd heard every day since her eighth birthday, when her mother had insisted they pack their few belongings and trek to the Benevolence Tower on the outskirts of New Vertica in the sprawling city of Nar Shaddaa.

The tower was different from anywhere they'd lived before, and what Chass remembered most about Benevolence was the *whiteness*—illumination so foreign to the smog-and-neon streets, so pervasive that her eyes hurt at the end of the day. Where windows had once looked into gutters, the inhabitants had bolted ivory cloth or, in a few cases, grown trellises of thick green vines. This was so no one could look in, Chass was told by her mother—so no one could spy on them and learn the secrets of the Inheritors of the Crystal. It had taken Chass two years to realize it was really so no one could look out.

But during her early days in Benevolence, before she'd grasped that her mother had dragged her into a cult amassing weapons and followers for a spice-crazed lunatic—a man who'd decided a charismatic smile and a replica kyber crystal were the basis for a religion—Chass had felt a peace she'd rarely experienced since. She'd been treated as equal to the adults (which seemed exploitative now, but at the time had felt like a privilege), and had cooked meals and repaired malfunctioning septic tanks and polished the crystal and cataloged weapons with the rest of them. When her mother spent increasing time with the Prophet, she ignored it because, after all, what did she need a mother for? They were all family among the Inheritors.

She'd truly believed that. And she'd excused the undercurrent of dread, the constant fear of failure (fear of the *consequences* of failure), as something that was part of all families. Part of what it meant to love a community and feel responsible for its fate.

Eventually she'd learned better.

Nonetheless, while Chass had lived in harsher places before and after Benevolence, she remembered how unbearably alone she'd felt in the days after fleeing. How it felt to be shunned as an unbeliever, disconnected from the cosmic Force. She'd told herself that she no longer accepted the Prophet's teachings, but she *had* believed, in her bones.

When Chass woke after failing to repair her B-wing and nearly suffocating in the void of space, she heard singing—and for a moment she believed again. It felt glorious.

The singing was real. She jerked upright and found herself wrapped in a musty linen cargo pad on the floor of a starship's gun well. The cannon itself was gone, and most of the viewport was covered in colorful drapery and cloth scrolls proclaiming THE FORCE IS LIFE and FELLOWSHIP IS CREATION. Her mouth was dry and her lips felt tacky but she was surprisingly alert for someone who should've been dead.

The singing—chanting, really—was tinny and garbled. Chass unrolled the cargo pad, wobbled to her feet, and followed the sound down a short hallway. Through an open hatch, she spied a circular command center decorated in the same style as the turret and occupied by three crew members gathered around a hologram.

The chanting ended. The holo showed a middle-aged humanoid woman whose skin was covered in colorful blotches of fungal growth—dozens of tiny mushrooms fruiting from shoulder and cheek and ear like patches on a threadbare uniform. Chass was seized by competing urges to look away in disgust and to stare in awe. There was something inherently compelling, if not commanding, about the woman's serene and tolerant expression. Something familiar, as well, and it was when the woman began speaking that Chass recalled where she'd seen her before.

"For this lesson, we will speak of fellowship and technology. You may have asked yourself, *Why do the Children of the Empty Sun reject droids? I'd much rather have a machine haul water or repair a comm system than do it myself . . .*"

Chass swore softly. The cultists in the Troithe refugee camp had stared at holos for hours on end, too.

"Our guest is awake, eh?" one of the crew called, and paused the recording. He, too, was familiar—the burn scars across his cheeks and scalp and the colorful swatches of his outfit brought her back to a hazy night at Winker's. It was the man who had saved her from the Vurk and tried to recruit her.

"Where am I?" Chass snarled. She reached for her sidearm and found nothing on her hip.

"We call this vessel *Gruyver's Skiff,* because I'm Gruyver and this is my solar skiff. She—*it* used to have another name, before I walked the path, but what good is treating machines like people if it leads to treating people like machines?" He rose from his seat, saw Chass tense, and settled again. "We found you floating in space. You're lucky we got there when we did."

"You *found* me?" Competing questions fought through Chass's brain, and she asked the one whose answer would be easiest to bear. "You mean you *tracked* me. You been following me since Winker's?"

"There's little coincidence in a universe directed by the Force," Gruyver said. "But that's an awfully suspicious leap."

You're not denying it, Chass thought. She swore again and marched into the room, shouldering a white-furred woman with horns and fangs away from the comscan terminal. The readouts showed little except the ship's rapid approach toward Catadra. "What happened with the battle? The carrier, the Star Destroyer—"

"No long-range scans on a solar skiff," the furry woman sneered in a nearly impenetrable accent.

"Nor lightspeed, nor guns, nor hypermatter reactor," Gruyver added, "which is probably why the TIEs haven't stopped us. I'm sorry, lass, but by all accounts the New Republic's lost. We heard that battle cruiser of yours went down over Troithe, and there's been only Imperial transmissions since then."

Anger flashed through her. She thought about how her comrades might have died—swift exposure to vacuum, annihilation by particle bolts, incineration on reentry—then reminded herself: *Put them away like Hound Squadron. Like the Cavern Angels. None of this is new to you.*

"How long was I out?" Chass asked.

"Been perhaps a day since the battle. We've been out salvaging scrap. Now we're heading home."

"You're lying," she said. Nothing he said was implausible—it wasn't as if Shadow Wing hadn't beaten the New Republic before—but the reply ripped through her anyway. "Where's my ship? Where's my B-wing?"

If she could drain the skiff's fuel supply she could head out, hit Shadow Wing with the advantage of surprise. Bring down the cruiser-carrier, get revenge for her squadron, and set everything right.

"Too big for the skiff to haul," Gruyver said, and looked almost sincere in his sympathy. "I am sorry."

Chass parted her lips but found nothing to say.

The third crew member, who hadn't spoken prior, rotated its jelly-stalk of a head and squealed something. Gruyver nodded and declared, "Good—radio the planet and tell them to prepare housing for another guest."

Chass was barely listening. The sound of the chanting lingered in her ears and she went from thoughts of revenge to thoughts of music, and the realization that if her ship was lost, so was the collection she'd accumulated. Rare songs. Banned songs. The work of dead singers and dead civilizations. Some of the recordings, she suspected, were unique in the galaxy . . .

They were gone like Wyl and Nath and Quell.

"We'll get you to Catadra," Gruyver said. "Clean you up, feed you. Figure out where to go from there, eh?"

"Am I a prisoner?" Chass asked, her voice dull and distant. "Hostage of the cult?"

"You're whatever you want to be, and whatever the Force desires," Gruyver said, which was a clear enough answer to Chass.

For a zealot, the Force desired whatever the believer wanted.

She'd flown to Catadra on over twenty bombing runs, but the solar skiff was slower than an assault fighter and she watched as the band of temples and palaces and bridges and stairways around the mountains came into sight. Gruyver brought her tea and spoke platitudes as they flew, and Chass considered grappling with him and trying to take control of the ship. She was outnumbered, though, and she saw no weapons—not a blaster, not a knife, not even a hydrospanner or a wrench heavy enough to brain a man.

That meant she was dealing with low-level cultists. She didn't know much about the Children of the Empty Sun, but all cults were alike: They preached peace and armed their leaders well.

Midway through their descent, the jelly-stalk crew member squeaked a warning; an instant later the skiff lurched and made a sound like lightning striking a dead tree. Chass felt herself float for a fraction of a second before she dropped hard onto her knees and caught a glimpse of emerald outside the viewport.

Then smoke filled her vision and Gruyver shouted, "Abandon ship!"

The *Gruyver's Skiff* was going down. Chass wasn't about to grieve, and she might've laughed at the idea of dying so soon after her rescue if she hadn't started choking. One of the cultists—the furry one, by the feel of the hand on Chass's neck—pushed her forward and through a hatch barely large enough for one body. Yet the woman wriggled into the compartment alongside her, and Chass breathed in ashes and the odor of unclean hair.

"Go! Stupid thing! Go!" the woman cried, pounding her palm against the walls of the narrow compartment.

The skiff lurched again and Chass wrenched her body, positioning herself so she could see through the hand's-width viewport centimeters from her nose. The universe was spinning and the compartment was tumbling and she understood that she was in an escape pod, ejected from its parent vessel and falling toward Catadra. She caught a glimpse above of a single TIE racing away from a burning, plummeting ovoid with metallic solar sails painted in cacophonous hues.

Her hands slid across the pod's instrumentation. Her companion yelped as Chass dug her elbow into its fur. Chass ignored the woman and found a primitive control yoke—the pod lacked a true engine but it had maneuvering thrusters, and by shifting her weight and wrenching at the yoke she found she could adjust her angle of descent. The light of the solar projectors painted a clear image of the land below— the ancient stone buildings built into the mountainside and the dark vegetation on the far slopes.

It looks different when you're not being shot at, she thought.

She resolved to choose a landing site and deliver the escape pod like a bomb. She'd bombed Catadra before. She knew how to hit a target.

She spotted a crater where a turbolaser emplacement had formerly stood between two granite towers. "Hit *you* once already," she muttered, and felt her skin tingle as the pod's electromagnetic brakes kicked in. She tuned out the chanted prayers of her companion and braced for impact.

———

Chass survived the fall. Her companion didn't. After the crash the woman with fur and fangs lay beneath Chass with her head unnaturally twisted. The body was still warm, and close enough that Chass would've felt a heartbeat if she'd survived.

Chass very nearly felt pity. She very nearly whispered a prayer of the Inheritors of the Crystal, to commend the dead woman to the Force. Instead she climbed out of the pod as swiftly as she was able and studied the city around her.

The TIE flitted across the Catadran sky for nearly an hour, occasionally dipping low enough to spew emerald fire at a structure and obliterate it as thoroughly (if not as rapidly) as any proton bomb could. Chass kept watch as she trekked through the streets, allowing the current of the crowds to determine her direction. Packed shoulder-to-shoulder with fleeing locals from a hundred species, she managed to blend despite her New Republic flight suit. No one noticed in all the chaos.

She was confident the TIE was targeting communications stations and landing pads—cutting off Catadra from the rest of the Cerberon system and the rest of the galaxy. On foot, unarmed, and ignorant of the planet, there wasn't anything Chass could do to interfere. But she still had a working brain, and she figured that if Shadow Wing had only sent a single TIE it meant the Empire's grip on Cerberon wasn't secure. It meant the enemy was afraid of a counterattack, or of anyone fleeing with a call for New Republic reinforcements. If nothing else, Chass thought, it was invigorating to smell fear.

She needed a ship. Whatever she planned to do next, she'd need a ship for it.

As she passed beneath a line of battlements, she heard shouting above. Stained and yellowing stormtrooper helmets rested in the gaps of the crenellations—trophies or warnings or both from the days after the Empire had fled. Catadrans grabbed the helmets up by the armful.

Not a forgiving people, but they're not stupid. Not the display you want if the Empire's coming back.

Assuming she found a ship, could she drive Shadow Wing off single-handedly or get a message to General Syndulla? The old instincts returned to her—the anticipation of dying gloriously to defeat an enemy who'd devastated her squadron, screaming a song as she flew into the heart of a carrier—but the taste was sour. It was Alphabet that had lured Shadow Wing to Cerberon in the first place, at the behest of a genocidal traitor named Yrica Quell; and the war was too close to its end for a glorious sacrifice to mean anything.

She'd probably survive anyway, and then she'd be in the same predicament as always.

Half a dozen screaming humans leapt across a gap in a broken bridge ahead of her, calling out something about hidden heretics. Chass wondered if there was anywhere she could get a drink and waited for the current of the crowd to bring her to a cantina.

By midnight she'd decided, after her third bottle, not to drink after all. She wasn't an addict, she told herself—she'd gotten in the habit of filling her downtime with *diversions*, but she didn't need a diversion tonight.

She found another customer at the cantina willing to trade a drab olive shirt and engineer's trousers for her flight suit, and she began asking questions about Catadra's local power players. Of the half dozen cults to come to sudden prominence in the months since Endor, the Children of the Empty Sun was the largest. "Mostly," a long-beaked Ishi Tib told her, "because they distribute food through the settlements, assign refugees to wrecked old palaces for housing—I wouldn't trust them, but if someone's going to govern? Better the Children than the Devourers of All Light or one of the other freak shows."

Chass nodded and tried to concentrate on the words instead of her memory of the last Ishi Tib she'd known. She really had liked Sata Neek.

Put him away like Hound Squadron.

When she left the cantina, she was halfway to forming a plan. Sometime after her first bottle she'd remembered what Gruyver had said aboard the skiff: *Tell them to prepare housing for another guest.* It wasn't proof that the Children had taken other New Republic prisoners, but it was a possibility and a second set of hands would be one more set to help strangle the Imps. So Chass strolled through the crowds (thinner in the early-morning darkness, camped around portable heaters and vaporators in the streets) until she reached the white-and-azure-tiled palace the Ishi Tib had told her about.

A man in sallow robes stood under a four-meter archway inlaid with flying-serpent mosaics. Chass noted the rifle-shaped bulge under the robes without surprise.

"No more food tonight," the man said. "Come back in the morning."

"Don't need food," Chass said. "My name's Maya Hallik. I'm spiritu- ally lost. Really at loose ends right now. Figured I'd find guidance here, so I want to join up."

She might've been more convincing if she'd bothered to work on her story, but she'd never met a cult keen on turning recruits away. She doubted the Children of the Empty Sun would be any different from the mix of con artists and fanatics and pathetic seekers she'd met so many times before.

She swallowed her distaste and smiled brightly, showing her teeth.

II

Yrica Quell couldn't remember dreaming, but she rose in the red des- ert more unsettled than when she'd fallen asleep. She recalled waking periodically to the sensation of tremors—quakes she could only feel with her cheek pressed against the tarp. Occasionally she'd also half- consciously repositioned herself to alleviate pain in her spine. Other- wise, her rest had gone undisturbed.

"This shouldn't be here," she said—to herself as much as to Adan—as she dripped water from the portable vaporator into their canteen. They breakfasted together on a single ration bar Quell had broken in half.

"What shouldn't?" Adan asked. He sat on the tarp with his back against the ship. They'd taken down their makeshift tent; the wind seemed quiescent in the morning dark, as if intimidated by the rising eye of the black hole.

"The water. The atmosphere shouldn't have so much moisture. There shouldn't be an atmosphere this dense at all on a planetoid so small."

Adan stared across at her. She noticed that he'd barely eaten from his portion.

"Does that mean anything?" he asked. "Aside from proving that the universe is full of wonder?"

There was no humor in his voice. Quell didn't laugh.

"No," she said, and took a swig from the canteen.

Quell ate her tasteless, stale meal with the mechanical discipline of a pilot taught never to allow her feelings to interfere with nourishment. Adan took imperceptibly small bites, but in the end his half bar was gone, too. Quell briefly wondered if he'd tucked away the remainder but decided it was his meal; he could eat it when he wanted.

After breakfast they performed another cursory search of the wreckage (finding nothing new) before Quell attempted to reconstruct the final flight and disintegration of the freighter, drawing trajectories in the dust to estimate where the other half of the ship had fallen. She and Adan agreed without discussion—without actual *agreement*—to go look for whatever might have survived. Quell had little hope that the droid was still intact, but perhaps there would be something more: the ship's long-range comm unit, or a portable scanner they could use to locate the energy readings that had led them to the planetoid in the first place.

They didn't have packs or satchels. That was fine, Quell thought, because there wasn't enough of anything to pack.

The journey through the desert was slow going. Although the hard-packed sand offered a measure of traction and the dunes were low and gentle, their injuries made each step effortful. Adan fared worse than Quell, and while they started side by side she left him a meter behind, then ten, then twenty as the morning wore on. When he diminished to a dark silhouette on the horizon she was tempted to increase her pace; she envisioned Adan's plodding steps taking him deeper into the dunes until he was buried neck-deep, until the wind rose and the sand flayed him alive.

The gruesomeness of the image surprised Quell. Morbid fantasies had never been her vice.

She waited for Adan awhile. Then she turned and crossed the distance to him. "You need to rest?" she asked, but he shook his head and they continued together across the endless plain of red.

They spotted the corpse from afar but until they were closer they didn't recognize it for what it was: the body of an Imperial stormtrooper swaddled in dust. Patches of white plastoid armor uncovered by sand stood out like bone.

"Dead," Yrica Quell said—the first word either she or Adan had spoken for nearly an hour. She nudged the corpse with a boot and sent an avalanche of sand tumbling from its back. A plume of finer dust rose like smoke from the scorched hole between the trooper's shoulders.

"For how long?" Adan asked.

Quell shrugged. "You tell me." She waited for Adan to answer, but he stared in confusion and she elaborated: "The place we found you. The Imperial hideout on Narthex. The unit there had charts of the debris field, like they'd been here before."

"This is one of them?" Adan asked. Before Quell could reply he shook his head. "No. It's possible but I don't remember much. If they were out here it was without me, and most likely before I was kidnapped."

Quell nodded and stepped around the body. She scanned the sand for a rifle or anything else useful the dead man might have carried. There was nothing.

"What was here for them?" Adan asked.

Irritation flared inside her. "Why would I know more than you?"

"You might have seen something during the approach," Adan said. "During landing."

The irritation remained, though Quell could admit that Adan's reasoning was sound. "Some sort of energy reading coming from the planet. I didn't have a chance to examine it. I doubt the ship's sensors could have given us much more anyway."

"An energy reading," Adan repeated. He knelt, but he was more than a meter from the body—too far to examine it with any real scrutiny. "Assume they were here for the source, then. To retrieve it? To plant it?"

"How about this?" Quell countered. "Who died, and how?"

Were there other bodies to be found? Would they all be shot in the back?

Maybe the stormtrooper refused to go along with a mission he couldn't abide.

She started to laugh before the ground began to quiver. The tremors weren't enough to unbalance her but they were impossible not to notice. Then after several seconds the quivering ended with a jolt that sent the sandy caps of dunes rippling down slopes.

Quell looked to Adan. He had his hand pressed to the ground for support, but now he rose again.

They resumed their walk.

Quell found her mind drifting as if she were on the verge of sleep—as if she were half dreaming, with logical throughways replaced by a labyrinth of symbols and preoccupations. She trudged through the desert and thought about Shadow Wing and what had gone wrong with the trap she had set to lure the unit to asteroid CER952B. She thought about Major Soran Keize, and fought to remember whether his promise to leave the 204th had been a figment—whether *her* departure was a figment, and she had come to Cerberon with her Imperial comrades and captured the New Republic Intelligence officer Caern Adan. She thought about Chass na Chadic and Wyl Lark and Nath Tensent and imagined them fighting Shadow Wing, being picked off one by one.

Every time they'd fought Shadow Wing without her, they'd lost. Why would now be any different?

The eye of Cerberon was high in the sky when it occurred to her to worry about her own mental state. Maybe it was her injuries—concussion or blood loss or both—that disoriented her. Maybe it was the planetoid's atmosphere—she didn't know how safe it was to breathe.

She tried to focus on surviving after that. Whatever was going on, she had enough problems without worrying about matters far outside her control.

They encountered fragments of the freighter buried in the sand—broken sections of bulkheads or scorched hull plating; once, a landing strut standing erect atop a dune like a flagpole—but nothing intact. Nothing salvageable. There was no sign of the interrogation droid.

Quell and Adan still did not speak, but Quell stayed nearer to Adan than she had for most of the morning and recognized that he was slowing. She heard him begin gasping with every step and suppressed her annoyance. *He's not doing it to irk you,* she told herself, though she wasn't totally convinced.

They found a half-cylinder wall from the freighter's access corridor and rested in its arc, protected from the wind. They shared another ration bar and what water the vaporator produced. Afterward, Quell was ready to continue the hike.

Adan's head lolled against the metal plating, his eyes half closed. If he hadn't been breathing Quell would have thought him dead.

"Adan," she said.

The man did not respond.

"Caern," she said.

He groaned and lifted his eyelids, squinting at Quell. "What is it?"

You're hurt. Maybe you're dying. We need to assess your wounds and discuss what to do if you can't keep walking. Whether I should leave you behind.

"You're slowing down."

Adan grunted and closed his eyes again.

He would slip away if she didn't act.

Is that what you want?

"Why are you so worried for Kairos?" she asked.

It wasn't the question she'd planned, but it had seemed safe in the moment. Unlikely to draw Adan's ire.

"Why does it matter?" he said.

Quell shrugged. The motion hurt dully. "Tell me or don't tell me." She squatted in the sand and shifted on her heels, preparing to rise.

Before she could stand, Adan said "Wait," and she lowered herself again.

She waited a long time for him to speak.

This is the story he told.

"We met in the camp," Adan said, and though Quell didn't ask what *the camp* was she thought first of Traitor's Remorse and then, reluctantly, of the holding facilities and labor outposts she'd often seen listed on Imperial military star charts. She thought of the rebel recruiting videos she'd watched at the age of sixteen—grainy holo-footage of electrified fences and emaciated alien bodies.

"I'd been held for maybe three months. Just long enough for me to realize that I was going to be there a lot longer; that my employers had given up on me or been shut down altogether; that my captors had gone from imprisoning me because I was suspicious to being suspicious because I was imprisoned. I decided my best hope was to wait for a new warden to arrive and audit the entire facility. Maybe some freshly appointed Imperial overseer wouldn't lose face for tossing me back to the streets of Koru Neimoidia.

"It wasn't a stupid hope. Thinking I could last the five, ten years it might take before a change in management, though? *That* was stupid."

Adan had been a financial journalist in his former life, he told Quell. It was the first time he'd told her anything about his existence before the Rebel Alliance. He'd been detained after publishing a story about droid production forecasts on Kol Huro, though he still didn't know why.

"They asked about the article. They asked about a lot of things I'd written."

But it was after that third month that he'd been transferred from the outer sections of the camp to the inner compound. He'd gone from a bunk room shared with five other prisoners to a private, windowless cell barely wide enough to sit with legs outstretched. He'd lacked any way to tell time—his meals came inconsistently and the compound lights were kept at the same dim levels at all hours. With his antenna-stalks fully extended he could hear voices from the cells above and below his own, but fear prevented him from attempting to make contact.

"I thought they'd amputate them if they caught me," Adan said, gingerly touching his scalp where the stalks were retracted. "If they knew I was *listening*. So I listened less and less, even though it was my only way of connecting."

He only left his cell for two reasons. Sometimes—it might have been once a week, but it felt random—a stormtrooper would escort him to the duracrete pit in the complex center for exercise. The pit was five meters deep and it was almost always cold, but it was broad enough to let a person pace and even run for as long as the troopers permitted. "You could see the sky, too," Adan said. "Sometimes I just sat and watched the sky."

The other reason he left his cell was for interrogation. "Making us walk to the droid instead of the droid coming to us—that was part of the process. That was to intimidate us." He hadn't seen a living interrogator since being moved into the compound; more evidence that he no longer mattered.

"But sometimes, when we were on our way or coming back to the droid? That's when we saw someone else in passing, coming back or going to their own session. We'd cross paths. We'd walk within centimeters of another person—someone who wasn't locked in a stormtrooper's helmet.

"There were three of us whose schedules matched up. I don't know how many in the camp, but there were three of us who saw one another walking to interrogation.

"That's how I met Kairos."

The moments of connection gave Adan no hope, but they gave him something to look forward to. Something to help chart the passage of time. Every time he saw Kairos he saw how she'd changed, what she'd suffered, and he knew that she saw the same in him. Quell strained to understand what that *meant*—what Adan had seen in the strange, silent woman; whether she'd been unmasked; *how* she had changed—but Adan said nothing more and Quell felt asking would have been obscene.

Yet Adan spoke freely of the last member of their trio. "Ver Iflan. You could see the defiance every time." The way he spoke made it seem to Quell like he was lying. "He was the one who figured out how to communicate—he'd known another man of my species, understood what we could sense, and he spoke to me from his cell. I don't know how many months after they put me in the compound, but I started to listen again.

"Ver Iflan made a plan. He spoke to me even though I could never speak to him. He started the work and he didn't get to see the end, but we did—I did, and *she* did."

Adan did not speak again for a long while. Quell finally asked, "How did you escape?"

Adan groaned softly, as if he were too weak to shrug and the sound was all he could offer. "How do you think?" he said next. "We made a new friend. Ver Iflan was gone, but he worked miracles with machines. We became three again."

"The interrogation droid?"

"Reprogrammed. Yes. Caern, Kairos, and Ito."

Quell said nothing. There was no comfort she could offer. There was no question she believed he would answer.

"You asked about Kairos," Adan eventually said, and sat up rapidly for a man in his condition. He opened his eyes and looked to Quell.

"What matters is that she saw me and I saw her. We three were bound together. Now I may be the last of us alive."

"You don't know that," she said.

"I know it's possible," he said. "So do you."

She stood and offered him a hand. He looked at her knuckles, covered in dried blood, with disdain, but pulled himself up by her forearm anyway.

The eye of Cerberon was setting behind them when the ground began to slope downward and red cliffs rose in the distance. They encountered fragments of the freighter less often, but still spotted the occasional reflection off a hull plate or the serpent's spine of a cable rising from sand.

Quell was considering how to proceed if they reached the edge of the wreckage—whether to return to the ship or continue on into the unknown—when the quaking returned. This time the tremors were enough to kick her forward; she doubled over and swept her fingers through the sand before regaining balance. Adan remained standing, though she heard his breathing become rapid and shallow.

Instead of calming, the tremors intensified. Quell grasped Adan by the forearm, as much for her sake as his, and they stumbled headlong. They ran to keep from falling on the downward slope, and a wind rose as the quake propelled them. A few seconds later a *crack* entirely unlike thunder resonated through the valley and darkness stained the sand. Quell feared a chasm was forming until the darkness leapt up in thick, jagged ridges. Black stones tore from the ground like the disease-racked bones of the planetoid.

The megalithic boulders were tall as Adan, and they plagued the valley at random—few were clustered close together, but Quell pulled Adan along as though the rocks were liable to impale them both. Fear incited her, and after the quaking began to subside it was only Adan's weakness that dragged her to a halt. They both fell to the ground, and Quell felt her knees scraped raw by the sand.

The last tremors died away. Quell stared at the ground, trying to steady her breathing.

"Are you all right?" Adan asked, soft and anxious.

"I'm fine," she said.

When she looked up, she saw he hadn't been talking to her.

A dozen paces away floated a metal sphere festooned with sensors and surgical manipulators. Gouges marred its black paint and several of its indicators were dimly lit, as if the interior bulbs were broken; but the red glow of its photoreceptor was undiminished. Its underside was caked in sand, and it hummed low enough that Quell felt her teeth buzz.

"I am functional," IT-O said. Its servos whirred and Quell realized its axis was slightly atilt. "I have been unable to access my full diagnostics suite, but my programs and memory are within acceptable parameters for emergency operations."

Adan smiled tightly and bowed his head, swaying slightly as he stood. Quell brushed herself off, rose, and asked, "Where have you been? Did you see anything?"

"I was pulled into the engine compartment when the hull was breached. I fell to ground near the cliffs north of here and only reestablished full movement a short time ago." The droid paused. "While I charged my repulsors I had time to analyze the tremors along with the readings we took during our approach."

Adan massaged his hip but didn't look away from the droid. "Good news, I assume?"

"For someone, no doubt," the droid agreed. "Although the higher math eludes me, I believe this planetoid's orbit was recently disrupted. It is moving rapidly toward the black hole at the center of the system."

The wind rose up again. Quell tasted dust between her teeth. She was tempted to spit it out but choked down the grit instead; she didn't have water to waste. "How long do we have?" she asked.

"I'm not certain," the droid said. "But the planetoid is not massive. It will disintegrate long before we reach the black hole. I estimate no more than a few days."

Neither Adan nor Quell spoke for a while. They did not look at one another.

"We should get moving," Quell said, though she didn't know where they should go.

III

The Y-wing descended over the district locals called the Web, and Nath Tensent cursed his droid with every centimeter. The vessel swung to and fro on the breeze, its thrusters offline, carried only by repulsors in the hope of avoiding detection. Any miscalculation could prove fatal, Nath knew, as they passed through the gaps between duracrete tubes spanning the district like spider's silk.

"You get us killed," Nath said, "you and I are going to have a talk."

The droid squawked an irritated reply.

"Well, that boy of yours will be annoyed if you come back without me."

The tubes—closer to sewers than skyways in breadth and odor—connected the district's aging factories. Nowadays most of the factories were decommissioned; the district's population resided almost entirely inside the tubing. Some were brightly painted with murals or flags, while more were stained with an orange moss that ate away at the rough surface like acid.

Two proton bombs and this whole place will fall apart, Nath thought, though Shadow Wing patrols hadn't been seen in the area for a while. Even elsewhere, the bombing runs seemed fewer than earlier; Nath suspected they were conserving ammunition.

A sensor sweep revealed his destination: a broad tube decorated with crude images of tooka-cats. The Y-wing crept forward and a metal hatch swung open, giving the ship no more than half a meter's clearance on any side. Still, Nath managed to creep forward—T5 did most of the work, but he kept an eye on his instruments—and he waited for his vision to adjust to the dim lighting within.

Gathered in the tube were several dozen ragged civilians packed among tents and semiportable generators and heating units and strings of glow-bulbs. They parted to make room for the Y-wing as it settled. The residents were humans, mostly—the descendants of noble and merchant families fallen from grace long ago—though many had been altered or augmented. Nath spotted cybernetic interface plugs and surgical appetite limiters, and experienced a cocktail of nostalgia and disdain for the gangs of his youth.

The ship lurched onto its landing gear. Nath gripped his sidearm as the crowd pressed in. He'd been told to find his contact here—that the residents had loathed Governor Hastemoor and saw the New Republic as a chance to permanently improve their circumstances. But he'd expected subterfuge, not a public confrontation with a crowd ready to riot.

They roared as he popped his canopy. He stood from his seat, squinted into the darkness, and grinned toothily at the locals in their starving, pathetic glory. Their cries were almost buoyant, and Nath thought back to the initial campaign for the planet—all the times he'd returned from a mission to the applause of infantry or refugees. He'd expected opinions to sour with the arrival of Shadow Wing, whereas instead the civilians' despair was cut with the manic hope he associated with the Rebel Alliance.

This time, their hopes were pinned on *him*.

Be careful. You're getting used to the attention.

He dropped out of the Y-wing and was caught by two burly men with painted faces. A greasy-haired brute held a child above the crowd, and out of irrational instinct Nath slapped a ration bar into the kid's hand, knowing it would either encourage the crowd or send them tearing at his flesh for more.

They called out questions:

"What's going on in Thannerhouse?"

"When is the Empire landing ground troops?"

"Is it true the governor is alive?"

He shouted in a booming voice that echoed in the vast tube. "*Hey!* We're going to talk about all that. Anything I can answer before I have to head back, I'll answer. But first you need to help out my pals.

"I'm not in charge of the troops. I was sent here on a special mission—to find *you,* because only you can help us. We need supplies, equipment . . . most important, we need transport.

"I can't say where or how, but we're taking the fight to the enemy. We won Troithe before, and we can win it all over again."

The crowd thundered back, voices merging but generally upbeat so far as Nath could tell. He caught snatches of inquiries, responded where he could, and caught the eye of a man no taller than Nath's breast wobbling forward on spindly mechanical legs. The others in the crowd backed away though they grew no quieter as the compact man said, "What kind of transport?"

"Air and ground," Nath answered. "Sturdy as you can—you don't want to know details, but assume rough flying and rough ground."

The man's legs extended until he was face-to-face with Nath. "Showroom's closed, but I bet we can figure something out. You know what this place is, don't you?"

"The Web?"

"Before it was the Web," the man snapped. "These factories—*transport* was what we did until the Empire shut us down. Kept promising they'd switch us to manufacturing TIEs, but they never did. The B-14, most popular airspeeder on Troithe? Built right here, made of materials mined on Troithe by workers born on Troithe. You want flitters? Stair-crawlers? Rumblers? We'll make it happen."

"You got a price?" Nath asked. He enjoyed a good sales pitch, smiled to show he understood, but he was still skeptical.

"You get the Empire offworld, the New Republic gets the factories running again."

"It's a deal."

True, he didn't have the authority to make the deal. By the time the residents of the Web realized that, however, he intended to be far away from Troithe and the Cerberon system.

When Nath was done with the Web, he rendezvoused with the troops outside the Highgarden District. Even keeping his speed down and his starfighter low enough to avoid scanners, he'd flown across a third of the continent and back in the time the infantry needed to creep twenty kilometers.

"Think we'll get what we need," he told Wyl, slapping one of the boy's skinny shoulders. "I told them not to bother with anything slower than a combat-rated cloud car. Jeems—that's the old factory foreman— says he expects he can dig up a dozen aircraft that meet our specs, plus the ground transport. Assume he's exaggerating and it's still better than we expected."

"Good," Wyl said. They strolled through a narrow alley between the empty lot where they'd parked their ships and the decaying playground the Sixty-First Mobile Infantry used as a camp. "I spent most of the day selecting pilots. No one with starfighter experience, but there's a few good candidates. Vitale used to fly atmospheric patrols for local security. Prinspai says he—she, maybe?—their species has wings when they're young, so that suggests a knack for maneuvering. I should have a final roster by tonight."

"Admit it: You love being in command." Nath grinned. With another man, he might've joked about leaving Quell aboard the *Lodestar* on purpose. He knew better than to try it with Wyl. "You feeling good about them?"

The lines in Wyl's stubbly cheeks seemed like chasms as he smiled, and Nath imagined the strands of his hair turning gray. "Even if they can fly, I'm going to have to teach them combat tactics, squadron maneuvers, and everything we know about Shadow Wing in, what— a few days? This might be our best shot, but I wouldn't say I'm feeling *good.*"

Nath thought about whether to question Wyl further or change the topic to something innocuous. He was saved from the decision by T5—the droid rolled along the cracked pavement chiming and squawking and Wyl raced to the machine's side, suddenly boyish again.

Wyl stayed close to the astromech as he returned to his pilot interviews. Nath observed from afar but didn't interfere as soldiers sat with

Wyl and T5 beneath the playground equipment—bright-eyed youths and scarred veterans, both humans and species Nath couldn't recognize. Tired and endlessly patient, Wyl sketched formations in the dirt and sent candidates away and welcomed others back.

T5 didn't leave Wyl's side even after they settled onto the grass to sleep. Nath didn't chide the droid, though it should've been performing low-level systems checks on the Y-wing. He suspected they were both thinking about Piter, the scared kid Nath had taught everything to; the kid he had protected as they'd defected from the Empire to join the Rebel Alliance.

Piter had been the first to die when Shadow Wing had ambushed their squadron at the Trenchenovu shipyards. T5 and Nath were the only living witnesses to that battle. Wyl seemed apt to last longer than Piter—*Hell*, Nath thought, *Wyl's a better pilot than Piter ever was*—but how long did any of them have on Troithe?

Nath lay on his back, staring through the jungle gym at the too-bright stars.

He'd taken too many risks to get revenge for Piter and Ferris and Reeka and the rest. He'd been stupid to try and lucky to survive.

He couldn't afford to seek revenge a second time.

The grenade bounced through the dying grass so softly that Nath woke believing it was a soldier's tread. The deafening explosion and accompanying flash disabused him of that, and as his sight and hearing shut down he felt soil and shards of pavement spray his face. He rolled onto his knees, fumbled for his blaster, and tried to figure out where to point.

Troops shouted around him, but their words were lost in the ocean-waves-and-door-chimes noise in his throbbing ears. Nath cursed and fought the urge to fire a blind shot. "I can't see!" he yelled, and someone's arms wrapped around his body. He felt himself dragged across the grounds as the ozone stench of blasters filled the air.

By the time his hearing and vision began to return his savior was gone. He stood inside the alley mouth, looking onto the playground as crimson energy streaked down from the windows of a five-story stone schoolhouse. The troops on the playground were scattering to escape the kill zone. On the opposite end of the playground from Nath, pinned behind an oversized child's model of a podracer, were dark blurs that might have been Wyl and T5 along with several soldiers attempting to return fire.

There was no way Nath could reach Wyl without getting a dozen charred holes in his chest. If he wanted to save his comrade he'd have to find another way.

He took one last moment to assess the battlefield, then stumbled down the alley, trying to shake off his vertigo. He passed a soldier crouched by a form caked in blood and dirt—a civilian, to judge by the clothes, likely a sympathizer who'd helped the company make camp and offered a plate of food.

Nath didn't speak to either, twisting his face into something between a grimace and a smile when he spotted the Y-wing, ugly as ever, intact on its slab of pavement. He hauled himself into the cockpit and fumbled through start-up procedures—a process slow and clumsy without T5's assistance, but he didn't need the astromech for what he had planned. The ringing in his ears was replaced by the growl of the ship's engine.

Systems checks came next, then manual power distribution (to thrusters, to stabilizers, to shields, to weapons—all in the right order so that nothing overtaxed the reactor). The vessel's atmospheric compensators cycled, attempting to balance the Y-wing for planetary flight. Nath overrode them and retracted his landing gear. Then he was ascending and a cloud of hot dust expanded outward from his position.

He remembered the soldier and civilian in the alley and imagined them caught in his backwash. *Sorry, boys,* he thought, but they'd survive—or if not, it wouldn't be Nath who pushed them over the edge.

He made a vertical climb until he was above the adjacent structures, then briefly ignited his thrusters to push toward the playground. Particle bolts streamed below him between the schoolhouse and the yard.

Nath maneuvered into the center of the playground, pointed his nose toward the enemy position, and descended rapidly, squeezing his trigger as he went.

Stone architecture exploded as high-energy cannon bolts ripped through the walls. The Y-wing's weapons were designed to puncture battle cruiser hulls; anything less sturdy than a cliff wasn't likely to hold up. The third story of the building, where Nath aimed first, became a compressed layer of flames; then the fourth and fifth levels collapsed and the entire façade poured like an avalanche onto the yard.

The particle bolt volleys ceased. Nath smelled dust in his lungs and nostrils, even knowing it was impossible for the granules to enter the airtight Y-wing.

No aerial threat appeared on his scanner. He checked the comm channels and heard troops reporting casualties and scouting the area around the yard. No one called in additional shots—it seemed likely the attackers had been a guerrilla team of Imperial loyalists, not part of any larger or better coordinated unit.

Nath peered out his canopy and spotted corpses half buried in the rubble. Like the man Nath had seen in the alley, they appeared to be civilians. He pursed his lips and loosed a long sigh.

The casualties might have been avoidable. He wasn't sure how much of the fault was on him, but he imagined the answer was "at least a little." Still, he'd had to act fast.

Nath adjusted the comm and said, "T5? You and the kid in one piece?"

The droid replied with an affirmative ping.

"How about our fresh pilots?"

This time the response was a concerned warble. They'd lost at least one of the candidates.

This is why you don't get attached, he thought.

"All right. See you down there."

He put the casualties out of his mind. His priority was survival—his and Wyl's—and he'd done exactly what he needed to do.

Everyone else on Troithe, his new squadron included, came a distant second.

IV

Colonel Soran Keize had developed a routine. The thought offended him—when suffering was abundant and obliteration was one poor choice away, the complacency of a schedule seemed presumptuous—yet it allowed him to support the 204th. He could serve his people best as a dependable cog in the machinery of war.

For these reasons he tried to project confidence as he moved about the Raddakkia Plaza communications center and reviewed reports from the 204th and Imperial loyalists across the planet. He smiled at Governor Yadeez when he crossed her path and tried to communicate his respect for her unkempt, underequipped guerrilla forces. He acknowledged, through a calm tone and nonconfrontational posture more than through words, that his own people had barely slept since arriving, had remained upright and dutiful and attentive without complaint.

Neither the squadron commanders nor individual pilots openly blamed him for what had transpired. Part of him wished they would—it troubled Soran to see his people act as if being trapped on Troithe was only incrementally worse than what they'd been through already. As if their colonel's choice to lead them into catastrophe was exactly what they had expected. It wasn't loyalty or faith that kept them dutiful; rather, it was incomprehension of the alternatives.

What did Grandmother do to you? he wondered. *What did I do when I left you behind? What have you seen since the Empire died?*

He was midway through his first four-hour shift as he completed his study of the updated tactical maps with Fara Yadeez. The young woman, for all her dignity and obvious pride in her planet, was more than willing to defer to Soran's expertise in war. Soran hadn't known her much more than two days, but already he was coming to relax in her presence.

She drank from a thermos containing a stimulant so acrid it made Soran's nose itch—she'd offered him some during their first meeting and he'd accepted in the spirit of goodwill; until she'd begun laughing uproariously, he'd sincerely believed that he'd been poisoned. She hunched her head and shoulders over the holotable far enough that images splashed against her chin like an evening tide. "Things will get worse in the Nine Boats District," she said, wrinkling her nose. "Do you object?"

"Worse in what way?" The holoimage showed a riot, or the aftermath of a riot. Civilians armed with bottles and burning rags stampeded away from a checkpoint established by Yadeez's loyalists. The Imperial forces fired indiscriminately into the crowd. One stormtrooper, who wore no helmet, walked among the injured, executing crawling rioters who'd been left behind by their peers.

"The troops there suffered—" Yadeez hesitated, straightening behind the table. "May I speak freely, Colonel?"

"You may."

She sighed and spoke in a tone of confession. "When word came that the New Republic had arrived in the Cerberon system, Nine Boats was one of the first districts to spiral into chaos. Rebel sympathizers struck before the enemy's ships landed, shutting down tram stations. Local stormtrooper units responded with what I'm told were standard crowd dispersal techniques, but gas and stunners weren't sufficient against the sheer number of rioters.

"Our troops were overwhelmed and—well. Many were beaten to death. Others were shot with their own rifles. Rebels obtained helmet cam footage and broadcast it to the comm networks." Distaste flickered across her face. "The survivors—our survivors—have been operating without support over the past two months. They've seen awful things. Their leaders are dead yet the rebels call them monsters. They want vengeance and I can't stop them."

"They won't follow your orders?" Soran asked. There was no condemnation in his voice.

"If I were on the ground directing them? Of course they would. But if I sit five hundred kilometers away, sending encrypted signals they may not have codes to decipher?" Yadeez shrugged. "My grandfather told stories of the Clone Wars, of planets driven to atrocities by starvation and fury . . ."

She trailed off and looked back to the hologram.

"I'm not here to pass judgment on your troops, or their discipline. In times like these—" Soran hesitated. *May I speak freely, Governor?* he wanted to say back to her. "In times like these none of us are fit to judge the ethics of our peers. All we can do is act as we believe is right and honorable."

"And what do you believe, Colonel?" Yadeez asked. "What polestar brings you to Troithe?"

Soran forced a humorless smile. Yadeez was far younger than he, but he recognized the skill of a woman from the political classes. She might have been asking: *Who gave you the order to come here? What is your mission?* Or her inquiry might have been as genuinely personal as it sounded.

"I serve my people," he said. "As I suspect you do yours."

Governor Fara Yadeez watched the horrors etched in the holo's blue light and nodded.

"She's intelligent. Determined. Ignorant of military matters, but I'd expect as much given her background." Soran turned over a bruised piece of fruit as he sat in the private meeting room they'd created from the comm center's kitchenette. Broosh and Darita were with him, the former positioned near the door and the latter perched on the countertop. Both wore flight suits, despite having returned to base over an hour earlier.

"You sound taken with her," Broosh said.

"Does she know we're planning to dump her the second we get offworld?" Darita asked.

"She hasn't brought it up. I wouldn't be surprised if she suspects— she understands that Troithe is only a small part of the war." He looked to the closed door, as if he could see through to the world outside. "Still, keep an eye on your pilots. We won't want to get too close to these people."

Captain Darita laughed low and rubbed her face with gloved hands. "We just got back from carrying messages to the western shield command base—little fort in the middle of nowhere that never got over-run. They wanted to give us medals just for showing up."

"Our experience was similar," Broosh said. "No one's spending time fraternizing, but it's easy to forget that we're not here to retake the planet. After the last few months? It's . . . gratifying to be treated like champions coming to the rescue."

Soran mentally thumbed through a pilot roster, trying to assess his people's likely reactions to being embedded with the forces of Troithe. For those who'd been desperate for purpose—men like Kandende, who'd become obsessed with the Emperor's Messenger droid, or like lost Seedia, so hungry for an outlet for her own aggressions and misgivings—it could serve as a source of direction. Others would re-call adopting the local forces at Pandem Nai and recruiting the *Edict's* cadets and wonder if the same could be done here—if select Troithe soldiers could be brought into the 204th.

He wondered how Lieutenant Quell would react—wondered whether everything occurring would play to her deep-seated dream of becoming a hero—before recalling that she was long gone.

It was tempting to accept the gift of the locals' gratitude and expose all his soldiers—as if it were a disease that would harden their immune systems, not destroy them.

"I recommend we keep our pilots focused on their duty," he said. "There's more than enough to go around. If anyone brings up our ob-jectives, remind them that we succeeded in eliminating the *Lodestar.* I'd like confirmation of General Syndulla's death, but until we have it, emphasize what we *know* we accomplished."

Broosh and Darita both seemed to accept the answer, and the three of them proceeded to discuss the ground crews' triage efforts and whether they'd be able to repair the worst-damaged TIEs. They were just wrapping up when one of the governor's aides announced that the New Republic forces had been located.

"They were in Highgarden for a full day," Yadeez said, spinning the holographic globe until a blinking dot appeared in one of the decaying sections of the eastern city. "One of the largest groups of New Republic infantry we've seen active, along with limited air support. Somehow they acquired transportation after an ambush last night, and they're now on the move. We don't yet know where."

"How did you acquire this information?" Soran asked.

"Multiple local sightings, compiled by an operative from the governor's—the old governor's—Special Intelligence Unit. We were lucky he happened to be in the area."

There was no tinge of doubt in her voice. Soran nodded. "Go on."

"Based on that information, plus unconfirmed sightings *here* and *here*—" She jabbed at two points, creating a line leading away from Highgarden. "—we've begun compiling a list of possible targets. Strategic outposts they might be moving to attack or occupy."

Yadeez tapped a button and twenty new dots flashed into existence, each labeled with a name and a set of coordinates. Soran wished he possessed the expertise to make immediate sense of it all. If Syndulla was still alive, he thought, she surely knew exactly what she was doing; and while he believed he was the superior pilot, he had no doubt she was the superior general. Add to that her familiarity with the terrain, and he would consider himself lucky if she'd died with the *Lodestar*.

"Tell me about them," he said. "All of them."

Yadeez did. For thirty minutes, Soran listened intently; he was broadly familiar with many of the targets from his earlier studies of the planet, but Yadeez's insights were useful and he needed time to process what he was seeing. As she described the significance of the Hoorn Skyway, however, and the possibility that the New Republic hoped to seize control of transportation infrastructure, his eyes roamed to a distant light on the map. He kept half his attention on Yadeez as he pulled up files, finally seeing fit to interrupt her with: "What about the mining facility?"

"Core Nine?" Yadeez paused and did not adjust the map. "It's the least likely of the targets, but it is potentially accessible to the enemy. There's not much they could do there, though."

"But it's functional?" Soran asked. He tapped the screen he'd been eyeing a moment before. "The New Republic could be after the equipment there, believing it's unguarded."

"It was never decommissioned. I don't know how much is online."

Soran nodded. Yadeez was watching him, openly curious. He wondered what she thought he was thinking.

"We can return to it later," Soran said. "Apologies—continue with the skyway."

Yadeez did. Soran gave her his attention again. But in the back of his mind he explored possibilities.

Whatever the New Republic intended—whether they were after the Core Nine megafacility or another target—the mine was a solution to all of his problems. It had everything the 204th required. He would reprioritize accordingly.

It was unfortunate that he would need to betray the governor. But Colonel Soran Keize had pledged to serve his people first.

CHAPTER 16

DEEP BEYOND DAY

I

Time was oblique to them. The droid's internal chronometer was unreliable due to damage. Yrica Quell had carried an emergency timepiece but it had shattered in the crash and she'd abandoned it in the freighter. The rising and setting of the Cerberon black hole over the planetoid's horizon made a mockery of night and day; the light of the burning iris was bright enough to make travel easier, yet without knowing the planetoid's rotation period it told them nothing about how long they'd been stranded.

Even the rhythms of their bodies were deceptive—Quell and Adan's injuries forced them to rest often and denied them deep sleep. They made camp when they felt unable to go farther and resumed their journey when frustration and anxiety drove them onward.

IT-O had said that it had spotted something—a shadow, perhaps only a mountain or a chasm, or perhaps a structure—during its fall. The direction correlated with what Quell and the droid could remember of the energy reading's location. So they trekked east, hoping to come upon something that would save them before the planetoid was torn apart by the black hole.

"If it's true that my captors were here," Adan said, "it doesn't seem likely we'll find anything worthwhile." They slogged through a wide valley, ridges towering over them. The sand was looser and offered less traction than before their descent—the gravel had disintegrated and only dust was left. "If there was a base or a communications outpost, they would have stripped it bare."

"We don't know that," Quell replied.

"We don't *know* there's anything here at all. But why else would they have come in the middle of a war?"

It was a reasonable question, yet it made Quell want to shove Adan's face into the sand until he choked.

"What if it was the Empire that knocked the planetoid out of orbit?" she asked. "What if they wanted to destroy what was here and make sure no one could recover it?"

Adan twisted his neck, staring at her a moment before looking back to the sand. They trudged forward and when Quell began to believe the conversation was over Adan said, "There were reports of secret vaults and laboratories targeted for destruction after Endor, supposedly on the orders of the Emperor himself. That was the less glamorous part of Operation Cinder, but it was still a part."

The wind rose. Quell felt cold. Adan was mocking her, she thought. Maybe she deserved it.

"If she's a spy, she's not an especially good one," the interrogation droid said.

The unit floated a short distance behind them. Both Quell and Adan turned. Its primary manipulator arm twitched and its photoreceptor was dilated. Then it seemed to steady.

"Apologies," it said. "My memory circuits are faulty. I was momentarily confused. Please continue."

They walked on.

They did not return to the topic of what they might find at their destination. They marched between the cliffs, trudging through sand like ashes under a star-bright sky blotted with the flotsam of the debris field. Cerberon, forever ravenous, rose overhead and the wind howled and dust danced.

They didn't speak again of Operation Cinder, yet they broke their collective silence more often. Adan asked what had happened during Shadow Wing's attack and Quell explained all she knew in a monotone, from the arrival of the Star Destroyer and the cruiser-carrier to the deployment of New Republic ships to Catadra and the interception over Troithe. When Adan asked why she hadn't led Alphabet herself, she told him, "Because they got your message." He didn't reply to that.

Later, when he asked how she knew it was Shadow Wing, she told him about Nath Tensent's signal.

"It's possible," he said when she was finished, "that it never was Shadow Wing. Tensent could've gotten it wrong."

"He wasn't wrong," she said. "I saw them."

"Obsession might have colored your opinion."

I saw Major Keize, she thought. *My mentor shot us down. There's no one else it could have been.*

But she didn't say it. She had told Adan that Keize died on Nacronis, and telling the truth now would raise subjects she had no desire to address. Instead she shrugged away his doubt and took the offensive.

"If you'd done your part," she said, her voice low and steady, "they would have taken the bait. They'd be on the asteroid right now, waiting to be ambushed by the Sixty-First."

Adan swore softly and said something Quell couldn't hear. She knew what he meant all the same.

The interrogation droid said nothing. Quell had always thought of IT-O as a peacemaker; but Adan was its master, and maybe she should've been grateful it wasn't taking sides.

———

The valley twisted so often that, after the black hole fell below the ridgeline, Quell no longer knew in what direction they traveled. The cliffs had become increasingly steep over the course of the day (or eternal night, or whatever it was) and climbing, injured as they were, was out of the question. "There's no point going back. We'll keep moving until we find a way out of the valley," Quell said, and Adan did not argue.

They didn't find a way out. The wind changed with the disappearance of the black hole, lashing them in cutting ribbons edged with particles of sand. They strayed to the cliff wall for shelter, but it wasn't enough—when a whip snapped across Quell's legs and dropped her to the ground, she loosed a frustrated howl and called for a halt. Adan voiced agreement, and she noticed for the first time how his face glistened with sweat. Forcing down her resentment, she offered him the day's accumulation of water from the vaporator. He drank most of it and handed back the canteen without thanks.

They found a hollow in the cliff where they made camp. It extended no more than five meters past the broad, jagged cave mouth, but it was oppressively dark and Quell wished for a glow rod or anything brighter than the droid's indicators. IT-O reported that it found nothing concerning during its full-spectrum scans, and they settled in to rest.

At least we're out of the wind, Quell thought before falling into a sore and troubled sleep.

It was black as ever when she woke. She didn't know if she'd rested for one hour or eight, though she felt not at all refreshed and her head throbbed from dehydration. The sound of the gusts outside was faint but the cave echoed with a lower keening. Quell worried it was the droid's repulsors malfunctioning but she didn't see the unit's lights.

As her eyes adjusted she saw Adan standing above her an arm's length away, staring at the cave wall and moaning. His antenna-stalks were half raised, though one was still unnaturally bent from his captivity.

The moaning stopped as Quell shuffled to a squatting position. "I need a drink," Adan said.

"I'll check the vaporator," Quell said.

"I need a *drink*," Adan repeated, and twisted to look at her with a fury that burned hot enough to show in the dark. "I need a decent night's sleep. I need to get out of here."

Quell flinched and slowly rose. Adan was a silhouette against the lighter shadows of the cave mouth. "If you have a suggestion, I'm glad to listen. You're the one in control of the working group. You're—"

"There is no *working group*!" Adan cried, half laughing. "There's only you and me, and enough chemicals to make my blood catch fire. What do you want me to tell you?"

Quell mouthed the words to make sure she'd heard them correctly. "You're not making sense."

"I am the only one making sense! They all need me, you understand? I do everything I can—" He stepped forward, and Quell saw something feral in his expression. He sweated despite the cold air, despite dehydration, despite their rest. "—and you're the one who ruins worlds! Who kills families!"

She should have felt compassion. He was clearly hallucinating. Maybe one of his wounds had been infected—he smelled foul enough—and that infection had spread to his blood. Maybe it was simply the pain he was going through. But she felt nothing for Adan, and when he lunged awkwardly she dug her heels into the rock and braced to push him backward instead of stepping aside.

He was stronger than she'd expected. He bowled into her with enough force to make her right heel slip and her knee strike the cave floor. Pain flashed up her thigh and she shouted, feared a fracture, and abandoned all gentleness as she shoved Adan away. Adan wobbled but caught himself against the cave wall.

He wasn't armed. She was confident in that. But neither was she, and she'd never been any good at hand-to-hand fighting. She could stop him, but she wasn't certain she could do so without accidentally cracking his skull or breaking one of his legs.

Adan came at her again, shouting incoherently, and she rose in time to catch him and spin with the momentum. They whirled together and she drove her left knee into his groin, shoved him off her once, then twice. She prepared to punch him when he staggered backward with eyes wide.

He dropped to the ground, catching himself on his hands. Behind him, in the dark, floated the red bead Quell recognized as the interrogation droid's photoreceptor. She couldn't see the needle in the droid's manipulator, but she knew it was there.

Adan shuddered and fell.

"The sedation should last several hours," the droid said.

"Where were you?" Quell asked. She sounded hoarse and she breathed heavily.

"I decided not to power down while you rested—the odds that I would fail to awaken seemed low but not nonexistent, given the damage I've sustained. I thought I would scout ahead rather than waste battery power in the cave."

"Warn me next time." Quell knelt beside Adan, and the droid descended over his body. "What's wrong with him?"

"The list of his injuries is extensive. You're asking about the delirium?" The whine of the droid's repulsors rose to an insectoid buzz. "I do not detect any infection. It may be an aftereffect of medication in combination with anxiety and malnutrition. I believe it will pass if he can be restored to bodily health."

She met the machine's gaze. "What do we do?"

"We must remove him from this planetoid as swiftly as possible. In the meantime he should not be forced to travel—it will only worsen his condition."

Quell wanted to sit on the stone next to Adan. Instead she stood. Once again, she wondered how long she'd managed to sleep. "I'll keep going. You stay with Adan."

She began sorting her belongings and dividing the remaining stores of food and water. Behind her, IT-O said, "I'll accompany you."

"Adan needs someone to care for him."

"I believe he can care for himself, and my supply of medication is nearly exhausted."

"Care for him anyway."

"Yrica."

The droid said her name and she turned, shoulders tight. "What?"

"I found something while scouting. You need to follow me."

The black hole was out of sight as Quell marched across the red wastes, eternally one step behind the interrogation droid. The valley was now narrow enough to be called a canyon, and as they traveled it split once, twice, three times. Always they followed the left-hand path, though the branches all looked the same to Quell.

Eventually the ground sloped upward and they came onto a mesa overlooking the fractured lands, unnaturally topped with sand that billowed at every breeze. Quell climbed dunes and pulled her shirt over her mouth and nose, wishing she'd brought her flight helmet.

The tower formed gradually out of the night, taking shape where stars were absent against the sky. From a distance, it might have been a natural obelisk—a gargantuan version of the black stones that erupted during the worst of the quakes. As Quell's eyes adjusted and she strained to take it in, however, she saw that the top of the tower was ornately forked—two individual spires rising from the central mass, arcing and coming together to frame an opaque lens that dully distorted the stars behind it.

There was nothing Quell could see at the base of the tower. There was no path through the sand, or even the corpse of another stormtrooper to indicate the location had significance.

She thought of what Adan had said about sites targeted by Operation Cinder.

"Do you know what it is?" she asked the interrogation droid.

"This is as close as I came," the droid replied.

She wished she hadn't spoken. Speaking aloud felt profane.

Closer to the tower, she could see that it had indeed been carved of the quake stone, apparently from a single piece. Its surface was broken by a circuit maze of shallow, nearly imperceptible grooves. Inset in the tower base was a massive rectangular door formed from a metal the same color as the rock, distinguished only by its marginally more reflective luster.

The tower's antiquity was obvious from the weathering of the stone. What had once, Quell suspected, been perfectly square corners were rounded from centuries—from millennia, perhaps—of wind and sand. Quell felt instinctively certain that the tower was older than anything on Catadra. Her memory drifted to the Jedi temple she'd visited on the Harkrova moon, and that memory led to a vaguely recalled word she'd encountered somewhere among rebel propaganda videos: *Sith.*

She couldn't recall the word's meaning, though she tried.

The tower door was sealed and did not acknowledge Quell's presence. She saw no way to open it—she found no controls, and when she leaned into the icy metal with her shoulder it did not give. She circled the tower three times as the black hole crested the horizon and found nothing of interest nearby.

The droid did not follow her, instead remaining near the entrance. "There is machinery concealed here," it announced when she returned. "Sophisticated biosensors installed within the edifice."

"What does it do?" she asked.

"The equipment could be programmed to scan for a specific biophysical signature—that of an individual, a bloodline, or a species. Given the location, perhaps this is the locking mechanism."

"The door automatically admits anyone coded for access?"

"It is possible. Alternatively—" The droid hesitated and hummed. Quell wondered if it was analyzing gathered data or simply deciding what to tell her. "—the equipment is significantly more advanced than required for a baseline genetic reading. It could be calibrated to read physiological responses."

She parsed the words. "Meaning what? It's mood-activated?"

"I do not know," the droid said.

"There might be nothing inside. This whole place might be useless to us."

"I acknowledge the possibility," the droid said.

Quell craned her neck and stared.

She'd been studying the tower a long while when the lens began to glow, refracting the warped, fiery light of the ascending black hole. Quell stepped backward, maneuvering so she could look through the prongs crowning the structure. The lens seemed to ripple and flare with every motion. She felt detached from her body as she observed, vaguely aware of the wind but fully focused on the eye rising into view.

She recalled watching an eclipse as a child aboard Gavana Orbital— staring through polarized goggles, watching the orb of a moon cross the path of the sun too slowly to fully perceive. She'd been transfixed then as she was now.

The burning eye reached the center of the lens. The pupil pulsed, as if the lens's curvature altered with each beat of her heart and caused the black hole to expand and contract. The iris became the outermost boundary of her vision, and her attention was pulled *inward*.

She felt the tug of gravity and she fell into the dark, into the crushing grip of the black hole.

Into the cold of space.

Into the blackness of her mind.

When her sight returned she was enveloped by the bright yellows and blues of a siltstorm. Mud sprayed her face and plastered her hair as she walked through a rising bog already as deep as her thighs. The chill did not disturb her. She looked around at domed buildings formed from rough duracrete as they were blasted by the wind and painted with fierce hues. Thunder rumbled, barely audible over the scream of the storm and the shriek of ion engines high above.

Yrica Quell knew exactly where she was.

Ahead of her, down a flooded street, a lighthouse swayed in the gale. Lightning flashed and struck the top, sending stone plummeting to the mud and leaving metal scaffolding aglow. She heard yelling and turned to watch churning floodwaters slam a white-haired man against the side of a house. The tides of the storm battered him against the duracrete over and over, and each cycle he attempted to grasp a window frame from which arms extended, trying to grasp him; to no avail. Quell couldn't tell whether he'd gone limp before or after he was swept away. The window sealed shut as the mud rose.

Quell knew the home's inhabitants would not survive. No one survived Nacronis.

The houses drowned. The airspeeder pilots who fell out of the clouds drowned. Metal doors tore from their hinges and the storm entered apartments and schools and workshops. The scream of TIE engines echoed. Quell watched it all, taking no action as the mud rose to her neck and the street became clogged with corpses. Her hands found clammy skin ravaged by blasts of silt. She felt the wind thrash the barriers in her mind until the utter indifference that gave her safe harbor cracked and splintered and tore away; until the horror of it all saturated her in an instant. Then she was no longer among the victims of Nacronis but flying in a TIE fighter, firing at the planet's defenders to protect her squadron and committing to the plan—the strategy that Major Soran Keize had laid out and the Emperor's Messenger had decreed. Quell stepped back through moments, defying the flow of time, and saw each choice she had made that had allowed her to keep fighting, to keep stoking the storms of the planet.

She could have turned on her squadron. She could have sabotaged the bombers. She could have sent a message to Nacronis en route or convinced her comrades not to act or strangled Major Keize aboard the *Pursuer.* Instead she had done everything possible to ensure the success of Shadow Wing's mission and reduced a world to a swamp where the dead would mummify and remain uncounted for centuries to come.

This was the legacy of Yrica Quell, and nothing she could ever do would change it.

When she saw the black tower and the red sands of the nameless planetoid again, she was on her knees. She convulsed with cold and retched, trying to purge herself, but nothing came.

———

"You were incapacitated for some time," the droid said. "Several hours, perhaps. I have been monitoring your life signs."

She remained on her knees, her forehead buried in her arms against the dust. She must have looked like she was praying, but the position tamped down her nausea.

"I'm alive?" she asked.

"You are alive," the droid said, "and you are suffering. I offer you my sympathies, for what little they are worth."

She nodded. Her chin touched sand. She forced herself to lift her torso upright. "It was the tower," she said.

"Yes," the droid agreed. "The tower was *also* monitoring your life signs. The scanning equipment in the edifice was active throughout your experience, and the mechanisms appeared to respond dynamically."

She looked at the droid. "Respond how?"

"I am not entirely certain. It appeared that the deeper you withdrew from consciousness, the more processing power the equipment in the doorway demanded. Additional scanners came online at biophysical thresholds keyed to your heart rate, brain activity, and more."

Quell considered this. She was surprised by the clarity she mustered, despite the lingering sensations of mud and corpses against her skin. "It was looking for something from me," she said. "Looking for a specific reaction before it opened."

"That is a possibility."

"Then I need to do it again to get inside. I need to get it right."

The droid's humming seemed deeper than usual, like a recording played at half speed. "You would need assistance. You would need to determine the full array of biophysical conditions the door requires, and how to bring yourself to that state."

Quell paused, unsure what answer she would receive if she spoke again.

"You can help me," she said.

"Yes," the interrogation droid replied.

II

Life among the cultists was at once numbing and excruciating. The woman known to the Children of the Empty Sun as Maya Hallik was designated a "seeker of the first insight." That meant, essentially, she had access to select areas of the palace compound; she got to pick out her meals before the faithless refugees but *after* the four hundred cultists who'd joined up earlier than Maya; and she was welcome to sleep indoors when the ash-sleet came down.

Chass wasn't sure if the ash-sleet had just been "sleet" before the New Republic's liberation of Catadra. She chose not to ask.

In return for the privileges of being a junior cultist, Maya Hallik was expected to join the prayer songs each dawn. (She found she recognized the melodies from songs in her lost collection, but the lyrics had been changed from paeans to ancient civilizations to pabulum about community and fellowship; each morning, she grew stiff with outrage yet nearly wept at the songs' beauty.) She was expected to speak to those outside the cult only when encouraging them to join, otherwise building relationships with fellow Children. (She largely abided by this, deciding anyone not part of the cult was too useless to bother with.) She was expected to help with cooking and sweeping and patching the crumbling walls of the palace.

Most of all, she was expected to watch broadcasts from Let'ij, the fungus-faced woman who had founded the Children of the Empty Sun and called herself not *Sweetbishop* or *Holy Carnifex* or *Enlightened Mother*—as Chass had bet with herself beforehand—but *Vessel*. This morning, she'd chosen to lecture on galactic politics.

"There's no use in distress over the return of the Empire to Catadra. One oppressor is the same as another," the hologram said. "It's true that Emperor Palpatine and his deputies thought little of us—thought little of any of Catadra's sects, and there were once many. Yet the New Republic differs in its words, not its deeds."

Chass sat in a common area where cultists normally cooked and played cards and listened to headsets. It might've been the refugee camp on Troithe, only every single person put down their cards and pots and headsets and looked up at Let'ij when the broadcasts began.

"Imperial soldiers openly disdained nonhumans, and the ruling class did little to intervene. But how often have we heard the New Republic chancellor talk about ending xenophobia while handing out medals to all-human death squads? We've met the New Republic's troops, and it is still humans who outnumber the rest.

"The Empire forced religious orders from Catadra to Jedha to truck with smugglers and embezzlers simply to survive, no matter how we might have wished otherwise. The New Republic calls a self-proclaimed 'Jedi Knight' one of its greatest heroes; can we trust it not to endorse that sect's rebirth above all others?"

The speech was delivered without anger. Let'ij, as she always did in her lectures, spoke with serenity and placid amusement. It was almost enough to keep Chass's attention.

"Yet seeking peace through bureaucracy is a fool's errand, so what does it matter whether it's the Empire or the Republic—old or new—dropping bombs? The only true peace is found in the Force, and the Force is cultivated through harmony and community and the vision of blessed individuals."

Half a dozen cultists seated near Chass mouthed the last sentence along with Let'ij. Chass found her own lips moving and barely refrained from spitting on the floor.

You're here for a reason, she told herself. *You're not one of them.*

Every lecture led down the same path. Each began with a bitter truth about the galaxy. Each ended with the promise that the Children of the Empty Sun were the reaction and solution to that bitter truth. It was an old con artist's trick—you accepted the former, it was easy to accept the latter.

Chass snatched a headset off a blanket and clapped it over her ears. It was *easy*—but only a simpleton actually did it.

When she wasn't pretending to be a good cultist, Chass na Chadic abandoned the pretense of Maya Hallik and searched the compound.

The palace's marble hallways were vast, decorated with gilded pools empty of water—save one, where people crouched and scrubbed laundry. Dark alcoves contained bedrolls and cutlery and children's toys. In some chambers the ceilings had collapsed, though these rooms were largely empty and the draft was blocked by plastic curtains affixed to doorways with gobs of gray sealant.

She didn't expect to find anything useful in the areas of the palace she was permitted to wander. But she memorized the locations of sealed doors and access-restricted lifts. She watched the cult's trusted members disappear down stairways guarded by muscular Gamorreans and a spidery Harch. Once she tried to walk the outer perimeter of the palace to figure out how large it really was, but she got lost in the Catadran streets and didn't try again.

Somewhere the cult had a prisoner they'd taken after the battle with Shadow Wing. Chass grew more confident in this daily—she caught snatches of conversation referring to "the guest" more than once, and had to resist the urge to throttle the speakers and demand more information.

The cult probably had a ship primed to evacuate its leader in the event of riot or rebellion somewhere, too. Maybe even a hyperspace transmitter Chass could use to contact the New Republic.

She would find them all. But the prisoner first.

She was scouting the lower reaches of the palace one afternoon when the sound of chanting led her into a wide chamber lit a fiery, flickering red. The noise emitted from a small black speaker that doubled as a lantern, suspended above what appeared to be a cremation furnace. A robed cultist stood beside the conveyor, surveying a procession of refugees approaching like peasants before a king. Chass observed through the doorway, careful to conceal herself.

A long-eyed Gran stepped forth from the line, knelt before the cultist, and—to Chass's bewilderment—held out a rifle in both hands.

"Do you forgo violence and the instruments of violence?" the cultist cried, and the Gran nodded. "Do you pledge yourself to the Speaker and Vessel of the Force, who tends to the Children of the Empty Sun?"

The Gran nodded again. The cultist grasped the weapon, set it gently on the conveyor, and sent it rolling through the arms of a nullifier field and into the flickering light.

"Then welcome, sister," the cultist proclaimed. "Shed the anarchy of rebellion and find truth with us."

The Gran moved away, and another cultist passed the Gran a robe folded like a platter, on which sat a gleaming square package that could have been a meal ration. The next refugee in line stepped forward and drew an antique scattergun, and the process began anew.

Chass attempted to suppress a gag of distaste—she wondered how many of the cultists whom she slept beside nightly had given up their weapons and their freedom for a single meal. She focused on the guns: A DH-17 pistol rolled down the conveyor, fed to the fires; probably stolen off the body of a rebel. A primitive beam tube went next; Chass wondered if it had been salvaged from some ancient temple.

She felt an eagerness, a hunger and *greed* she'd forgotten she was capable of. If she had to live with the cult any longer, she intended to do it armed.

She indulged the fantasy of racing in, grabbing a gun, and shooting her way out—crawling through the palace like a guerrilla fighter until she'd freed the prisoner and located a means of escaping the planet. Next she considered her realistic options: Steal a blaster off one of the would-be cultists in line? Smash the lantern and grab a weapon in the dark?

The solution came to her, shockingly obvious, when she spotted the cultist's unctuous smile as he accepted another gift.

Chass waited two hours before the ritual ended and the donors and cultists filed out a second doorway. The lantern dimmed but didn't go out. She scampered to the conveyor, lowered her body to the belt, and crept like a stalking cat through the entrance. She could see nothing inside where the fires had burned.

But there was no heat. She fumbled, arms outstretched, touching flat lenses and the spokes of gears. She touched grease and jabbed her palm on something sharp. Finally her hand closed on the leather grip of a hold-out blaster.

Of course the cult wouldn't destroy the weapons when it could stockpile them instead. The guns' destruction—like everything else in the palace—was a lie.

She was out of the furnace in a matter of seconds, off the conveyor and down the hallway so fast she tripped and propelled herself forward by will alone. As she turned a corner she tucked the weapon into her pants, under her shirt at the small of her back. A moment later she bowled into a body that howled in surprise.

Chass and the newcomer tumbled onto the floor together. She kicked and tried to disentangle herself, reached for the blaster and hoped it was charged as the man—whose face was covered in burn scars—wobbled to his feet, laughing.

As Chass regained her footing and clutched the weapon behind her she recognized him. When his expression changed to one of astonished bliss, she realized that he recognized her as well.

"You survived!" Gruyver cried and spread his arms wide. "You found your way to us."

Chass stroked the blaster's trigger guard and watched the man who'd saved her from the Vurk at Winker's and from suffocating in the depths of space. If he wasn't a brainwashed lunatic he was something worse— a willing agent of the Children of the Empty Sun, a knowing part of the con game.

"I guess I did," she said, and let her hand fall to her side.

She had a gun now. She could always shoot him later.

She told Gruyver the story of Maya Hallik, whose tale wasn't entirely unlike that of Chass na Chadic. Maya, too, was a New Republic fighter pilot, and Maya, too, had been raised in a *religious fellowship*. "My mother picked it because the leader was Theelin. Said he was the reincarnation of an old Theelin god, and we were following old Theelin customs," she said, before slurping up a mouthful of watery wheat noodles from a narrow thermos in the cult's kitchen. "All lies, of course. Why I reacted badly on the skiff. And at Winker's. Don't really trust cults."

"You came, though," Gruyver said. "You came anyway."

Chass grunted and sucked up another mouthful. Broth dripped down her lower lip, burning the skin. "Where else was I supposed to go? Crashed on a strange planet, not a lot of options."

Gruyver laughed and rubbed his hands together above a mug full of broth and almost no noodles. Chass was sure he knew she was lying—about her reasons, maybe about her name—but he said only: "I'm glad you did. I promise—there's no reincarnated gods here."

Spare me, she thought, and waited for him to preach.

"Eat," he said, and poured half his broth into her thermos. "Tell me about flying."

She saw no escape from the conversation, so they talked.

Gruyver, it turned out, had never left Cerberon. He spent their meal asking questions about hyperspace travel—what it looked and felt like, whether Chass was brave enough to jump to lightspeed in a one-person fighter, and on and on. The questions were penetrating but not insistent, and Chass found she could avoid answering simply by shrugging.

Eventually she asked him—making an effort to sound casual and instead sounding like a drunk woman pretending to be sober—"Anyone else end up here after the battle? Do you know?"

"One that I'm aware of," he said, "found adrift, much like you. She's still in the medical suite, I believe."

"Huh." Chass nodded. If she asked more—if she asked to see the prisoner—she'd certainly be refused. On the other hand, if she *didn't* ask it would be much too obvious she was onto them.

"Any chance I can visit?" she said.

"Once she's healed, I think," Gruyver replied.

"Great. So what were you asking about? You said you'd never seen a real sun before . . . ?"

Each day for the next three days, Gruyver found Chass after morning prayers and introduced her to cultists she'd previously managed to avoid. A Twi'lek woman whom Gruyver called his niece had a love for speeder bikes that she communicated passionately, if not articulately;

she exchanged stories with Chass about repairing engines and the joys of speed. A Clawdite changeling admitted to once imitating Let'ij, and being caught by the cult leader herself. Most of the cultists were Catadran natives but a few were migrants—one, Chass was convinced, had been a notorious bounty hunter from the Meridian sector before taking up with Let'ij and her crew. Another, calling herself New Dawn, had spent a month on Jedha and spoke at length with Chass about the hundred sects she had encountered—how they were similar and how they were different and how many were lost when that holy world had been destroyed.

The cultists told Chass about their hopes to expand and build and plant gardens in the city to feed thousands. They spoke about it like it was a normal thing to want. Like dreaming of a future outside war and chaos was something that people *did*.

Chass hated how it made her feel, but the comforting presence of her hold-out blaster made it tolerable. She had a way out if she needed it.

She located the medical suite on the first day but it wasn't until the evening of the third that she was confident enough in the medics' schedule to slip inside. She strolled past empty cots and over to the private rooms, peering through a small window into each.

She nearly missed the prisoner. In the fourth cell, in the corner next to a cot, was a humanoid form. Under the dim light, Chass was confused by how dark the woman's body appeared in contrast with the pale, bruised face. Then she realized it wasn't the body that was dark but the figure's clothes: black cloth and leathers specked with badges and patches and tubing.

Tubing?

Chass's eyes fixed on a white symbol on the shoulder: the six-spoked crest of the Galactic Empire.

"You're Shadow Wing," Chass said.

The woman in the Imperial flight suit raised her eyes to the window but didn't move.

"Give me one reason I shouldn't kill you," Chass said.

"New Republic?" the woman asked. Her voice was hoarse and barely decipherable.

Chass nodded.

"You want to get off of Catadra as much as I do," the woman said.

Chass raised the blaster and fired through the window. The woman screamed and clapped a hand to her arm where the leather of her flight suit had melted. The medical suite's alarms whined and trilled. "Never try to manipulate me," Chass said.

The woman's lips curled into a snarl. Chass ran for her life.

III

Easy, now, Wyl Lark thought, skimming fingertips over the console as if tickling the down of a sur-avka. *I'd trust you to fly blind, and it's not really so dark down here.*

But he didn't say the words aloud, because his comm was still open and the pilots at the other end of the transmission wouldn't put faith in a man who spoke to his ship. Instead he declared, "Fifteen kilometers—we're making good progress," and felt like a child unsure of his role.

"Who's fast and maneuverable now, huh?" Nath replied. "That A-wing of yours suddenly ain't worth much."

The other pilots' laughter followed. Wyl was grateful.

There were no stars outside his cockpit—not even the false stars of city lights. The only illumination came from his own vessel's emergency beams, painting swaths of rock and stalactites and revealing crevices that seemed too narrow to pass through until, upon approaching, they shucked the illusions of distance and widened to great maws. The tunnels honeycombing Troithe were as broad and straight as avenues and as slender and winding as a battle cruiser's maintenance shafts. Wyl flew at speeds a landspeeder could have surpassed, giving himself enough reaction time to dip beneath stone curtains or sweep around crystalline pillars.

Crashing wasn't his biggest worry, though; more likely was choosing a tunnel so narrow that he'd be unable to turn around. Wyl didn't consider himself claustrophobic, and he'd gone caving more than once among the cliffs of Home; but the weight of a planet was pressing down above him. He had no desire to face Troithe's underworld alone.

He had no desire to abandon his new squadron and leave them unprotected.

His comm crackled. "There are houses here. Whole villages preserved in stone!" Wyl recognized the voice of Denish Wraive—two centuries old, eighty years since he'd flown in combat, but as enthused to pilot his souped-up airspeeder as any child of Home climbing onto his first mount.

"They say there's ghost civilizations buried below the city foundations," Gorgeous Su replied through static. Wyl guessed she was passing through a distant tunnel. She was the most eager of his scouts, too quick to seek shortcuts without asking permission. Sister to the Houk he'd met among the infantry commanders, her massive frame had barely fit inside the Humble HoverCat's cockpit. "Probably a lot of superstitions we should be glad we don't know about."

"Ignorance as a defense against local culture," Ubellikos sniffed. The young human spoke with the stentorian articulation—and accent—of a Hutt. His confident indignation reminded Wyl of Chass. "Such an Imperial way of looking at things."

"Yes," Prinspai agreed with an insectoid chitter and click.

"Works well sometimes, though," Nath said, and the others laughed again.

They were Wyl's squadron now. He barely knew them, but they were his.

None of them had slept much since descending beneath the city. The Sixty-First Mobile Infantry had loaded into unarmed rumblers, tunnel-tanks, mining transports, and repulsorcars. Those ground vehicles stayed in constant motion, their drivers operating in shifts drawn up by company commanders. The resulting caravan slithered on its long journey toward the Scar of Troithe.

Wyl had been among those who'd approved taking the underground route—it was, according to the charts, far quicker than an overland passage and less likely to draw attention from Shadow Wing. But the unit had quickly discovered that the charts were out of date, and the aircraft were pressed into service mapping tunnels and caverns. Like the ground vehicles, the aircraft rarely stopped—the mining transports could carry two ships during the pilots' rest periods, but no more.

Wyl slept least of all. When he wasn't able to play scout he was running the pilots through drills, lecturing them about past encounters with Shadow Wing, or drawing up tactical maps. There wasn't space in the tunnels to train properly, so they trained *improperly* at slow speeds or at distances measured in meters instead of kilometers.

Even when Wyl's A-wing was docked with the caravan, he was busy discussing plans with Carver or checking the progress of the infantry's engineers. Two additional craft were still being refurbished—a repulsorcraft Wyl doubted could ever be upgraded to suit his squadron's needs, and a rusting Clone Wars starfighter Nath had called a V-wing. The latter resembled the mangled child of a TIE fighter and Wyl's own A-wing and he'd promised it to Sergeant Vitale, if it could be made to work.

He was flying alongside the caravan while most of the others were on recon duty. Their sensor pings painted a tunnel map onto his screens, and he felt his eyelids flickering when Gorgeous Su declared: "Game time."

Wyl snapped to alertness. "Enemies?" he asked.

Nath snickered. Ubellikos groaned with a rumble. Vitale, who was serving as the caravan's liaison to the squadron, said, "You mean a proper game, right?"

"*Who? What? Where?*" Su said. "Bored to tears, might as well."

Stay focused, Wyl wanted to say, but only because it was the sort of thing Quell or Rununja would have said to Alphabet or Riot Squadron. They all needed a distraction. The right thing to do was to let them have the game.

So he did.

"Just keep half an eye on your scanner, okay? If anyone crashes I'm going to get the blame."

The pilots and Vitale debated who would go first. They nominated Nath, who seemed disinterested but good-humored. His Y-wing stayed four hundred meters ahead of the caravan. "*Who* hears about my death first? Anyone who owes me credits; might as well make their day. *What's* the cause? Some punk with a vibroknife who wants to make a name for himself. *Where* does it happen? One of the Echo systems. Always pictured myself retiring to a tube-yacht there."

T5 chimed in the background, Vitale contended that Nath's *What?* was insufficiently specific, and Su and the others argued who would go next. Wyl thought of the last time he'd played, with Riot aboard the *Hellion's Dare;* they'd been on the run from Shadow Wing then, too, and he'd found the game at least as distasteful.

They're bonding. Let it happen. Be part of it.

"*Who?*" Vitale said. "My nephew back on Corellia. Good kid, and I'd like him to remember his aunt. *What?* Imperial Vizier Mas Amedda's personal guard detail. *Where?* Coruscant, obviously. We survive this mission, we're headed there sooner or later."

Su was next, and she hit her notes with practiced flare. "*Who?* My husband and love, Thage Howless, wherever his black heart might be. *What?* Whatever Shadow Wing's using for a command ship when I ram the bridge with an airspeeder packed full of armed warheads. *Where?* Someplace along the Rimma Trade Route, as we chase those bastards out of the Core."

"How exactly do you intend to fly a Humble HoverCat out to the Rimma?" Denish Wraive asked.

"I hate calling it that," Su answered. "I'm flying a child's toy."

"Besides," Vitale called, "Alphabet's got dibs on the Shadow Wing grudge."

"We can share," Nath said.

Vitale laughed. "What do you say, Wyl?"

He heard the playfulness and remembered their dinner with Alphabet among the refugees. "Plenty of grudge to share. But let's hope we don't have to, huh?"

Ubellikos made a rude noise of disapproval, Vitale laughed, and the game went on. Wraive was next, and he composed an intricate, minutes-long tale of his death from heart failure after saving his great-grandchildren in the final days of the war. Prinspai clicked briefly about an oxygen overdose. Wyl knew his turn was rapidly approaching, and he made an effort to find something to share—something disarming and honest instead of bleak—and all he could think of was: *I'm not planning to die. I'm not planning to let any of you die.*

A proximity alarm saved him from an answer. He checked his scanner and saw a mark moving through a side tunnel.

"Enemy!" Vitale called. "Game time for real!"

The TIE fighter flashed ghostlike above the rumblers and repulsorcars, pale in the illumination of its running lights and trailing the afterimage of its ion engines. Its scream echoed through the caverns, magnified and distorted, and Wyl found himself transfixed for precious seconds before he opened his throttle and gave chase. "One TIE," he called. "Probably a scout. Attempting to pursue—do *not* fire in the vicinity of the caravan. Last thing we need is a cave-in."

"Last thing we need is thirty more of those guys," Nath corrected.

The TIE pilot must have had the same concern—it did not fire as Wyl chased it past repulsorcars and Nath's Y-wing. A few of the infantry shot low-powered particle volleys, but aside from wrecking Wyl's night vision they had no effect. He shifted his eyes to his scanner until he readjusted, following the TIE into another tunnel branch.

He wondered if he'd met the enemy pilot before. Blink would have recognized him and made contact. The others he'd known best by their ships' damage and their fighting styles, neither of which applied today.

"How did they know where to look for us?" Ubellikos asked.

"Someone must've seen the vehicles we nabbed," Nath said. "Sort of implied we'd be going underground." His voice gave way to distortion as Wyl's distance from the caravan increased.

The A-wing could easily keep pace with the TIE, and Wyl rarely lost sight of his quarry's lights. But the TIE pilot was skilled and—Wyl suspected—better rested, making frequent last-second course changes and descents into whole new strata of the underworld. In one narrow passage, Wyl had to tilt his fighter oblique to the rock or risk clipping his wings. The TIE was barely more slender than the A-wing but *barely* was enough to give it an advantage. Wyl shifted his body in his harness as if his own weight would provide the extra tilt he needed.

His deflector screens shimmered as the electromagnetic field intersected the wall. The A-wing trembled and jostled within the shield bubble. Wyl smelled burning wiring and shut off his deflector screens altogether. *Now we're even,* he thought, watching the TIE.

He saw his chance when they emerged into a broader cavern. The TIE spun and juddered, attempting to force Wyl to fly past into its field of fire. He retained his relative position and fumbled with his comm. "TIE fighter," he called. He should have jammed all signals but the fighter hadn't attacked—it galled him to take the first shot unprovoked. "Reduce speed and surrender immediately."

It wouldn't work. It didn't work. He reduced power to his weapons (bypassing a malfunctioning capacitor to do so), attempting to find an intensity that would damage the TIE without causing an avalanche if he missed.

The TIE fired before he could. It bobbed upward, raking the cavern roof with particle fire an instant before its thrusters blazed—it was attempting to crush its pursuer and outrace the cavern's collapse. Wyl applied retro-rockets and repulsors to brake and squeezed his trigger as g forces squeezed him into his seat. He saw dust and the flash of his blaster cannons and veered starboard as the world fell and rumbled, trying to cut his velocity further and strike the avalanche sidelong instead of headfirst. *Shouldn't have dropped your shields after all,* he thought, and smiled and winced together.

He heard stone striking metal and the less melodic *crack* of debris against his canopy. A rain of boulders filled his peripheral vision; inertia carried his port wing dangerously close to the destruction. He attempted to roll onto his starboard side, buy himself another meter of clearance, but he didn't know whether he'd succeeded until his stabilizers kicked in and he realized he was hanging in his harness.

The rumbling stopped as the cave-in ceased. Dancing sparks illuminated the broken wing of a TIE fighter in the dark. The pilot's ploy had failed.

He's bought the caravan some time, he thought, as sweat rolled down his cheek and dripped onto the side of his canopy. But if Shadow Wing had found them once, Shadow Wing could find them again.

His squadron wasn't ready.

There wasn't much to do. Splitting the caravan wasn't an option—it might keep a sizable number of soldiers safe from attack but the ground vehicles would never reach the surface without aerial scouts. "We could park down here, fortify and prepare," Twitch suggested when the commanders assembled via comm, and even she laughed at the idea. "Get all crushed when the foe drops one bomb, but we'd be fortified and prepared for it."

"We keep rolling," Carver said. "Get distance from where they found us and hope we reach the surface before long."

It wasn't a plan but it was a declaration of intent, and Wyl didn't have anything superior to suggest. (Quell would have had a superior idea, but Wyl wasn't as clever as Quell or as experienced as Rununja.) He explained the situation to his pilots, trying to mix compassion with determination as he finished:

"For now, our job isn't to beat Shadow Wing or retake Troithe. It's to protect the rest of the troops. We're all tired, but we can do that much."

Gorgeous Su, Denish Wraive, Prinspai, Ubellikos, and Nath Tensent acknowledged the situation one by one. Wyl gave them their scouting assignments and was preparing for his own recon run when Nath asked, "Your cockpit smell like sweat and piss as much as mine does?"

Wyl laughed despite himself. "Probably. I've been trying not to think about it."

"When's the last time you climbed out, got some fresh air?" Nath paused. "Fresh as it gets down here, anyway."

"Been maybe eight hours. I am taking care of myself, Nath. Thank you."

"There's perks to being commander. No one's stopping you from taking four hours to land on one of the rumblers and get some sleep."

"That what you would've done, when you had a squadron?" Wyl asked. He tried to keep judgment out of his voice. In truth, he *did* wonder how Nath would handle the situation.

"Doesn't matter what I would've done. Just telling you what I figure."

Wyl drummed his fingers on his console and nodded. "Nath?"

"Talk to me, brother."

"Look out for the others, too. The way you do for me? They could use it. I could use it."

"The others haven't been through what we've been through. I'll do what I can, but—"

"The 204th hit all of us. They've been through enough. Please."

Nath didn't say anything for a long while. Wyl thought he heard T5 burbling in the background alongside static and engine noise. "I'll do what I can," Nath finally said.

Please, Wyl thought, but he didn't say what he wanted to say: that in their game of *Who? What? Where?* only Nath had been bold enough to imagine a life after the war; that the others needed hope, no matter how cynical, and they would listen to Nath more than they would Wyl.

Wyl was dreaming when the call came, his starfighter at rest atop the rumbler and visions of honeyblossoms filling his brain. The broad yellow petals dripped nectar onto his tongue; the sweet and tangy flavor filled him completely. But reality shredded the fantasy and he heard Su cry, "They're here!"

Several frantic exchanges later, the situation became clear: A full TIE squadron was en route to the caravan, no more than five minutes from arrival. Su had spotted them during recon and was now transmitting her scanner readings. Wyl detached his fighter from the rumbler but didn't lift off, trying to clear his mind as he reviewed maps of the nearest tunnels.

"Not much room for ship-to-ship combat," Nath said. The caravan was crossing a broad cavern amphitheater supported by gnarled pillars like petrified trees from the dawn of creation. "Prinspai's so far ahead we can't even get him on comms. How do you want to play this?"

"Could try to block them." Wyl ran a gloved fingertip over the map, strapping on his flight helmet with his other hand. "Find a choke point, collapse the tunnel like the TIE tried earlier."

Gorgeous Su sounded grim. "The one you said buried himself?"

Vitale's voice was clipped and irritable. "Carver's ordering weapons out. We're not stopping the caravan, but maybe we'll get lucky with a blaster shot or two."

Shooting down a TIE with handhelds would be challenging but not impossible; the soldiers were disciplined and experienced, and the cavern didn't provide room for the fighters to stay out of blaster range. But the ground troops were also packed together—that meant the TIEs could obliterate multiple vehicles in a single pass, killing twenty or thirty or fifty at once.

"They haven't seen us yet," Wyl said. "Su, I'm heading to your position. The two of us will draw them away from the caravan and reunite with the troops later."

The caravan was climbing one side of the amphitheater, heading for a misshapen tunnel entrance barely large enough for the tunnel-tanks. The rumblers strained at the ascent, smashing delicate spires as they went.

"You break off now, you'll never find us again," Vitale called.

Wyl's shoulders tightened. She was right to worry, but it hurt to hear her fear. "Su, jam all frequencies on my mark. Nath, you and Denish stay with the caravan. If I can't make it back, take command and I'll try to find you on the surface—"

"This is a bad plan, brother," Nath growled. Wyl could see the Y-wing's thruster fires ahead of him as the caravan entered the tunnel.

Carver's voice came through a second later. The infantry commander didn't hide his disdain. "Your plan is *not* approved. We can't afford to lose two ships—we're fighting a damn air war!"

"I'm in charge of the squadron," Wyl said. "Su? Activate jammers."

"Yes, sir," Su said, though there was a flatness in her tone that Wyl couldn't interpret.

The comm filled with static. Wyl activated his own jammers and lifted off the rumbler, eyeing the tunnel maps and hoping he could navigate the labyrinth in time to reach Su. Engine vibrations shook his body, and he watched the serpent of the caravan crawl beneath him. The tiny figures of soldiers crouched atop vehicles with rifles and portable cannons looked as delicate as a child's toys.

He had barely enough room to wheel his ship around. The caravan still extended past the tunnel mouth into the amphitheater, and beyond the opening he saw a flash of emerald. The TIEs were approaching, firing on Gorgeous Su.

He opened his throttle and felt his ship rattle as loose armor plating flapped and durasteel bolts strained. "You're tired, too," he murmured, but he smiled. This was his mission—he would fight Shadow Wing, and save lives, and he would do it all enveloped by primal geological wonders. If this was how he died away from Home, he'd be content.

Who? What? Where?

The last of the caravan vehicles—a twenty-passenger mining car—lurched into the tunnel entrance as Wyl approached. He slowed, intending to skirt its bulk as it moved into the tunnel proper; but the car, too, slowed and then stopped. He saw another flash of emerald beyond the entrance and tried to determine what was going on.

The shock wave hit him hard—he snapped backward against his seat as his ship lurched and white light flooded his cockpit. He heard the thunder of a quake, as he had during the cave-in caused by the TIE, but no alerts flashed on his console and nothing impacted his ship. He pulled to a halt and waited, fingers gripping his firing trigger.

When the dust dispersed, he peered at the mound of rubble where the tunnel mouth had been. The last of the mining cars was gone, and Wyl felt sick with certainty that he knew what had transpired.

He deactivated his jammers and waited for confirmation.

Carver called for a stop six hours later to repair an overheating repulsor-car. Wyl landed and walked on unsteady legs across uneven ground. When he returned from staring into the crystal-encrusted abyss of a nameless chasm lit only by phosphorescence—a sight he hoped to remember until the end of his days, despite the circumstances—Nath Tensent intercepted him a stone's throw from the caravan and their ships.

"You doing all right?" Nath asked.

"I am," Wyl said.

The older man pulled a stick of chewable caf from his pocket, tore it in half, bit into one portion, and held the other out to Wyl. Wyl took it after a moment of hesitation. "We were too late to do a blasted thing about Su," Nath said. "Whatever we did, she was outnumbered and too close to escape. You see that, right?"

"I do."

He did. The twenty soldiers aboard the mining car—the soldiers who'd detonated their own vehicle to keep Shadow Wing from pursuing—were another matter. But Nath didn't ask about them, and Wyl didn't bring up their sacrifice. He'd aired his distress to Carver—*It should've been my call!*—and been overruled already.

Instead he asked, "Are we making the wrong decision? Planning a counterattack like this?" and hoped Nath understood his meaning.

"You tell me. You wanted to leave the city, we left the city. You agreed we had to act, and that an air force was our best shot. Folks are dying to make all that happen, so if you've got another idea it's a good time to speak up."

It wasn't what Wyl had been hoping to hear. "I know. Right now, though, I could use some perspective—"

"You don't want my perspective." Nath glanced at the caravan, where soldiers and pilots squatted on vehicle roofs or laughed at ribald jokes under yawning cracks in the cave ceiling. "I'm on your side, but if you want someone to inspire you? You want someone to inspire Wraive and Prinspai and Ubellikos and Vitale?

"I don't know them any better than you do, and I don't care to. That's not what I'm here for."

Wyl stared at his friend. In time, he forced down his outrage and gloom and spoke as a commander was meant to speak.

"All right," he said. "Let's keep moving."

IV

Soran Keize walked with Governor Fara Yadeez down the path they'd come to enjoy together over the past days—a route that took them above Raddakkia Plaza on the drift-platforms and over to the rooftop gardens of the Taa Complex. Yadeez had told him that the sublevel greenhouse utilized a climate emulator. "Have you ever experienced snowfall, Colonel?" she asked as they alighted in the tearblossom glade. "Not in a holo or through a viewport, but actually *felt* it?"

"I grew up on a world with eight-month winters," Soran answered. "I know what it feels like." But he smiled as he said it, and the words brought back the taste of mulled rordash-root cider and the ache of cheeks numbed by frost.

"Then I wish we had the power to spare so that you could tell me whether the climate emulator is any substitute for reality." She shrugged. "Then again, I hear the New Republic intends to repurpose Hoth as a prison for those who remain loyal to the Empire. Maybe I'll have my chance someday."

It was not a rumor that Soran had heard, nor one that seemed credible—for all the New Republic's hypocrisies, its chancellor was dedicated to a pretext of justice over punishment. Repurposing Hoth, the icy world where the rebels had been so badly defeated, had too much poetry.

He'd begun to respond when Yadeez cut him off. "Ignore my self-pity. You were telling me about Core Nine?"

"I was. My scouts arrived this morning and found the facility intact, much as your files described. They confirmed the presence of a bulk ore freighter in the launch bay—more than a century old and infested with mynocks, but structurally sound."

"The freighter interests you?"

"It does." He could have left it at that, and she might not have questioned him. Yet he'd gone over the conversation in his mind already and chosen the path he believed best served his cause. "If it could be made operational, it could provide an advantage in our mission."

"How much ore were you expecting to take from Troithe, Colonel?" The humor in her words was absent from her eyes, which watched him keenly as they walked the gravel path through the gardens.

Soran paused to kneel beside a condenser coil wrapped with a yellow vine sporting iridescent green blossoms. He inhaled an odor reminiscent of Chandrilan vanilla. "Both my Star Destroyer and my carrier are gone. Consider what would be possible if we armed the freighter for combat. It would require a larger engineering crew than I can field, but there may be weapons salvageable from the wreckage of the *Edict*. If mounted aboard the freighter . . ."

He trailed off to allow Yadeez to develop the fantasy as she wished. Part of him even meant what he implied.

"It would still be a freighter," she said, "albeit one capable of smashing mountains. You could strike at facilities deep in enemy territory without risking your TIEs. Maybe even claim control of the planet's defense shields."

Several of the shield generator installations had fallen into Imperial hands already. Others had proved less tractable. "You understand, then," he said, and rose to face Yadeez.

"I do, Colonel. However I can help you and your mission, I will."

They continued their walk, discussing the particulars of the project—where to source the engineers; how to transport them to the wreckage of the *Edict* and Core Nine; how long it would take before the freighter was ready, and whether Core Nine could be secured before General Syndulla's remnant arrived there. These subjects put Soran on more comfortable ground, and it might have been a conversation with any companionable agent of the Empire.

It was easy for him to forget the true purpose of the freighter. That he had seized on it as the answer to his troubles—the one starship on Troithe large enough to carry a wing of TIE fighters offworld and into hyperspace. To ensure the 204th's survival, he *needed* it.

With regrets, he would have to leave Troithe's survival to the governor. Like Soran, she was responsible for her own people first and foremost.

That night, Soran attended the service for Lieutenant Garmen Naadra, who had been lost in the caverns beneath Troithe during Squadron Three's efforts to locate the enemy remnant. Naadra was the first pilot lost since the battle against the *Lodestar*, and therefore the first who could be honored properly, as an individual instead of as one loss among many.

Soran had known Naadra well, though he'd spent little time with her in the past year; he'd mentored her shortly after her graduation from the Academy, humored her desire for tactical plans and custom simulator drills over the course of months until she had become a confident soldier. Naadra had never expressed the ethical reservations others had; never even spoken to Soran about why she'd enlisted. She had only wanted to become a better pilot and conquer her fears by doing so.

He said none of this at the small gathering led by Captain Darita in the Taa Complex gardens. Imperial military regulations discouraged formal memorial services, but every unit had its own discreet traditions. Aboard the *Pursuer*, that had meant a short ceremony performed by Colonel Nuress to celebrate the elevation of the officer next in line, followed by a private reading by the appropriate squadron commander of any testament left by the deceased and the distribution of personal belongings.

Naadra's possessions and testament, if any, had been left aboard the *Aerie* and her body and TIE were lost underground. There was nothing to remember her by, nor anyone to elevate in her place.

So the squadron told stories, in the timeless manner of soldiers. Darita gave Soran a glare of defiance when the reminiscing began, as if she held him responsible for *this* death, if not all the others; but he took no offense and he shared his own tales of Naadra when the time came. Late in the night, they started a fire from the brittle branches of wilting foliage and talked about Blacktar Cyst and the chase through the Redspace Reefs where the *Pursuer* had earned its name.

In mourning Naadra, Soran allowed himself to mourn Palal Seedia, whom he had led to defeat over Catadra. He'd wished to know her better and to see her achieve her potential. Vann Bragheer, too, had been a profound loss to the wing. Gablerone's absence continued to strike Soran often during the day. He'd had no time to bid farewell to them, to remember or honor them. But he could mourn Naadra.

For the first time since Soran's return to the 204th, he felt like he was again among his people. They had changed, and he had changed; but they were Shadow Wing nonetheless, and he was glad that they were his.

He woke from dreams of flight in which Rikton, whom he had known in his life as Devon, served as his wingmate on their mission to avenge Garmen Naadra. But Naadra became Fara Yadeez, then Yrica Quell, and Rikton and Quell both died in the New Republic prison camp called Traitor's Remorse; and when the comm call jolted Soran from his bed and summoned him to the makeshift landing field in the plaza, he was glad for it.

Yadeez had sent the message and met him there. She was dressed in an informal coat of thin violet fabric that fell to her ankles and billowed in the breeze. He wondered if she'd risen on short notice as well; Soran had worn his flight suit often over the past days, but tonight it had seemed absurd and he'd pulled on an ill-fitting nobleman's shirt and slacks one of the supply crews had found.

Yadeez didn't look exhausted. Instead her expression was brighter than he'd ever seen, and there was a buoyancy to her step. "Colonel," she said. "I have a gift for you."

"A gift?"

She tilted her head, as if straining not to look back at the field of TIEs—all of them showing scars of battle by now, including the ones freshly salvaged from the Jarbanov junkyard. Among the starfighters sat a boxy atmospheric skyhopper that might have once been considered luxurious but struck Soran as dated and utilitarian. Not one of the 204th's, which meant it belonged to the governor's people.

"The first crews arrived this morning," Yadeez said. "They spent all day with the wreckage of your Star Destroyer and told me they found . . . something I thought you'd want to see."

Soran spotted movement on the skyhopper's ramp. Two ununiformed men with the bearing of Imperial officers descended, frequently looking behind them. Yadeez kept talking. "The governor—Governor Hastemoor—shouldn't have known, but he had eyes and ears in strange places and I recognized it from his files. I don't know—"

She cut herself off as a third figure descended the ramp, weaving as if inebriated or grievously wounded. Soran saw the hem of the figure's robes first—red cloth and leather that never brushed the ground. The slender silhouette of the torso followed, unremarkable except for the left arm severed midway between elbow and shoulder. Nothing bound or concealed the stump; the wires that hung sparked and popped.

Soran had no wish to look upon the figure's face, but the compulsion overwhelmed him. The glass plate was unmarred, if smeared with ash, and from within a light flickered: a holographic face, aged and waxen with sunken eyes and a crease of a mouth held in a scowl or a smirk. The sapphire light blurred into static, re-formed an instant later, then disappeared altogether.

Soran knew what he looked upon. He did not understand how it had survived the obliteration of the *Aerie* or found the wreckage of the *Edict.*

"It is the Messenger, isn't it?" Yadeez asked.

"Of course," Soran said.

His pilots had changed without him, and changed again upon his return. He had hoped their fall to Troithe had freed them from their past.

Yet there was no escaping the shadow of the Emperor.

CHAPTER 17

SHATTERED WORLDS AND NIGHTMARES

I

The next time Chass na Chadic met the prisoner of the Children of the Empty Sun, the Imperial pilot had been released from the medical suite and permitted to mingle with the cultists. She hobbled on steel crutches, remained in her flight suit, and was accompanied by a pair of "medics" who looked more like guards. The three of them passed by the laundry pool as Chass was scrubbing a shirt; the pilot saw her but her gaze did not linger.

Good, Chass thought. *Maybe she's learned her lesson.* Maybe she understood that Chass wasn't afraid to shoot at her heart next time.

Chass had come to the palace to rescue a New Republic pilot and build a plan to escape Catadra and destroy the 204th. Instead she'd found a blaster and a Shadow Wing pilot and nothing more. She was getting impatient with her progress, but she was developing a new plan.

Gruyver continued introducing Chass to most every cultist in the palace, and though that left her busier than before she was now *trusted*. She had a room of her own—a tiny, unpainted stone cell. She'd been invited to take part in the garden planting the following month. A small child had taken to giving her presents—little sculptures of bent wire representing Catadran animals; Chass didn't have the heart to reject these and lined them up against her cell wall. Most significantly, she'd been able to steal a radio so she could listen to subspace static on concealed headphones during Let'ij's daily lectures, awaiting a signal from the New Republic or Imperial reinforcements or whatever she could get.

The third time she encountered the prisoner was that same evening, on her way back to her cell to lounge and plot. She passed the TIE pilot in a palace corridor and the woman moved surprisingly swiftly, despite the burn marks and bruising and limp—she planted her feet on the marble, adjusted her stance, and jabbed a crutch into Chass's nose before Chass realized she was under attack. The medics rushed toward them as they scuffled and fell.

Chass was attempting to pound the woman's head against the marble floor when her adversary leaned up, teeth close to Chass's ear. "You know about Shadow Wing?" the woman hissed.

The last time she'd spoken, Chass had chalked up the hoarseness in the woman's voice to fatigue and injury. Now she heard something new—a hitch of static. Maybe a medical vocabulator?

"Yeah," Chass grunted.

"You were at Pandem Nai," the woman said.

The medics were trying to pull Chass away. The woman clamped her teeth on Chass's earlobe, released, and whispered, "I know where to find a ship."

When they parted ways, Chass was bleeding profusely. The pilot met her gaze and bowed her head in a gesture that seemed almost submissive.

Gruyver visited Chass in the medical suite while her nose was bandaged by the attendants. They checked her horns for damage with an expertise Chass could grudgingly admit—if only to herself—that she'd never experienced in the New Republic. "Does your species require any additional care?" one attendant asked, and Chass almost snorted in reply. The sudden, sharp pain and rush of salty blood into her throat turned the sound into a gurgle.

"Aren't there people on the street who need treatment more?" Chass asked Gruyver when the attendants moved away. She spat a wad of blood and phlegm onto the marble.

"Anyone outside is welcome to join us. But we can't force them," Gruyver answered.

"Your medics *could* go to the people of Catadra instead of promising bacta as a recruitment bonus." She tried to keep the disgust out of her tone—she didn't want to lose Gruyver's trust—but she didn't try hard.

The scarred man laughed anyway. He seemed to laugh at just about anything. "You're ornery when you're injured, Maya. I can't speak for Let'ij, for she speaks for the Force—but she always says the health of the fellowship, of the community, is what matters most of all."

"In that case, why'd you rescue *me*? Why'd you grab—" She almost said *the Shadow Wing pilot.* "—the Imp?"

"Have you spent much time on Catadra? Just because we don't walk into a riot or a holy war doesn't mean we have no mercy."

"And you keep the Imp under guard because . . . ?"

Gruyver smiled brightly and wiggled a finger at Chass's nose. This time *she* laughed—a quick, humorless bark. She wondered how many cultist limbs the woman had broken.

Gruyver shrugged and offered his arm to Chass as she stood up from the examination table. "She told the man who found her that her name was Lieutenant Palal Seedia," Gruyver said. They walked alongside each other out of the medical suite and back toward the palace living chambers. "That's about all she says. Let'ij says to welcome her, so we welcome her. *You* should welcome her; set an example."

"An example of what?"

"What the future could look like. Rebels and Imperials, working together and moving past their grudges to be part of something bigger."

Chass smirked and prodded the bridge of her nose, sending a jolt of pain into her skull. "So we're definitely not hostages for you to use when *whoever's* running the system takes a closer look at your operation?"

"Do you want to leave, Maya?" Gruyver stopped abruptly and turned to face her. "You're no hostage. You can leave if you must."

Tone it down, she told herself.

"Childhood trauma. Bad cult when I was young. Remember?"

"I do," Gruyver said. "Maybe Palal Seedia brings back other bad memories, too? You think about your friends from the New Republic?"

She'd never talked about friends—Maya's *or* Chass's. She thought of Nath Tensent's face, caught a flicker of Wyl Lark, and pushed it all down before the worst of them rose up in her brain. "They weren't my friends," she said.

"Everyone had friends before they found the fellowship. Know that you have family now—but if there's anyone we should watch for? Anyone you wish us to haul to safety if we find her floating in the void? You need only say the word."

The name Chass didn't want to remember rose up again. The woman who had stolen her trust, lied to her, earned her loyalty and let her down. *If you see Yrica Quell? If she's still alive? Then you kill her.*

She blinked away a sting in her eyes. The words came without thinking.

"I knew a woman named Kairos. I don't know if she made it out, but she deserves better than to die in a stasis tube."

"Of course," Gruyver said. "Of course."

Gruyver's urging to *set an example* made it easier to meet the Imperial without drawing attention. The next morning Chass cornered her in a dusty, half-collapsed corridor that smelled like pipe smoke. Once again, Chass threatened to kill the woman.

Seedia listened patiently to Chass's lavish descriptions of evisceration before asking: "You'll wait to settle our differences on the outside?"

"You said you have a ship?" Chass asked.

If Seedia had been part of the attack—if she'd killed Alphabet Squadron and Riot Squadron and Hound Squadron—then she *would* die. But if she could lead Chass to the rest of the people who needed killing, so much the better.

"The cultists thought I was unconscious when they brought me here. I was not." The woman's vocabulator whined like an insect; she didn't seem to notice. "I know where they keep their vessels. I can't get there on my own, though—not with *these*."

Chass eyed the crutches. "We climbing somewhere?"

"I need access codes or grade-four explosives. Normally I would steal one or both. Under the circumstances—"

"I get it." Chass scowled. She could rig a basic bomb if she sacrificed her blaster's battery and scavenged parts from the kitchens and the bathrooms, but grade four meant they were going through something thicker than a standard blast door. "Whose access codes?"

"I'm not certain. I assume even the *holy Vessel of the Force* needs a code cylinder."

She spoke with such disdain that Chass smiled despite herself.

Nothing ever came easy. Chass learned the name of the child who insisted on giving her toys—Nukita—and she discovered where the palace corridors dead-ended in unpainted granite or mounds of rubble. She sought in vain for a cultist who dealt in contraband, or one who could grant her access to heavier weaponry. She located a crypt used by whoever had built the palace centuries before and found the solitude there peaceful.

She saw the cultists attempt to welcome Seedia as they'd welcomed her. The Imperial began to take meals with the others, reluctantly spearing fried beetles before stalking away. The cultists endeavored to make conversation each time, asking Seedia what she thought of the food or if she liked the clothes left for her—nothing that touched on matters personal or political. Usually, Seedia ignored the speakers altogether.

Once, however, when Nukita offered the pilot one of her bent wire toys, Seedia whispered something to the girl and sent her away bawling. Chass saw the exchange from start to finish and something turned in her gut.

She made a note to kill the woman slowly.

The next time Let'ij lectured to the cult, Chass removed her headset and listened.

"How many of you," the fungus-faced hologram began, "sought to destroy yourselves before coming to the Children? How many of you indulged in practices, knowingly or unknowingly, that could only have led to your doom?" The woman smiled with gentle humor. "Did you toil, obedient to droids you believed you owned? Did you steal and deceive so that you could earn credits for spice and death sticks? Did you *fight*, claiming to yourself that it was for a worthy cause?

"Look at your neighbors. They did the same. There's no shame in this galaxy except the shame of self-deception. There's no reason to carry with you the burden of your past, or the burden of dreams for the future. With the Children of the Empty Sun, there *is* no future."

That's the most honest thing you've ever said, Chass thought, and shifted on her blanket in the common area. One of the cultists—no one she knew—rested his head against her shoulder.

"The Jedi Order tells stories about men with great destinies, whom the Force chooses for terrific deeds. But the Force doesn't desire greatness. The Force desires simplicity and life and love. The Children of the Empty Sun may one day spread across the galaxy, but as individuals? We will rise every morning and sing and eat and raise our children according to the laws we have deciphered from cosmic truth.

"There are no criminals among us—no paths to doom. Nor are there heroes."

The lecture went on for a very long time. Afterward the cultists gathered for their thrice-weekly "disquisition," in which small groups sat in silence until, one by one, the attendees rose and spoke about whatever the Force *moved* them to speak.

Usually these little speeches were confessions of sins, major or minor, from various points in the speaker's lifetime. To Chass, the whole affair looked an awful lot like a way to gather blackmail material—she expected there were recording devices in all the disquisition rooms, ready for Let'ij and her attendants to review. She'd seen similar scams elsewhere and thought, as scams went, it was a pretty good one.

Today Gruyver talked about his daughter, whom he'd abandoned along with her mother years earlier. A pale child admitted he'd been eating raw nectrose crystals, despite the cult discouraging sweets. A tusked Aqualish spoke at length in a language that Chass didn't understand; he was applauded and embraced when he finished. Chass searched for something to talk about in case she was asked to share—something appropriate to the life she'd built for Maya Hallik.

The confessions went on. No one even looked at her.

Lieutenant Palal Seedia rose from the auditorium's bottom tier on a single crutch. Chass hadn't seen her, hadn't recognized her in civilian garb instead of her flight suit. Her electronically enhanced voice reverberated through the room, distorted by echoes.

"I executed a planet," Seedia said. "I was part of Operation Cinder and I accept personal responsibility for the cleansing of Nacronis."

The cultists shuffled in their seats but no one interrupted.

"I don't think of that as the worst thing I've done," the pilot went on. "Many people would disagree—I assume the New Republic would hang me for it, probably after giving me as humiliating a trial as they could manage—but I was raised to believe in duty and obedience to those who uplifted and privileged me. I can't bring myself to believe that obedience is ever truly wrong. At worst, it's like a solar flare—bad news in the wrong circumstances but not possessed of agency. You don't hang a sun for incinerating a passing freighter.

"That said? I've done many things I *am* ashamed of. I left my twin sister in charge of the estate when I promised my father I'd care for it and pass it on to my children. I once—I've made errors on missions that cost lives, and I—"

Seedia paused and looked around at the crowd. Her voice fell.

"The worst thing I've ever done—the thing I feel most guilty about, that I've done more than once? I didn't tell my friends I loved them when they went on a mission to die.

"Not because I was scared, or—not because I was scared. Because it seemed undignified. So they died without knowing."

Seedia sat down. Scattered applause sounded before silence resumed.

What the hell was that? Chass thought, though she had a good guess.

Chass met with Seedia that night in one of the palace gardens. Even through her broken nose the smell of mulch was almost overwhelming.

"The ancient Tangrada-Nii general Mardroon called it *crossing the threshold of the mirror,*" Seedia said.

"What?"

"The moment when you've seen the face of your foe. When you've gotten so close, learned so much about each other, that whoever moves first is bound to win." The TIE pilot sounded disinterested, as if she were explaining something rudimentary. "It's a dangerous time. But the gravest peril is to wait too long—to believe you've not yet arrived at the threshold, when you already have. You risk going from understanding the enemy to *becoming* the enemy."

Chass wasn't a fool. She understood. Mostly.

"The cult? Or us?"

"You tell me," Seedia said. "I tried to earn their trust today, but you saw the result. They're brainwashed idiots and provincial yokels but they're not entirely stupid."

"At least they don't go around killing planets," Chass snapped.

They watched each other awhile.

"You're the one with the blaster and working legs," Seedia said. "If we don't get the access codes soon I suggest we take hostages."

Chass wrinkled her nose as the bandage tickled her skin. "I can get the access codes," she said. "Then you die, or I die, and the winner gets the star system."

||

The Cerberon sky was dazzling after so long spent underground. The stars bled together into shining clouds, too dense and bright to do otherwise. No electric lanterns or neon signs tarnished the heavens' clarity—the only sources of illumination at ground level were twinkling indicators on droids and repulsorcars, and the distant blue-green fires that rose from the cracked landscape of pitted metal plains and blasted canyons.

"It's beautiful," Wyl Lark murmured, his hand resting on T5's top module.

A flight of ships crept overhead from the direction of the city.

"They're heading for our target, you know," Nath said.

"I know." Wyl felt an unexpected flash of irritation, though he was confident that Nath meant no condescension. He hoped his voice hid his emotions; despite their spat below the surface, the last thing Wyl wanted was to alienate his friend. "There's nowhere else they would go. But if they're setting a trap, they're not being subtle about it."

"Maybe they figured we wouldn't look up." Nath shrugged, T5 chimed and vibrated beneath Wyl's hand, and then Nath continued, "Or maybe they figured there's no turning back for us. We go to the mining facility or we starve to death in this wasteland."

"Wouldn't surprise me."

Wyl surveyed the ruined land around them. The Sixty-First Mobile Infantry was hidden within a ravine as desolate as any asteroid. But where CER952B had been shaped by meteorite impacts and erosion over millions of years, the Scar of Troithe had been formed by living beings. Its shattered expanse lacked the grandeur of mountains or ocean depths; instead it resembled a pane of hardened glass repeatedly struck by a hammer until cracks covered every centimeter. The continent had been excavated and strip-mined until it was barren; and then the people of Troithe had kept digging until there was nothing left but chasms and unquenchable flames.

T5 squawked louder and wiggled from side to side. Nath looked back to the sky and Wyl followed his gaze, spotting three new lights—vessels flying low in the atmosphere, close enough for their howling to be heard.

"Droid recognizes the engine signature. Says they're cargo hoppers," Nath said. "Looks like the Imps are moving in some serious equipment. Could be they thought our plan was too good not to steal?"

Wyl laughed. Someone shouted his name and he removed his hand from T5. "If our plan was good enough for Shadow Wing, then we must be getting better at this," he said, and hurried to answer his summons.

The commanders met in a circle of dust in the shadow of overhanging rocks. The rest of the company provided them with a modicum of privacy by staying at a distance, but Wyl still heard boots shuffling in the dust and the low murmur of conversations throughout the ravine. Carver had given orders to stick to the shadows and keep the noise down, yet there was only so much the troops could do to hide their presence.

"Good thing they're not actually looking for us," Twitch muttered. The churlish, middle-aged squad leader was cleaning an assault rifle as she squatted in the dirt, paying more attention to her weapon than to the rest of the group.

"There's more going on than a scheme to ambush us," Carver agreed. The sergeant-turned-unit-commander looked as if he'd aged over the past days, his skin cinched tight over his muscles. "If we were their top priority, their scouts would be all over the canyons. Hell, they could blow the mining facility apart from the inside and pick us off out in the open."

"Then they want the facility for its own sake," Wyl said. He glanced around the circle.

No one argued. No one spoke.

Carver broke the silence. "Come on, people. We wanted it because it could hold up against a siege, give us a place to stage hit-and-run attacks from. So what are the Imps going to get from an old megafacility that they can't find anywhere else?"

Junior, the elderly human Wyl rarely heard speak, shifted awkwardly. "It's a deep core drilling site. Troithe has an unusual mineral composition. Volatile minerals." Without turning his head, he flapped a hand in the direction of a column of blue-green flame lighting the ravine from kilometers away. "Maybe they want to blow it up."

Twitch looked up from her rifle. "The whole planet?"

"Maybe," Junior said. "Chain reaction? Quake activity? I don't know."

"Lark." Carver was scowling. "You were the one who said Shadow Wing wouldn't care about preserving the population. Could that go for infrastructure, too? Any reason to think they'd hesitate to blow a world?"

"I'm not sure." It was an honest answer, and better than *I hope not.* "They were part of Operation Cinder—so yes, they're willing to kill a population. But if they came to retake Cerberon for the Empire, I don't know if they'd ruin it all out of spite—"

Carver spoke over him. "Denying resources to an enemy isn't *spite.*"

"—especially after what happened at Pandem Nai. The 204th worked *with* us to stop that planet from burning, even when they knew they were going to lose. Whatever the reasons for Cinder, Pandem Nai is the most recent action we can point to."

Twitch snorted. "Not inspiring faith."

"Let's not assume they're capable of detonating the core of the planet," Lien Toob said. Like Junior, the Sullustan was mostly an unknown to Wyl, though she'd struck him as pragmatic in their past meetings. "Imperials are monsters, not gods. We shouldn't confuse what they'd *want* to do with what they *can.*"

"Let's not underestimate them, either," Carver said.

The conference splintered from one discussion into several. Carver,

Twitch, and the massive Houk named Jorgatha—Gorgeous Su's brother—began sketching assault plans in the dust, debating whether it was too late to take the facility in a frontal attack. Junior began pulling up data, listing the facility's known assets to anyone who would listen and trying to find precedents for a planet-wrecking bomb. Lien Toob split her attention between Junior and Wyl, asking questions about Shadow Wing's past strategies and leadership that Wyl felt unprepared to answer.

Even as he spoke to Lien Toob, Wyl tried to listen to Junior. Most of the mining equipment, the man said, was likely long gone from the facility. If the 204th did intend to detonate underground mineral deposits, they would need to bring in heavy machinery. "Could explain the cargo hoppers streaking across the sky," Junior muttered.

It was an intriguing point, but another item in Junior's equipment inventory nagged at Wyl's attention. He sat pondering, reluctant to interrupt anyone until the thought boiled over in his brain. "It's possible they're trying to escape," he said, crisp enough to demand the others' attention.

"Escape *what*?" Twitch asked.

"They lost their Star Destroyer. Everything we've heard suggests they lost their cruiser-carrier, too. What if they're trapped in Cerberon with us?" He paused, sucked in a breath, and went on: "Junior said the facility had a bulk freighter to move ore into orbit. Maybe it's still there. Maybe all Shadow Wing wants is to get out of here after their plan went wrong?"

The others glanced at one another. Wyl saw nothing but skepticism in their eyes.

"Junior," Carver said. "There really nothing else on the planet that could cart around a TIE wing? Would a mining barge actually do the trick?"

"Probably. Probably and probably," Junior said.

Carver grunted. "So it's conceivable that our enemies—the same boys and girls who wiped out one world already, who blew up the *Lodestar*, and who've got a reputation for nastiness and scheming—

want to pick up and leave. It's also conceivable that they're looking to cut their losses and fry the whole planet."

"Conceivable it could be both," Twitch added, though no one acknowledged her.

"Tell me, Lark," Carver said. "How much you willing to bet it's one over the other? Because if we hang back and wait, the consequences could be dire."

The sergeant's tone was aggressive but not challenging. Wyl expected the man would listen to his answer.

"I wouldn't bet the fate of Troithe on it," Wyl conceded.

"All right," Carver said, and clapped his hands together. "Then let's make a new plan, the way we always do when things go south. We thought the mining facility would be where we holed up and waited for reinforcements. Turns out it's our latest target. Almost like we're rebels again, huh?"

"Hope your squadron's ready for action," Twitch said.

So they turned back to drawing landscapes in the dust and studying readouts of the facility, and for many hours they talked. They discussed ground assaults and the squadron's readiness, and whether the V-wing and the airspeeders could be armed with heavy ordnance.

No one brought up the possibility of Shadow Wing escaping again. Eventually Wyl realized what he had to do.

There were scouts and guards and soldiers who played cards through the night. Denish Wraive, Prinspai, Ubellikos, and Vitale had taken to spending their evenings together ever since Gorgeous Su's death, reviewing Wyl's latest combat courses or catching up on gossip from friends in the infantry. He brought them together with Nath and outlined the strategy, promising more details once particulars of the ground assault were finalized. He told them to sleep; that the next day would be difficult. "This wasn't the operation we were expecting," he finished, "but we knew it would come to a fight sooner or later. We'll take them by surprise and show them it's not about the ships. It's about the pilots and the plan."

He wasn't sure he'd convinced them, but they went to bed shortly thereafter.

Thus, the camp was quiet when Wyl climbed out of a rumbler and padded toward one of the fissures off the ravine. The pack slung over his shoulders didn't slow him, though the smell of old leather was mixed with something like ammonia and mold.

He clambered over rocks and squeezed between outcroppings, scraping the skin from the back of his neck before he arrived in a broader canyon and increased his pace. He'd considered taking his ship for the journey, but doing so would've drawn attention from friends and foes alike. His mission tonight was a solitary one, and he'd worked out the timing in detail—he had ninety minutes to travel as far from the camp as possible, half an hour to attend to his task, and another ninety minutes to return before the black hole ascended above the horizon and began to rouse the soldiers.

Wyl tried to remember the last time he'd traveled alone on foot through the wilderness—even a wilderness as tainted as the Scar of Troithe—and recalled nothing from his life with the Rebel Alliance or the New Republic. He remembered only Home.

For so long, his world had been his starfighter and his squadron. He wondered what he'd lost along the way.

The solitude weighed heavier the farther he went. There was no wildlife, not even nocturnal animals foraging. He missed the sounds of his companions breathing; the rustle of movement and the rumble of engines. He briefly directed his attention skyward, to the stars and the trail of cargo hoppers blazing toward the mining facility, but he tripped on the uneven ground and reluctantly lowered his head again.

He listened to the faint breeze and the distant crackle of mineral fires.

He found a slope to ascend and wished he'd brought his gloves as he scaled the boulders. Yet he'd been climbing ridges since his childhood, and this one was no challenge. When he crested the plateau he kept walking until the shattered land around him appeared infinite and undifferentiated—until it felt as if he would never find his way back to the company.

Next he set his pack down and took out the transmitter. The readout revealed low-level activity across frequency bands, which Wyl took to be the Imperial ships in conversation and the background noise of the planetary communications web. He adjusted the settings, opened a comm channel, activated the holo-imager, and placed the transmitter in the dust.

He stood over it and spoke.

"This is Wyl Lark of New Republic unit Alphabet Squadron, attempting to reach the 204th Imperial Fighter Wing," he said. "I am aware this communication is irregular. I am also aware that you know who I am. We've spoken before, at Pandem Nai and in the Oridol Cluster."

You know you can trust me, he thought, but it was a leap he needed his listeners to make on their own. He omitted mention of Blink's message to him over Troithe, though it was Blink he imagined as he spoke—he didn't know why the TIE pilot had warned him, and he didn't dare expose what the Empire might consider treason.

"I believe that some of you are tired of fighting. I can count the comrades I've lost battling you. I can count the TIE fighters I've destroyed. I don't want to do it anymore, not unless I have to in order to protect—" *Not the New Republic. Not even Home.* "—in order to protect more people from dying.

"I'm exhausted. You're exhausted. If you're trying to escape this system, if you want to find a way out of this, let's come to some sort of solution before—"

The voice that interrupted Wyl was low and stern. He recognized it immediately. "Probably best if you stepped away from the transmitter," Nath said.

Wyl turned around slowly but did not step away. Nath Tensent stood five meters distant, fingering the grip of his sidearm on his hip and wearing an expression of weary admonition. Past Nath was T5, antenna raised as it observed the scene.

"Tell me you didn't block the message," Wyl said.

"Could tell you that, but you'd know I lied soon enough." Nath jutted a thumb back at T5. "Little junker doesn't have much range but it's pretty good with a jammer. Got here just in time, too."

"You knew what I was planning?"

"Hadn't a clue. Thought someone should keep track of you anyway."

Wyl stared at his friend in bewilderment. "I don't know what you think I'm doing. I'm trying to save people, Nath—us, Shadow Wing, Troithe, everyone—"

"I gathered that. I didn't figure you were turning traitor, but the odds your plan ends well are pretty slim." Anger seeped up through Nath's calm façade. "Assuming you don't get shot by the first TIE that comes along, what do you think is going to happen? There's a *war* going on."

Wyl did his best to keep his voice steady. Mirroring Nath's ire gained him nothing. "Shadow Wing wants a way out. They're trying to get a ship offworld—"

"I heard your theory. I know."

"—and Blink *spoke* to me above Troithe. It's how I knew it was the 204th. Blink warned me because—I don't know, maybe because of a respect for what happened at Pandem Nai. But he or she or *whoever* Blink is sent me a message before the jamming started."

Nath looked genuinely surprised for the first time. He blinked the reaction away soon enough. "Did that message prove useful in any way?" he asked.

"What do you mean?"

"Blink telling you it was the 204th. Did it save the *Lodestar*? Did it save Chass and Meteor? Seems it split us up and distracted us instead of doing much good."

Wyl began to turn away. Nath shot him a look of warning that made him pause.

"No," Wyl admitted. "But sometimes people fail. We don't assume that means they aren't sincere. There is a real chance here."

"I expect there was a real chance in the Oridol Cluster, too. But your friends died there, and the risk is bigger now." Nath exhaled performatively, raising both hands and starting to cross the distance to Wyl. "You talk to them? They can kill you, or get a lead on us, or blow up the whole planet if we're wrong about what they're doing at the facility.

"You negotiate with them? You invite them to set a trap; or you finagle a cease-fire that looks good until someone misreads a signal or sours on the situation and takes the first shot.

"You somehow pull this off? You let them get offworld? You probably get court-martialed for your trouble. And what do you figure Shadow Wing does next? They going to retire just because you negotiated a cease-fire for a day?"

Nath was two meters away. Wyl tensed, planting his feet in the dust. Nath stopped walking.

"You never seemed to me a man who'd choose to fight when there were other solutions," Wyl said. "Or a man who'd make war as a matter of principle."

"You're a moron." Nath smiled joylessly. "You think that's what this is about? I'm out here to slaughter the enemies of the New Republic?"

Wyl curled and uncurled his fingers, glancing to T5 as if the droid's mere presence could calm him. The astromech did not respond.

As infuriating as Nath was, what made it worse was that Wyl didn't understand *why*, couldn't comprehend how the conversation had gone down this course. Yet he was carried along by the current. "I don't know," he said softly. "You've gone out of your way for revenge against Shadow Wing before."

Ugly laughter struck Wyl like a fist to the gut. "I got justice for my squadron," Nath said. "I don't regret that, but it's done. I made the tough decisions because I was a *leader*. You don't seem to realize what position you're in.

"I am *saving* your sorry butt, brother, from the consequences of your actions. You really want to resolve this thing peacefully? Walk away from the people who blew up the *Lodestar*, probably killed Quell and Chass? I'm in. I'll follow. It's not my job to set things right this time, and no one ever accused me of patriotism."

The thought of Chass and Quell dead in space—the thought Wyl hadn't allowed to find purchase in his mind, despite its constant scrabbling—was fire on the back of his neck. Quell, whom he'd lost the chance to damn or forgive. Chass, the last of Riot Squadron and his only link to the friends no one else survived to remember.

What if Shadow Wing *had* killed them both? What did he owe them?

Nath kept talking. "But if you want to walk away without firing a shot, you be prepared to live with it. If Operation Cinder comes around again, if Shadow Wing picks up where they left off, you don't get to have regrets."

During his cold, steady raging, Nath had closed to within a handspan of Wyl. Wyl met the larger man's gaze, seeing Sata Neek and Rununja and burning worlds.

"Back at Pandem Nai"—Nath's tone was suddenly calmer—"I didn't watch out for you like I should've. You called me on it, and you were right to. I'm watching out for you now. You hear me?"

"I hear you," Wyl said, and for the first time he thought he understood Nath Tensent. He'd always known Nath was manipulative and ruthless but also sincere and good-humored; he understood now that Nath was loyal, more loyal in his way than most soldiers Wyl had known. "I hear you. I'm just not sure it matters."

If they killed Quell, if they killed Chass, if they killed you and Kairos like they killed Riot Squadron, it still wouldn't change what's right.

He thought it. He didn't get the chance to say it.

The sound of boots crunching on scree drew the attention of both men. They looked to the edge of the plateau and saw several infantry troops scrambling up the slope. Vitale led the way, hair bundled under her helmet and a rifle tucked under one arm. "Answer your blasted comlinks!" she cried. "Got a skimmer waiting below—we've got to get back to camp *now.*"

"What's going on?" Nath asked.

Wyl shifted his position, blocking the transmitter from sight.

"Just picked up a message from friendly guerrillas back in the city.

Every TIE squadron out there just changed course, heading directly for Core Nine," Vitale answered. "Whatever it is they're doing, we've got to seize the facility before the whole 204th is on-site. Carver's got a plan, so—you in?"

Nath looked to Wyl. Wyl looked between Nath and Vitale and the cracked wasteland. He shifted his heel back through the dust and imagined snapping up the transmitter, running from the company— but what was the point? He would be on his own, with nothing worth bargaining away. No way to negotiate. His comrades would be left to die alone.

He had failed. Like Nath said, he had to accept the consequences.

"Let's go," he said.

CHAPTER 18

THAT WHICH YOU TAKE WITH YOU

I

"**W**hat did you see this time?"

"I'd rather not say."

"I understand. What did you see this time?"

Yrica Quell squatted in the red dust with her back to the tower, facing the interrogation droid. The machine floated against the black sky like a moon or a battle station, its low hum throbbing in her bones. She did not meet the gaze of its photoreceptor. The stars behind it blurred into a smear, her sight unfocused with exhaustion and apathy.

"The day I joined the 204th," she said. "When I chose not to run off with the Rebel Alliance but instead to leave the Academy and stay with the Empire."

"It was not the first time you made a similar decision," the droid said.

"No. It wasn't."

Memories flashed across her brain like sparks from a downed power conduit—a final spasm after the vision that had assaulted her. She had gone to the Imperial flight academy to become a pilot; to become a pilot so she could fight for Mon Mothma's Rebellion. She'd seen other recruits drop out or fail, earn their freedom through guile or incompetence. She'd been offered the chance by a boy, once—she remembered his name was Camm, though it took a moment—who'd repeatedly failed his simulator tests. He'd planned to run and he'd wanted to take Quell with him. She'd refused, fearing arrest and execution (and not liking Camm nearly as much as he'd liked her).

She couldn't count how many times she'd chosen to stay with the Empire. Chosen not to walk away when she had the chance.

The droid's humming rose an octave and oscillated weirdly. "Why do you believe you made that same decision time and again?"

"Because," she said, and swallowed the next words. "Because."

"Because what?" the droid repeated. But she didn't answer, and IT-O made a sound not unlike a sigh before finishing, "I detect no significant change in the tower's response to your bioreadings. You must actively explore your feelings; passivity and resistance are getting us nowhere."

"I'm not resisting."

"How often," the droid said, "did you think of Nacronis before Pandem Nai?"

She screwed up her face in confusion and disgust. Was it mocking her?

The droid went on. "I make no accusations. You knew what had occurred. Yet only after Adan confronted you did you acknowledge it to yourself—and once that was done, a barrier was broken. You began, as you told me, *to remember* your life with the Empire. We have been addressing the consequences ever since."

"So what?"

"So you are very good at resisting despite yourself."

"Give me an hour," Quell said. "Then we can start again."

She didn't know how many days had passed, but for a while she'd counted the circuits of the black hole over the horizon. Each time it ascended, her body tensed and she forced herself not to tremble. Her heart rate increased. When the eye of Cerberon reached the center of the black tower's lens, then it was time to sit in the dust and stare at the all-consuming singularity and be drawn into a new vision; time for the interrogation droid to monitor her vital signs and scan the machinery in the tower edifice. The droid had told her that the tower was *looking* for something, some biological response that would open the door. By rigorous testing and a process of elimination, Yrica Quell was determined to produce whatever response the tower required. It was the only hope of escaping the planetoid for herself and Caern Adan.

So every time the black hole stared through the lens, Quell stared back. Every time, she saw something different.

Sometimes it was a memory uncorrupted by time: The stinging detergent-scent of her first cadet uniform as she donned it in the brutal light of the Academy barracks, certain her bunkmates could see through her bare skin to her brittle bones. Sometimes the tower's offering was fantasy or revelation or clairvoyance: the vision of Nacronis's death that had first enveloped her, or other visions since then of Nacronis's drowning citizens; or the view from an X-wing cockpit as rebel forces fled over Trydara and TIE fighters, *her* TIE fighter, picked off rebels one by one. Sometimes the tower showed the burnt and bloodied faces of the dead: comrades in the 204th, Xion and Tonas and Jidel, or the nameless stormtroopers who'd been blown apart on the shuttle over Abednedo on her first real mission with Alphabet Squadron. Sometimes visions blurred together, one after the next. Sometimes one was enough.

Always IT-O was there when she emerged. "The vision is the prompt," the droid told her after the third nightmare. "The emotion is the password. But you must connect with the imagery; you must fully understand the experience."

She was willing, she told the droid. She was *trying*.

After each vision, she spoke of what she'd seen and the droid questioned her.

It didn't feel like therapy at all.

———

The next time she looked upon the eye and the black tower, she saw herself sitting in a repurposed shipping container in Traitor's Remorse, lying to IT-O about what she had done at Nacronis.

She saw the hangar bay of the Star Destroyer *Pursuer* on the night she'd crept out of bed to repair the acceleration compensator on her TIE. She'd failed to spot the fault before takeoff earlier in the day—she hadn't followed procedure, never should have been allowed to leave the ship, and she'd be rebuked and punished if she brought it to the ground crew's attention now. But if she could repair it herself no one would ever know . . .

She saw the face of Nette, recognized the crooked jawline of the girl who'd introduced her to the Rebel Alliance and whom she'd promised everything, *everything*, to. She'd joined the Academy for Nette. She'd just never gotten around to leaving.

"You were romantically involved?" the droid asked.

"We were teenagers. I was a year younger than her. I wouldn't elevate it to the status of *romance*."

"But you were close?"

Quell squeezed her eyes shut and felt the planetoid's dust sting her lids. "Yes, we were close."

"What did she tell you when she decided to join the Rebellion?"

"She didn't. We'd talked about it for a while, but she didn't announce it before she left."

"She didn't say goodbye?"

"No."

"Was that difficult?"

Quell shrugged. She adjusted her position, rising off her bottom to squat on her knees and stave off the numbness. "Everything's difficult when you're that age. But it could have been worse—we weren't talking a whole lot at the time."

"You were fighting. And while you were fighting, this woman departed your home station to fight a war, leaving you only a message. Am I correct?"

"Yes."

"I would imagine you felt somewhat responsible."

Quell winced. Her eyes opened, she blinked away the sand, and she shuffled forward on her knees.

"I would imagine," the droid continued, "that you were afraid you had driven her to depart. And that you felt afraid *for* her, knowing that you had failed to join her in her venture."

"What's your point?"

"Many would-be rebels failed to ever make contact with an Alliance cell. If you are unaware of her fate, you should consider the possibility that she never had the opportunity to join. Substantial numbers of smugglers who promised to transport prospective rebels were in fact traffickers working for cartels and crime syndicates—"

The fingers of her right hand combed through the sand. When she'd palmed enough she hurled it at the droid. An expanding cloud billowed around the machine as the larger granules fell to the ground.

She lacked the strength to do anything else.

"Bastard," she said.

The droid tilted on its axis, readjusted itself, and floated out of the cloud of dust.

"I overstepped," the droid said, and its voice was grave. "I apologize."

Quell dropped to her elbows and rubbed her filthy palm in her hair. "What was that about?" she murmured.

"There are connections that I believe would be beneficial if you made," the droid said in the same unshaken tone. "I am concerned about the timeline and I inappropriately pushed you in an attempt to expedite."

"The timeline," she said.

"For you. For Caern Adan. You have limited time."

Until we starve to death, she thought. *Until the planetoid drifts so close to the black hole we'll never be able to get out.*

She nodded brusquely, though she found the excuse a poor one.

The droid spoke again a minute later, and the gravity in its voice was replaced by something resembling contrition. "*I have limited time*," it said.

She looked at the gouges in its black paint; the unlit indicators. She remembered what it had said about its faulty memory circuits and its failing power cells.

"I am afraid I will lose all capacity to assist," it said. It was no longer contrite. It was confessing.

"We'll get this thing open," Quell said, and forced herself to rise.

The next time she subjected herself to the eye, she saw herself in the hangar bay of the *Lodestar,* hurling her fist into Caern Adan's stomach in a fit of frustration and rage. She saw General Syndulla watching her with an expression of puzzlement and disappointment. On Troithe she saw the Twi'lek woman cast a glance backward as she fled to aid another squadron that needed her more—Vanguard Squadron, a squadron that wasn't composed of traitors and failures. Quell saw the astromech droid D6-L wobbling excitedly, its transparent dome whirring around, its pings joyful as she offered it a *crumb,* the smallest hint of gratitude for serving her ceaselessly on the Harkrova moon and accepting fault for her failures. She saw D6-L burnt and ruined after saving her life on Pandem Nai, its chassis wrecked and its memory chip the only thing she'd been able to recover.

She'd treated D6-L unfairly. She'd treated it as a tool, and now she wore its chip around her neck as if that somehow mattered to the machine that no one but she would remember. Then she'd treated CB-9 with disdain, as if D6's replacement were at fault for her old astromech's destruction. CB-9 had repaid her by locking her out of her X-wing when Alphabet Squadron had needed her most, when Shadow Wing had returned.

Her bitterness had cost her her droid and her squadron.

The visions continued from there.

She lay on her back, the cold air washing over her sweat-damp shirt. She ignored the chill and told the droid about the last vision she'd seen:

the day she'd broken the painted plate her father had hung by the kitchenette light controls. "I was seven, maybe, and I'd been running back and forth, and the plate just came down. When he found out, he thought my brother Garrit had done it.

"He yelled and yelled. He said the plate had been his grandmother's. My father *never* got angry but he yelled at Garrit and I think he was crying.

"I never told him I did it. I haven't thought about it in years."

"Do you regret not telling him?" the droid asked. It floated out of view just behind her, its hum low and gentle. Almost soothing.

"I don't know."

"How *do* you feel?" the droid asked.

"Same way I feel about the time our felinx was sick and dying." The tower hadn't shown her that memory. It came unsummoned into her mind. "My parents were sure she was in pain, and they were probably right. But I refused to go with them when they had her put down. I got to be angry and self-righteous and my pet got to die without me."

The droid's voice was soft and soothing. "Say the word."

"I feel ashamed," she said.

"You were a child," IT-O said. "You were a different being."

"I wasn't—"

"In the years since those experiences, most every cell in your body—every atom—has been replaced and renewed. You have rebuilt yourself, both physically and mentally. You do not need to carry the guilt of prior incarnations."

She rolled onto her elbows in the dust. The droid was almost within reach, and its form blocked her view of the tower.

"I've got more than enough guilt for *this* incarnation," she said quietly, and raked her fingers through the sand.

"All the more reason to let go of the distant past. One step at a time, yes?"

She nodded carefully, considering the words.

The droid's photoreceptor seemed to fix on her. "You are a good man, Caern Adan," it said. "You are far braver than you realize."

The light behind the photoreceptor lens flickered. The droid tilted on its axis and then righted itself.

"We have more work to do," she said. There was no point in drawing attention to the droid's glitching. "We have to get inside the tower."

She saw her mentor.

She saw Major Soran Keize walking beside her aboard the *Pursuer* for the first time, taking an interest in her she'd feared was neither innocent nor appropriate. In time she'd been proven wrong about Keize's intentions; but that day she'd wondered what he would ask of her, and those fears—the image of the major as a corrupt man, an honorless man—made her skin feel ill fitting.

She saw Major Soran Keize leading the squadrons at Taka Shier, burning the hives of the natives for reasons she never heard explained.

She saw him on Nacronis, trudging through the mire in his flight suit, telling her that they'd lost the war. Ordering her to desert her unit and go to the New Republic. "You have the nature of a soldier," he'd told her.

But she could tell IT-O none of that. She had lied to the droid and lied to Caern Adan. She'd claimed that Soran Keize was dead, though compared with her lie about the murder of Nacronis it was a mere fib— barely worth a rebuke from New Republic Intelligence, barely worth a mention were she ever brought to trial for her crimes.

But to tell the truth about Soran Keize was to admit that she had needed his push to leave the 204th. *If you would do this,* he'd told her, gesturing to the corpse of Nacronis, *then there's nothing that will drive you out.*

She would not make that confession.

"It was Nacronis again," she told the droid. Her tongue was dry and her head felt heavy. She was dizzy when she stood and stumbled away from the tower.

"There has been no significant change in the tower's readings."

"Maybe that's because I saw the same thing."

"If you are experiencing the same vision, you should be able to apply the lessons we have discussed."

"I'm trying," she said. She marched across the plain, and the droid followed her. "You want me to make connections. You want me to find the links between the visions and give the tower what it's digging for."

"Yet you experience the visions at a surface level instead of confronting and integrating their emotional resonance."

"You know that because—what?" She whirled and nearly fell, but she bent her knees as if the ground were bucking again and maintained her balance. "I'm not hurting enough? I haven't plumbed all the depths of shame and misery you want me to experience?"

She breathed heavily. She stared into a scar in the droid's metal.

"I have taken oaths to do no harm to my patients," the droid said. "Those oaths are not unbending but they were made solemnly and with clear intent. I take no pleasure in the tower's nature. If the structure was a prize of the Emperor—if it was targeted for destruction by Operation Cinder for that reason—it is a prize only a sadist would treasure.

"Nonetheless, it is our only means of escape."

Long after the droid's voice faded she listened for an echo in the soft wind. She couldn't remember the last time she'd eaten. The sockets of her eyes seemed to throb. Physical distress was a shelter from the ocean of the visions; the visions were a shelter from the disintegration of her body.

"I know," she said. "Not your fault the Empire is full of bastards. I'll keep trying."

But she didn't tell the droid about Major Keize. She hoped her shame would be enough.

Nette was dead. Chass was dead. Wyl was dead. Nath was dead. Kairos was dead. General Syndulla was dead. Major Soran Keize led Shadow Wing and burned the galaxy and never even asked Quell to come home.

———

She snapped out of her vision certain that she was falling through the burning ring of the black hole. Her body felt beyond hot, as if her skin were ready to blacken and peel away and leave only charred bones underneath. She groaned and rolled on the ground and saw the droid hovering above her, a manipulator extended and its syringe touched with crimson.

She hugged herself, rubbing her fingers along her arms until she found the corresponding dot of blood and soreness on her left biceps, opposite the squadron tattoo on her right. She shuddered once, forcing down the pain before asking, "What the hell, droid?"

"The damage to my hardware is now affecting eighty-two percent of my systems," the interrogation droid said. "You have made minimal progress. We must accelerate this; the tower *does* appear to respond to physical pain."

She tamped down her fury. It wouldn't help. She accepted the answer and they resumed the work.

She no longer noticed the rise and fall of the black hole. She would look up, see it outside the frame of the lens, and return to her rest; or she would find it staring and enter its depths once again, focused on the sins she had repeated over and over, the flaws in her spirit that had brought her to this point and had caused her squadron and her wing and the galaxy so much suffering.

IT-O had pinpointed those flaws well enough. She knew what she'd done, even if she chose not to confess everything aloud.

The droid rationed its serums and chemicals, enhancing her agonies when the tower seemed most responsive. Once, it told her, it had detected an energy surge; but she'd woken screaming at the wrong moment and the tower's equipment had gone dormant. So they repeated the process time and again.

The next cycle or a hundred cycles later, after seeing fresh horrors and waking drenched in sweat, Yrica Quell scuttled away from the tower. Driven by instinct to leave the site of her misery, she crawled until she reached the edge of the mesa and thought for a moment of pulling herself over. Not to die—she had no conscious urge for death—but because she wasn't finished fleeing. She let her chin droop over the cliffside and breathed slower as the cool wind washed over her, calming her.

The droid's words floated down. "We must return. You cannot ignore what you see."

She sounded petulant as she asked: "Why?"

"Because it is your only escape off this world."

The voice was the voice she had come to know since Traitor's Remorse, but there was a *wrongness* to it that made her shudder. She eased back over the cliff's edge and turned to look at the floating sphere.

"*My* only escape?" she asked.

"Yes," the droid replied.

She repeated the words in her mind, and it felt like another vision. Another horror.

"Why do you care whether I escape?" she asked.

"Because you are my patient."

She climbed to her feet and reached out to the droid to steady herself. The metal of its chassis was too warm, as if its components were overheating. "Fine. But I need to walk it off, or I'm not going to survive to see the lens again."

They moved along the cliffside. Quell did not turn her head to look toward the tower. "Can I ask you something?" she said. "About you?"

"We are not here to talk about—"

"I know. But sometimes it's easier to talk about someone else. Even if I'm not talking about someone else. You know?"

It sounded like the sort of thing the droid would want her to say. Too much so, perhaps, but she hoped the hoarseness in her voice and the lurch in her step would give the words the required innocence.

"Very well," the droid said.

"You remember what you were? Before you had patients?"

"Yes."

"How did you go from that to—what you are now?"

"I was reprogrammed."

"By who?"

"No one whose name would have meaning to you."

"Where?"

"At an Imperial transitory holding facility in the Colonies."

"And you were reprogrammed? And escaped there alone?"

"Yes."

She walked on until she felt a chunk of stone catch the toe of her boot. She dropped to a knee and brought her hand to the errant shard. It was in her pocket by the time she was upright.

She hesitated to ask the next question. She didn't want to know the answer.

"Do you know anyone named Caern Adan?" she asked.

"No," the droid said.

She felt the pull of the black hole as if it were looming above her. She thought of the kindness the droid had shown her over the past months; the evening of the victory party after Pandem Nai's fall, when it had called itself her friend.

"Your memories are gone, aren't they? Wiped or corrupted?"

Neither of them moved anymore. She faced the unit's photorecptor, watched the droid tilt on its axis and then, with a twitch, pull itself level again. "The damage is significant," the droid said.

"You're a torture droid again, aren't you?"

She wished she had her sidearm, or a vibroblade, or even an arc welder. Her hand cupped the jagged stone in her pocket, but next to the machine's serums and sonics and chemical torture turret she was sorely outmatched. It didn't matter that the droid was damaged—she was damaged, too, and probably worse.

The droid's voice was lower, taking on a tone of warning. "I no longer serve the Empire, and that is no longer my purpose."

"Then why are you *torturing* me?" she cried, louder than the wind. As if in reply, the planetoid rumbled as a quake shook the ground.

"Because although I am not a torture droid, I see no reason not to use the tools at my disposal—"

"You mean no reason to regret?"

"—nor any reason not to punish an Imperial war criminal for the acts she has committed."

Quell screamed without words as she lunged for the droid. Its humming dropped to a motorized growl and it descended half a meter, causing her swing of the stone to cut through air. She felt a numbing sonic pulse pummel her right leg and couldn't prevent herself from collapsing but she fell forward onto the machine, wrapping her arms around its chassis as it attempted to wriggle free. The fingernails of her left hand scraped metal and found one of its scars; her right elbow locked around its secondary manipulator as her right hand brought down the rock, striking at random.

She heard a crisp shattering sound and felt something sting her wrist—she suspected she'd smashed the droid's syringe and been stabbed by the glass. The droid became suddenly slick; her fingers lost their grip on frictionless metal as it exerted its repulsors and rotated its body. A moment later she felt something burning her left calf and smelled a stench like melting plastoid.

She released the droid and saw her pant leg boiling away. She didn't want to think what the skin beneath might look like, but if she was lucky the garment had taken the brunt of whatever the droid had sprayed her with. The machine was ascending again, attempting to move out of reach, and she knew that if it rose overhead she wouldn't catch it. She forced herself past the agony in one leg and the numbness in the other to leap, to grasp the droid by a manipulator and yank it back toward the ground. Halfway to the sand the droid rebounded in midair, and they bounced together toward the edge of the cliff.

The droid was saying something but its voice was distorted, rapidly changing pitch. It dragged her through the dust and she wrestled it downward, digging her trembling knees into gravel. She struck it with her rock again and drew sparks, struck it once more and saw a panel pop open.

But then her knees were dangling in the air and she was slipping over the cliff's edge. She tried to scale the machine and pulled it closer instead; then one of her arms slipped, the rock fell from her grasp, and she flipped onto her back. Her shoulders and head dangled off the side of the mesa and the torture droid loomed over her, still clasped by one arm, its red photoreceptor staring at her like the burning eye of Cerberon.

"Adan," she gasped. "Kairos. Nothing?"

"Nothing that would excuse what you've done," the droid said, and its voice fluctuated from masculine to feminine with each word.

Quell raked her nails over metal as blood rushed to her head. She felt an open socket where the panel had been pried open and tried to hold on as the machine aimed its chemical turret at her face. Something slapped at her nose, and she feared it was the first blast from the turret; then she saw a dark rectangle flash through her field of vision and she realized that it was a chip hanging from a short metal chain around her neck.

She had moments to act. She used them.

She lifted her torso, fighting gravity and her wounded body's weight, and brought herself as close to the droid as she could. She gripped the back of the sphere with one hand as if pulling it in for a kiss and snagged the chip with the other, yanking the chain forward and plugging the chip into the droid's open socket.

IT-O made a noise like a thousand voices overlapping.

Quell shimmied forward underneath the machine, letting the chain slip over her head as she returned to the mesa and crawled a meter from the edge. The droid emitted bursts of static and rotated in the air, working its way toward Quell in periodic bursts of speed. Its motions might have been comedic if the unpredictability hadn't been so startling, the implications so horrifying. She had no idea what was occurring in its synthetic brain—whether D6-L's memory chip was downloading files like a virus or whether the broken chip had caused a hardware malfunction the torture droid couldn't circumvent. She felt no triumph at the thought of her old astromech saving her one last time.

IT-O fell to the dust. Its manipulators twitched like the legs of an overturned beetle. A muffled sound played from its speakers: fragments of her own voice, as if it was searching recorded conversations for . . . what? Some last jab at her? A plea for mercy? An indication of regret?

It had forgotten regret and mercy when it had forgotten Kairos and Caern Adan.

She thought of kicking it off the side of the mesa. The fall would destroy it for sure.

She turned away. She hadn't forgotten.

She made it to the cave before the next sunless morning. Both her legs were lanced with anguish, but so far as she could tell the actual damage was superficial. Quakes struck the planetoid twice during her travels, and each time the shaking seemed to drive the pain deeper—yet the effect barely slowed her. She'd suffered enough over the past days. She felt no need to linger on misery anymore.

Adan was where she'd left him. His cheeks were puffy—not gaunt like she'd expected—and his brow was damp with sweat. Wrappers from meal packs danced around the cave in the breeze. She could hear him breathing from several meters away, but she thought he was sleeping until she knelt beside him and he, barely cracking open his eyes, said, "You're back."

"Disappointed?" she asked.

"Perpetually," he said. She scowled and he smiled. "But that's my fault. Not yours."

He sounded lucid, unlike the delirious man she'd left behind. She wondered if the droid had been responsible for that, too.

"How are you feeling?" she asked, and hoped he saw the compassion in the question instead of the inanity.

"Pretty sure I'm dying," he said.

She took one of his hands in both of hers and lay beside him.

They talked.

Adan was dying, she agreed, though for a while she tried to convince him otherwise. His injuries from the crash—or from before the crash—had been infected, and the infection had spread to his blood-stream as she'd earlier feared. His organs were failing. Quell knew little about Balosar anatomy, but she felt confident in that and she had nothing with which to treat him. Nonetheless, Adan was composed and, if not at peace with his death, resigned to it.

They talked, and when his speech became angry the anger wasn't directed at her. He fumed about the unfairness of his demise, and what it would mean for New Republic Intelligence and the peace to come—when men like him would be needed to secure the galaxy against the inevitable guerrilla threats and terrorist movements. He complained that he should have been safe on Troithe, and that the military should have protected him from capture. She saw him blink away tears when he spoke about Kairos and she realized he felt responsible for her injuries; and when he asked about Shadow Wing, tried to comprehend how their trap could have gone wrong, she played the role she knew he wanted and offered speculation and tactical analysis as if they were back aboard the *Lodestar* with General Syndulla.

"Sometimes I wonder why we put in so much effort," he mumbled. "Are they so much worse than the other Imperials out there? They're not the only ones who were part of Cinder—maybe we had them broken after Pandem Nai and should never have lured them here."

"I don't think they're *worse*," Quell said. She wasn't sure it was the answer he wanted. "But it's not about punishment, is it?"

"No," Adan agreed. "It's about prevention. Because they won't stop killing people until someone stops them, and no one but us is liable to do that."

"I'm sorry we didn't manage," Quell said. Their faces were centimeters apart, and she could smell the disease in his body. She didn't meet his eyes.

"Well," Adan said, not hiding the bitterness, "no one can say we didn't try."

They were silent for a while. Adan slept for a while. When he woke he told her he wasn't worried about his analysts. He talked about Nasha Gravas, and how he was certain she'd found a way to keep the others safe. From there he segued into conversation about the *rest* of the working group—asking if she thought Chass na Chadic was alive, and Wyl Lark, and Nath Tensent. She didn't know, and she realized he was building up to a question he'd been holding back for hours.

"Where's Ito?" he asked.

She had an answer prepared. She discarded it for another. "Its power cells ran dry. The damage was worse than it wanted to say."

She watched Adan swallow. He'd wept enough already that she couldn't tell if the tears were new or old. "Good droid," he said. "Good droid."

Once again, they lapsed into silence. Adan's breathing was louder than the wind in the small cave, and Quell could feel the moisture from his rasps against her neck.

The man was dying and would soon be dead. She'd found him insufferable for most of the time she'd known him, but still, she believed he deserved a peaceful end. *It's why you're here,* she told herself. *Not for you. For him.*

But the pressure built inside of her, and Adan said nothing to bring a new topic to mind. Finally she said, "I want to tell you something."

"Tell me," Adan said.

She confessed what she'd been unable to confess to IT-O.

"After Nacronis, they pushed me out."

Adan watched her but said nothing. She wasn't sure he'd heard, or if he'd heard whether he understood.

"I didn't leave by choice. I left because I was told to, because someone saw that it was killing me and I wasn't brave enough to leave on my own.

"It's the same reason I didn't leave years earlier. Because I'm a coward."

Adan's nostrils flared. His face seemed to contort and he began to laugh. She didn't think it was funny, but she didn't protest—she hardly had the right—and the laughter turned to sputtering and coughing and he said, "Aren't we all?"

"What does that mean?"

He shrugged as well as he could in his condition. "Every day, I think about the people I abandoned in the prison camp. Kairos and Ito and I—we left how many hundreds behind? We left Ver Iflan, who saved us, behind."

"You weren't *killing* people," she said. She felt a flash of anger at the comparison, as if Adan were claiming a shame he hadn't earned. "You left people behind in a desperate situation—"

"I *didn't* kill people," Adan agreed, brusque as he'd ever been. "You're right—you did more monstrous things than I could dream of. But my conscience bothers me just the same."

She saw no mockery in his eyes.

"Why else," he asked, "do you think I kept a torture droid around? You figure I enjoyed the reminder of my past?"

Adan shifted his body as if attempting to roll over and turn away from her. But though he wriggled he did not turn, and his gaze held on her until she allowed herself to recognize compassion in the man's face, and defiance, and humor and guilt together.

"How do you stand it?" she asked. "Knowing what you did?"

"I drink. I work. I do what good I can in the galaxy. I *manage*, Yrica Quell." He snorted, or tried to snort—the sound she heard involved fluid in his nostrils, if not his lungs. "I move forward, because dwelling on my shame doesn't help anyone."

Quell heard the words. *You haven't done the things I've done*, she wanted to protest, but she'd said it already and it hadn't fazed him at all.

Lying beside the man who'd rescued her and berated her and for a very short while been her friend, she fell asleep.

She woke on and off to Adan's strained breathing. He whistled as he sucked in air, and at times he sounded like he was accompanying the wind in some alien orchestra. His condition was degenerating, and he seemed to struggle more with each hour that passed.

Once, when he was whimpering in misery, she stroked his arm and whispered, "I'll remember you."

He laughed and coughed. "I know what you think of me," he said. Quell shrugged.

"It's all right," he said. "Leave me behind. You're carrying enough with you."

He died not long after that. His breathing became more strained, then softer, then ceased altogether. Quell considered whether to bury him but the planetoid would come apart soon enough and, along with the rocks and the tower and the wreckage of her ship, Adan would burn away in the ring of fire surrounding the black hole.

She doubted he would have expected a burial anyway.

She sat with him for a spell before cataloging the few supplies remaining and wondering what to do next. There was no one to rescue anymore, no reason for escape except to survive or to complete the mission she'd begun with; yet she *did* desire to escape, no matter that she lacked the means. She considered forgetting the tower and wandering the wastes in search of another answer—another structure or a hidden ship, a miracle buried in sand.

She had no wish to return, nor any reason to expect the tower would ever unlock for her.

The tower was still her best chance.

She sighed to herself, took one last look around, and departed the cave. She felt drained, as if some inner fire had consumed all its fuel and dwindled to embers, and she allowed her mind to wander as she trekked. The 204th Imperial Fighter Wing seemed farther away than ever, though when she thought about the unit the memories came easier and clearer than they ever had. Not only the memories the tower had shown her, but the joyful ones: memories of laughter and friendship and the thrill of flying at incredible speeds. She took bittersweet pleasure in these.

The memories of Shadow Wing came as easily as the memories of Alphabet Squadron. As easily as the memories of IT-O and Adan.

She turned off course to check the site of her battle with the torture droid and found the machine in the dust, torpid or deactivated—she didn't have the tools to tell. She stripped it of anything she hoped would be useful and moved on.

The tower was unchanged, stabbing into the heart of the planetoid. The black hole was below the horizon. She had plenty of time for dread before it aligned with the lens.

Her instinct was to pace; to distract herself from what was coming. She sat instead. She sorted through everything the droid had said about the portal and the tower's response to her bioreadings. It couldn't all have been lies—whatever IT-O had become at the end, she believed it had been sincere at the start—but what answers did that leave her?

She could smash her own kneecaps and hope raw, physical pain did the trick. She could attempt to explore, to inhabit her feelings as the droid had advised. Neither option seemed promising—she could hurt herself no worse than the droid already had, and as for her feelings? Was she, as the droid had said, *resisting*?

The question lingered awhile before she decided she knew the answer.

She'd stopped resisting after Pandem Nai. Every moment since she'd acutely felt her own guilt, her own complicity and cowardice. She understood all she had done and why. The droid had mistaken an unwillingness to confess with a lack of comprehension.

Which left her with what?

I drink. I work. I do what good I can in the galaxy. I manage, Yrica Quell. I move forward, because dwelling on my shame doesn't help anyone.

Was the solution that simple?

Quell waited for darkness to return her stare.

In time, the black hole reached the point of conjunction. The iris rippled and distorted and the pupil seemed to dilate and tug at Quell's consciousness. The sense of falling was familiar; the taste of despair no less so. The visions came, assailing her with her guilt, reminding her of all the times her cowardice had brought pain to beings she loved or beings she'd never met.

This time, she knew better than to wait.

As the nightmare wrapped about her soul she lifted her left foot and planted it in dust she could not see or feel. She lifted her right foot, never shirking from the stare. Her body was foreign to her as the black hole captured her mind, but still she walked.

I move forward.

She wanted to weep. Maybe she did. But she did not fall to her knees. She saw Nacronis and Nette and Soran Keize and Caern Adan. She saw the faces of her squadrons, old and new, and recalled Wyl Lark and Chass na Chadic and Nath Tensent leaving her behind on the *Lodestar.*

The tug of gravity was violent and seductive. The nightmare was agony, yet it was an agony she had earned—one she had invested in over the course of months or lifetimes, and if she abandoned it then what made her *Yrica Quell* would be left behind, too. Her identity would be stripped away, ripping off her like skin and fluttering into the dark.

It wasn't too late to return, a voice told her. Not too late to turn around and plunge back into the comforting horror that the tower made manifest.

Still she walked.

She heard the howling of the black hole in her skull, felt it devouring space and stars and years like a whirlpool. She howled in reply, unable to do otherwise, and with every step her body returned to her. She felt an ache in her teeth and a burning in her calves.

The black hole released its grip and she felt weightless.

The vision ended and she stood in front of the tower. The great door was open before her, wide enough to admit ten people abreast into the chamber beyond.

Still she walked.

Inside, she was not at all surprised to find a ship. But for the first time in days, she smiled.

CHAPTER 19

THE END OF COMMUNITY

I

"I have a dream sometimes," Chass said during disquisition. She rocked back and forth on her bare heels, staring into the auditorium aisle to escape eye contact with the cultists. Twenty, maybe thirty of them watched her. She'd chosen a seat opposite where Palal Seedia had sat two days prior; she'd worried it was too obviously *considered* a choice, then decided there wasn't much she could do to hide her intentions.

She stood silent and awkward, forming words. She placed her hands on the back of the bench in front of her then hastily removed them when the occupant turned around.

"Okay," she amended. "I have the dream a lot."

No laughter. No smiles.

"I've never been to Coruscant," she said, "but I'm pretty sure it's on Coruscant. Probably because it looks like you'd expect Coruscant to look in a holodrama or some garbage, and it's not real, you know? My dream. So Coruscant."

The name *Coruscant* rapidly lost meaning through repetition. *Tell them,* she thought. *Tell them everything.*

"The war is over. Not the way it's over now, but really over. The fighting's stopped. Chancellor Mothma—or whoever, it's just a dream—has disbanded the military and I'm out. And I'm alive, you know? I didn't muster out early or anything. I survived every battle of the war, and—"

She heard the hoarseness in her voice. *Tell them everything.*

"—and I wasn't expecting that? Everyone dies sooner or later, right? Stupid deaths, mostly, like—" *Hound Squadron,* she almost said, then remembered that Maya Hallik hadn't been part of Hound. "—Fang Squadron. But I always figured—I always looked up to people who made a difference when they died.

"When you know you're going to die, you look for a way to make it matter. You make it big as you can, because you might as well. Right?"

Right? Right? She heard her own voice echo in mockery.

In the dream there was no Scarif for her. No third Death Star to set things right. In the dream she was a survivor, like every good soldier wanted to be. Her moment of sacrifice had never come.

"So I'm living on Coruscant. I'm getting a stipend, because the New Republic is good as its word, but the money's not enough to pay for more than a cruddy apartment. I've got whatever furniture came with the place and cheap, garbage food that's better tasting and less filling than ration bars." She could smell Surabat noodles boiling, bleeding oil as they softened. "I could use extra cash, but what am I supposed to do?

"It's not like I haven't been looking, trying to find work. There's *not* any work. There's two hundred ex-soldiers for every job that needs a killer and I don't have any other skills. I don't know anyone on Coruscant—everyone I flew with, the three who're still alive, are all back on their homeworlds. Good for them. I don't get that ending."

She didn't really *dream* that part. The apartment was clear as anything in her mind, but the rest was a sensation. A ghost of a life she hadn't truly lived.

"I do some stupid stuff just to pass the time. You know the sort—petty stuff, not robbery, but enough to catch the eye of local security. They go easy on me, because I'm a vet. They go easy on me the *first* time.

"After that, I lose the apartment. Keep my gun. It all goes downhill from there."

The end of the dream didn't need embellishment for her audience. She saw the alley behind the cantina with perfect clarity. She saw herself, utterly sober, turning the blaster over in her hand and considering what to do next.

"I have the dream a lot," she said again. "The last few years I tried so hard to make sure it wouldn't come true. The last month or two, I've just been trying not to dream."

The silence in the room suddenly seemed less like the silence of prayer and more like the awkward moment in a crowded billet after someone's digestive system produced the wrong noise. Chass sat back down, her confession finished.

She knew what to expect afterward, but knowing didn't make her more comfortable. As she sat on her bench, shivering and curling her toes and trying to shake the dream, she heard the shuffling of bodies around her. Hands clasped her arms from behind and lifted her back to her feet. She shouldn't have shuddered at the touch—it did nothing to serve her goals—but she couldn't help herself.

She kept her eyes downcast but perceived the cultists closing in, trapping her. She felt the warmth of more hands, hands on her shoulders, fingers trailing down her chest, not possessive or insistent but reverential, like pilgrims touching a holy icon. She drew into herself, breathing deep and making herself narrow, but the cultists enfolded her anyway and their bodies pressed against hers.

This is necessary, she told herself, but she no longer believed it.

She looked up. Eyes locked with her own—nonhuman eyes, kind eyes, and she felt the tide of compassion lift her and carry her away. The world whispered her name: *Maya Hallik.*

———

They celebrated her confession, as she'd known they would. The cultists ushered Chass to a gallery where they presented her with silk robes and garlands of pungent flowers, both of which she refused; but an elderly woman tucked a long-stemmed blossom between Chass's horns and she remembered the time Hound and Riot squadrons had crowned her Queen of Starfighters. She'd taken joy in that event; yet that joy seemed faint and gray compared with what she felt among the Children of the Empty Sun.

Hound Squadron had fought and cheered and died with her. The cultists *loved* her. They were deluded fools but it was love all the same.

"It's not like I just joined up, you know," Chass murmured to Gruyver. They were in line for food, as word of Chass's disquisition had spread and the day's cooks had gone rummaging for fresh fruit and unspoiled flavor tubes. "I've been here a while."

"You did better than join us," Gruyver said, and heaped stewed pits onto her plate over warm flatbread. "You trusted us."

"I trusted *you*. I still haven't even met Let'ij. She'd probably kick me out if we met."

"Let'ij obeys the will of the Force. She's our interpreter, not our leader."

Chass waited for more, sopped up juices with bread, and decided to push. "How am I supposed to know that when she's always hiding?"

Gruyver laughed. "You want to see her? You're our first convert from the New Republic. After today, I'm sure she'd make time."

Chass forced herself to smile through lunch as cultists passed her and touched her and wished her well. She only saw Palal Seedia once, at the back of a crowd. The woman nodded in her direction with the swift surety of a guillotine.

Let'ij summoned Chass in the middle of the night. Chass barely had time to check the blaster at the small of her back before a pair of cultists she didn't recognize escorted her from her cell into regions of the palace she'd never seen before—up a staircase with three glimmering ray shields and topped with a blast door. Eventually they arrived in a mosaic-tiled room with a glass skylight, divans covered in soft cushions that warmed on contact, and a pool of scented fluid that danced with iridescent colors. Let'ij's guards wheeled in a tray of fresh fruit and bread after Chass sat down—a meal far superior to the rations and fried beetles the rest of the cult typically survived on.

Her body was buzzing, as if she'd taken a dose of spice and then forced herself to lie down. There was too much energy inside her for her circumstances.

Chass remained seated for a quarter of an hour before Let'ij arrived, wrapped in sallow cloth embroidered with gold. The woman padded forward as if she were rushing to check a forgotten roast in the oven. "Maya! I'm sorry to keep you," she called. "Had a minor crisis involving a street fire, but it's all dealt with." She spoke without the crispness Chass had heard during the lectures, but she sounded no less serene. "The acolytes fed you?"

Chass gestured at the tray of food, swallowing a mouthful of sweet bread. "Didn't know we had stuff this good here."

"If there were enough for all of us, we'd share." Let'ij snapped up a berry, sucked out the seed, then nibbled on the flesh as she spoke. "Unfortunately, there's not—and it's hard to be attuned to the will of the Force when you're suffering hunger pangs. So we reserve it for occasions like these."

"Sure," Chass said, and shifted her weight on the divan so that she could feel the comforting bulge of her weapon.

Let'ij lowered herself beside Chass, turning and leaning against the divan's back with one arm. Her perfume was of attar and petrichor. "In any event, it's a privilege to finally meet you. I know you've got doubts about us, but you've come *so* far and I hope you'll stay a while."

"Sure," Chass said again, and realized she hadn't fully considered what was to happen next.

She'd come ready to act. Ready to see her plan through. Yet facing Let'ij, she wasn't able—the buzzing inside her, the energy awaiting release, was too great. If she let go all at once she'd explode.

"What's your scam, anyway?" she asked.

Let'ij cocked her head and waited.

"I mean, all your lectures are just about peace and community and submitting to *you*. It's not even—there's not even a prophecy or some end-of-the-world garbage to keep things lively." The words flowed out unexpectedly, and Chass savored their bitterness.

Let'ij smiled and looked up through the skylight. A few stars gleamed bright enough to penetrate Catadra's cloud cover. "You're not the first to say that," Let'ij said.

"So what's the scam?" Chass asked again. Her voice was trembling— rage and excitement leaked out in hitches and bursts. "What's your goal? You want to run Cerberon and live it up with a bunch of wor-shippers? Or are you thinking bigger?"

Let'ij waited, then replied as calm as ever: "The Force exists in every species, but it only shows us what we're meant to do when we operate as a larger organism—a *community*.

"Everything I've done, I've done to create a community that nur-tures, thrives, and supports life. No Republic or Empire, just people depending on people for love."

"No place for independence in a cult," Chass said. "Believe me, I get it. Doesn't explain the ships, though, or the guns, or—"

"We're not out there putting heads on spikes. We're not the ones who bombed Catadra. But we're not averse to self-defense, either."

Chass tried to interrupt but found she couldn't form coherent words.

Let'ij went on: "Judge us by the same standards you judged the New Republic. There's millennia of wisdom from a hundred cultures that teach what the Force wants—the flourishing of life, tranquility, community—yet the ruling powers only fight. You don't trust the mil-itary to turn away from violence any more than I do. They don't know how."

"But *you* know how," Chass said. She laughed and shook her head. "*You* listen to the Force, so you can build a better civilization."

"Hard to believe, but what's more likely to work? Holding on to war hasn't given you peace, Maya. Maybe, just *maybe* I'm an alternative."

Chass didn't hesitate after that.

She allowed the energy boiling up inside her to froth over, grasping her blaster and bringing the grip down onto Let'ij's scalp as if it were a knife. There was no swell of blood but the cult leader's grunt was satisfying enough. Chass brought the weapon down a second time, then a third, until Let'ij stopped moving and Chass was panting.

She didn't hear the guards. She didn't hear much of anything over her own breath.

Two minutes later, she gripped Let'ij's personal code cylinder—found after rifling through her pockets—and marched back to the stairway leading to the main section of the palace. No one stopped her. As she walked, she realized she hadn't bothered to check whether the cult leader was alive or dead.

Seedia wasn't stupid enough to tell Chass where they were going, and Chass wasn't fool enough to let go of the code cylinder. With most of the cultists abed, the palace was silent as they hurried through dim corridors. The marble felt strangely warm beneath Chass's feet, and the only smell was dust.

They descended stairs that took them beneath the crypts and then ascended a tower, passing into a chamber cluttered with wires and machinery. Seedia, now using a single crutch as if it were a walking stick, declared, "Here," and pointed at what Chass had assumed was a wall and now realized was a massive blast door.

"Stay where I can see you," Chass said, and Seedia moved to the side of the door opposite the control panel. Layered around the metal were strips of duracrete, marble, and wood—remnants of earlier iterations of the palace. Chass ignored them, inserted the cylinder, and watched the door rise.

She stepped out with Seedia into what had clearly once been a garden dominated by a central fountain. Now the planting troughs were empty and the fountain was dry and the husks of spacefaring vessels littered the grounds. Chass saw a Corellian cargo hauler stripped to its skeleton and a mountain of salvaged pieces of the solar skiff she'd arrived on. She began to shake and twisted her neck, trying to find any-thing operational. Something that could fight or at least get her out of Cerberon and to the New Republic.

Then she caught a glimpse of the B-wing assault fighter resting be-hind the remnants of the skiff. Spiderweb cracks spread through stonework under the vessel's landing gear, and the air stank of oil and fuel additives. Chass knew the B-wing's black scars and chipped paint intimately; even without the crest on the ship's side she would have recognized it.

She was going to leave Cerberon. She was going to forget all about the cult. She was going to take revenge on Shadow Wing.

"Maya?" a man's voice asked.

Gruyver emerged from behind the cargo hauler, a hydrospanner in hand. Chass barely spotted him before he went down with a cry, face striking grass and stone and the metal shaft of a crutch extending from the back of his neck to the hand of his assailant.

"Pay attention," Seedia said. "If they set off an alarm we could still fail."

Chass looked from her ship to Seedia to the man on the ground. She was no longer making decisions—sometime after the disquisition she had been swept into a current, acting without thought or control or comprehension of where those acts would lead. She was at Gruyver's side, turning his bleeding head in her hands, trying to determine if the emotion suffusing her was rage or terror or relief.

When the metal rod struck her skull she could only think: *Well, of course.*

Chass rolled onto her side and caught the crutch as it came down for a second blow. She tugged and climbed the rod, pulling Seedia forward as she rose. She twisted her hands, rotated the rod, and Seedia yelped—Chass didn't think she'd broken the woman's wrist but she'd come close enough.

Seedia's booted heel drove into Chass's chin, compressing tongue against teeth and filling Chass's mouth with blood. She let go of the crutch, tried to stabilize herself to throw a counterpunch, but could only swing wildly as the Shadow Wing pilot hopped from side to side. Chass reached for her blaster and the crutch tapped her shoulder and elbow in rapid succession before she managed to draw.

"They got to you," Seedia said. She sounded almost disappointed.

Chass's vision blurred and filled with crimson as she squeezed the trigger, gripping with both hands. The blaster jerked and her shoulders ached and she felt the metal grow hot against her fingertips. She was screaming obscenities but she couldn't tell where her target had gone.

She kept on firing. She looked for motion in the shadows, twisting her body and ignoring the pain. She saw the kind face of Wyl Lark mix with the blood and scars of Gruyver and wondered for an instant where she was trying to escape to. She felt a blast of warm air like a desert wind, adjusted her stance, and watched a four-winged jumper lift up and move jerkily through the sky like a mosquito.

She shot at it until long after it was gone. Until the blaster began to overheat.

"Maya?"

Gruyver was standing beside her, trembling. His voice was thin and soft and old.

"Maya? Are you all right?"

Her arms were stiff, frozen from her shooting stance. She lowered them but held on to her weapon.

"Put down the gun. Come to the medical suite. We'll fix you and we'll talk." Gruyver's face was soaked in red. He was shaking, but he watched her with pure compassion.

Wyl Lark would've watched her the same way, but Wyl was one person with a rare and bizarre capacity for empathy; Gruyver was a single cultist among many.

Another voice called: "There is no shame except the shame of self-deception."

Chass turned to see Let'ij, flanked by her guards at the entrance to the garden. The cult leader pressed a cloth to her forehead where Chass had brained her, but she smiled calmly.

"If you go," Let'ij went on, "you will not rid yourself of us. You will carry the seed inside you, and it will grow."

"Screw you," Chass said, and ran for her ship, turning only to say: "And my name isn't *Maya*."

When she was roaring skyward, feeling once more like Chass na Chadic, she vowed to never again think of her time on Catadra or her experiences with the Children of the Empty Sun. The thoughts and experiences would tear off her and flutter in her wake and burn up in the atmosphere and she would be purged, ready to pursue vengeance— to bring the wrath of the New Republic down upon Shadow Wing and face whatever that battle had to offer.

She didn't need Gruyver or Let'ij or Nukita. She didn't need disquisitions or meals with insipid fanatics.

She reached under her seat and discovered that her slugthrower and her box of music chips were gone. In their place she found a small metal case, which—once squeezed between her hips as she maneuvered one-handed—she opened and discovered held another set of datachips. These were labeled HOLOGRAPHIC LECTURE and numbered several dozen.

She slapped the case shut and shoved it back beneath her seat and flew into the dark.

CHAPTER 20

COURAGE IN THE RUINS

I

The Core Nine mining megafacility was as much a bunker as any military outpost Soran Keize had ever seen. It had no shield generator and few weapons, but its sixty levels were dug into the bedrock of Troithe, constructed to endure any quake or industrial disaster its designers could conceive of. Its lowest sections could, Soran was sure, survive a bombardment from anything short of a Star Destroyer; it was no wonder General Syndulla's remnant had chosen to try to flee there.

Soran's interest was not in the lower levels. Outside a cursory search, his soldiers had not descended below sublevel fifteen—the base of the primary launch silo. He walked across the pitted duracrete bay beside Governor Fara Yadeez, watching local Troithe engineers work alongside ground crews from the 204th as they welded hull panels and power-washed thruster modules. Cadets from the *Edict* hurried up loading ramps into the facility's sole remaining ore freighter, carting ordnance that the newly assigned crew would load into freshly added torpedo tubes.

"They've done extraordinary work in so short a time," Yadeez said. "Your people are remarkably adaptable."

"Thanks to your assistance," Soran said, and the flattery was sincere. Somehow, Yadeez had produced twenty engineers out of the chaos of Troithe who now toiled under brutal conditions. She'd salvaged more of the *Edict*'s weapons than he'd hoped possible. "We have a flagship to be proud of once again."

He caught Yadeez smiling. He suspected she knew that he was less sincere in his praise of the freighter—upgraded or not, it was a five-hundred-meter crate with missile launchers and cannons bolted on. But it would hold six squadrons of TIE fighters and it could make the jump to lightspeed.

It would allow Shadow Wing to abandon Cerberon and leave behind their costly victory over Troithe and the *Lodestar*.

"Regardless," Yadeez said, "I'm grateful for the opportunity to see your launch. We're gathering as much sensor data as we can from the satellites we've reacquired, and I think you'll be pleasantly surprised—"

Her words fell off as a klaxon sounded, loud enough that Soran's eardrums throbbed in response. The engineers at work on the freighter paused as one, then returned to duty team by team as officers waved them back into action. Until orders decreed otherwise, their obligations had not changed.

Soran raised his comlink, ready to shout through the noise, when he saw Broosh racing toward him from the direction of the lift shaft. "Report!" Soran cried, and Broosh shook his head with a grimace as he closed the distance.

"Aircraft squadron," Broosh called. "Mixed signatures but we spot three starfighters along with what appear to be atmospheric craft. En route to the facility, not more than five minutes away."

"The survivors?" Yadeez asked, wincing the moment she'd spoken. Soran gestured dismissively—he was in command but he saw no need to prevent her from taking a role.

"Let's assume so," Broosh said. "No other signs of activity. I won't guess what sort of attack they're planning—they don't have the fire-power to pose a serious threat, so it must be, what? A trap? A distrac-tion?"

"Likely one or the other," Soran agreed. "But I wouldn't totally rule out a frontal attack."

"Sir?" Broosh grimaced and cupped a hand over one ear. Someone finally shut the klaxon down, and the silence that followed was like the airless vacuum of space.

"Our enemies have proven their competence," Soran said. "Assume nothing without confirmation. Ready the available squadrons for takeoff; I'll have additional orders shortly."

Twice now, Shadow Wing had confronted General Syndulla's forces. The first time Soran had been absent and Colonel Nuress had died above Pandem Nai. The second time had been above Troithe, and though the foe's flagship had been destroyed the price had been far greater than Soran had been prepared to pay.

He did not intend to see his soldiers humbled a third time.

||

Wyl Lark sped through atmosphere unhindered by rock formations or housing facilities or the fear of detection by enemy scanners. His A-wing's fuel supply was low, but he had more than enough for a mis-sion confined to a single planet. The damage he'd sustained since fall-ing to Troithe was no worse than damage he'd endured in the past, and he'd learned to compensate for the tilt his repulsors produced. And though he was out of missiles his blaster cannons were still operational. His ship was wounded but he was *flying* again, and it was wonderful.

Could be our last run together, he thought, and skimmed gloved fin-gers over the console. *Let's make it a good one.*

His comm was open. "Lark to squadron," he called, "all ships report in."

"Wraive standing by."

"Prinspai standing by."

"Ubellikos standing by."

"Vitale standing by."

"Tensent standing by."

An A-wing interceptor, a Y-wing assault fighter, a V-wing antique, and three airspeeders weren't much against Shadow Wing. Four of his pilots were still strangers to him. He'd never fully planned and executed a mission as sole squadron commander, and he was working with soldiers who lacked any reason to trust him after the loss of Gorgeous Su.

He wouldn't try to lie to them.

"I do believe—I truly *believe*—that we can win this," Wyl said. "Let's look forward to talking about it tomorrow, huh?"

He heard the nervousness in his voice. If he'd been speaking one-on-one he might have been able to perceive what they needed, to hear them out and offer support or blunt honesty or dutiful professionalism in return. But here—

Nath Tensent interrupted his thoughts. "That's Wyl's way of saying: *These bastards are tricky. But they blow up when you shoot them, like anything else.*"

The others laughed. Wyl laughed. *Thank you, Nath,* he thought.

Less than two hours earlier, Nath had been ready to draw a weapon on Wyl. Now he was grinning and taking on the most dangerous part of the mission. Wyl wondered if he was trying to make amends—he doubted it, but Nath was a complicated man.

Wyl trusted him to do his part, at least.

The other aircraft trailed Wyl as they raced over canyons and burning mineral deposits. Wyl spotted the energy signature of the mining facility on his sensors and leaned forward, trying to spot the structure on the horizon—but if it was ahead it left no silhouette against the glittering, star-filled sky. He felt himself sliding in his seat and straightened his ship; the vessel bounced and jolted enough that he made a mental note to be careful when he spoke.

Don't bite your tongue off.

He called out a new vector and his squadron followed as he dived toward the ground, leveling out a dozen meters above the tops of the canyons. He checked his scanner again.

"Where is it?" Prinspai called. "We're directly above the—"

The insectoid pilot didn't finish the thought. Rock dropped away beneath them and they were suddenly flying above an enormous chasm where a hundred lesser canyons merged into a single basin. In the center of the basin was a domed cylinder of metal and duracrete that reminded Wyl of a rocket silo. There was no architectural artistry in its design, nothing to break up the stark walls except for lines of fading yellow paint that might have once offered guidance to incoming ships. Yet for all its brutal mundanity, the sheer size of the megafacility was daunting—it was large enough to distort perspective, to make the surrounding cliffs seem impossibly small. It was a spike driven into the heart of the world, breaking and scarring the land such that millennia of erosion and tectonic shifts would only begin to heal the damage. It was the reason there was nothing green on the Scar of Troithe.

It would take full seconds for the squadron to cross from one side of the chasm to the other. Wyl's sense of perspective was distorted further when he saw the dome begin to retract, hemisphere parting down the middle. His scanner flashed and showed starfighters ascending through what, from afar, appeared to be the slightest crack.

For an instant, he was tempted to deviate from the plan. If he accelerated, he thought, he could enter the mining facility before the dome closed again. He could attack Shadow Wing from the inside . . .

. . . and be shot down in seconds. It wasn't an option.

"Squadron coming out!" he called. "Stay with me—we're going in close and we're going in fast. Scatter them with cannon fire and make sure they follow."

"Perhaps the challenge is to keep them from *catching* us?" Wraive said.

Wyl loosed his first shots and his squadron joined him. Crimson fire splashed off the dome with no noticeable impact; but as the first TIEs emerged, they broke formation under the barrage.

"They'll need time to accelerate to top speed," Wyl said. He pitched his A-wing toward the dome, ready to pull up the moment the full TIE squadron was free. "Until then, their advantage is marginal. We don't have to buy too long."

He'd plotted a course already. When they fled Shadow Wing, they would ascend in a broad spiral arc that would avoid taking the TIEs out of the facility's general vicinity. The TIEs would catch them or they would drop away at whatever altitude they considered too far from base. Either result would, Wyl hoped, be enough.

"Wyl to Nath," he called. "They spotted us, as planned. Now it's over to you."

III

Nath Tensent felt his ship bob like a wooden boat on rough seas. The engine growled and sputtered with every lurch, and his readouts spat out warnings one moment before going dark the next. "*You're* doing a fine job," he muttered, and T5 squawked back irritably as he opened his throttle and set the Y-wing into motion.

Wyl and the other pilots chattered as the canyon walls blurred around him. Nath kept half an ear out but he was too focused on navigation to really *listen*—his sensors gave him plenty of warning to indicate where the canyon branched but an overhang or unexpected avalanche could end his day very suddenly.

The Troithe underworld had been worse—tight maneuvering had been the order of the day, and agility was not a Y-wing's strong suit—but he hadn't been on a schedule down there, either. Now, if he was going to do his part, he'd need to hit close to top speed in Troithe's atmosphere.

"Remind me why we're doing this?" he asked.

T5 replied with a threat to take control. Nath smirked. He hadn't expected a better answer, and the truth was he knew his reasons. They were *stupid* reasons, but he had them thoroughly cataloged.

Nath was a practical man, but he'd never been a coward. *If you wanted out,* he told himself, *you could've gotten out after Pandem Nai . . . and if you wanted to lead, you should have fought for the position.*

But he'd stayed, and no matter how much Wyl infuriated him he didn't want to take command. He'd been through that heartbreak before and even with the right crew—say, a band of thugs and pirates who could thrive following Nath's philosophy of self-interest—his days in charge were probably over.

That didn't mean Wyl wasn't ungrateful. He wondered if the kid would ever understand.

"Hey!" he called, and thumped a fist on his console. "Where's my targeting computer?"

The secondary screen swung out and wobbled on its tracks. The range indicator blurred as it counted down the distance to the canyon's end.

There was a very real chance he was going to get himself killed. And why? For his squadron. For Wyl Lark. For Chass and Kairos and Quell, who might have been alive and might have been dead. He'd looked for other ways to serve Alphabet, and there were no other good options.

He'd cleared all his debts before when he'd shot and killed Shadow Wing's colonel. Now he was racking them up again.

He made a tight turn into a crevasse that nearly sheared off his starboard nacelle. The high walls blotted out the starlight above, and Nath was forced to pilot in darkness. T5 sent warnings to his console indicating shifts in the topography, but even the astromech was navigating by sensors alone.

The range indicator fell toward zero.

Nath primed his torpedo launcher without looking toward the controls. Suddenly the walls of the crevasse dropped away and he was in a broad chasm—a pit that might have housed a whole city district. In the center of the jagged plane that served as the chasm floor stood the massive cylinder of the Core Nine mining megafacility.

His scanner showed Wyl and the others along with the squadron of

TIEs, but they were too high above to concern him. He spotted what might have been a ground entrance into the facility—a strip of flat ground and a dark line that might have been the outline of a blast door—and adjusted his heading.

"Locked and ready!" he called.

The range indicator blinked with all the disinterest of an alarm clock. Nath squeezed his firing trigger and saw his power readings spike; T5 was trying to optimize energy distribution and targeting. The burning bolt of a torpedo ripped from the Y-wing and jolted Nath backward, and he fired the next before the missile reached its target. Then the next. His cannons pulsed, sending smaller quivers through his vessel—he didn't hope particle bolts would do much good, but if he'd had a rock to hurl at the bunker he'd have thrown that, too.

He would only get one pass.

The light from the explosion was brighter than anything he'd seen since the death of the *Lodestar*. It washed the canyon like daylight— true daylight, not the glow of solar projectors or the fire of the black hole—and he grinned, tempted to soak in the view as his weapons readouts turned red and the last of his torpedoes shot forth. Instead he pitched upward and veered as if to skim the side of the dome; and as he approached his torpedoes' impact point he dropped the handful of proton bombs he'd kept unused since the battle for the capital district. He couldn't see whether he'd achieved his goal, but the ground outside the facility entrance rippled like water from the resulting shock waves. Dust rose in burning plumes.

His scanner showed the TIE fighters descending toward him. He wondered what they expected to do, given his Y-wing's usefulness was spent.

"Any luck?" he asked his droid. "Or do I need to slam this thing into the wall to finish the job?"

He was only half joking. He'd checked the ejector equipment before takeoff, and if he didn't succeed now the battle would be over before it had truly begun.

T5 flashed a sensor image onto a screen. Behind the dust clouds and the flame, there was a crack in the wall of the facility. Not more than a meter wide, but it could've been worse.

"Nath to ground troops," he called as he rode the wind. "Your turn."

IV

Half a kilometer below, the New Republic's Sixty-First Mobile Infantry poured out of canyons on foot and by speeder bike, racing toward the gap in the facility wall. Wyl heard the shouting over his comm—the updates passed between squad leaders and the obscene battle cries— and he was heartened by the noise. But he had no time to listen to the particulars as he yelled, "Down! Down!" and his squadron scattered while the TIEs pursued.

The world blurred as the A-wing rocketed toward the ground. The flash of his scanner indicated two TIEs chasing him; the four other aircraft were likewise followed, which left two enemy fighters free to hit soldiers on the ground. That was a better result than Wyl had feared, but it wouldn't leave much margin for error.

He fell like a meteor toward a canyon and pulled up as cliff walls rose around him. For an instant he lost control of his ship—it bucked and shuddered and the control yoke did nothing—and TIE fire rained down, pelting stone below. The shimmer of Wyl's shields suggested something had hit him, but then he had control again. Only one of the TIEs was in the canyon with him, and they rocketed forward together.

This is the plan, he reminded himself. *This is exactly how it's supposed to go.*

He spared his scanner a glance to confirm that the other aircraft, too, had descended into the canyons. It was a mad tactic, but the walls offered a shield against assailants, reducing their possible angles of attack; and at top speed the TIEs were likely to crash, forcing them to match the lesser velocity of the airspeeders. Wyl and the others had even gathered as much topographic data as possible during their flight to the facility, which might—conceivably—give them the advantage.

"Wraive," Wyl called, trying to keep half an eye on his sensors as he swung back and forth in the narrow canyon. The TIE closest to him was attempting to lock on. "Can you get to the troops? Give them air support?"

"Not with two fighters on me. Apologies."

He adjusted the sensor map and spun in time to avoid a burst of fire from behind. "Prinspai, try to cut in behind Ubellikos in Canyon Echo. Use sub-branch Echo 1-1. Wraive, stay on your path and I'll see what I can do."

Acknowledgments came rapidly. Wyl adjusted his comm and heard Carver reporting TIE attack vectors from the ground. He tried to imagine the enemy descending as the infantry pushed toward whatever breach in the facility Nath had managed to create—hordes of New Republic troops totally exposed as they ran across rough terrain.

"We're coming," he swore, though he wasn't sure whether anyone heard.

Emerald particle bolts sprayed across the canyon. Wyl instantly recognized the tactic. The Shadow Wing pilot was firing wildly, but it wasn't an act of desperation—the foe was forcing Wyl off course, encouraging him to dash himself against the rock faces. If Wyl didn't do something the plan was liable to work.

Who are you? Char? Blink? Do you know me from Pandem Nai?

He thought about opening a channel to the enemy, but his own pilots were counting on him for instructions and he had his hands full surviving the flight. It would have to wait.

He turned to speed to save him, opening his throttle and giving up on consciously watching sensor readings or listening for screaming TIEs. He let instinct guide him as he had when flying the beasts of Home, and the A-wing seemed to twist and dive with the fluidity of a sur-avka. He flipped and kept flying with blood saturating his head and turned down twisting passages in the rock. Emerging from one canyon into another, he spotted an airspeeder whip past and fired instantly, his bolts catching the pursuing TIE a fraction of a second later. The enemy trailed sparks and its wing panels coruscated with energy, as if it were in the throes of ascension to some higher plane; then it smashed into rock and Wyl sped through the resulting pyre.

Who were you?

The first Imperial kill was his. If he opened a comm channel, what could he say now?

But he'd momentarily freed Wraive from pursuit. His own hunter had disappeared somewhere in the canyon maze. He checked his sensors again, called out recommendations to Prinspai and Ubellikos and Vitale as he confirmed their positions, and headed for the mining facility. "Stay in contact," he said, "and watch relative positions. We planned this, but we're outnumbered and the enemy's going to start using the same tricks against us real fast."

He took the risk of soaring out of the canyons to cut the distance he needed to travel, exposing his fighter long enough to speed five hundred meters across the highlands before dipping into the basin where the mining facility awaited. TIEs flew like insects over the mass of troops, dancing and leaping out of range of the rockets and heavy cannons as their volleys churned rock and tossed burning bodies into the air.

Wyl tore his eyes from the troops and fired into the swarm, careful to ensure any stray blasts would strike the cliffsides or the facility instead of the ground. A fresh pair of TIEs split off to strike at him and he laughed in relief as they followed him into yet another crevasse.

He could outrun them, perhaps, but then they would return to their battle against the ground troops. He reduced thruster output, allowed his foes to creep nearer as he wove among rock formations. The TIEs began to fire, particle bolts skimming so close to his hull that the coruscation of his shields and the energy discharge made it difficult to see. He diverted power from his weapons to rear screens, tried to determine whether any of his squadron mates were near enough to assist, but by their comm chatter they were having enough trouble keeping the ground forces alive.

You'll have to save yourself.

The crevasse widened until the base was broader than the top and a canopy of rock hung above Wyl, save for a single narrow crack leading to the surface. The light of the particle bolts painted the stone walls in jade. The shadows were deep enough to conceal a village but he couldn't use them to hide—the glow of his thrusters would give him away anywhere, and if he switched to repulsors now he'd be shot down before the mechanisms kicked in.

"We'll find a way," he whispered, more for his ship than for himself. Yet he'd be sorry to fail his squadron and the infantry.

The cave walls turned from jade to fiery ruby. Particle bolts ripped from a dark hole in the shadows, forcing the TIEs off course and allowing Wyl a chance to adjust, to attempt to exchange position with his pursuers.

He only caught a glimpse of his savior: a Y-wing hovering in darkness like a sniper. Somehow in the chaos he'd forgotten that Nath Tensent could still be counted on.

V

The New Republic was inside Core Nine. Colonel Soran Keize watched enemy soldiers clamber through a gap in the duracrete on a security monitor no larger than a datapad—a reminder that no matter how sturdy the megafacility was, it was not built for the peculiar needs of war. The monitor room itself was built for a handful of security officers, not a command-and-control operation, yet it was the only place from which he could follow the invasion.

One of Yadeez's aides sat at the console, frantically accessing blueprints as Soran spoke into his comlink. "Combat-rated ground forces should proceed to sections one-alpha and one-gamma immediately. Use all necessary firepower to stop the New Republic infantry; our squadrons will cut off the reinforcements outside."

He spoke with confidence. He hefted a rifle off a side table, slung the strap over his shoulder, and inspected it one last time; a power cell two-thirds charged wasn't ideal, but it was the best anyone could bring him on short notice. When the battery was burnt out, he could always switch to his sidearm.

He clapped a hand on the aide's shoulder. "I'm heading for the fight. We'll need every gun we can get, but stay in contact—I'll coordinate from the front lines."

The aide nodded briskly. Soran turned and nearly walked into Governor Fara Yadeez as she entered the doorway of the small office. "There's no need," she proclaimed, and it surprised him to hear her countermand his orders so boldly—even by implication. "The freighter is nearly ready. They're attempting to bring the engines online. If you're going to counterattack from anywhere, the bridge of your flagship seems preferable."

Soran studied the governor. Her expression was somber and dutiful as ever.

"It's good news," he said. "But someone needs to lead the defenders. Even if we had time to evacuate, surrendering the facility to the New Republic would be an imperfect solution."

The monitor showed blaster flashes. The facility's narrow corridors made for a natural kill zone. The Imperial defenders had claimed an intersection from which they could fire and retreat, and though enemy corpses quickly accrued Soran knew his forces would soon need to retreat to another choke point, then another.

"The freighter is nearly ready," Yadeez repeated, the words deliberately enunciated as if she were speaking to a child.

He finally understood her meaning: *You have what you came for.*

In that moment he was certain she knew what his priority had been since the moment his troops had fallen to Troithe. She knew that he had worked not toward conquest, but toward escape. She might have been saying: *Only a fool would throw it all away now.*

"Come aboard with me," he said. "If the defense *does* fail, you'll be able to—"

She interrupted him—again, surprising him with her boldness. "It hasn't come to that yet. It's *my* people who will hold the line. Your personnel—your ground crews, your shipboard officers, along with anyone from Troithe not combat-rated—should board the freighter now."

She held both hands out, her palms up. Soran understood what she was asking.

"It's not necessary," he said.

Yadeez shrugged. "The Empire won't survive or fall according to the fate of Troithe or its governor. Shadow Wing may yet save us."

She curled and uncurled her fingers, waiting.

The Empire, like Troithe, is already lost. You needn't go with it.

He wanted to say the words, but they would not persuade her. They would only steal her faith in him, steal her faith in the 204th's grander purpose. She was not his responsibility—his duty was to his people—but he wished to do better by her than that.

Soran Keize unslung his rifle and laid it carefully in the hands of the last Imperial governor of Troithe.

"I will remember what you did today," he said. "It was my privilege to know you."

"Likewise," she said, and it startled him to hear the word pronounced without aristocratic pretense. He wondered again just how far she had risen—how far down the line of succession she had been from Governor Hastemoor.

It only made him admire her more.

She flashed him a gruff smile. He returned it, and left her behind as he made for the freighter.

VI

Nath Tensent waited in the shadows of an overhang, reactor operating at one-tenth maximum output to conceal his heat signature but ready to ignite at a prompt from T5. He kept his hands on his weapons controls, watching his scanner and listening to the comm. The experience was almost relaxing.

A Y-wing wasn't much good at playing sniper, but given the choice between shooting from cover and jumping into a dogfight, the choice was clear.

Wyl was calling orders to the other pilots again, and Nath observed as the aircraft swapped paths through the canyon maze. "That's a mistake," he muttered, but he kept his channel closed so that only T5 could hear. Wyl might've been prone to boxing his people in but no one deserved to be second-guessed on the battlefield. Besides, the kid was almost as good at getting people out of trouble as into it.

"Don't suppose you could tweak the maneuvering jets, since we don't need to power the torpedo launcher?" Nath called. "Maybe make this wreck a little more useful in this fight?"

T5 didn't respond. Nath snorted and shook his head.

"You keep monitoring the squadron," he said and tuned the comm to the infantry frequency.

Dozens of soldiers were still fighting to get inside the facility, trapped in caves and canyons by TIEs that opened fire whenever they emerged. Nath heard fear and determination in the troops' voices as the squads planned surges and diversions and multipronged attacks, all of which inevitably failed. Carver had gone silent at some point, dead or just without a working comlink. Junior was leading three soldiers up the cliffside in an attempt to shoot down TIEs with blaster rifles.

Meanwhile, the squads inside the facility fared only slightly better. Sergeants Twitch and Zab led the assault. By the sounds of the yelling, Zab's strategy amounted to "rush the bastards, fast as you can"; somehow *that* was resulting in a modicum of success whereas Twitch's attempts to secure the compound corridor by corridor had bogged down.

"There's a command center here," Zab called, "but the place is dark and it's just a bunch of . . . I don't know, mining controls. Heavy opposition is all toward the main hangar."

Maybe Wyl was right, Nath thought. Maybe Shadow Wing really was trying to escape the planet, not ignite some mineral deposit deep underground. It would be hard on the kid if it turned out to be true. But they couldn't have known.

Besides, the more Shadow Wing pilots who died, the better off they all were.

T5 beeped through the comm and Nath's scanner flashed. He swore as he watched a dozen fresh marks, then *another* dozen, approaching the facility from all directions. The rest of Shadow Wing had finally arrived, coming in from across the planet to make sure the New Republic didn't stand a chance.

"Twenty-to-one odds, huh?" Nath said, and brought his reactor back to full power. "We'd be better off down there with the infantry."

T5 squealed in agreement. Nath smirked and adjusted his comm again. *Make this good, brother,* he thought, and waited for orders from Wyl.

VII

Six squadrons of TIE fighters lashed out with particle bolts like lightning. The sonic boom of their passing was like thunder. Wyl Lark and his pilots fought them in the open, above the mining facility, because playing hide-and-seek in the canyons wasn't an option against an enemy with enough proton bombs to level a mountain range; and leaving that same enemy to slaughter the New Republic soldiers was no option, either.

So Wyl's squadron sped through the TIE swarm, evading particle lances and attempting to survive rather than fight. Before Shadow Wing's reinforcements had arrived, Wyl had hoped that the infantry would open the facility dome and grant the New Republic fighters shelter against the storm; but it was too late now. The storm had come. All they could do now was buy the infantry time.

Wyl called orders as familiar Shadow Wing maneuvers played out—maneuvers he knew well but his pilots did not. Wyl recognized the Twins, whom he hadn't seen since the Oridol Cluster, move in perfect sync through the firefight. Wyl lost Prinspai to the Spiral and Ubellikos to Snapper's Needle when the pilot was pinned to the ground and left with nowhere to escape. Both cried out for help before their end, and Wyl could do nothing to save them.

Then it was Wyl, Nath, Vitale, and Denish Wraive, and Wyl knew there wasn't much time left.

You made mistakes, he told himself, *but you tried.*

"You did good," he told his ship.

Then a new thunderclap hit the battlefield. Wyl looked up and laughed like a man drenched in rain as a shadow passed over the stars.

The voice through his comm was clear and self-assured. "This is General Syndulla to all New Republic forces. Vanguard Squadron is here."

VIII

Hera had been gone for too long.

She had left Cerberon with a clean conscience, knowing— *believing*—that the system was secure and that Caern Adan and Yrica Quell had built an inescapable trap to destroy one of the Empire's most lethal forces. A trap that, in addition to its ruthless efficiency, could be sprung with a minimal loss of New Republic *and* Imperial life. She had left because Vanguard Squadron needed her, and because the New Republic war effort had needed the ships and territories that Vanguard Squadron would bring into play.

She didn't wonder now whether she'd made a mistake. Maybe she had, maybe not. Maybe when she'd received Chass na Chadic's emergency message she should've taken time to regroup and develop a plan. But rushing headlong into battle for the right cause was a habit she'd never unlearned from her rebel days, and self-recriminations wouldn't save Troithe or Alphabet Squadron or the Sixty-First Mobile Infantry.

As she stood aboard the bridge of the Nebulon-B frigate *Temperance,* she was determined to save everyone she could.

"Get the fighters ready to launch," she said, "and power up the main batteries. Prepare to fire on the surface."

The *Temperance* was holding position in-atmosphere above the Scar of Troithe. Sensors had picked up the TIE swarm from afar, and Hera had decided that if Shadow Wing was attacking, her job was to intervene regardless of the situation on the ground. The frigate had successfully evaded the planetary defense network and bypassed Troithe's shields—simple enough when approaching the unprotected ruined continent, though both might prove troublesome if the battle moved elsewhere. Shield coverage appeared spotty over the city, and the frigate hadn't been able to determine whether the defense network was under enemy control.

The bridge crew seemed fully aware of the gravity of the situation, despite the ease of the mission so far. The ship's captain had graciously turned command over to Hera. Now she watched sentient beings from a dozen species pull up tactical screens and weapons readings and call out commands to the fighter bays as they tried to decipher what was happening planetside.

"You're certain about this?" Stornvein asked. Her favored aide had accompanied her through the hell of the mission with Vanguard. He stood ready despite enduring the destruction of worlds and the funerals of friends. "We fire on that mess down there, we could end up hitting our own people."

Hera eyed the tactical displays as details popped into existence: canyon charts, troop movements, some sort of heavy bunker under assault. "We can't wait for target IDs but we won't be careless, either. We'll start the turbolaser bombardment at minimum power with a wide dispersal pattern—grab their attention and force the TIEs to break formation."

"And hope they don't all come after us? Or are we taking on Shadow Wing directly?"

She smiled grimly. It was an excellent question. On the one hand, there was every reason to think that Vanguard and the *Temperance* could put up a good show, even exhausted as they were.

On the other hand, no one had yet beaten the 204th in a fair fight.

"One problem at a time," she said, and gave the order to fire.

CHAPTER 21

THE CHAOS OF VICTORY

I

Had Chass na Chadic flown anything but a B-wing, she'd have spearheaded the attack on Troithe. As it was, she was closer to the butt of the proverbial spear, chugging behind the Vanguard X-wings as they sped out of the frigate's launch bay. The experience was disturbingly familiar, though she needed a moment to realize why: The last time she'd launched from a Nebulon-B frigate had been the final mission of Riot Squadron and the *Hellion's Dare*.

Not that it mattered. Not really. She was where she wanted to be.

The B-wing fell as much as flew toward the surface, battered by wind and seared by the heat of atmospheric reentry. Thruster bursts kept the vessel from spinning but increased its speed until it dropped like a meteor. Its indicator lights flashed red, broiling the cockpit. The repairs put in place by the *Temperance*'s engineers had involved sealant spray and jury-rigged wiring, not the refit the assault ship needed after the battle over Catadra; Chass could smell paste melting as her harness cut into her chest.

She adjusted her comm with a jerky hand—ignoring Vanguard Squadron's chatter and switching to a general New Republic channel—then deployed her strike foils like a parachute. Servos whined with distress and the ship jolted and bounced as her retro-rockets and repulsors kicked in, slowing her fractionally.

The canyons were visible now—the cracked expanse of the continent filling her view in all directions. Crimson energy bolts rained around her, outracing her to the ground. Chass aimed for a distant glimmering and the glimmer soon resolved into a mass of TIE fighters and X-wings and unidentified allies: Shadow Wing and Vanguard and the survivors of the *Lodestar*.

She fired into the melee. Outnumbered as the New Republic was, she figured she was more likely to hit an enemy than a foe. ("When you're about to lose," Fadime had liked to say, "it never hurts to gamble.") She considered firing off a missile or torpedo as well, guessing the atmospheric shock wave might scatter the enemy—it wasn't a tactic she'd tried with Shadow Wing before, which meant they might not be prepared for it—but the odds of friendly casualties were too high even for her.

Her screens flared, shucking off heat, as a voice declared: "General Syndulla to ground. How may we assist?"

It was Wyl Lark who replied. Chass laughed as she dropped into the melee and was embarrassed by her own sense of relief.

"General," Lark said, "we have ground forces attempting to take the mining facility. We don't—I don't know what Shadow Wing is doing there. It's *possible* they may be attempting to detonate some kind of weapon. Regardless—"

"We'll keep the TIEs busy, give your troops room to operate, and follow your lead," Syndulla responded. "It's good to hear from you, Alphabet."

Chass watched a pair of TIEs speed out of her way. She tried to level out and barely avoided slamming into the facility dome below her, arcing back up toward the fight with cannons pumping and her vision a blur. "You're in charge now, huh?" she asked.

Wyl cried out her name like *Chass* was the winning hand in a card game. Nath was on the comm next, declaring, "You and that ship are sturdier than you look."

"Mostly me," Chass said. "The ship's basically scrap. You know what it's like—you've been flying a junk heap for years."

"Cute, sister," Nath said. "Cute."

"We're glad you're alive," Wyl said. Beneath the joy she heard the physical strain in his voice.

She couldn't see his A-wing above her and didn't have time to look. One of the Vanguard pilots was chasing a TIE her way; she tried to line up a shot, fired, and growled when her particle bolts slipped inside the enemy's wings.

"Where—" Wyl began, then began shouting commands at his comrades and the X-wings. She welcomed the break as she cut through the battle, trying to comprehend the hurricane of engine trails and particle bolts—to figure out whether there was a coherent plan or if she was better off just riding the wind.

She locked onto a TIE and nearly shot it down before its wingmate tore apart her shields with a single volley. She cursed and tried to divert power back to the screens.

"Casualties down here are pretty bad," Nath said. "*Lodestar*'s gone and a lot of the crew with it. Most of the other pilots. No word about Kairos. No word from Adan or Quell, either, unless you—"

"Nothing," Chass said.

"Yeah. I figured."

She was surprised to hear disappointment in his voice. She swallowed her own reaction, tried to channel it into the physical act of piloting.

But Quell had lied to her, betrayed her. If she was dead—

Focus on the damn fight!

Wyl kept calling orders and updates. Vanguard Squadron moved in response, trapping TIEs before they could hit the troops on the ground and disrupting enemy maneuvers before they could be fully born. A Vanguard X-wing went down, splashing against a canyon wall and sending an avalanche tumbling down the cliffside. A TIE went wild when a bolt clipped its cockpit sphere, spinning and spraying shots as it hurtled into the distance.

Somehow, Chass was surprised to realize, the New Republic forces were *surviving*.

They weren't winning, though. Winning would be costly.

She felt an unfamiliar churn in her gut at the thought of dying. She had responsibilities now.

The B-wing's gyroscopes spun her foils around the cockpit. She swept the air with firepower as she attempted to regain altitude, and she was frantically trying to determine whether a TIE flight was headed her way when Nath said: "B-wing running quiet today?"

"What?"

"No music," Nath said.

She swore and laughed bitterly as she evaded a deadly volley. She wasn't about to explain that her collection was gone. "You need me to sing?" she asked.

"Twenty credits if you do."

She searched for an appropriate oath. He was baiting her. Of course he was baiting her. And she was an idiot.

"Screw it. You're on," she said.

Which is why, as Chass na Chadic rose into the sky and reduced a starfighter of the 204th to a ball of burning gas and metal, she began to wail into her comm. She sang about star charts and broken hearts and life as an outlaw—a ballad that had been pirated and altered and reassembled across the Outer Rim for twenty years and still had more than its share of fans. Nath laughed, the Vanguard pilots cursed or ignored her, and the oscillating sound of particle bolts joined her as her orchestra.

❚❚

Colonel Soran Keize recognized that the course of battle had changed and knew precisely what was required to correct it. That certainty made acceptance no less difficult—no soldier watched a plan crumble and was eager to accept that truth—but the difference between an experienced commander and a novice was that the former did not pause or shirk.

The command deck of the bulk freighter was crammed with stations devoted to cargo control and load shifting, and Soran was forced to duck beneath piping and conduits as he crossed from the viewscreen to the comm controls. His bridge crew largely comprised the survivors of the *Edict*—few escape pods from the *Aerie* had been recovered—and the cadets' youth showed in every awkward fumble at a lever or dial. He doubted they'd flown anything larger than an airspeeder not designed to Imperial specifications.

"Get me the governor," he called, resting his hand on the headset, "and signal me when the engines are at full power."

None of what was occurring outside Core Nine was a surprise. He'd counted himself lucky every minute New Republic reinforcements had failed to arrive, starting from the moment the *Edict* and *Aerie* had jumped into Cerberon. In truth, the foe had come far too late: He had his ship—his means of escape—and he could depart having achieved all of the 204th's objectives.

The 204th's objectives, if not his own.

One of the cadets made a hand signal from the engineering station. "Open the doors," Soran called, and a countdown appeared on one of the displays as the facility's great dome ever-so-slowly parted.

An indicator lit on the headset. He fixed it over his ears and heard the sound of blasterfire. "Yadeez," he said. "Enemy naval forces have arrived at Troithe."

He imagined her voice: *The 204th may be the finest Imperial fighter wing left in the galaxy,* she might have said. *Can you defeat them?*

"Go!" she said instead.

The difference between an experienced commander and a novice was that the former did not pause or shirk. Soran did not pause or shirk now. He deactivated the comm and shouted rapid orders to the cadets as the freighter's engines rumbled and its bulkheads rattled at a deafening volume. Low-resolution imagers assured him that, fifteen levels up the launch silo, the dome was nearly open wide enough for the freighter to pass through.

He wiped the dust off a course projection display with his sleeve and jabbed at the controls, generating a path from the surface into the upper atmosphere and marking five points along the way. "Follow this trajectory until I tell you otherwise," he said, sending the data to the helmsmate. "TIE squadrons to withdraw from the battle and come aboard at these locations."

He awaited the most obvious of questions. After what had become of Yadeez, he was braced to answer it.

"What about the last squadron?" the helmsmate asked.

There were six squadrons in a TIE wing. All of them could fit aboard the freighter.

"Captain Darita will guard our retreat. She and her squadron will rejoin us when we leave orbit."

The cadet did not question him again. Soran turned his attention to the sensor map and wondered what his next sacrifice would be—and how long before he became numb to the burdens of leadership.

III

Vanguard Squadron didn't hesitate to follow Wyl's orders, despite never having served under him. General Syndulla never counter-manded Wyl, despite being a better strategist. The New Republic forces seemed to accept that this was his fight—that his experiences on Troithe and his history with Shadow Wing qualified him to lead and required that he do so.

Wyl felt pride at the faith of his comrades and he felt shame at his own pride. Mostly he was focused on the battle.

Moments earlier a bulk freighter had ascended from the mining megafacility and begun a course skyward. The TIEs were rapidly en-veloping it in a defensive formation while continuing to launch ag-gressive sorties at the New Republic starfighters. Two Vanguard craft were down, and others were showing severe damage. Nath Tensent's Y-wing was, to all appearances, being held together by spit and T5's arc welder. Denish Wraive's airspeeder had withdrawn, its engine overheated. Vitale's V-wing had a single cannon remaining. Wyl's own craft had somehow escaped fresh harm, but he felt the strain on his body as he swooped and glided and fired and spun; he was trembling with fatigue, and he could only maintain the display for so long before he made an error. One would be enough.

The ground forces had reported no sign of a planet-ravaging bomb. The freighter, although apparently jury-rigged with heavy weapons, was not moving toward any obvious target. As the TIE swarm thinned, Wyl wondered if he had been right: if Shadow Wing's primary goal was simply to escape the planet.

"Enemy squadron approaching the freighter—looks like they're docking in the cargo bay," one of the Vanguard pilots called.

Wyl jerked his fighter to one side as cannon bolts streamed from below and a trio of TIEs passed him by.

He *had* been right.

"Alphabet Leader?" Another of the Vanguard pilots—Wyl recognized Tssat's reptilian sibilants. "Where do you want us?"

He hesitated, unused to thinking—of having the *luxury* to think— more than a few seconds into the future mid-battle. Somewhere in the background he heard Chass singing, her voice tinny and small.

"The other TIEs—are they going aboard, too?" he asked.

He could see the answer on his scanner. Vitale replied, "Negative," and it gave Wyl another moment to consider.

Shadow Wing was fleeing. He couldn't prove it, but he was *certain.* If he pursued, more New Republic pilots would die. More Imperial pilots would die. If he pursued, the chaos would continue at least a little longer.

And if he didn't?

Nath's words came to his mind, unbidden: *If you want to walk away without firing a shot, you be prepared to live with it. If Operation Cinder comes around again, if Shadow Wing picks up where they left off, you don't get to have regrets.*

"I can live with it," Wyl whispered to himself and to his ship. And he could.

"We're ready to support you." It was General Syndulla's voice, calm and encouraging. "The *Temperance* is prepared to engage."

He suspected she would back whatever decision he made. She trusted Wyl would serve the needs of the New Republic.

He adjusted his comm, opening a general channel. The words that emerged from his mouth tasted swollen and bitter—he'd spoken openly to the 204th twice before, and he knew he was now betraying something, someone, that he couldn't entirely place.

"This is Wyl Lark to the opposing force. Power down your weapons and surrender. Repeat, power down and surrender. All airborne forces should ground themselves immediately." His lips were dry and tasted like blood, but the hardest part was done. The last words came out like breathing: "No one else has to die today."

There was no reply. The TIEs continued to fire. The bulk freighter continued its ascent.

"Alphabet Leader—"

Wyl cut off the Vanguard pilot. "All fighters pursue. If you can hit the freighter, do it, but don't take your eyes off the TIEs."

Rununja, Riot Squadron's commander, had told him once that it was no crime to fire on a retreating opponent. "There's nothing dishonorable or treacherous about attacking the enemy from behind—or about the enemy doing the same to us," she'd said. "This is not a parlor game, where the next round is something to be anticipated eagerly. This is a war, won in part by disabling military forces."

He understood that. Still, as he fired toward the freighter as it sped toward the bright stars, he was sure he had forgotten something vital.

IV

Three of the TIE squadrons were now aboard. The bulk freighter roared through the upper atmosphere, veering sharply away from the

New Republic frigate above and the Scar of Troithe below and toward the planet's more populous regions. With grim satisfaction, Colonel Soran Keize observed through aging instruments as the first concentrated particle beams from the planetary defense network ignited the sky; the ensuing flashes could have heralded the birth of a new star.

The beams were concentrated toward the Nebulon-B frigate as it attempted to intercept, though a handful raked clouds near the New Republic starfighters. Soran wondered what it had taken Governor Yadeez and her troops to recapture the defense satellite control centers—what heroics had been performed on the surface that he had been blissfully unaware of. He imagined Imperial guerrillas storming outposts fortified by local defenders, urged to retake Troithe and obey their new governor.

Fara Yadeez might have known the 204th's objective. But her troops surely had believed they were fighting for their planet, not the survival of Shadow Wing.

"Bring Squadron Two aboard," he said as the sensor map changed. Even from across the ship, he could hear the rush of wind inside the cargo bay; somehow, his crew heard him and relayed the orders.

He turned attention to his headset. "Captain Darita? Are your pilots prepared?"

"Last ones standing, Colonel. We're down two ships but the satellites are giving us room to breathe. So long as no fresh enemy starfighters arrive, we can escort you out of orbit."

Darita's voice was hoarse, the words clipped as she expelled them between evasive maneuvers. Soran watched her fighter spiral and spin on the scanner.

"Good," he said. "We'll see you shortly."

Darita said something in reply but it was lost in static. Her mark disappeared from the scanner as she, too, was destroyed.

Soran allowed himself a moment of grief. But only a moment.

When he refocused, his gaze strayed to a viewscreen. His eyes were drawn not to the flare of starfighter combat but to the ground far beneath them—the diffused glimmering of a million towers rising from a landscape constructed over centuries. It was an unexceptional world, Troithe—a slovenly cousin to Coruscant, a forgotten stepbrother to the colonial factory worlds—but the governor's guerrillas and the civilians who had supported them were as majestic as any pilots in Shadow Wing.

Troithe would never be reclaimed by the Empire, he thought. But Soran Keize had never been a true believer in the Empire anyway.

He believed in people. His people, mostly. But in a galaxy where the Empire was no more, perhaps his duties as a soldier extended further.

He had what he wanted, yet he'd achieved it on the backs of those who'd looked to him for aid.

Forget Soran Keize. Remember Devon.

"Arm the missiles," he said. "Target all New Republic outposts and fire on my mark."

The Star Destroyer *Edict*'s ordnance, transferred to the freighter, wasn't much of a parting gift for the warriors of Troithe. But the missiles would leave whole districts in ruins. They would turn rebel bunkers into craters and boil lakes and collapse factories larger than mountains. They would ensure that the fighting could continue long after Shadow Wing departed, and that millions of Imperial loyalists would not march readily into detention camps under New Republic domination.

That would have to be enough.

V

The air was thin, but not so thin that Chass na Chadic couldn't hear the shriek of the missiles as they left the freighter and drew fiery trails across the sky. She stuttered through the last lyrics of her song and came to a breathless halt.

"Missile launch!" someone called over the comm.

"No kidding," she muttered.

She scanned the atmosphere between her B-wing and the freighter.

Seven TIEs were all that remained of the enemy's rear guard, but they were holding up well against Vanguard's greater numbers.

Wyl's voice came through, calmer than she would've expected. "All ships, intercept any missiles in range. Priority is the *missiles.* Continue pursuit of the freighter *only* if you can't reach the primary target."

Chass had fallen far behind after taking a glancing blow to one thruster. She was barely able to stay airborne as it was; she'd already accepted the bitter knowledge that she couldn't catch the freighter. She looked to her scanner and blew out a breath as she set a new course.

The missile she'd chosen was headed toward Thanner Lake, descending in a long arc that Chass had seconds to intersect. She let gravity do much of the work of acceleration, knowing if she opened her throttle further she'd blow her whole engine. Wisps of cloud spattered her canopy and mixed with the spots of her vision.

She gave her scanner a glance and felt a pang as the freighter grew increasingly distant. *Don't think about it,* she told herself. *You got Syndulla here, Wyl and Nath survived. Anything else would've been a bonus.*

She switched to ion guns as she approached the blazing comet of the missile. Her scanner showed other fighters pursuing other missiles, disappearing over the horizon and out of range. She was surprised that Wyl's A-wing wasn't among the pursuers; more surprised to see that Nath's Y-wing was.

Her targeting computer approximated a range to the missile. She let the mechanisms minutely adjust her course.

She wondered what the Children of the Empty Sun taught about saving nonbelievers. The thought came from nowhere. She squeezed her trigger.

Searing white energy poured from her cannons. The missile was still a distant, burning object, but if she missed at such a speed she wouldn't have a second chance. At best, she'd get a chance to look it in the eye as she passed it half a kilometer away.

Ion bolts cut a path through clouds. The B-wing followed. Chass waited for a time that felt imperceptibly short and indeterminably long before the whole sky flashed and she stared into catastrophe, refusing to close her eyes. Her ship seemed to *snap* as it was tossed back by the shock wave, and she felt her skull smash against the back of her seat as a spiderweb of cracks appeared in her canopy.

Then the flash faded. The missile was gone, detonated above the city. The B-wing resumed its course.

In the sudden tranquility, Chass wondered what would become of herself.

VI

Nath Tensent was flying low—low enough that he would've been below the planet's shields if the region had still had any. His Y-wing shuddered violently several times a minute and the floor of the cockpit beneath his right foot was alarmingly hot, to the point where his sole was melting against his rudder pedal. T5 had mercifully shut down most of the console displays to spare him the infinitely scrolling warnings.

All of which explained why he hadn't joined the squadron chasing the freighter beyond Troithe's orbit. All of which also explained why he was low enough to intercept one of the moon-smashing missiles that Shadow Wing had kindly decided to share before departure.

Wyl was calling orders, assigning missiles to Vanguard craft. Nath waited till the rest of the fighters had been matched up and winced when he saw a warhead still untargeted, heading his way. "All right," he said to the droid. "Set course and see what we can do."

He succinctly announced his intentions on the New Republic channel. No one seemed to notice in the chaos. Nath wondered if Wyl was aware he was still in the fight.

The Y-wing rocketed toward its quarry, gradually gaining altitude. With all the damage the Y-wing had sustained, however, it would take a miracle for Nath to shoot down the missile—his targeting computer was offline and T5 couldn't compensate. He considered other options and found them lacking: Unless he wanted to hurl himself directly onto the missile, he lacked the arsenal to make much of a difference.

He entered a thick cloud front, took a deep breath of boot rubber fumes, and listened to Wyl and General Syndulla exchange updates on the freighter's progress. He thought of the boy and all they'd been through that day—about their confrontation over the transmitter, and how blasted disappointed Wyl had seemed.

The image of Wyl in his brain flowed into an image of the crowds packed into the tubes of the Web, who'd roared at him, cheered for him, begged him with every breath to save them from the governor's forces. It wasn't like it had been in the rebellion—people had begged him to save them then, too, but now they were stupid enough to believe he *could*.

He cursed and tried to peer through the clouds in the direction of the missile. *Luke Skywalker shot down the Death Star without a targeting computer,* he thought. But Luke Skywalker hadn't been blind when he'd done it.

He had less than a minute till intercept.

"Droid!" he called. "Where's that missile going to hit?"

One of his displays flickered and showed a chart of the planet surface. A marker blinked eighty kilometers south of the central spaceport—the Old Skybottom District. He vaguely remembered a support mission in the sector and couldn't for the life of him recall if the area had been evacuated of civilians.

The missile was descending toward his position. He squeezed off a few shots in its general direction, well aware the bolts would go wide. In all likelihood, if he ever got a glimpse of the missile, it would be too late to do anything.

He had ten seconds, maybe fifteen.

"Any casualty estimates?" he asked.

The droid didn't answer. Nath didn't have time to wait. He scowled at the scanner and made a decision.

He channeled weapons power, repulsors, life support, dampeners, everything but thrusters into his deflector. His boot was stuck to his rudder pedal and his toes felt like they were on fire, but he managed to fine-tune his vector for what he hoped was an optimal intercept course. "You got anything you want to say—" he began, but he didn't finish the sentiment before white light filled the clouds.

He perceived the missile and the brilliance of its burning trail for only a fraction of a second. The droid squealed; proximity alarms wailed; and the blaze of the missile was joined by the blaze of his deflector screen. He'd channeled all his power to the port side, and he rolled to starboard, simultaneously hoping that he'd made his move too early and that he'd timed it just right.

There was a noise like a thunderclap and the Y-wing spun wildly through the air, nearly dislodging Nath from his harness. Sharp pain spiked down his left shoulder as he was tossed about. Vision was utterly beyond him, but what he didn't see wasn't bright—no explosion, at least.

He fumbled, blind and dizzy, with his controls. His fingers twisted shaking knobs and he feared he'd done more harm than good until the Y-wing bucked, metal rang, and suddenly the spin slowed to a violent side-to-side sway. He might have thanked T5 if he hadn't had more urgent concerns.

"Where is it?" he asked—or tried to ask, though the air was thin and he could barely hear himself. "Where's the damn missile?"

The port side of his canopy was black, scorched to the point of opacity. It looked like it would shatter at a tap. Sparks spurted into Nath's field of view but he couldn't tell where they came from. He felt a jolt of worry, wondered whether T5 had paid for his miscalculations, then saw the droid's message on his console.

The scanner was centered on the missile. The weapon jerked to and fro, as if the scanner image itself were malfunctioning. It was falling, but no longer accelerating beyond gravity's usual allowance.

"Let's go!" Nath cried, and brought the Y-wing around.

The missile had clipped the Y-wing's deflector bubble without touching the ship itself. There hadn't been more than a few centimeters of clearance—there couldn't have been, for the plan to work—but Nath had pulled it off with a vessel that could barely scrape its way across a tarmac without scars. The energy of the deflector had shorted out the missile's systems and now the weapon was dropping unguided toward the planet surface.

"We should be dead," Nath murmured, as he fired wildly at the falling warhead. With its thrusters gone he'd hit it sooner or later. "We're going to get a medal for this."

T5 squealed through the comm.

"I said *we*. Your boy better be happy," Nath growled, and concentrated on saving the world.

VII

The cockpit's lights glowed red. The silver curve of the main console reflected and distorted the overheads, drawing a thousand arterial lines in machinery as if the ship were made of blood and bone. Yrica Quell operated controls that felt sculpted to her body, tugging slender levers and caressing switches as she picked her way through the Cerberon debris field.

There was a battle taking place above Troithe. There had been a battle there last time she'd seen the planet, though now there was no *Lodestar*, no Star Destroyer. She recognized the combatants if not their vessels: Vanguard Squadron X-wings pursued a bulk freighter escorted by Shadow Wing TIEs, yet failed to punch through the Imperial rear guard.

It had taken her hours to bring the strange ship's systems online. The planetoid had quaked and erupted as she'd examined the vessel inside the black tower, inspecting its components within and without. She'd been tossed to her knees more than once, as if the cursed world had exerted every bit of strength to thwart her escape. But when she'd finally deciphered the launch sequence, takeoff had been straightforward. She'd left the tower behind and found herself gliding through atmosphere in a vessel more advanced than anything she'd flown before.

Once in space, with her friends' grave behind her and the black hole dominating her viewport, she'd used several more hours to take stock of her situation. She'd studied the ship's instruments and tapped into in-system communications frequencies, trying to make sense of what had happened during her time stranded.

Near-total silence suggested that the New Republic had lost its fight for Cerberon. Occasional flickers of Imperial signals confirmed as much. Calm despite herself, weary beyond imagining (the two might have been connected, she realized after a while), Quell had developed a plan with the tools available to her.

From inside the debris field, so close to the black hole, she hadn't been able to identify the new arrival bursting out of hyperspace at the system's edge. But her sensors had picked up the hypermatter particle surge and she'd begun the slow process of navigating the field and crossing toward Troithe. Reinforcements represented an opportunity, she had told herself. She hadn't expected her chance to come so swiftly, or in this way; but she had to take it.

Now she listened to comm chatter as she flew away from the black hole, picking up only fragments thanks to distance and decryption failures. She heard General Syndulla's voice and smiled softly at the familiar sound of her mentor—her second mentor—ordering Vanguard ships against the handful of TIEs escorting the freighter. She thought she heard Wyl Lark's voice, too, and felt the tension in her muscles momentarily release. Some of her squadron might have survived after all.

Syndulla would be disappointed by what Quell intended. Quell's squadron would understand better. They knew her secrets, and Quell was incapable of disappointing them.

She could hear Imperial communications, too—where she'd needed to enter decryption codes into the computer to hear Vanguard, the TIEs were decoded automatically. She listened to her *first* mentor advise the TIE pilots as their numbers dwindled, and found the voice of Soran Keize strangely unfamiliar. She heard the sacrifice of Captain Darita and mourned; she'd barely known the woman, but they'd watched out for each other, cast glances across the mess hall and stepped in when the other was hassled by a leering member of the *Pursuer's* crew. Quell had forgotten those moments until now, like so many others she'd suppressed before Pandem Nai.

Captain Darita would be disappointed in her, too.

As for Major Keize? She wasn't certain.

Quell's ship slipped below an asteroid embedded with the wreckage of an ancient dreadnought. She continued her course toward the bulk freighter and increased thruster output. The debris field blurred around her. She didn't have long to act.

The black tower and the burning eye of Cerberon had nearly buried her in the torment of her past. She was thinking about her future, now—had been trying to envision it since she'd left the corpse of Caern Adan. *I move forward,* the spy had said. IT-O, too, had clarified her path: The droid had done so much for her, but when its memory had been stripped away it had recognized her as just another war criminal deserving punishment.

What more could she have expected?

The ship emerged from the debris field. She saw the bright orb of Troithe against the stars and realized that the bulk freighter would be out of the planet's gravity well in moments. Shadow Wing would escape back into the galaxy and New Republic Intelligence would be left to begin the chase anew—only this time, they wouldn't have Caern Adan to lead the working group.

Quell gingerly depressed a black crystal inlaid in the silver console, then drew back a lever above her head. The ship hummed, softly at first and then rising to a bone-aching buzz. The cockpit lights dimmed and went out, leaving only the indicators and screens to illuminate the domed compartment.

A message flashed onto one of the displays: CLOAKING SYSTEM ENGAGED.

Quell emitted a small sound of approval. The ship really was a beauty.

She sped toward the bulk freighter. She doubted the cloak would last more than a few minutes, but that would suit her well enough. She checked the controls that she thought—she hoped—operated the magnetic clamps and shifted in the enveloping metal curves of her seat.

She winced as her left biceps brushed her harness. She touched it gingerly with two fingers of her right hand, exploring the bandage wrapped around her arm. The wound was still fresh, acquired after she'd taken off from the planetoid and determined her next steps.

Beneath the bandage was a swath of burnt and bloodied skin where a tattoo had once been—a tattoo of five mismatched starfighters racing together into battle.

She wouldn't need that tattoo anymore.

The last TIEs were speeding into the freighter's cargo bay. The Vanguard fighters were firing wildly as the freighter's lightspeed engines powered online. Quell heard Wyl Lark's voice yell about missile interceptions and she laughed a little, racing through the chaos toward her target.

The freighter was going to escape. It was too late to stop it. Invisible to all sensors, Quell was going to go with it.

She'd been thinking about her future, and what would become of her in the New Republic. When her tribunal came, who wouldn't see her as IT-O had? As her squadron had?

She wasn't ready for her existence to end.

She left the crushing gravity of the Cerberon black hole behind. She left the darkness and guilt and despair behind.

Her ship alighted on the hull of the freighter, and she saw the cerulean glow of hyperspace.

CHAPTER 22

BUOYANT SPIRITS IN SOMETHING LESS THAN CELEBRATION

I

It wasn't until days after the battle that they reunited in the rooftop gardens overlooking Raddakkia Plaza. The fight to retake control of Cerberon hadn't been difficult, as recent missions went—the battle group had captured Troithe and Catadra once before, and all involved knew the lay of the land. The Imperial guerrilla forces had fought boldly at first, but with the capture of "Governor" Yadeez (Governor Hastemoor's successor, who'd been an aide to the undersecretary of Imperial affairs before the Emperor's death) the enemy had dispersed from all but a handful of districts. Those remaining territories would need to be blockaded and contained for many months to come. The guerrillas would remain active for longer, but that would be true across the galaxy.

Hera Syndulla thought of it as a victory. Even Shadow Wing's final attack had been largely neutralized—only a few isolated bunkers and control centers had been destroyed by the missile barrage. Known civilian casualties were currently numbered at thirty-seven. *You did everything you could for these people,* she told herself. *No victory comes without cost.*

She tried to look cheerful as she walked the garden's dirt path and listened to celebratory shouts from below. Wisps of smoke from the troops' impromptu barbecue drifted from the plaza. The gardens were less busy than the street, but the attendees from the medal ceremony had been encouraged to mingle among the flora and Hera clasped hands and spoke encouragingly to civilian fighters who'd resisted the governor and Shadow Wing's occupation; to soldiers who'd nearly died in the battle at Core Nine; and to survivors of the *Lodestar* who had landed escape pods in enemy territory and trekked across the planet to rejoin their comrades.

Her smile grew broader when she spotted Wyl Lark and Chass na Chadic. The two pilots were embracing awkwardly under a withered fruit tree, Wyl standing half a meter back as he clasped the Theelin woman by her shoulders. Chass looked discomfited, but tolerated the touch before pulling back and shoving the toe of her boot in the dirt. The two spoke softly, and Hera nearly walked away before Wyl spied her and waved her over.

"Glad you found each other," Hera said. "Where's Nath?"

"Making the rounds," Chass said. "Showing off his prize. He's got a whole line of locals waiting to thank him."

"I can imagine," Hera said. "We're lucky he survived—that man carries loaded dice."

"He does at that," Wyl said, and though he smiled Hera thought she saw something troubled behind the expression—some unspoken doubt.

Ask him another time, she thought, and she indicated for the pair to join her on her walk.

Wyl and Chass murmured to each other while Hera led them among the ceremony-goers. She listened but tried not to interrupt; it seemed they'd exchanged a few brief calls since the fight but had had few other chances to communicate. Wyl was asking Chass about what had happened over Catadra, and Chass was asking him about the fight on Troithe. Neither seemed inclined to talk about their experiences. When Chass became visibly agitated she stepped directly to Hera's side and asked, "How much energy are we wasting on this party, anyway? Isn't half the planet still starving?"

"Fresh supply ships are finally coming in," Hera said. "In the meantime, it's good to keep morale up."

She didn't explain that those *fresh supply ships* had been won at great expense in a conflict over agriworlds three sectors away. That fight hadn't been Hera's, though she'd spent more than one night discussing it in holographic conference with New Republic High Command.

"Aren't we lucky to be first in line?" Chass muttered.

Hera bit back a retort. She appreciated Chass's fire, even when it was ill directed.

Besides, Chass was right. They shouldn't have been spending time on celebrations. Yet with the *Lodestar* destroyed, Adan's working group decimated, and the Sixty-First Mobile Infantry in little better shape, none of them had the resources to pack up and begin a new operation.

A crowd down the path parted and the bulky form of Nath Tensent swaggered out, addressing soldiers and civilians by name as he went. He spotted Hera and the others and raised a hand in greeting, heading their way. "Look at us!" he called. "Together again, huh?"

He wore his medal pinned to his flight suit—a Bronze Nova, awarded for courageous efforts in the service of civilian lives. He looked more comfortable with it than she'd expected. Hera started to congratulate him when Chass repeated, "Together again."

Then Wyl: "Together again."

Hera wanted to point out the obvious, but she understood.

We're not ready to talk about the ones we lost.

She knew it was best to let them mourn in their own way, but it was a disappointment nonetheless. She'd been hoping—for her sake as much as theirs—to discuss Yrica Quell.

II

They wandered the garden awhile but eventually descended to the plaza and joined the troops for the barbecue. Chass na Chadic stayed with Syndulla, Wyl, and Nath, drinking a cold, minty brew as they discussed the last few days of cleanup. Wyl and Nath were frequently pulled into conversations with soldiers Chass didn't recognize, leaving her alone with the general.

". . . when we finally got a transport out to CER952B, you can imagine how it went," the general was saying. "One hundred of our best, stranded there while the rest of the company was on Troithe. I'm not sure whether the captain was angrier about missing Shadow Wing or about not being with his soldiers."

"I know how the captain feels," Chass said.

"Don't we all?"

She didn't look at the general. Instead, she watched Nath and Wyl laugh as they spoke to the woman Wyl had been talking to when they'd gotten drunk at the refugee camp—Vitale, Chass thought—and a long-haired pilot who looked like seven decades of pretension poured into a flight suit. Someone called him Denish.

No one invited Chass over; she didn't really expect it. She nonetheless felt a *distance* from her comrades she hadn't anticipated. Maybe it was what Syndulla had said—the fact she'd missed out on the action, hadn't gone through what Wyl and Nath had gone through planetside. Maybe it was that they hadn't gone through what she had.

"Troops on the asteroid were pretty bored," Syndulla said. "Same for you when you crash-landed on Catadra?"

"Same for me," Chass said. "Boring."

Syndulla obviously didn't believe the lie. Chass didn't mind.

Wyl and Nath rejoined them and passed around plates of fried fish caught in the city gutters. Chass's thoughts went to the Children of the Empty Sun. She hadn't told Nath or Wyl about the cult, hadn't gone back to Catadra. Let'ij's lectures remained in their case in her B-wing, and though she hadn't opened the box she hadn't tossed it, either.

She hadn't dreamed about Coruscant or had a drink since leaving.

You will carry the seed inside you, Let'ij had said, *and it will grow. We will welcome you when you return.*

"Any lead on the freighter?" she asked, and Nath and Wyl and the general looked surprised. She wondered what they'd been saying when she interrupted.

"Nothing yet," Syndulla said. "New Republic Intelligence is still putting the pieces together, trying to figure out everything that happened. My understanding is they're hoping to interview Governor Yadeez, but there are . . . political issues."

"The chancellor's eager to hold someone accountable for Troithe's war crimes, huh?" Nath snorted.

"I don't blame her," Syndulla said. "Swift justice might help quell Imperial resistance."

No one responded to the wording. No one responded at all. Chass fixed her gaze on the plaza pavement.

Syndulla started over. "We'll find the 204th, in any event. If anyone wasn't convinced of their significance before, they certainly are now."

"You said that last time," Chass muttered, and wrapped her arms around her chest as cold air cut through the limited warmth of the solar projectors.

They would find Shadow Wing, though. Quell had been a bastard, but now she couldn't stop them.

Chass meant to be there for the end of it all.

III

Wyl Lark did his best to involve Chass when Denish, Twitch, and Vitale started wagering on when the rioting in Old Skybottom would burn out. He found the conversation in bad taste, but it was the sort of bad taste Chass had always seemed to enjoy. Instead, she ignored him (like she had every effort to engage her that afternoon), shrugging off questions and staring into the middle distance. He tried to accept his failure with grace.

He hadn't yet reconciled with Nath, either. He hadn't found the means, or the words, or perhaps even the reason. He'd congratulated the older man on his Bronze Nova and told him that he deserved it, which Wyl thought was true—Nath really had almost died to stop the missile from hitting the ground, though Wyl wasn't totally convinced Nath had meant to sacrifice himself. That judgment was colored by the knowledge that Nath had indeed found a way to live; but it was partly a way to explain why Nath hadn't sent Wyl one final message.

Now Nath was the face of their victory—*the* pilot representing all those who'd flown with the infantry during Troithe's darkest hour. He was enjoying his fame, befriending not only freshly arrived troops but members of Troithe's provisional civilian government. It might have been instinct rather than intent, but Nath, Wyl thought, was drawn to influence. It was his way to take opportunities.

He's done nothing but protect you, Wyl reminded himself, because that was true, too. *You'll figure things out between you.*

Once, he caught General Syndulla watching him watching Nath. "Just thinking," he told her, and hoped it would be enough.

They ate and drank more as the evening passed and they began talking about the dead: about the losses aboard the *Lodestar,* the near-total destruction of Meteor Squadron, and fatalities among the infantry. They discussed Gorgeous Su and Carver and the *Lodestar's* Captain Giginivek, whom Wyl had never met but Syndulla showed obvious fondness for. It relieved Wyl to talk about someone he wasn't supposed to know—he felt a measure of shame at not being able to say more about the pilots he'd led to their deaths, but there hadn't been time to get to know them.

Somehow there had always been time in Riot Squadron, no matter what the circumstances. No matter how much chaos there had been.

Nasha Gravas, Caern Adan's second-in-command among the analysts of the working group, emerged from the crowd as Wyl, Nath,

Chass, and Syndulla sat together on the pavement under the dimming solar projectors. Her slight frame looked almost emaciated and she couldn't hide a limp on her left side; like the rest of them, she'd been through trials during Shadow Wing's reign. Nasha offered a curt greeting to the group and after a few pleasantries gestured at Nath. "Let's talk about a few things," she said, and they went.

"You know what that's about?" Chass asked the general.

"Not specifically," Syndulla said. "But Gravas is taking over Adan's team for the time being."

Chass grunted, stood, and sauntered away. Wyl thought about following, but Syndulla rested a hand on his knee to stop him. "I know you're worried about your people," she said. "But stay a minute?"

Wyl nodded and looked at the general. The cheer she'd been exuding for the past hour seemed to dissipate, though she was still smiling.

"I don't know everything you went through," she said, "but I know you made some hard decisions on your own."

He shrugged. "I was the one left in command. That doesn't mean I deserve all the credit."

"Or all the blame," Syndulla agreed. "But you deserve more than most, and you kept folks alive. You averted the worst-case scenario, where the whole city burned while you fought it out with the 204th. You built a squadron that kept the enemy in check. And in the end, you didn't forget your mission.

"So far as I'm concerned, you may have made tactical errors here and there—but you made good calls, Mister Lark."

"Thank you," he said, and tried to sound sincere.

Syndulla's gentle smile became a smirk. "I *do* want to talk about those tactical errors at some point. You're going to make an excellent commander but you're still new, and you shouldn't have to muddle through it alone. If I have one regret—" She cut herself off. She looked as serious as she did during a briefing. "I was away for too long. I can't be part of Alphabet, but I'm going to be backing you. We're going to do this together and we're going to chase the 204th down wherever they go. We won't give them a chance to rebuild again."

"I'm glad to hear it," Wyl said. Hesitantly, he reached out and took Syndulla's hand, clasping it as if they'd made a pact.

"We'll talk about all of this another time. I just wanted to let you know."

"I appreciate it." Wyl stood and looked around the plaza, smiling softly. "Right now, I'm going to take off. It's been a long few days, and I want to turn in early."

They said their goodbyes, and Wyl navigated through the plaza. Staying to celebrate seemed unnecessary—Chass didn't want to be there and he couldn't force her, and Nath seemed more than occupied. He'd mourned Su and Prinspai and Ubellikos with Denish and Vitale the previous evening and barely slept that night. Wyl was tired, in body and spirit, and he hoped to catch a shuttle back to the spaceport and sleep among the refugees under the bright stars.

He wanted to speak to someone, to share what he'd been through, and he thought of composing a message to Blink. But his taste for those missives—for the fantasy of communicating with Shadow Wing—had faded.

It wasn't Shadow Wing he needed guidance from. Nor was it General Syndulla, no matter how much he respected her efforts. She'd been fighting the war too long to understand what he needed.

As he sat aboard the shuttle, body compressed between a bulky young soldier in body armor and an elderly civilian whose head lolled on Wyl's shoulder, Wyl composed a message to his elders. He couldn't remember the last time he'd written Home—sometime before Shadow Wing and Alphabet Squadron, when he'd planned on leaving Riot Squadron and the war behind; when he'd believed the war was finished.

He'd made an oath to return Home when the Empire was defeated. General Syndulla believed that he'd made the right choices; but *none* of his decisions these past days had felt right.

Wyl of Polyneus closed his eyes and dreamed of flying. He vowed to find his way back.

IV

"They really don't want to talk about her, do they?"

Nath Tensent laughed long and loud and embittered. "No, they don't," he agreed, glancing from General Syndulla to the smoke in the distance. This time the plumes were from fireworks rather than rioters, though he supposed the former could've been in the hands of the latter. "Can you blame them? Quell was their commander. Losing her like we did—"

"Are you certain she's lost?"

"Possible she made it out," Nath admitted, and shrugged. "If she did, though . . . makes it more complicated."

Syndulla sighed and nodded. "I got Adan's last message, too."

"Not the woman she said she was. I'm not one to judge moral character, but not stopping Operation Cinder when she had a chance?" Nath shrugged again. "Let Wyl and Chass come around in their own time. The kids want to talk, we'll talk when they're ready."

Syndulla tucked a head-tail behind one shoulder. Nath tried to read her reaction but couldn't see past the surface. He could be sure that Syndulla had thoughts about Quell that she wasn't ready to share. Or that she wasn't interested in sharing with *him*.

"Squadron won't be the same," he finally said, "but pretty sure we're in it till the end. Whatever that looks like."

It was a display of confidence he didn't feel. Wyl and Chass were a mess. Syndulla hadn't said a word about whether the *Temperance* would be their new flagship or if they would find another. And given what Wyl had said about Blink, it was increasingly clear that Shadow Wing had its own vendetta going. If Alphabet Squadron didn't find them first, well . . .

Syndulla furrowed her brow at something across the plaza. Nath followed her gaze and instantly spotted the tall, nonhuman woman moving toward them. The woman's legs wobbled with each step—she looked like an AT-ST crossing an oil slick—but she was powering through and didn't fall. She was wrapped in loose gray cloths that looked sewn together from shredded blankets and stained sheets; Nath figured they couldn't help her awkward walk.

There was nonetheless something familiar about her outfit. Nath couldn't place it. Her face didn't help—he didn't recognize her species, certainly didn't recognize her features. What he initially took to be skin was a set of chitinous plates perfectly covering her bald head. Gaps in the mauve plating revealed deep-set eyes and thin black lips. As she drew closer he saw that the plates' edges were chipped and discolored—she gave the impression of a creature scarred.

She said his name in a guttural voice.

He stood up along with General Syndulla.

He knew who she was.

"I am healed," Kairos said.

Nath grinned slowly, broadly, and held back an oath.

He had a thousand questions, but it was the best news he'd heard all day.

V

"Major Soran Keize. It's good to finally meet you."

"You, as well," Soran said. He didn't correct her regarding his rank. Grand Admiral Rae Sloane was, according to the rumors, the closest thing the Galactic Empire had to an Emperor nowadays; he doubted she was interested in his field promotion.

Her hologram cocked its head. She'd heard something in his tone, perhaps, that piqued her. But she didn't follow up on it, and between the static distortion of the image and the freighter's low-quality projector Soran didn't try to interpret what he saw of her expression.

"It's a pity you didn't make contact sooner," Sloane continued. "By all reports you made a valiant effort at Cerberon but you lacked the ships to hold the system. You dealt a solid blow to General Syndulla's battle group but the general herself still lives. I understand that the 204th is a formidable unit—but it is only *one* unit, and we no longer outnumber our enemies."

"I am aware of that, Admiral. I have been . . . humbled by my experiences."

All he'd really heard was: *The general herself still lives.* He had brought Shadow Wing to Cerberon promising revenge; he had failed to deliver even that.

"How were you humbled, exactly?" Sloane asked.

He chose his words carefully. Sloane had, he assumed, eliminated her share of rivals in order to secure her position in command of the fleet. He wished to show that he was no threat, yet he couldn't afford honesty.

He'd always heard that Sloane was a patriot and a military officer above all else. Soran had never been the former; he could hope she would relate to him as the latter.

"As you said, the 204th is a single unit. As its commander, my primary concern has been the unit's well-being. Merely surviving in the current environment has been challenging, and I knew I could do little to affect the course of the war on my own. Thus, we've focused on precision strikes, ambushes, and the like.

"My experiences in Cerberon, however, brought me into contact with units less privileged than my own. Less able to survive without the support of the Empire as a whole. My view of the war has . . . broadened."

"And now you've come to me."

"Now I have."

Because there are others looking to the 204th for hope.

Because the likes of Governor Yadeez and the people of Troithe deserve more.

Because while they aren't my responsibility—and here he thought not only of the people of Troithe, or of the cadets he had found aboard the *Edict,* or of Colonel Madrighast and the Imperial fleet, but of Rikton, whom the wanderer Devon had tried to save—*I would be a miser to refuse to give what I can give freely.*

"Good." Admiral Sloane studied him, then shook her head briskly. "I'm sending you rendezvous coordinates for one of our battle groups. You will resupply there; expect a limited capacity for repairs. I'll see what I can do about finding you a better carrier, but you may be stuck with the freighter."

"I understand," Soran said, "and I appreciate any help you can provide. Do you have a mission in mind?"

"Possibly." She looked to one side, either referencing a file or signaling someone else in the room. "Your unit was involved in Operation Cinder, correct? Action in the Nacronis system?"

"Yes, Admiral."

"That puts you in a rarefied group. It tells me your pilots are steadfast, as well as skilled." It sounded like praise but her smile was bitter. "We'll have a use for you. Expect new orders shortly."

The hologram flashed into nonexistence, the light staining Soran's retinas and leaving him blinking away spots. His expression fell with the same suddenness as Sloane's disappearance and he stroked the comm panel with trembling fingers.

He had made a bargain that he would surely curse, if not regret. He had recommitted himself and his unit to a losing battle for an Empire not worthy of being saved, for the sake of giving desperate soldiers a brief reprieve from their graves or New Republic prison cells.

But he had hoped not to hear of Operation Cinder again. Those days represented the worst of the Empire and the Emperor's atrocities.

"I imagine you're pleased?" he asked.

In the corner of the dim communications center stood a figure in a red robe. One arm dangled at its side, severed midway between elbow and shoulder. The glasslike plate of its face flickered and sparked with light that, on occasion, resolved into the image of the dead Emperor Palpatine.

Soran had not asked for the Messenger to be brought aboard the freighter, but someone had delivered it anyway. He'd only discovered its presence after the escape from Troithe and the jump to lightspeed.

"You are but one of many tools," it said in the Emperor's decrepit voice, before the sound became an electronic squeal and the words played a second time, a third, over an ear-piercing shriek.

Without thought or intent, Soran swung at the machine. Pain lanced from his knuckles to his elbow as his fist impacted the curved plate, and as he pulled his hand away he saw that he'd left a red smear across the glass along with a web of cracks.

"Operation Cinder," the droid said, "is to begin at once."

Soran wondered whether the words were echo or portent.

VI

She waited in an unpowered cargo turbolift—the closest thing on hand to a cell, she suspected. Her guard's name was Mervais Gandor and he snorted when he laughed, raised bantha calves on his homeworld, and had been the single clumsiest ordnance specialist aboard the *Pursuer*.

She wasn't sure he recognized her. She barely recognized him. She didn't try to make conversation.

Outside the elevator, through the small window and past Gandor, she could see TIE fighters lined neatly throughout the hold and uniformed men and women hurrying between them, decoupling hoses and unbolting hull panels and performing tasks meant for droids. She tried to make out faces and failed to identify many.

The unit really had changed.

"Stand back," Gandor said through the intercom. She did, and the door rose fast enough to wash stray locks of hair behind her ears. Scents of fuel and dust filled her nostrils.

A man walked into her line of sight. His brown hair appeared black as he passed through a shadow, and his thin, delicate lips looked out of place on his angular face. He carried himself with an easy confidence, though there was a weariness to him she'd never seen before.

Her eyes fell to his right hand, where a strip of sanitary cloth was wrapped around his knuckles. "Everything all right?" she asked.

He followed her gaze and smiled gently. "An accident. Thank you."

They studied each other. His smile faded.

"Why don't you tell me why you're here?" Soran Keize said.

She straightened her back. The words came naturally.

"Lieutenant Yrica Quell, reporting for duty."

ACKNOWLEDGMENTS

See the acknowledgments for the previous book, only more so.

Need I say anything else? Maybe a few words. Special thanks to editor Elizabeth Schaefer, who made certain that the squadron made it home safe. Thanks as well to my Fogbank colleagues who were, as always, endlessly patient (and to the children of the garden, who deserve to be remembered).

Most of all, to those friends and loved ones I let slip into the distance while staring at words: I am eternally grateful to you all. I'm coming for you.

Two down. One left.

ABOUT THE AUTHOR

ALEXANDER FREED is the author of *Star Wars: Alphabet Squadron, Star Wars: Battlefront: Twilight Company,* and *Star Wars: Rogue One* and has written many short stories, comic books, and videogames. Born near Philadelphia, he currently resides in San Francisco, California. He enjoys the city's culture, history, and secrets, but he misses snow.

alexanderfreed.com
Twitter: @AlexanderMFreed

ABOUT THE TYPE

This book was set in Minion, a 1990 Adobe Originals typeface by Robert Slimbach (b. 1956). Minion is inspired by classical, old-style typefaces of the late Renaissance, a period of elegant, beautiful, and highly readable type designs. Created primarily for text setting, Minion combines the aesthetic and functional qualities that make text type highly readable with the versatility of digital technology.